THE ROMAN ENIGMA

Also by Walter F. Murphy

THE VICAR OF CHRIST

For Brandy and Elly,
the best of spies,
the dearest of friends

CAST OF CHARACTERS

AMERICANS

Col. Brian Patrick Lynch, professional soldier assigned by OSS to assist John Winthrop Mason with Operation Bronze Goddess

John Winthrop Mason, Wall Street lawyer assisting OSS by directing Operation Bronze Goddess, an effort to hide from the Germans the fact that the British have developed a machine called Ultra, which can read messages enciphered by the supposedly secure German machine Enigma

Lt. (j.g.) Roberto M. Rovere, Italian-American naval officer whom Mason selects to carry out Operation Bronze Goddess in Rome

Paul Stransky, OSS officer on duty in the Vatican as secretary to President Roosevelt's personal representative to the Pope

Rev. Fitzpàdraig Cathal Sullivan, S.J., American priest in the Vatican's Secretariat of State, who is also an OSS agent and controls Roberto Rovere while he is in Rome

C. Bradley Walker, Associate Justice of the Supreme Court of the United States, who without fully understanding it lays out the basic plan for Operation Bronze Goddess

BRITISH

Sir Henry Cuthbert, brigadier assigned to liaison with OSS on Operation Bronze Goddess

GERMANS

An Augustinian monk, a noted moral theologian who teaches at the Lateran (Papal) University and is also an Abwehr agent

Adm. Wilhelm Canaris, head of the Abwehr, the German military's intelligence service, who conceives the notion of Operation Rigoletto to allow an Allied spy to "kidnap" a phony Enigma

Capt. Erich Danzig, SS officer specially assigned to arrest and deport the Jews of Rome

Col. Manfred Gratz, Abwehr officer in Rome whom Admiral Canaris appoints as local commander of Operation Rigoletto

Sgt. Walther Hoess, chief torturer for the Gestapo in Rome

Field Marshal Albert Kesselring, commander of Army Group A, opposing Allied military forces in Italy

Gen. Hans Mueller, military commandant of Rome

Lt. Col. Viktor Olendorf, SS officer in command at Rome of the recently merged Gestapo (political police) and SD (the Nazi party's intelligence and counterintelligence service)

Maj. Kurt Priebke, SS officer, assistant to Lieutenant Colonel Olendorf

Maj. Otto Schwartzkümmel, head of cryptography in Rome; his sexual proclivities make him vulnerable to blackmail

Capt. Karl von Bothmer, Colonel Gratz's assistant

ITALIANS

Anna Caccianemici, young woman who works for the OSS, the Abwehr, an Italian resistance unit, a well-known Roman restaurant, and herself; Roberto M. Rovere reports to her on arrival in Rome

Fabriziana Donatello, a *dondrona* from Trastevere, a neighbor of Anna Caccianemici

Msgr. Ugo Galeotti, a Vatican diplomat with a reputation for a shrewd mind and a hyperactive fork

Msgr. Giovanni Battista LaTorre, one of the Vatican's undersecretaries of state

Eugenio Pacelli, Pope Pius XII

Rebecca Piperno, wife of Tommaso Piperno

Tommaso Piperno, a street sweeper in Trastevere who works for the Commune of Rome, the Abwehr, the OSS, several Italian resistance units, several black marketeers, and himself

Sister Sacristy, mother superior of a Franciscan convent in Trastevere

Stefano, a sexually ambivalent young barman whose puppy love Anna Caccianemici exploits to help blackmail Maj. Otto Schwartz-kümmel

PROLOGUE

Oh, Rome! my country! city of the soul!
The orphans of the heart must turn to thee,
Lone mother of dead empires! and control
In their shut breasts their petty misery.
What are our woes and sufferance? Come and see
The cypress, hear the owl, and plod your way
O'er steps of broken thrones and temples, Ye!
Whose agonies are evils of a day—
A world is at our feet as fragile as our clay.

GEORGE GORDON, LORD BYRON,
"Childe Harold's Pilgrimage"

Washington, D.C., Tuesday, 22 June 1943

It was exactly 2:00 in the afternoon of a blisteringly hot day. At the top of the massive stone steps to the Supreme Court's white temple, the colonel hesitated, then turned to enjoy the magnificent view of a neat marble plaza, followed by a broad avenue, and continued by trees shading a green lawn rolling toward the Capitol, all topped by a blue sky spackled with tufts of white cotton. After that brief pause, Col. Brian Patrick Lynch fell in step and marched alongside his companion. As was proper for the junior officer, Lynch walked on the left, so that the senior officer would have his sword arm free. It was only a small matter of protocol when the senior was, as here, a civilian, but Colonel Lynch unconsciously, albeit very meticulously, followed the rules of military courtesy. The lessons of West Point die hard, if at all.

Once inside the huge door, the two men trooped the long marble corridor, enjoying the cool respite from the fierce heat of Washington's summer. Both were lean and tall, though the civilian was a full inch shorter than the colonel and perhaps ten pounds heavier. The demands of his law practice on Wall Street had denied him the benefit of the colonel's months in that gigantic steambath called New Guinea. Still, by the standards of civilians in the year of Our Lord 1943, John Winthrop Mason was slender: exactly six feet tall, and 170 pounds according to the scale of the Yale Club in New York, 171 according to that of the Cosmos Club in Washington.

Lynch was wearing the suntans of an army colonel. His close-cropped, thinning brown hair was all but hidden by a barracks cap. Like his former commanding officer in the South Pacific, he wore no ribbons on his jacket. Mason's suit was dark blue, single breasted with

3

vest; a gold chain across his flat upper stomach connected a pocket-watch to a Phi Beta Kappa key. The suit had been custom-made on London's Savile Row before the war and still fit with the trim elegance its tailor had created.

In Washington during the second summer after Pearl Harbor, one saw many faces like that of Brian Patrick Lynch—a gaunt look accentuating a hawk nose and blue eyes that reflected the anguish of having survived combat. Nowhere, however, was one likely to encounter a replica of Mason's face, except perhaps in the Prado's collection of Goya's sketches. Mason was not a small man, but his head was much too large for his body, and his salt-and-pepper hair, deliberately kept long and shaggy, magnified that discrepancy in size.

His facial features seemed the work of a genetic disaster or a misanthropic plastic surgeon. A pair of huge ears protruded from his head at almost right angles, producing an effect not unlike that of the handles of a Greek amphora. His nose was flat, as if the cartilage had been removed and the flesh pressed and spread firmly against his cheeks. His lips were thick and his mouth shaped rather like that of a permanently petulant pig. His slate gray eyes bulged slightly, making him appear perpetually surprised by what he encountered in life. One soon learned, however, that his expression reflected myopia and boredom far more often than surprise or even interest; it seldom changed, no matter what scene floated into view.

The two men marched in perfect step down the corridor. Their strides would have been the same had they been at the head of a triumphant but sacrilegious army violating the Court's sacred chambers. At the end of the hall, they turned right then left and entered the marshal's office. A bored female receptionist looked up from her Remington typewriter. Mason's strange physiognomy startled her for a brief instant, but she quickly regained her composure.

"Mr. Mason and Colonel Lynch to see Mr. Justice Walker." Mason's tone was clipped, almost curt, its authority evident.

The young woman hurriedly scanned a notebook, then pushed a buzzer and returned to her typing. A few minutes later a black man wearing a black suit and a black knit tie appeared in the office. "Haskins, please take these gentlemen to see the justice," she ordered. Her eyes did not leave the paper she was reproducing.

"Sirs." He nodded and led the two visitors farther down a side corridor, where they turned and paralleled a reverse of their original course to the marshal's office. Near the end of the high passage, they halted as the attendant tapped gently on an oak door. "Come in." The voice came from a male secretary whose desk was situated in the very center of a large room. Its ample windows provided a generous but uninspiring view of the Library of Congress. That sentence was the sum total of the secretary's lines in the drama, for no sooner had he spoken when a cyclone of energy, not quite five feet, seven inches in altitude, came bounding out of the inner office and enveloped the civilian visitor.

"Mason, my dear Mason! How good to see you!" The Honorable C. Bradley Walker, Associate Justice of the Supreme Court of the United States, loosened his grip on his former student's elbows only long enough to make a sweeping gesture whose orbit encompassed the entire building. "It's not like the seminar room at Yale where we had our oral encounters, but one manages, even during a war one manages. How grand to see you! This must be Colonel Lynch. Welcome!" The colonel felt himself pulled into the vortex of the justice's energy. There was no opportunity for reply, for as his hand was being pumped his ears were being similarly engaged. "I doubt that our Mason here has told you of his penchant for upsetting seminars. As one who has spent a lifetime in the academy, I am not at all unskilled, my dear chap, not at all unskilled in the arts of seminarmanship. But in Mason here, we meet the master, the ultimate master. I have never-heard a colleague, much less a student, able to pose such tempting but un-answerable questions and to do so with such fiendish deception, bait-ing a trap for the expert no less than for the neophyte with an occa-sional and quite appropriate Shakespearean aphorism. He is the master of a black art, a black art indeed."

The two quickly found themselves propelled into Walker's inner office, a room dominated by overcrowded bookshelves and two desks, one a large walnut slab, the other a slender podium behind which the justice stood—miming Oliver Wendell Holmes, Jr.—when he wrote his opinions. The Danish elegance of the podium's design belied its strength. There was, of course, no fire in the marble fireplace, but such an affectation on a hot June day would not have surprised Lynch. The colonel was convinced from the way that Walker bounced across the thick carpet that he had blocks of sponge rubber inside his shoes;

a similar product inside his head would have made a certain kind of symmetrical sense.

The two men settled into a black leather divan, as the justice plopped himself into the high-backed leather chair and, with an oft-rehearsed air of casualness, put his dainty feet in the midst of the papers strewn about the desk. "Well then, you did say that you had something of the utmost importance that the President wanted you to discuss with me. What was its essence?—But first, how is dear Franklin?" he interrupted himself. "One of the less bearable hardships of this war is that we can't see each other as we did in the old days. I have my work here, he downtown." The justice tossed his head to indicate the generally northwesterly direction from which the executive power of the United States flowed.

"The President . . ." Mason began. It was a vain effort. Justice C. Bradley Walker was not to be stopped by an answer to his question.

"War is but organized violence, and violence is not my cup of tea, not my cup of tea at all. On the other hand, a lifetime's struggle to advance the values of Western civilization has instructed me that, at times, violence can only be countered by violence. And so, after much deliberation, and not without severe soul-searching, I have concluded that I could be useful doing something more directly connected with the war effort—and I've told Franklin so. I've asked him—no, begged him—to enlist me. Let me run OPA or WPB or some similar agency. But, no; he insists that he needs me here. Well, if we are to function efficiently as soldiers in the Grand Army of Democracy, we must obey without question or complaint. Still, I wish Franklin wouldn't give so much power to Jimmy Byrnes.

"Just among us girls"—the justice lowered his voice to a conspiratorial whisper—"I could never trust a man who would desert our august tribunal to accept a post in the executive department. That sort of choice reveals—oh, how it reveals—a still throbbing pump of political ambition; and you know full well, full well, the chameleonesque morality of ambitious politicians. But come now, Mason, you haven't yet told me about dear Franklin."

"Basically well, Mr. Justice, tired but well. He sends his warmest personal regards."

"To be sure, to be sure; and please convey mine to him."

6

"Are we secure here?" Mason asked.

"Secure? Secure? Ah yes, I see." Walker laughed nervously. "You mean are we, how do you fellows put it, bugged? Hardly. No one bugs the Supreme Court of the United States."

"Sorry, but our mission involves a matter of the highest national security. I cannot tell you specifically to what my questions relate. The President would appreciate your not even remembering that this conversation took place. He will remember it, but you should not."

"That goes without saying, my dear Mason, without saying. A lifetime's experience in public service has left me not unappreciative of the veils of secrecy that, of necessity, surround wartime decision making. Now, how may I be of service?"

"Let me put a hypothetical case."

"Ah, these former students, Colonel. How they enjoy turning the old man's ploys against him. Yes, indeed, let us put hypothetical cases." The justice's eyes glistened with anticipation.

"Suppose, Mr. Justice, that you were at war against a powerful enemy who had a secret weakness that you understood. You need to exploit that weakness not once but many times. How would you keep him from knowing that you have his secret even while you are using it against him?"

The justice removed his rimless pince-nez and carefully cleaned the lenses with his handkerchief. He waited for more information. When it became painfully apparent that no more was forthcoming, he finally spoke. "Mason, you have disappointed me—no really, embarrassed me, and in front of the colonel, too. After all, I made such marvelous claims about your capacity to construct conundra, and, my dear chap, you hardly pose a problem at all."

Lynch glanced at Mason. The lawyer's bulging eyes revealed nothing. They seldom did.

"The solution," the justice went on, "is as plain as the moustache under Adolf Hitler's nose: You search for the secret as if you did not know it, search for it and let the enemy ascertain that you're searching for it. Meanwhile, you use what you know and attribute your victories in the field to superior skill and superior equipment—mostly superior skill in planning. That will drive the enemy crazy with anger. He'll believe you're only lucky, and when he discovers you're still

7

ferreting around for his secret, he will know, absolutely *know*, my dear chap, that bad fortune alone has produced his defeats. Use his own ego to help him deceive himself."

Mason rose and extended his hand. "Thank you, Mr. Justice. You will probably never realize how helpful you have been. But the President will understand."

"Is that all?" The disappointment in Walker's voice was genuine. "Just that trifling poser?"

"Yes, sir."

"Well, my dear chap, one does what one can—and where dear Franklin is concerned, there is seldom a limit to what one can do."

The two men marched silently until they were back in the afternoon heat glaring up from the white marble of the piazza in front of the Court. When they entered Mason's own LaSalle, which had been patiently, if illegally, parked at the curb around the corner on Maryland Avenue, Lynch spoke. "Is he real?"

"Real?" Mason asked.

"Yes, sir. I've never seen so much horseshit so tightly compressed."

Mason was silent. For a moment he glowered angrily; then he pressed the button that caused a heavy glass partition to close the passengers off from the driver. As the lawyer removed a short, thick cigar from its silver case, he smiled. "Compressed horseshit." He repeated the phrase, then chuckled out loud. It was the first occasion on which the colonel had heard Mason laugh. He was not a man noted for his own—or his tolerance of others'—humor. "Compressed horseshit," he said once more. "You military have vulgar but picturesque words and phrases. Still, you are right. There is a great deal of that substance compressed in him, but there is also the shrewdest brain you will ever encounter. And the quickest. He provided the solution to Operation Bronze Goddess in less than ten seconds. All your experts—and mine—have been trying for weeks without a single promising idea." The lawyer lit his cigar and inhaled it as if it were a cigarette. "Do you like his stratagem?"

"Well, it has a certain appeal." The colonel dragged out his words. He wanted time to think because he was afraid that Mason was about to leap—indeed, probably had already leaped—to the obvious conclusion. "The first part, crediting our military skill rather than Ultra's

8

ability to read Enigma, is easy. We don't have to encourage that. The second part is pretty hairy. Faking an effort serious enough to convince the Germans would be very difficult and damned expensive."

"Money is not important."

"I wasn't thinking of money or of time. A lot of people would have to die to convince the Germans that we were trying to steal—or kidnap—their enciphering machine."

"In war many people have to die. That is the way this world operates. It is not a nice place for nice people. Long ago the chiefs learned to advance their interests by having the Indians slaughter each other."

"I wonder if the Indians would approve."

"I should not care to inquire. It would be much ado about nothing. This plan will produce the greatest good for the greatest number. Artistically, it is also a stroke of genius." Mason half-closed his eyes and let the breeze from the open side window cool his body as he savored the aroma of the fat cigar.

Lynch recognized the signal that conversation was over, but he chose to ignore it. Mason was neither a friend nor a benevolent superior. In the five weeks they had been together, the lawyer had shown neither warmth nor concern for those who worked for him. And Brian Patrick Lynch did not like cold fish. Or cold people, especially those who found it easy to plan the deaths of other human beings. On Lynch's scale of values, Mason's character was as ugly as his face. But he was also in command. The general had made it clear that whatever and whomever Mason wanted for Operation Bronze Goddess were his for the asking—and without question. Protecting the secrecy of Ultra's existence and its ability to read the Germans' communications—Operation Bronze Goddess—had absolutely top priority.

The colonel decided to probe how far Mason had ranged in seeking support for the mission. "I hadn't realized that the President was personally involved in Bronze Goddess."

Mason opened his frog eyes for a moment, then half-closed them again. He spoke with the strained patience of a parent whose day has been long and whose child has been inordinately inquisitive. "Do not be absurd. The President has only the most general notion of our efforts. But I had to invoke his name. The speed of the justice's brain is exceeded only by that of his mouth. He is without peer as a transmitter of gossip, even in this town of rumormongers. The President's name is the only thing in our galaxy short of death that can still Justice Walker's tongue."

Mason leaned back in his seat and snapped open his watch. "We have only three minutes and fifty-two seconds before we arrive at our destination. I need silence in which to meditate . . . if you please."

Rome, Wednesday, 23 June 1943

The Roman morning was a bright blue, so clear that one could see far beyond the giant statues atop the Basilica of St. John Lateran deep into the mountains of south central Italy. A tall, dark-haired Irish-American priest, Fitzpàdraig Cathal Sullivan, S.J., halted his walk only a dozen yards from the crest of the steep Gianicolo. Below him the Tiber coiled languidly around the old city. Straight ahead but more distant, the twin towers of Trinità dei Monti rose above the Spanish Steps; to the right the white marble of Vittorio Emanuele's garish monument reflected the sunlight; and even farther to the right the clay around the ruins on the Palatine glowed a dull bloodred. From this height, the panoramic grandeur of the seven hills and their halo of history screened the mud of the river, the decay of the ancient buildings, and the artistic horror of modern architecture that Mussolini thought majestic.

The Jesuit loved that view. Indeed, the opportunity to enjoy its magnificence had been the real reason for his climbing the Gianicolo this morning. He had, he knew, merely rationalized to himself that it had been necessary to talk to the nursing nuns in the pediatric hospital on the hill. It was essential for a spy to keep in close touch with his agents, but these women would have sent a message to him if they had had anything of importance to report. After all, his position as an official in the Vatican's Secretariat of State made it easy for clergy to contact him.

He was paying for his pleasure in the Roman vista with a heavy pressure in his chest that was radiating down the inside of his left arm, making the knuckles of his little finger tingle as if they were receiving mild electric shocks. As usual, just before the pain gripped him, he had found it difficult to breathe. There had been a burning in his lungs and a slight giddiness, as if he had not been getting enough oxygen.

10

The priest leaned against the hospital wall, hoping that the pain would subside. He took out a large handkerchief and mopped the sweat from his face. What he really wanted was a towel. The climb had been hard. It was much hotter on the open walk up the hill than it had seemed down in the shade of St. Peter's. And having to wear a long black cassock, as Roman custom required, increased Father Sullivan's discomfort.

The pain was not ebbing. Reluctantly, he reached inside his cassock, took two small tablets from the vial that he carried in his trouser pocket, and placed one of them under his tongue. He hesitated, undecided for several minutes, then kept the second tablet between his fingers and closed his eyes as he waited for the nitroglycerine to open his coronary arteries.

Stop all physical activity and try to be calm, the doctor had said, think pleasant thoughts, perhaps meditate. Father Sullivan had tried the last, several times. But, he had to admit, he was no more a mystic than he was an ascetic. He prayed, of course, but his prayers consisted mostly of direct confrontations with the Almighty: appeals for help, brief reminders of unanswered requests, thanks for past favors, and petitions for forgiveness of sins. Even though he was a priest, Fitzpàdraig C. Sullivan could never imagine himself approaching, much less attaining, a contemplative state that lifted him into some sort of transcendent union with the divine. He happily settled for a quick act of contrition—it was always possible that a major heart attack was beginning rather than only a transient bout of angina—and then some pleasant thoughts.

His mind focused on the small party his friends at *America* had given him when he left for service in Archbishop Spellman's chancery. Fiorello La Guardia, the Little Flower himself, had popped in. He had stayed only a moment, but he had shaken the priest's hand and had told him what a wonderful job he was doing. Then there was that day when he had been in Washington on an errand for the diocese and had met Sen. Robert Wagner. To talk to him, Spellman's emissary, Wagner had interrupted a conversation with no less than Sen. Arthur Vandenburg, and Wagner had introduced him to the great man. Sullivan could remember every detail of the occasion, even to the dark pinstriped suit that Wagner had worn. Most of all, the Jesuit recalled the bulldog determination that had flashed from Wagner's and Vandenberg's eyes. They were powerful people, dedicated men. They were also his friends. After the war, when the truth could be told, "Father Christmas," the American spy in Rome, would become a legend, and famous and important people like La Guardia, Vandenberg, and Wagner would seek him out.

The pain was rapidly easing now. It would be gone in a few moments and he could resume the climb to the hospital. Perhaps the nuns would have something to report. One of them regularly visited the child of a cabinet minister. She might have heard something to confirm or contradict the rumors that were rife in the Vatican that even a majority of the leading Fascists had had enough of the war and were preparing to oust Mussolini and sue for peace when the Allies invaded Italy.

SPIES IN ROME

I see before me the Gladiator lie:
He leans upon his hand—his manly brow
Consents to death, but conquers agony,
And his droop'd head sinks gradually low—
And through his side the last drops, ebbing slow
From the red gash, fall heavy, one by one,
Like the first of a thunder-shower; and now
The arena swims around him—he is gone,
Ere ceased the inhuman shout which hail'd the wretch who
  won.

GEORGE GORDON, LORD BYRON,
"Childe Harold's Pilgrimage"

ONE

Rome, Monday, 27 September 1943

"*LAHH-buoh-nahh!*" From the street below a male teenager's voice sang out in the dialect of Rome, as a pair of fourteen-year-old girls walked toward the school farther up the hill. The youngster was calling to the world to witness the beauty of the taller girl. They scampered on, pretending not to notice, even as they smiled. The response came from up above. "*Ah-boo-ree-noh!*" It was a very fat, middle-aged Trasteverina whose rasping voice rebuked the boy as a "peasant" for his vulgar panegyric.

Roberto Michele Rovere knew without looking over the railing of the rooftop garden that the woman was leaning out the window of her apartment. It was not a conclusion that required scientific deduction. Leaning out the front window was the standard occupation of the housewives of Trastevere; and, by the time their second child was out of diapers, the vocal cords of most of these women had long been scarred by the loud shouts that were the normal method of communicating with any person with whom one was not at that very instant making love. Fabriziana Donatello's grating yells differed in painful pitch from those of her cohorts stationed in neighboring windows. Perhaps her raucous tone was different because she had had no children. But that was another matter, the will of God, inscrutable and final despite hundreds of candles lit in the San' Dorotea.

Except to cook, eat, sleep, use the toilet, dump the garbage out of the window, and very occasionally earn her keep by sweeping and mopping the inside marble staircase of the decaying palazzo (it was, by American standards, a tenement, but in Italy even a tenement is entitled to be called a palazzo), she spent her days and evenings positioned like an overweight gargoyle grimly watching life ripple across

15

the cobblestones of the street below. Trastevere was her country; it was almost her universe. The garbage did not matter. Not even Mussolini had been able to convince the Trasteverini to put their refuse in trash cans. After all, if the good God did not intend Trasteverini to throw their garbage out their windows, why did He send men with brooms to sweep it up each morning?

Unlike many of her neighbors, Fabriziana knew something of the world across the Tiber. When she was young, she had crossed the river many times to help take care of the children of a Jewish family who lived in the old ghetto. She could not recall exactly when, maybe 1928 or was it 1929? That had ended a good period in her life.

Fabriziana's traveling, however, had not been confined to her youth. Several times a year her husband had made her put on her best (and only) Sunday black dress and walk with him all the way to the Piazza Venezia, several kilometers away, and hear il Duce. Paolo had applauded vigorously—and frequently—and she had followed suit, though more slowly. She had never been good at understanding the Tuscan dialect that foreigners mistook for the language of Italy, and much of what Mussolini said in his northern accent was little more than gibberish to her.

That difficulty with language contributed to Fabriziana's problems in deciphering the letter from the Red Cross. It, too, had been in Tuscan. The man who ran the wine and oil shop was the most educated in the neighborhood. He had attended an entire year of middle school and was able to translate for her. Yet even in Romanesco the words had conveyed little: Paolo Donatello, her husband of fifteen years, was in a prisoner-of-war camp in *Carolina del Sud*. The earlier letter from the War Ministry had made much more sense: Paolo was missing. She could have told the army when they drafted him that, if there was to be fighting, they'd be missing Paolo soon enough. He might applaud il Duce and even argue in the wineshop that Fascism was good for Trastevere—or even Italy, if that word had any meaning. But risk his neck for strangers? Not likely. Not Paolo, not very many Trasteverini. They could be fierce fighters where personal or family honor was at stake, but risk one's life for a stranger or an ideal? Never.

But where or what was *Carolina del Sud*? At least Fabriziana had the comfort of knowing that any place with such a strange name must be very far away and therefore very safe. To be a prisoner was not the best

16

fate; on the other hand, it was not the worst. Moreover, it was one to which Paolo could bring some experience. On several occasions he had been a nonpaying guest at the Regina Coeli—the Queen of Heaven—jail, conveniently located along the Tiber between Trastevere and Vatican City. Paolo would know how to survive, perhaps even prosper.

Two floors above Fabriziana's small apartment, Roberto Michele Rovere, sometime instructor in Romance languages at Princeton, currently lieutenant (junior grade), U.S. Navy Reserve, on loan to the Office of Strategic Services, sat on the rooftop terrace. He was doing his best to absorb the weakening rays of the autumn sun. He needed the warmth to restore some sense of reality to his life. A week ago he had been in Virginia. Now he was in German-occupied Rome, in the apartment of his contact, Anna (or An-NAH, as the Trasteverini would have pronounced it, had they ever spoken her given name).

He closed his eyes and dreamed about what life had been all about before the OSS had tapped him. "Tapped"—the word was exact. "They" had chosen him; he had certainly not volunteered. Nor had he tried to prepare himself to be a spy. After all, a doctorate in comparative literature hardly forms the usual gateway to espionage, especially when one's interests run in the direction of modern poetry.

Roberto had enough ego to admit that the OSS's choice had not been irrational. He had never—never before, that is—been exposed to any of the arts of cloak and dagger, but in other ways he was superbly qualified to spy in Italy. He had been born in the United States, but he often felt more Italian than American.

On his father's side, he was descended from an old—and mildly noble—family from Savona. Roberto's paternal grandfather had taken what family fortune there was and moved to Florence, where his son had become a well-known professor of literature at the university. On a visit to the University of Chicago, *il professore* had met and married an American woman. Her ancestry was what the Italians would call a *misto*, a mixture. She was the product of a union between a slender, dark Jewish girl and a red-faced Irishman, straight from the Old Sod of County Mayo to the Back of the Yards district of Chicago. His mental shrewdness and quickness with his fists brought him from slop boy in the slaughter pens to president of a meat-packing firm.

As a result of his mother's inheritance and his father's share of the family's holdings that ran twisting Sangiovese vines among gnarled

17

olive trees in the hills south and west of Florence, money had never been a problem in Roberto's life. With his parents and two younger sisters, he had spent the months when the university was more or less in session, from October until May, in Florence. During the summers, the family moved back to the United States, staying either with relatives on Chicago's Gold Coast or at their own summer home on Lake Michigan.

Much to his father's pride, Roberto had received his *laurea* from the University of Florence in a nascent field that in a more specialized educational environment would have been called linguistics. Then he had gone to graduate school at Harvard in comparative literature. He took and passed his doctoral examinations after only three terms and returned to Italy to do research for a dissertation on the still living Roman poet, Carlo Alberto Salustri, who used the pen name of Trilussa.

The dissertation had been a labor of love. Not only did Roberto admire Trilussa's artistic skill, but he found the old man *simpatico*. They shared a love for literature, good wine, and Roman grandeur, as well as an intellectual contempt for Fascism. Trilussa delighted in deploying the indirect language of his folksy poetry to ridicule Mussolini, leaving "the pig" to writhe impotently under the laughing whip of allegory.

Perhaps as a conceit to demonstrate his literary virtuosity, the poet had chosen to write in the Roman dialect, Romanesco, or Romanaccio, "ugly Roman," as northern Italians dubbed it. That choice made his writing less accessible, but it allowed him to appear even more wisely enigmatic, a status that civilized Italians rank far above sainthood.

Outside of Tuscany in north central Italy, the "Italian" language was, in the 1930s, as often a legal fiction as a popular tongue. Historically, each region had had its own language that sometimes differed from other dialects as widely as German from Spanish. As part of its efforts to unify the country in the later half of the nineteenth century, the House of Savoy had christened Tuscan, the dialect of Florence and Siena and the language of Dante, as Italian. The effect was not much greater than that of the usual governmental decree in Italy. People continued to use their own dialects, and it was not until Mussolini that the government made rigorous attempts to ensure that Tuscan would be strictly taught in all schools, wherever located. As a result, most younger Italians became fluent in two languages, Tuscan and their own local dialect, with the latter the tongue of neighborhood, friends, family, joke telling, and lovemaking; the former the means of communicating with strangers and public officials—to whom, of course, one owed no duty of candor or even clear pronunciation.

Decoding the secrets of the verse—and long conversations with Trilussa—left Roberto a master of the dialect. Nevertheless, the poet complained that he spoke it as a scholar, lacking the Roman's instinctive disdain for grammar when those rules got in the way of vivid imagery or an opportunity to bewilder the gullible.

Roberto's romance with Romanaccio was a cause, not a result, of his interest in Trilussa. Although his father, as a learned *professore*, had treated Rome, Romans, and Romanaccio with the contempt that only Florentines and Parisians can muster toward those who do not speak their language with perfect inflection, Roberto had loved Rome and its guttural dialect since he had been a small child. It was a love that had come from his mother. She was always manufacturing excuses to spend a few days in the city, and Roberto's sisters were happy to have him go with her and allow them a chance to beguile their father into all sorts of rashly expensive promises.

While his mother shopped in the fashionable district around the Spanish Steps and took coffee at the outdoor cafes on the chic, if sleazy, Via Veneto, Roberto would spend the day in the ruins of Republican and Imperial Rome. Sometimes he would sit in the sun, among the rubble of the Forum, near the spot where, local lore had it, assassins' daggers had struck Julius Caesar. (Roberto preferred to ignore the more probable truth that the assassination had occurred a half mile away in an area near the Largo Argentina, now ingloriously paved over.) He would dream of himself wearing a toga and striding the ancient streets, rallying the Senate and people of Rome to oppose tyranny.

On other days he wandered across the open avenue to the shell of the Colosseo and sat on the stone bleachers and pictured himself as a gallant gladiator whose courage and fierce skill had long ago earned him freedom, but who returned every few weeks to the sand below to prove his mettle by once more engaging in mortal combat. The crowds would shout his praises, and the emperor and his court—and lovely courtesans—would liberally shower their favors on him.

The people of modern Rome, at least those who lived in the old parts of the city like Trastevere, "the Romans from Rome," also fascinated Roberto. He made friends among the shopkeepers, the trashmen, and the boys of his own age. He sometimes wandered across the river to Trastevere to enjoy the warm atmosphere of a neighborhood bar—the gathering place for working-class families from squalling *bambini* to ancient grandparents. Older people sat at tables and drank coffee or wine and discussed the fate of the world or at least of the immediate vicinity; children raced around, alternately slurping and spilling ice cream; and teenagers drifted in and out, making the shy beginnings of courtship under the sharp eyes of their relatives.

Unlike his father, Roberto was pleased by the way Romans gargled rather than mouthed their words; and, like a normal teenaged male, he was morbidly attracted by the vulgarity of the common expressions. He had to be careful around his home, however. The usual earthy negative—often heard even at family dinner of his chums in working-class Rome, *"Fa' in culo,"* Do it in your ass—was not one that his parents tolerated, though his sisters thought it almost as funny as the slap across the mouth his first—and last, when his parents were within earshot—use of the phrase had triggered.

Later, when his hormonal balance had begun to restore itself, he saw some reason in his father's judgment. The dialect was as studded with obscenity as the speech of a marine sergeant, and conversation was peppered with gibes that were far more cruel in their callous capitalization on humble origins, physical infirmities, and psychological insecurities.

Roberto's parents, evidencing what for them was a rare exercise in foresight, had decided not to return to Italy after the Germans invaded Poland in September 1939. It did not take a military genius to gauge the superiority of German arms and fighting spirit over those of the French, or a psychoanalyst to know that Mussolini would pounce on the body of France as soon as he judged that the Germans had torn her throat out. Nor did one have to be paranoid to fear what would happen to a family that was partly Jewish if, as seemed probable from the anti-Semitic noises the Fascists were increasingly making, Italy took Nazi racial policies seriously.

What made the judgment unusual was that it was practical. The

20

Rovere family, most of all *il professore*, was noted for not knowing—
or caring—enough about the real world to make practical judgments.
Money was. Florence was. Chicago was. Lake Michigan was. Beauty
and literature were. To the Roveres the real world was not that of
Hitler, Mussolini, Stalin, Chamberlain, or Roosevelt, but of Dante,
Guicciardini, Tesauro, Manzoni, Muratori, or even Moravia. It was
shared by a few foreigners like Shakespeare and Goethe, or perhaps
Hesse and Melville, but not by politicians, living or otherwise. Mussolini was a clown, Hitler and the others figments of journalists' hyperactive imaginations.

In any event, the Roveres settled comfortably in Larchmont, New
York, and *il professore* joined other and poorer refugees from Fascism
in gracing the New School for Social Research. Roberto had remained
in Rome that summer and risked staying on through November 1939
to finish his research. He knew that his father's defection would expose
him to the wrath of Mussolini's bullyboys, but he gambled on their
being too slow witted to link him to his father for many months.

When he had completed a draft of his dissertation in the spring of
1940, after the Nazis had humiliated the British navy and conquered
Denmark and Norway and were in the process of crushing the nu-
merically far superior armies of Britain, France, Belgium, and Holland,
Roberto accepted an appointment at Princeton as an instructor. He
spent the summer revising the dissertation for submission to a pub-
lisher, a task that proved easier than persuading an editor to accept the
manuscript. Outside of Italy, Trilussa was still considered, when he
was considered at all, a minor poet; and most British and American
critics considered Italian poetry, when they considered it at all, to have
begun and ended with Dante. The peninsula's main contribution to
modern poetry, the bulk of those pundits believed, lay in providing
inspiration for artists like Shelley, Keats, and the Brownings.

After a grim year divided between preparing to teach sections (pre-
cepts, they were called at Princeton) in introductory courses and
reading publishers' letters of rejection, Roberto received a brief note
from Columbia University Press expressing enthusiasm for the work
and a desire to publish it "after certain revisions." Along with a hard-
earned reputation for caring about his students, acceptance of the
manuscript set his academic career off to a promising start. True, it

21

would have been better to have had a more prestigious press than Columbia's; but, it was, as *il professore* succinctly commented, *abbastanza*—it would serve.

Then, a few months later came Pearl Harbor, followed by a rapid finish to the fall term, a hasty search for appropriate military service, weeks of waiting for assignment, and three months of training to be a naval officer at a small college in the New England wilderness called Dartmouth. With his commission in June 1942 came orders to Washington to join a small group of officers drawing up plans for the eventual military government of Italy. Given the way that Allied forces around the world were in disorderly retreat, Roberto thought the work just a tad premature, but he was not ready to protest safe duty. According to the *New York Times*, the *Washington Post*, and assorted newsreels, there were places in the world where opponents were exchanging live ammunition rather than angry memoranda. And he had absorbed enough modern Roman philosophy to temper his hatred of Fascism with a concern for personal survival.

It had been good duty. He had merely to survive for twelve months to be promoted to lieutenant, junior grade. At first, however, when he had been crowded into temporary offices along Constitution Avenue, boiling in the summer, freezing in the winter, survival had not always seemed a certainty. Then, in February 1943, shortly after the Pentagon was completed, his office moved to spacious, air-conditioned quarters and his desk became a pleasant corner of his life.

The work itself was interesting. Each of the dozen officers had once been associated with academia. That background plus the fact that all were reserves rather than regulars made relations easy, discipline slack, and production high. The team proceeded as its members were accustomed: They defined a set of problems and tried out alternative solutions until they found the plan that fit best.

The only onerous part of the duty was selling the team's ideas to the professional soldiers, who were dubious that for Italy "national character" meant more than mounds of spaghetti with heavy garlic and tomato sauce. But, while uninformed and not very interested, the professionals were intelligent men, willing to accept the pragmatic argument that a particular scheme, however incongruous to Americans, would work well in Italy and so spare time and troops for other

22

missions. There was, to be sure, some drudgery in preparing technical details, such as calculating the amount of food, water, and medical supplies that various cities would need and devising alternative plans to provide those necessities.

Washington, during the early stages of World War II, was an Eden for a tall, reasonably handsome, young heterosexual bachelor whose inhibitions about sex were social rather than moral. The town was filled with women working for the government. They outnumbered men, depending on the night, four or five or even six to one. Since teenage, Roberto had had a series of girls, had broken a few hearts with his brown-black eyes, and had had his own broken a half dozen times. But it was still a period when sex "all the way" was dangerous, though hardly unknown among the unmarried or unattempted by young males with young females who seemed sufficiently sophisticated to protect themselves against its perils or sufficiently unsophisticated to be unaware of the potential costs.

Roberto had been abstemious, not virginal but abstemious. He liked that word to describe his sex life. In Florence, he had rationalized that the political risks were too great; he and his family had had troubles enough being known as anti-Fascists. As a graduate student at Harvard, he had rationalized that, while one might take a Radcliffe girl to dinner or to bed, one simply didn't marry her. And, to the average American woman of that generation, sex meant marriage. At Princeton, temptations were minimal. The faculty and students were all male, and it was not cricket to seduce a secretary. That taboo, of course, did not preclude an occasional wild fling in Kingston or New Hope.

Sitting on a rooftop in Trastevere, with German troops moving down the Lungo tevere barely five-hundred yards away, Roberto could understand that he had spent much of his youth in libraries rather than bistros not merely, as he had once liked to think, because of a passionate affair with scholarship. There was something of that, perhaps even much of it. But there was also the less pleasant thing, competition with *il professore*. The old man was good, the best in Italy. But *he* could be better. That ambition drove an engine.

He could laugh at his Oedipal rivalry now that he was a spy rather than a scholar. How would *il professore* have been as a spy? Probably

23

damned good, Roberto had to admit. He appeared so bumbling and absentminded that no one, not even the Gestapo, would have suspected the power of his intellect or the iron of his will. He would, no doubt, have gone straight to the military headquarters at the Villa Wolkonsky and asked to see what Roberto had come for, the top-secret machine Enigma, and done so with such an unassuming and instinctive air of authority that some obsessively obedient Teutonic orderly would have brought it to him to photograph.

After a few carefree months in Washington, hopping among the beds of several female civil servants, Roberto had gallantly offered an attractive though much traveled ensign in the WAVEs the opportunity to share an old town house in Alexandria that a maternal uncle had willed him. The WAVE, like most people who came to wartime Washington, had had difficulty in finding a decent room; a town house had seemed a fantasy come true. Roberto's offer of a separate bedroom and bath with her own key to the house as well as to her room made the offer no more attractive but easier to accept. The lock was strong, but not nearly so strong as her libido. Besides, his bedroom was far larger and had a lovely view of the Potomac.

There was mutual affection in the arrangement, but the WAVE had reserved her heart, if nothing else, for another naval person, now on a destroyer in the Central Pacific. Thus, her relationship with Roberto assuaged several needs without causing emotional complications—as long as the valiant destroyer officer remained in the Pacific.

For Roberto, life was very pleasant. Planning to govern Italy was either ludicrously easy or absolutely impossible, but always interesting for one who loved Italians. In neither case, however, did it consume all of his intellectual energy. He found a great deal of time during supposed working hours to begin serious study of another Roman poet, Giuseppe Gioacchino Belli. As reservists and academics themselves, his immediate colleagues had no objections as long as he did his part of the assignments, and to the professional soldiers one book in Italian looked pretty much like any other.

Life was less pleasant in certain other areas of the world. In July 1943, British and American troops landed in Sicily and began a hard, bloody fight to sweep the Germans out. On the mainland, a few weeks later, the Fascist Grand Council demanded Mussolini's resignation.

24

Marshal Pietro Badoglio's interim government asserted with the bravado to which all Italians had long been accustomed—and most become immune—that Italy would be "faithful to her given word" and the glorious struggle for a Fascist victory would continue. The king echoed his marshal: "Let each resume his post of duty, faith, and combat."

Everyone in London, Washington, and Berlin who knew much about international politics and every Italian whosoever understood that these speeches were meant only to allay German suspicions while the new government bargained with the Allies for a separate peace. The Nazi high command knew its partner well enough not to need the transcript that a U-boat, listening to the transoceanic telephone conversations between Roosevelt and Churchill—supposedly safely scrambled—provided of Allied negotiations with Badoglio.

Roberto's idyll ended at almost the same time as Mussolini's. In late July 1943, barely a month after Mr. Justice C. Bradley Walker had entertained his former student and Colonel Lynch, Roberto had been amusing himself before lunch, reading some of Belli's poetry, his desk spread over with a large street map of Rome so that anyone who was not fluent in Italian would have thought him hard at work winning the war. A tight-lipped lieutenant colonel, scarcely older than Roberto and certainly not as handsomely educated, suddenly materialized in the office and, in a tone that indicated that "no" would be an unacceptable response, invited him to lunch with Col. Brian P. Lynch.

The colonel's set of offices was in one of the Pentagon's inner rings. There was only one word on the secretary's door: Planning. Inside, the colonel sat at a conference table with John Winthrop Mason, who despite the weather was dressed in an impeccably pressed three-piece suit, the gold links on his stiffly starched French cuffs just visible below the jacket's sleeve. To Roberto, Lynch looked much like fifty other regular army colonels, lean, tough, and battle weary. Mason was another kind of horse. The arrogance of affluence welled up through his protruding eyes, and the smell of power spread across the man's grotesque face like a heavy after-shave cologne.

The young lieutenant colonel made the proper introductions, then swiftly exited. An orderly immediately began serving a disappointing

25

collection of ham sandwiches, stale potato chips, soggy pickles, and sweetened ice tea without lemon. Between bites Roberto responded to the colonel's questions about life in prewar Rome, where, it turned out, Lynch had spent three marvelous years as an assistant military attaché. John Winthrop Mason said almost nothing during the meal. Nevertheless, Roberto was aware that the older man was listening to and weighing every word he said, doing so, Roberto thought at first, with surprise; then he realized that the look was almost frozen on Mason's unfortunate face.

After lunch, the orderly returned with cookies, fruit, and a pot of thin, overboiled coffee. Roberto would have much preferred thick espresso so that his adrenaline would start pumping and keep his mind alert. Mason took an apple from the tray, admired it, and put it back. Then, after two sips of the brownish liquid from the pot, he spoke his first full sentence. It came from a startlingly high voice. Roberto had expected far more resonance from a head that large. "Mr. Rovere"— the "mister" was technically correct for a naval lieutenant, but Mason did not pronounce the final *e* in Roberto's name. It was a typical American mistake. "What we shall discuss is so highly classified that you might suffer a fatal accident if we were to suspect you might ever reveal that this conversation took place."

He paused to let his message penetrate and to work some sort of magic with his thick lips so as to effect a smile that was as thin as the coffee. It did not occur to Roberto that Mason had intended the smile to indicate that he had spoken in jest.

"North Africa, Churchill said, was not the beginning of the end, but the end of the beginning. The beginning of the end will be our landing in Western Europe. That day is distant. Here is the most important reason."

Mason got up and turned on a radio receiver built into the wall. After a few minutes for the tubes to warm up, the room was filled with a farrago of *dahs* and *dits* from shortwave transmissions. In Officer Training School, Roberto had barely been able to send Morse code, and he could never read more than five words a minute. These operators—he knew enough to recognize several different hands on the keys —were transmitting almost as fast as one normally spoke in a conversation.

26

Mason listened intently for several minutes, then abruptly switched the radio off. "Could you read that?"

"I'm afraid not, sir."

"Neither can we. That is what is postponing the beginning of the end. You have just heard the German naval command and a U-boat. They're probably exchanging information about a convoy in a code we can't break."

"What they're using," Lynch broke in, "is a cipher and a ciphering machine. The Germans call it Enigma. The name fits perfectly."

Mason flicked his protruding eyes at the colonel but did not otherwise deign to acknowledge the intervention. "Those submarines are bleeding us white. Last year they sank six million tons of Allied shipping. This past March alone, they sank more than six hundred thousand tons."

"Six hundred twenty-seven thousand, three hundred seventy-seven," Lynch broke in again. He knew it annoyed Mason to be interrupted. In fact, the colonel had found that interrupting him was just about the only way of getting under the lawyer's cold skin.

"The average freighter," Mason went on, his facial muscles tightening beneath his eyes, "dispatches ten thousand tons. Thus we are losing a large number of ships and a tremendous amount of cargo."

"And human beings," Lynch noted out loud but still almost to himself.

"And human beings." Mason sighed. "We hear those transmissions, but we cannot read a word. You're a naval officer." Roberto felt flattered; he had never thought of himself as a real naval officer, only an actor in costume. "You know what it would mean if we could break their messages. We could divert our convoys and attack the submarines. We could be on the offensive. Later, when we invaded the Continent, we'd know where their troops were, where to land, and where to bomb. In sum, Mr. Rovere, learning Enigma's secret is the most important step toward ending this war."

Mason stopped as abruptly as he had begun. His mouth resumed its accustomed porcine pout. After almost a full minute of stressful silence, Roberto asked, "Why are you telling me this?"

Mason nodded to Colonel Lynch.

"What Mr. Mason has said is plain common sense. The Germans

27

know it as well as we do. What I'm going to add is the classified part of our discussion. It's Top Secret, TSNS. You know what that means, Lieutenant?"

"Yes, sir," Roberto half-smiled. "Top secret, no shit."

"You're damned right, no shit at all. We're planning to put in several teams of agents to 'borrow' an Enigma, photo it, diagram it if they can, and then put it back like the nice law-abiding folks we are. All without the Nazis knowing that any one of our people ever touched their little hummer. Stealing one won't do. If the Nazis know we have their baby, they'll redesign it or junk it for something else, and we'll be out in the cold again."

"Why me?" Roberto asked. "That sounds like a job for a professional second-story man, not a scholar."

"You're right." Mason joined back in. "We are putting in several teams. And the British will make a similar effort. Each team will have some specialty that will give it an edge. You're good in German, bilingual in Italian, and also fluently read, speak, and write the Roman dialect."

"Romanesco is the proper term. Most Italians say Romanaccio, though technically that term should only be used to refer to the slangy aspects . . ."

"Yes," the colonel interrupted. "I remember. You can blend in with the terrain. You've lived there. We can give you real papers and clothes that will make you out a local. We figure that that will be critical. Right now, we don't know where the Germans have an Enigma in Rome, except in their embassy. That one's too heavily guarded. The chances will be better if the military establish themselves in Rome. The Wehrmacht wouldn't dream that we'd try to snatch an Enigma from under their noses. They've got some operating with their troops in the south already. When they settle down to a real defense of Italy, they'll have to establish a major communications center in Rome. We want somebody who can work closely with our 'resident' and with the locals. They can do much of the stuff that requires technical knowledge, but we want *our* man there."

"It sounds pretty farfetched to me," Roberto said, then quickly added, "sir."

"So was Pearl Harbor," Mason put in abruptly. Then he twisted his mouth into that thin smile again. It was warmer than what was left in his coffee cup, but only a trifle. "You're right, it is farfetched. We hope one of our teams will accomplish the mission. But the odds are against it." Mason paused, picked up the apple again, admired it once more, then replaced it on the table. "The odds are about forty to one against you. It would take great courage to accept those odds, but the game is worth the candle."

"Literary research and analysis are a form of problem solving, a kind of detective work," Roberto said. "And, with all due respect, sir, I'd guess the odds at more like four thousand to one."

"You may be correct," Mason conceded. "And you are absolutely correct about your academic work having been a form of problem solving. That's why British MI-Five and MI-Six use dons from Oxford and Cambridge. That is another reason why we want you. We need someone with your skills to cope with a fluid situation."

"How much time do I have to decide?"

"Take your time, Mr. Rovere," Mason replied as he pulled a large gold watch out of his vest pocket. "The colonel and I have another eight minutes and forty-two seconds until we leave for our next appointment."

Roberto blinked. "Could I ask a few questions?"

"No," Mason snapped.

The room became quiet, very quiet. Within Roberto the cynical modern Roman argued against the gallant gladiator, the shrewd urban peasant from Trastevere debated the noble senator. Had shouting, screaming, and obscene gestures been permitted, the gladiator and the senator would have been doomed. The struggle, however, had to be waged in silence, making the modern Romans' defeat inevitable.

Nevertheless, Roberto waited until Mason stood up before saying he agreed. To his surprise, Lynch seemed saddened by his decision. He said nothing, however. His only response was a request for the keys to Roberto's house and car. "You'll be leaving immediately. We'll take care of everything."

"What about my roommate and my family?"

"Stay in this office and write your family that you've been suddenly assigned to sea duty to replace an officer who's had appendicitis," Lynch instructed. "The same cover will do for your roommate. And please tell her that an army friend will be by to put your things in storage. One of my assistants will take care of all the details."

29

"About your roommate," Mason commented as he was leaving the office, "the destroyer of a certain lieutenant, senior grade, is heading toward Mare Island for an overhaul. He will arrive on the east coast within two weeks."

Roberto had no way of hearing the conversation between Colonel Lynch and Mason as they marched down the corridor toward an elevator and a waiting staff car. "That's the last," Mason noted. There was a trace of triumph in his voice. "What's his date of birth?"

"Twelve November 1918, a peacetime baby."

"A Scorpio. Every one of our people is a Scorpio."

"I'm afraid I don't understand why you insisted that all of the agents for Bronze Goddess had to have been born between twenty-four October and twenty-two November."

Mason's voice took on its tone of exaggerated patience. "No, you probably would not; you're a Cancer."

"I'm a what?"

"Your having been born in early July makes your sign Cancer, and Cancers typically have no feel for this sort of analysis. Scorpios may not either, but they make the best spies. Even their negative traits are useful: They tend to be obstinate, secretive, and suspicious. But it's their positive traits that are critical: They tend to be persistent and determined and to have such a deep sense of purpose as to be willing to sacrifice themselves to accomplish their mission."

Lynch smiled. "Sounds like they'd also make great martyrs."

"Precisely. These people will, in all likelihood, become superb martyrs for our Divine Ultra."

"You really don't put any stock in superstitions like astrology, do you?"

Mason's eyes protruded a millimeter more than they usually did. "It would take a Cancer to categorize unwelcome patterns of behavior, empirically verifiable, as 'superstitions' while clinging to the mumbo jumbo of religion. You failed to notice that several times I used the word 'tend.' I spoke of probabilities. People do tend to behave according to the general characteristics described by their signs. Those characteristics were not arbitrarily assigned by some magi in the Middle East; they are the products of centuries of observation."

30

"You really do believe in that crap!" Lynch was unsure whether he was more appalled at Mason's basis of choice or delighted that he had found a weak spot in the man's crocodile skin of hard logic from which all emotional content had been drained.

"One: It is not 'crap.' Two: I do not put my whole faith in astrology nor, for that matter, in anything else except the power of my intellect. I merely follow the law of averages unless I have sound reason to do otherwise. Bronze Goddess requires dedicated spies—you put it more accurately, martyrs. Scorpios tend to make excellent spies and martyrs. Three: There is no reason here not to follow the law of averages. Conclusion: Prudence dictates that we choose Scorpios. I trust I have made myself clear."

"You have." Feeling both a dull ache in the pit of his stomach and a religious need to take a long, hot, soapy shower, Lynch did not pursue the matter.

Roberto's training took place at a base in eastern Virginia. The teams were triply isolated. First, the post itself was deep within pine woods laced with poison ivy and populated mostly by ticks, with an occasional snake for company. There were no furloughs or liberty even for a few hours. The response to requests for professional female visitors was a curt no. "Better to live horny than die satisfied—and soon" was the way one instructor put it. Second, the training area was several miles distant from any other activity on the base. Third, the individual teams—Able and Baker each had two men, Charlie and Dog were singles—were billeted in separate Quonset huts, several hundred yards apart. "The less you know about what the others will be doing, the tighter security will be. That could mean your lives if one team gets caught. What a man doesn't know, he can't tell."

All the agents did, however, share some common training. For the first two weeks it was mostly physical conditioning and practicing Morse code, a simple cipher, and a slightly more elaborate code. Later there was a crash course in photographing documents. Physical exercise was especially difficult for Roberto. Not only had his job in the Pentagon left him in poor shape, so had his entire life-style. Moreover, his cover called for him to have a slight but noticeable limp caused by a broken ankle that had been too hastily set during the battle of El

Alamein. "Poor bastard probably fell out of a jeep racing for Tripoli," Roberto's "coach" explained, "but his story was that he was wounded by a British bomb. The Italian army bought it, and you better stick to it." By clever use of rolls of adhesive tape, the coach made it easier for Roberto to limp; in fact, the tape made it impossible for him not to. Running was painful, jumping agony.

For Able and Baker, the two two-man teams, the training was a bore. They were professionals, a pair of Dutchmen, a Frenchman, and a Belgian who had worked at Rouen before the war. They were older, spoke poor English, and kept to their partners, talking to others only when absolutely necessary. They internalized the instructors' pitch about security. Team Charlie was a solo, a young Basque who had spent a year at Oxford. He, too, was an amateur. Roberto had tried to be friendly with him, but the young man also followed the instructors' warnings. He did so, however, less because he recognized their wisdom than because he accepted their authority.

After the first two weeks, the teams usually met before breakfast for thirty minutes of physical training, then fifty minutes of drill in Morse code. After that they saw each other only at occasional meals and special instructions. The latter included schooling in elementary burglary. The visiting lecturer had been a frequent guest at several state penitentiaries. That part, at least, was interesting. The most fascinating aspect of the training, however, was instruction in Enigma itself.

On a table in front of the trainees was a bulky machine about the size of a large cash register. On its front was a standard typewriter keyboard. "Gentlemen, what you see here," the instructor began, "is officially labeled 'The Glowlamp Ciphering and Deciphering Machine, "Enigma." ' It was developed after World War I by Dr. Arthur Scherbius. He offered it on the commercial market during the nineteen twenties. In 1926, the German navy adopted a modified version, a few years later the Wehrmacht and still later the Luftwaffe followed suit. The U.S. Army Signal Corps had the foresight to buy this gem while it was still available on the open market. The cost, including packing and shipping, came to less than a hundred sixty-eight dollars."

"If you have it," Roberto broke in, "what are we doing here?"

"Because, sir"—the instructor smiled—"this is an early and very simple model. It can't read the more sophisticated versions any better than we can. It helps us to understand what we're up against and what we need to know. With this model and detailed pictures—better yet, blueprints—of the later version, we can build an Enigma that can speak and read like a Prussian general.

"Let me explain how the beast works," the instructor went on. "Would you type out a word for me, Lieutenant?" He nodded toward Roberto.

Roberto hit the keys for "okay," but on the display on the top of the machine "ZABR" lit up. "Try again, please," the instructor asked. Robert hit the keys again. This time the display read "LEXJ." Once more, please." The third time "MPUQ" came out.

"There," the instructor beamed, "is the beauty of the beast. As you all know, a cipher is simply a system of substitutions of letters or numbers for other letters or numbers. In a simple cipher A might become C, B would be X, and so forth. In a more complex cipher, the first time A appeared it might be C, but the second time Y, the third time M, and so forth.

"Now, there are two functions a cipher must fulfill. It has to be secure so the enemy can't read it; and it must be usable by real people who're in the middle of a war and need information quickly. You can't have the CO of a Panzer regiment racing across the Russian steppes carrying a dozen books telling him that the four hundred and twelfth time today he uses the letter A it becomes the number seven and the two hundred and eleventh time he uses E it becomes an X. He could never send messages rapidly enough for them to have any meaning; and he'd have an even worse time trying to figure out what the hell higher headquarters was telling him.

"On the other hand, while a simple cipher allows you to shackle and unshackle messages quickly, it permits the enemy to read your mail. In every language certain letters appear much more frequently than others. The first thing any cryptologist does is to count frequencies. There's also the problem of certain recurring words and phrases. You can do a lot to mask those by transmitting only in letter groups of the same size. We send all traffic in five-letter groups, some other countries in three- or four-letter groups. So all words in the cipher that the enemy intercepts are the same length, though in the real language a particular word may be partly in one group, partly in another, and long words, like those the Heinies love, spread across two, three, or even four groups. Still, unless your cipher is pretty complex, you're stuck with the problem of repeating letters.

"A machine like Enigma solves all these difficulties. It's not tiny but it is portable, even this older model. The newer ones, so far as we can tell from the background of propaganda films, are smaller, like a big typewriter. It's possible you can hook them directly to a radio. We aren't sure. In any event, it can be transported by jeep or, in emergencies, by hand. And it's both simple and fast. All a man has to do to encipher or decipher is to put the machine onto a particular setting and type normally. Here, Lieutenant, type the ciphers and see what comes out."

Each time Roberto typed in the gibberish that had appeared earlier, the machine produced "okay."

"We must possess," the young Basque spoke hesitantly and diffidently, "many thousands of German messages. Is it not that one can find enough repetitions to permit the fracturing of the cipher?"

"Yes and no. In a short run, no. Let me explain something of the mechanics. Here." He lifted the cover from the machine. "Inside are three rotors and a reflector. Each time you strike a key it sends an electrical impulse through each of the rotors. As the impulse goes through a rotor, it changes the letter. Then the letter strikes the reflector and goes through the rotor gismos again, and is changed three more times. The fiendish part is that every time you strike a key, each rotor changes its position so that the next letter goes through a different set of changes. Each rotor on this model has sixty different settings, and, our people *think*, the newer models have at least four and maybe five rotors. If they have only four, then there are about thirteen million possible courses a letter could take each time an operator strikes a key—*if* the newer model does not have a reflector. If it has a reflector, then the number of possibilities is about thirteen million squared, or maybe it's cubed or to the fourth power. I don't know. I can't count that high. For the long run, however, you're right about Enigma. We can break the little hummer, but our mathematicians want a couple of centuries."

No one laughed.

"But how is it that the Germans read their own messages?" the Basque asked.

"There are two simple ways. Either for certain time periods, say a day, all Engimas have their rotors set at particular positions when they begin to transmit or receive. Or the early part of a message contains a coded instruction for the rotors' settings. One of the most critical things you people will have to do is to look around for anything like a code book or instruction sheet. You'll also have to note very precisely the rotor settings at the time you first see your target. If we learn those settings we might be able to use the messages we've recorded from that day to break the system. The code book or instruction sheet would be surer, however.

"Now, gentlemen, look at this monster carefully. During the next few weeks you will learn how to operate it; you will learn how to take it apart; you will learn how to put it back together; and you will learn how to diagram it—and you will learn how to do all of these things in your sleep. When you see the new model, it's going to look like an old friend who's had a face-lift."

The instructor had kept his word. Together, the teams had ten hours of lectures on Enigma, then each team spent a minimum of two hours a day on the machine, stripping it down, putting it together, and diagramming every one of its many parts. The last dozen diagrams were done from memory.

In early September, just before the American Fifth Army landed at Salerno, south of Naples, three of the teams shipped out of the camp. Roberto, however, remained for another week of thumb twiddling. Just as he was convinced for the hundredth time that he'd been forgotten, a staff car took him to the airport at Norfolk, where Colonel Lynch and John Mason were waiting on board a C-47.

One quick glance made Roberto realize he had forgotten how ugly Mason was. After their luncheon in July, he hadn't thought such slippage possible. The two men gave him a routine set of written orders and more complex verbal instructions. He would fly with them to Andrews Field, near Washington; there, he would board another plane that would take him to the Azores, Gibraltar, Sicily, a submarine, and finally Italy.

On the flight to Andrews, Lynch provided some hard information. "We're moving you into place. Your balloon is going up. As you know, Marshal Badoglio has surrendered, but the Germans have rescued Mussolini and some Fascists are still in the war."

"As much as they ever were," Mason interjected.

"Yes, the army put up a bit of resistance against the Germans' occupying Rome, but the Wehrmacht smashed that in quick order. The German embassy in the Villa Wolkonsky has shipped a lot of personnel north to Lago di Garda, where Mussolini is setting up a new government. But the Villa is still important to us. That's where the Germans have set up their military headquarters to govern Rome. Field Marshal Albert Kesselring has kept his command post for the operations of the German army in Frascati. The general who runs Rome is Hans Mueller, a fat drunk. The description we have on file says that he's personally slovenly and, to a lesser degree, professionally slovenly as well. Very un-German. He's too far advanced in his drinking to be trusted with an important command."

Conversation stopped while Mason lit one of his fat cigars. Then Lynch went on: "General Mueller is one weakness. Rome is a second. As you remember, it's a city that knows something of sin. Mueller is not likely to run a tight ship, at least as far as his own officers are concerned. He wouldn't mind terrorizing a few hundred thousand Italian civilians, but he will also expect his officers to enjoy themselves."

Mason muttered something unintelligible. Lynch paused, trying to catch the high-pitched mumble, then continued: "And Mueller has an Enigma in his headquarters. Security will be tight there, but probably not as tight as it was when only the embassy ran the villa. That's another weakness in our favor."

"There's still one more," Mason broke in. "Mueller's chief of cryptography is an academic like you, a mathematician. Herr Dr. Otto Schwartzkümmel—brilliant, overqualified for the post, but that's very German."

Lynch handed Roberto a file. "Here's what we have on him. Read it carefully on the flight leg to the Azores. Then seal it and give it to the pilot. He's a courier and will return it to us."

"The gist of it," Mason said, "is that Otto has a taste for boys. These things run along national lines, the Irish with whiskey, the Germans with pederasty."

Lynch started to speak, then thought better of it.

"How does that help me?" Roberto asked. "That's not my style, and there're limits to what I'll do for my country."

36

Lynch looked embarrassed, but Mason did not even blink. "We do not expect you to seduce him, merely to use this information. Such people are vulnerable."

"Blackmail?"

"Blackmail is a vulgar word," Mason noted.

"It sounds obscene," Roberto said.

"Obscene?" Lynch was suddenly angry. "Obscene? When I first got back to the States from the Pacific, I picked up a copy of *Life*. There was a picture of a dead marine—just a kid—washed up on the beach at Tarawa. Half his clothes were rotted off, and rigor mortis had set in. That was obscene—a dead teenager. I want to stop that kind of obscenity. Don't hand me any holier-than-thou shit. I don't give a rat's ass for some Nazi queer."

"We can now move beyond the basics," Mason said coolly. "But do not mention Otto to our 'resident.' He would not approve, and that would complicate your work."

"Your contact," Lynch said, almost calm again, "is a woman named Anna Caccianemici. You'll stay at her apartment. She lives on the Vicolo del Cedro in Trastevere. Here's the number. You know the street?"

Roberto nodded. He recalled the street—and the restaurant at its head, La Parolaccia—"the dirty talk"—where singing waiters insulted customers in filthy dialect songs while serving hearty Roman food.

"Watch Anna. It shouldn't be too difficult." Lynch handed Roberto a picture of a fair-haired young woman. Her facial features were attractive, but the expression in her eyes was hard. "Watch her, she's tough," Lynch went on. "Don't get any romantic notions because she's working for us. She's a Communist, and she's a professional."

"I'll be careful."

"That would be prudent. Your code name will be Raven. Tell Anna your Uncle Antonio sent you. In this packet is a sheet of dialogues you're to use for ID with our people. Memorize them and follow them. Our 'resident' you'll know only as Father Christmas. He knows all about you. He'll get you out when you've completed the mission. He can contact you, but probably he will only respond to your requests. The only way you can contact him is via a pattern of laundry hung outside Anna's window. That description is also in the packet. Make sure you destroy all the documents before you go ashore."

Roberto took the envelope. "What else?" he asked.

"A Minox camera with plenty of film. You've been instructed on how to use it. Keep it in this waterproof bag until you're ashore. And here's some cash." Lynch handed him a wad of old bills and a dozen coins. "Please sign the receipt. It's for a hundred thousand lire and three hundred German marks."

Roberto took the slip of paper and signed. "You don't expect me to buy my way into the villa, do you?"

Mason frowned. "At fourteen lire to the dollar, you have in excess of seven thousand dollars. And Father Christmas can provide more if it becomes essential."

"And if I sign a receipt. This summer the lira went to two hundred to the dollar on the *real* market. So I've got only five hundred dollars."

"Make do." Mason waved his hand to indicate the issue was closed.

"That's it as far as I'm concerned," Lynch put in. "And our timing is good." The plane was taxiing down the runway toward the terminal at Andrews. "Do you want to add anything, sir?"

"Nothing." Mason extended his hand and did his best to make the twisting of his mouth seem like a genuine smile.

The three men deplaned, Roberto awkwardly limping toward the administration building, Lynch and Mason striding toward the waiting LaSalle. When they had taken a dozen steps, the colonel halted and called for Roberto to wait a moment. The older officer came over and put his arm on Roberto's shoulder. "Look, I'm sorry I blew up. I get even more worked up than most people about how filthy war is. Just be very careful. Don't trust anyone, anyone. If you're in doubt, run. Father Christmas should be able to get you out or at least hide you. But for God's sake, don't tell him about Mason's blackmail scheme. He's a priest and might suddenly become very uncooperative. If you're caught—I hope you won't be, but if you are—it's all right to bargain if it gets too rough. You can tell them that Able dropped in near Utrecht three days ago, Baker near Rouen last night. Charlie should cross the border near Barcelona tomorrow. I don't have any details, but the British are putting in three or four teams. Their liaison officer hasn't arrived yet, so that's all I have."

"Wouldn't that hurt the mission?"

"Not likely. By the time you get to Rome the others will be miles from their entry points. And, if they catch one team, the Germans will realize we're making a major effort."

"Well, I guess I should say thanks."

"Don't say anything, just be careful." Lynch turned on his heel and marched away.

Back in the limousine, Mason asked, "Did you speak the speech as I pronounced it to you, trippingly on the tongue?"

"I feel like Judas," Lynch snarled.

"Judas has received a bad press. If your Jesus had to die to save the world, his betrayer was the real hero. It takes more courage to sacrifice a friend for a cause than to die for it oneself."

Lynch's face turned florid. He twisted uncomfortably in his seat. West Point's discipline ultimately beat down a Celtic urge to commit mayhem, but it was only a limited victory. "Bullshit," he muttered. "With all due respect, sir, you don't know anything about dying or asking other men to die." Then after a sullen pause, he repeated, "Sir."

"You're correct," Mason responded blandly. He brushed an unruly hank of hair from his forehead. "I also know nothing about heroes. Those departments fall under your jurisdiction. I know only about clients. And the government of the United States is my client. And keeping secret Ultra's ability to read Enigma is vital to the interests of the United States. Now, I would appreciate silence in which to ponder our next move."

The flights across the Atlantic and Mediterranean were jumbled nightmares of unpadded aluminum bucket seats, quick stretching of muscles on black tarmac, watery black coffee, paper-thin slices of ham and dry cheese on stale white bread, and used and reused airsick bags. Roberto found very little new information at the submarine base in Sicily other than that the rendezvous was scheduled for 3:00 A.M., Monday, 27 September.

When he awoke after a brief nap on the sub, he changed into the Italian clothes that were in his valise, recited from memory (again) the recognition dialogues for his contacts and the laundry code for Father Christmas, destroyed the paper, then checked and rechecked his Italian documentation: an ID card with photograph, a certificate of discharge from the Italian army, an *annonaria* (ration card), a driver's license (also with a photograph)—all made out to Roberto Carlo Umberto Esposito. He also filled his pockets with what the people in Virginia called "authenticating trivia": a half-used pack of *cerini*—Italian matches—a dozen small coins, an old pocket knife, a receipt from a Roman trolley, a key to the apartment in Trastevere, and a cork from a bottle of wine from the Abruzzi.

"*Esposito*," the exposed. There was too much irony to laugh at. In medieval Italy, when a woman abandoned her infant, she usually placed it on the steps of a church. Gradually the custom became so established that pastors built a rough equivalent of a lazy susan in one of the church doors so that a mother could push her "exposed" infant into the shelter of the building. The good nuns who ran the orphanages gave such foundlings the surname of Esposito (with the accent on the second syllable). Exposed, abandoned, poor bastard—all, Roberto thought grimly, fit him exactly.

The rendezvous went reasonably smoothly. A little below Civitavecchia, almost thirty-five miles north of the mouth of the Tiber, the submarine lay on the surface for twelve harrowing minutes until a faint light winked the prearranged signal. Sailors helped Roberto into a small, inflatable life raft of the kind used by bombers. It was marked with the numbers of a B-24 squadron based in North Africa. If the Germans found it, they would have no reason to doubt that it had contained an unfortunate flier or two.

Ashore in the sandy darkness, a burly Italian helped Roberto cast the raft adrift and led him to a truck pulled off the side of the road. The vehicle was half loaded with a cargo of chestnuts, zucchini, cucumbers, and several huge *fiaschi* of local wine. It was powered by *bombole* (bottles) of natural gas, towed behind in a small trailer.

They were halfway to Rome before Roberto realized that he had forgotten to begin his part of the ID dialogue. The driver had also neglected to go through his part, but the odds were astronomical that a person coming ashore in the dark was either an American, an Englishman, or Neptune himself. For a time, Roberto had wondered whether he would have to—or could—use the clasp knife in his pocket, but he soon dismissed the thought. The man had not asked for money, and no Italian traitor would lead his victim into a German trap while he still had a full purse.

Roberto went over his cover again. His family were Abruzzesi, peasants from the wild mountains east and south of Rome, where the Trebbiano grape produces the world's best white wine, or so the Abruzzesi claim. The Espositos had come to Rome in search of their fortune, or anyone else's that was unguarded. The father, uncle, and three sons knew how to plant and tend grape vines and how to open locked doors and windows. The mother and two daughters knew an even older skill, one, however, that family pride prevented their practicing except when the menfolk were short of cash.

Faced with small demand in the city for grape tenders, the Espositos had fallen back on their other talents. Quite naturally, they had settled in Trastevere. Eventually Roberto Carlo Umberto and his older brother were drafted. The third brother became a long-term tenant of the Regina Coeli when a sharp-eyed *carabiniere* caught him wearing a stately gold watch that had once graced the person of the policeman's father.

Soon after Roberto Carlo Umberto Esposito's discharge from the army, an event convinced what was left of the family to return to the Abruzzi, where life was safer and food more plentiful. The event was Roberto's death from knife wounds suffered in an affair of honor involving the lately virginal sister of a Neapolitan. Because reporting the death would have involved surrendering Roberto's ration card and perhaps also forgoing the pleasure of personal revenge, the Espositos had kept silent. Later, the resistance had obtained the identity papers through a combination of bribery and blackmail.

The two Robertos bore sufficient physical resemblance that the photographs on the documents would serve. A more accurate likeness might have raised suspicions, especially since the pictures were four years old. Roberto Rovere, however, was sufficiently sophisticated to realize that his cover was good enough to survive only a cursory check.

It was after six before the slow-moving truck reached the outskirts of Rome. Traffic was light as the driver negotiated the Via Gregorio Settimo, then turned off to cross the Gianicolo and reach the open market in the Piazza San Cosimato, in the heart of Trastevere.

It was immediately evident that the food supply was short. In prewar days, twenty or thirty bustling merchants would already have unloaded baskets of fish, slabs of meat, baskets of olives, fruit, and fresh vegetables. There would have been a babble of raucous voices, some talking, some arguing, others making catcalls at young, unmarried women. The men would have been using their hands to converse, cajole, or threaten, and their eyes to toss lecherous glances up at the windows around the piazza in the hope of glimpsing a woman who had forgotten to pull the shades while she dressed. The piazza's market had been Rome at its best, earthy, loud, full of raw sexual suggestion, ripe wine, good food, and the promise of a gloriously sunny day to enjoy.

Today, however, it was not the same place, except for the weather. There were a dozen men like Roberto's driver, each unloading only a few crates. They went about their work quickly and, for Romans, silently, even morosely. There was noise, but it came from the potential customers who were held back by a covey of police. Soon they would become an angry phalanx, each woman skilled in the art of kneeing or elbowing her way to the front.

Roberto thanked the driver—who only grunted something as he accepted a wad of lire—hopped down from the cab, and, carrying his small Italian valise, started around the huge palazzo that Pope Pius XI had built to house papal offices. There were two ways to get to his contact's apartment on the Vicolo del Cedro. He chose the more obvious route across the picturesque Piazza Santa Maria, a cobblestoned meadow in the gnarled forest of tenements called Trastevere. In better days, three open-air restaurants and two bars had fronted on the piazza. It was too early for the restaurants, but it looked as if they were all closed. The bars, however, were still functioning.

Across the piazza, he turned down the narrow Vicolo del Fonte dell' Olio. It twisted twice in ninety-degree arcs, allowing him to pause a full three minutes, unseen from the piazza, to make sure he was not being followed. At the exit of the dell' Olio onto the smaller Piazza Renzi, he stopped again. No one came from the Santa Maria, though several heavy, black-clad signoras, rosaries ostentatiously dangling from their hands, shuffled toward morning Mass.

As rapidly as his limp permitted, Roberto crossed that piazza to the Via del Cipresso, which fed into the other side. The second door had once been stained a bright red. It was darker now, and peeling. That door had been an affectation of a Florentine artist, one of Roberto's boyhood friends, who had bought an apartment on the tenement's first floor (second floor by American reckoning), gutted it, and converted it into a studio for himself and a convenient loft with a wonderfully pneumatic double bed for his mistress. The artist had abandoned the studio—and his mistress—when she produced a full-blown case of syphillis, contracted, she had dogmatically insisted, from the public toilets on the roof of St. Peter's. Roberto had labeled her claim as the doctrine of the immaculate infection.

The Cipresso twisted much like the dell' Olio, and he took advantage of the sharp turn to halt a third time. The only activity came from the slap of last night's garbage onto the street, the swish of a sweeper's vain efforts to stem Trastevere's flow of dirt, the scuffling of an aged woman swaying along on bloated legs supported by swollen feet encased in bedroom slippers, and the scampering of a scrawny, pregnant cat as she triumphantly leaped onto a reeking pile of freshly thrown refuse.

Roberto limped on and turned left onto the Vicolo del Cinque. There was more clatter here. It was a street of shops. Tradesmen were rolling up their clanking iron shutters, while two men unloaded great *fiaschi* of red and yellow Castelli Romani wine from a horse-drawn dray. From above came the sound of rattling silverware and dishes. Two hundred yards later, past the tightly shuttered Parolaccia, the Cinque, with neither reason nor warning, became the Vicolo del Cedro.

Empty wash lines were strung across the street. On a good day like this, in another hour the passage would have more cloth catching the sun and wind than a Spanish galleon beating home from the Indies. The windows were all still closed to protect the inhabitants from the night drafts, "the blows of air," which, Romans knew, carried every sort of evil in their inky currents.

Roberto could divert little attention to the upper stories. Navigating the scattered heaps of garbage, puddles of slimy, muddy water, and piles of steaming horse manure required concentration as well as agility.

Up ahead, on the right, a green door, half open, carried the proper number. He gently pushed it. Two filthy, skinny cats came bounding out, immediately followed by the heavy odor of feline urine mixed with last night's garlic. There was no electric bulb; but with the door open, the whitewashed walls and pale gray marble floor reflected enough illumination from a skylight on the top floor for Roberto to make his way up the stairs to Anna's apartment.

The top of the stairs was bathed in early sun from the skylight.

43

Ahead was a heavy metal door, next to it a bell. Roberto pushed it softly, although anyone in the building who was awake would have heard him limping up the stairs. In Trastevere, people made it their business to know who came and went and why. Three short rings, as he had been instructed. Then, after a few seconds, he inserted the large, old-fashioned key into the lock and turned it twice. The tumblers clinked into place, the door opened slowly, and he took a hesitant step into the room.

"*Chi è?*" Who's there? The voice was much lower pitched than Mason's, yet distinctly female. Because he was standing in a pool of light, Roberto could only dimly make out a woman sitting on the sofa. Reflections off the metallic object in her hand made it evident he was looking at a pistol.

"I am Roberto, also called Raven," he responded with the first part of his identification.

"*Dunque?*" she asked flatly. So? "Keep your hands in front of you and keep them very still when you talk." The pistol barrel focused its long eye on his belly button.

"So? So I've walked a long way. I haven't been followed. And I'm dead tired. You are Anna and I am Raven. I was told I could stay here."

"I am Anna but I don't know any Raven. I don't like birds, except plump chickens freshly roasted. Look around, bird, do you see any space here for a guest?" She swung the pistol in a very tight circle.

The apartment was small, tiny by American standards. The living room—dining room—kitchen, with a bathroom blocked off in one corner, was scarcely eighteen by eighteen feet. In the middle of the room, open steps, more like a ladder than a staircase, led to a platform. Roberto took the risk of putting down his bag and walking to the ladder to see the next level. In fact, there were two upper levels. Over one part of the multipurpose room and bolted to the walls was a loft that, much like the apartment on the Cipresso, held a double bed and an old-fashioned wardrobe; a few steps higher and more toward the kitchen part of the basic floor was a smaller platform, with its own supports attached to the walls. That second loft held a desk, a chair, another wardrobe, and three wire cages, each with a pair of rabbits.

"There is also a terrace on the roof," Anna said, without lowering the pistol.

44

"Uncle Antonio was very clear that—"

"How is Uncle Antonio these days?" she cut in.

Roberto suddenly realized that once again he had forgotten to complete the ritual of identification. "Uncle Antonio has not been well."

The pistol moved from his navel. "*Cretino*! Why didn't you give me Antonio's name right away? I was ready to shoot you. We are not part of an amateur drama here, Roberto Raven. When someone gives you lines to read, read them; and read them *exactly* as you have been taught. The alternative can be a bullet in your brain or a cell in the Fascist torture center at the Palazzo Braschi or the place the Gestapo are setting up on the Via Tasso."

"What do we do now?" Roberto asked. He was, in fact, very tired.

Anna got up and opened the drapes, letting the morning light flood the small apartment so that Roberto could see her clearly. Her features were more angular, her nose longer and more slender than in the photographs. She was also thinner, probably the result of the shortage of food. Nevertheless, she exuded the animal magnetism he had been warned about; and much of it came from her green eyes. "Do you have an *annonaria*?" she asked.

He nodded and flipped his ration book to her, along with a thick cluster of lire.

"From these we can eat. We'll do as well with the lire as with the ration stamps. One advantage of this apartment is that the Cinque conceals the best black market inside old Rome. While I look for food, you drag that bad leg up those stairs, feed the rabbits some of the grass I've collected on the roof, and clean out their cages. Then take them on the terrace for some sun. But don't let them out of your sight, even for a moment. Our Christian neighbors would steal them in a wink. They're professional thieves, and those rabbits are our only sure source of meat. We can catch an occasional cat, of course, but we have to entice them into the apartment. Some people get angry if we trap them in the street. The Romans say the geese once saved the city from the barbarians. I say today it's the cats' turn." Her voice was more sneering than ironical.

"They keep the rats away from the open garbage," Roberto noted.

"Soon we'll be eating the rats, too, if your American friends don't leave their whores in Salerno and start fighting Germans."

TWO

Rome, Monday, 27 September 1943

At noontime Roberto went up to the terrace. From that perch he had an excellent view of the street and the women in the windows who guarded its twisting way. He could see Anna when she was a hundred yards down the Cedro, just as she passed La Parolaccia. She strode like a haughty queen, head high, depending on some mysterious radar to guide her feet among the garbage. Above her the women passed on vulgar insults about her. To them she was *la Strega*, the witch.

She called out no greeting when she entered the apartment, but Roberto could hear clanking in the kitchen below. Thirty minutes later, she brought a tray up to the terrace and set it on the table. There were two plates, each with half of a small, broiled fish, two green salads without dressing, a half dozen chestnuts, and two chunks of brown bread. There was also the Italian equivalent of a silent butler. She motioned toward it. "That's for your crumbs. We save them. The ration of bread is only two hundred fifty grams a day; that's about half of one of your pounds. And we have to find it before we can buy it. When we do, it's usually made from ground chestnuts or chaff rather than wheat flour. The revolution makes for tight bellies."

"Use my lire for the black market."

"That will help with our neighbors down the street, but to get the best stuff, you have to go straight to the *contadini*. I don't have the time or the transportation to get out to the countryside, and it would be too risky for you. But we'll survive. I steal food from the restaurant where I work. We used to attract the Fascists; now the Germans are our clients. It's easy to rob them."

After eating, Roberto brought the rabbits inside, and Anna cleared the table, carefully brushing the crumbs onto the silent butler and then putting them in a bag. Downstairs she took a long toothpick from a pack near the stove and went to work with it while she put six table-spoons of what looked like coffee into an espresso pot and then added four demitasse cups of water.

"Chicory and barley," she explained as she poured two steaming cups of the thick syrup. "Liquid *mèrda*, but it's all we have. It can't keep you awake, and it's a way of getting the sugar down—I don't bake." She put a teaspoon of coarse brown sugar into each cup.

Roberto grimaced as he took a tentative sip. Anna laughed. "Drink it like a Roman. Once you get it past your taste buds, it isn't half bad." She quaffed hers in a single gulp, like a man standing at a bar. Roberto followed her example. It had the consistency of espresso, if not the flavor.

"You'll get used to it." Her voice hardened. "*Allora*, we get to busi-ness, Roberto americano. What I've been told about your mission sounds idiotic. Only a cretin would think you're going to sneak into the Villa Wolkonsky and photograph that machine, that Rebus."

"Enigma," Roberto corrected.

"Whatever. You must have some plan. Tell me about it."

As succinctly as he could, Roberto summarized the background and vulnerability of Otto Schwartzkümmel, the chief of cryptography. "How we could go about this business, I don't know. Frankly, I don't like it; but I don't have any other ideas."

Anna laughed, genuinely pleased. "At last, I see hope for you Americans. This will be fun, blackmailing a German *rottincuolo*. Your *capo* must have Italian blood. Let me think about it. I have some German 'friends' now. They might help us—without realizing it, of course."

Roberto made no reply.

"You don't seem pleased," she noted. "Why? Do you like boys, too?" She was sneering again, not teasing.

Roberto looked at her angrily. "I don't like boys, young or old. A natural mistake for you, I suppose, since you undoubtedly prefer women."

"I would prefer make love to a *stronzo* than to any woman I know. But don't get any ideas."

Roberto stood up. "Your virtue, if any, is safe. I'm too tired to chase you."

"There'll be no chasing," Anna said, reaching out to tap the pistol on the low mantel. "My virtue is my own concern. So is my survival, and that comes first. Use the sofa," she said curtly. "I'm due at work in a few hours, and I have some errands to attend to first."

Eight hours later she returned and woke Roberto out of a deep sleep. For a few moments he had no idea where he was. The whitewashed walls of the small apartment were strange, and no light came from the outside to help him with identification. "Don't be alarmed," she said as she closed the drapes and lit a pair of candles. She muttered something about Fascist swine not being able to make the electricity work. Then she opened her purse. "I have a surprise for you, Roberto Raven. *Ecco, guarda un po'.*" Behold, look. She took out an old piece of newspaper. Wrapped inside were two *bigne,* the Roman name for chewy but airy rolls, and six *mazzancole,* large marinated shrimp, already cooked. "In better light you could see what a feast we have. The *bigne* were made with real flour, and the *mazzancole* are fat and pink. They were grilled over a hickory fire. And I have a little wine."

She fumbled through the cupboard by the sink and produced a liter bottle of San Pellegrino mineral water, its contents replaced with the dark yellow of one of the Castelli Romani wines. "I'll set the table while you shower."

The "shower" in the tiny bathroom was a metal cubicle whose plumbing produced a thin trickle of water. The *scaldabagno,* a gas heater that ran only when water went through its pipes, flickered and huffed, but barely enough to turn the water into a slow, tepid stream. "Take care with the soap," Anna called. "It's all we have for another five days."

Roberto looked out the shower curtain and saw her in the same room, casually brushing her long hair. She made no effort to move when he turned off the water. For a few minutes, he hesitated to leave the metal cubicle; then Anna pulled back the curtain and flipped him a damp and not especially clean towel. "Don't stand there and catch pneumonia," she said, then went back to the kitchen area.

When he was dressed, Roberto joined her. "Where did you get this food?"

"I stole it from a very stupid German officer who likes to have his dinner in bed with two whores—any two whores. The peasant insists

48

on dinner at seven. Anyone uncivilized enough to eat at that early hour deserves to be robbed."

Roberto dropped the subject. He was not quite certain of her relationship to the German and his *ménage à trois*. He was, however, reasonably certain that he did not wish to know. "Have you been thinking about my mission?"

"Some, but I need to know how well you can perform."

"The United States government thinks my performance is adequate; otherwise I wouldn't be here," Roberto said stuffily.

"The United States government is an old woman. Her needs are not those of a young woman. Let us go into the loft and test your performance by higher standards."

Rome, Tuesday, 28 September 1943

Anna and Roberto slept late that morning. She suggested that they celebrate what she called their alliance by eating breakfast at the bar on the Piazza Santa Maria. It would cost a few ration coupons and too many lire. But, she argued, the small apartment was cramped with two people in it, the sun was shining beautifully, winter, with its short, dreary days was coming, and eating out made a morning seem festive, even if the coffee would be a *misto* of chicory and barley and the *cornetti* would not be made from real flour.

At the café the two seated themselves at a table out of doors and enjoyed the sun, the children climbing over the fountain, and even the ersatz coffee and rolls. After half an hour, Anna excused herself and went inside, toward the single rest room, beyond the end of the bar. She was wearing a gray, lightweight sweater that stretched tautly across her chest and slacks that bagged in the legs but were almost skintight across her hips and bottom.

As she walked through the outdoor tables, most of the males—all were under seventeen, over sixty, or else somehow crippled—leered at her, but they did so in hungry silence. Everyone knew she lived in Trastevere. And in an area where knives could flash as swiftly as tempers, an adult male did not make advances at a woman from the neighborhood, for fear of provoking a relative or lover. In the public market, where only women would be shopping, a merchant might get by with an occasional catcall or even a lewd comment to an unmarried woman, but not even a suggestive remark was safe in a bar that catered only to the neighborhood.

Anna returned the gazes with her hard stare. Roberto was fascinated by the scene. He pretended to be reading *Il Messagero*, Rome's Fascist newspaper, but he was able to notice that when she returned their stares several older men immediately grabbed their genitals. Touching one's privates was a historic Italian method of warding off the evil eye. But Trasteverini seldom took chances with such critical aspects of life; they preferred a definitive grope to a possibly less efficacious touch. The action was mute but substantial evidence of Anna's reputation in the neighborhood as *la Strega*.

As she walked inside the café, she motioned to Stefano, a handsome, slight fifteen-year-old boy who was working as barman, to join her at the far end of the room. One glance at his eyes showed that he shared the older men's admiration of Anna's body, but not their assessment of her character. He worshiped her as only a teenager can adore an "older woman."

There was only one other person inside, Stefano's elderly mother, and she was hard of hearing and stationed at the cash register at the other end of the bar. Anna stood next to the wall, in the narrow aisle behind the large espresso *macchinetta*. Given the height of the machine and of the bar itself, it would have been next to impossible for anyone coming into the dark room from the brilliant sunlight even to know she was present. Stefano walked daintily down the length of the bar and stood beside the *macchinetta*, within a few feet of Anna. She placed her left hand on his hip, her fingers pulsing gently. "Do you have a message for me, *caro*?" she whispered.

"*Signorina*," he stammered, "I do not think it is wise for me to become involved."

"I know, *caro*, I know," she purred. "Your mamma tells you to be careful. Your father is dead; one of your brothers is in Russia, a second went to the Palazzo Braschi and has never been seen again, and your sister disgraced the family by being raped by a German soldier after the fighting a few weeks ago. You are the youngest, the only one left. Her bambino, that's how she thinks of you, her bambino. Don't worry, *caro*, it's only natural. But you're not a bambino, you're a man now, aren't you?" She took his hand and gently cupped it under her left breast. "A man needs many things. Most important, he needs to make his own decisions." She could feel his hand tighten almost involuntarily. "Did you see the German this morning?"

"I saw him," Stefano spoke resentfully. "He said only '*Va bene.*'" Okay.

"That's all? You're sure?"

"Yes, I'm sure."

Anna stepped back, letting his hand slide away. "You are a good comrade, Stefano. And you are a man."

"*Signorina.*" It was a plea, a prayer.

"No, *caro*, don't touch me again. I might make you take me right here in this public place. When the war and the revolution are finished, we shall have weekends, perhaps months of weekends together. Just you and me and a huge, warm bed to make love in all day and all night, as we did in my apartment."

"But him?" The boy motioned toward the tables outside.

"Him? Don't worry about him. He is just a wounded soldier I am working with. He's stupid, but he could be useful to the party. He has nothing to do with you and me." She put her fingers to her lips and then touched his mouth. "Now, take back a message for me this afternoon: 'Urgent. Tonight.'"

"I don't think, I . . ." Stefano began.

"You must. For me." She touched his lips again. "Think of what it will be like for us when we get rid of these Fascist butchers. I lie in bed at night, Stefano, and pretend the war is over and you are taking care of me again, as you did after the Fascists let me go."

"*Cos' è?*" What is it? The old *signora* at the cash register was shouting suspiciously. "What's going on? *Bello*," she called to Stefano, "I've told you not to let that woman get close to you."

Anna winked slyly at Stefano and, with the bar between them and the *signora*, gently stroked his thigh several times. Then she turned and entered the rest room.

Outside, as Anna walked through the tables again, Roberto looked up from the newspaper. The performers were replaying their earlier roles.

"What dialect do you speak?" Roberto asked as she sat down. "I don't even know where you're from."

"German. I'm from the Alto Adige. *Basta.*" Enough. "There is no need for us to know about each other." Her mood had shifted to the frigid formality of the previous morning. "We work together and we sleep together. The first is important, the other is to amuse ourselves." She stopped as she heard Stefano's footsteps behind her. He brought two more cups of the phony espresso. He put Anna's down carefully, but skilfully managed to spill some of Roberto's half-filled demitasse.

Anna dismissed the boy with a flick of her eyes. When he was gone, she said to Roberto, "I work at the restaurant late tonight. I have been thinking of your problem. Have you?"

"I've been thinking of nothing else." Then he grinned. "Well, almost of nothing else."

Her laugh was nasty, almost cruel. "This whole war is nothing but a sack full of pricks." It was one of the more common Roman vulgarities. "Once I thought we'd have a revolution and kill all you bourgeois bastards dead. Now you're killing each other. That's good, but you're also killing us." She turned away and stared at the façade of the church of the Santa Maria.

"Do you really believe a communist revolution would make the world any different? Any better?"

She shrugged. "I believe nothing except that I've got you on my hands, not enough food in my belly, and Germans in Rome who would like to kill me. Those are troubles. Yes, I believe in something— trouble." She kept looking away.

Roberto was helpless. He gulped the dregs of the espresso and turned his attention to the children climbing around the fountain. After ten minutes of pained silence, Anna spoke. "It's time to feed the rabbits. Let's go."

As Anna and Roberto passed the corner where the Vicolo del Cinque became the Cedro, they walked by Tommaso Piperno. He did not look up from his big push broom as the couple went by. Neither noticed him. Street sweepers were part of the Roman landscape.

Vatican City, Tuesday, 28 September 1943

As Anna and Roberto were leaving the Santa Maria, Rev. Fitzpàdraig Cathal Sullivan, S.J., was returning to Vatican City from his morning constitutional around Rome. He was not quite six feet tall, but his long neck and slight, middle-aged stoop combined with his loping way of walking to give him a giraffelike appearance as he moved. Sullivan was a true "black Irishman," with skin almost olive and a

52

mop of thick ebony curls. In contrast, his eyes were fiercely blue, at least what one could see of them under bushy eyebrows. During his first few weeks in Rome, he had affected a full but neat beard that, he believed, imparted a distinguished diplomatic aura to its owner. The Jesuit vicar general had disagreed, and bearded Father Sullivan quickly became clean-shaven Father Sullivan once again, totally dependent on a spackling of silver at the temples to make him appear distinguished.

In 1939, when German tanks rolled into Poland, Fitzpàdraig Cathal Sullivan, S.J., had been a member of the staff of the Jesuits' magazine, *America*. Soon, however, Francis J. Spellman, the newly designated archbishop of New York, recalled Sullivan's writings and his gnawing political curiosity and persuaded the Jesuit provincial to loan the priest to the archdiocese for "liaison" work in the chancery office.

Fitzpàdraig's colleagues had advised him to object to the transfer. His earlier career in the Jesuits had been happy. Now his reputation as a priest-scholar was firmly established. His liberal articles on domestic politics were drawing wide national attention, and the people at Fordham were interested in his doing some part-time teaching. Moreover, he was making the beginnings of putting together a critical edition of Eusebius' *Ecclesiastical Histories*. Already several editors of religious presses had approached him about publishing it. Together these signs augured for a rich, if quiet, life of prayer, reflection, and writing.

On the other hand, even at the outset Spellman's chancery promised to become a nest of intrigue. Long ago His Excellency had set his ambitious eye both on a cardinal's red hat and a role as a major broker of political power. From his first day in office, he tried to put his hand into every political decision in New York in which he was interested— and into many in which he was not. A red hat would increase that influence, not only in the city but also in Washington. Franklin Roosevelt knew Spellman—and his views; but he was only one among many archbishops, lacking the prestige, though not the financial resources, of a cardinal.

Within the chancery on Madison Avenue, there was a coterie of bright young *monsignori* who had their own ambitions in the corners of their minds, even as they pushed the archbishop's. They, too, wanted to further social justice by increasing Catholic influence in American politics. By "Catholic" they meant "clerical"; by "clerical"

53

they meant the chancery of New York; and by "the chancery" each one meant himself. "They'll do the country a lot of good," one of Sullivan's colleagues observed. "The President is getting obsessed with the war in Europe and forgetting about the poor people here at home. Spelly and his boys will nip at FDR's social conscience; they'll remind him that a lot of people are still without jobs and food. But those same lads will do a lot of harm, too. They see Communists and atheists under every rock, and each one of them wants to be the next pope. You'd be going into a bear pit, F.C. The only serious thing you'll write is your will."

But intrigue and power fascinated Fitzpàdraig Cathal Sullivan. He loved to play around the edges of power, to watch and have a hand in the intricate processes through which pastors were assigned and removed, *monsignori* designated and aspirants disappointed, money allocated for missions, and special projects funded or denied, and the secular equivalents for which politicians would seek the chancery's help in promoting or opposing causes and candidates. Now, after four years on and sometimes almost off those edges, the good Jesuit felt much older than forty-four.

These last fifteen months had been especially rewarding, but also especially tiring. In early 1942, he had become Spellman's boy in the Vatican, a fascinating role to play. The archbishop's natural charity melded with his ecclesiastical aspirations. The union was augmented by his financial means and his influence among American and curial officials. He and Pius XII had known each other in younger, more peaceful years. Today, Spellman's coffers were open to help the Pontiff and the hungry in Italy; tomorrow, when the war was over, perhaps Papa Pacelli's heart would be open to New York and its needs for a cardinal as archbishop.

Officially, Father Sullivan was a minor functionary in the Papal Secretariat of State, with a primary duty of assisting the Vatican's relief efforts. Less officially, he was authorized to draw on Spellman's fiscal resources and political credit with the government of the United States to help *il Papa*. Even less officially, Sullivan found time, under the code name Father Christmas, to help the United States defeat the evils of Nazism. He was feeding the hungry, clothing the naked, visiting the imprisoned, and even occasionally making friends with the mammon of iniquity. That life was sparkling, exhilarating to an extent that approached sexual ecstasy, but it was also demanding—and, given his multiple allegiances and coronary problems, dangerous.

The most direct route from where Father Sullivan was walking along the Via della Conciliazione to his makeshift office in Vatican City's railway station ran through the Gate of the Bells, alongside St. Peter's, opening directly onto the gigantic basilica's even more spacious piazza. A visitor would have to satisfy several tiers of Swiss Guards—their usual brightly colored Renaissance costumes replaced by the camouflaged fatigues of modern battle dress—of the legitimacy of his business and then obtain a pass much like an excursion ticket, valid for this day and trip only, with no stopovers permitted.

Father Sullivan, of course, had no difficulty with such regulations. He walked briskly through the piazza, ignoring the armed German paratroopers patrolling outside the arcing double white line that connected the arms of Bernini's colonnade and marked off the Vatican's territory from that of Italy. Inside that double line, Sullivan also ignored the unarmed German soldiers gawking like the tourists they were at the splendor of the place. At the gate, he returned the sentry's salute with a jaunty wave and lithely jumped over the barrier before the other sentry could raise it. With a quick *"Buon' giorno,"* he proceeded to his office, pleased that the morning's physical exertion had not triggered any pressure in his chest or burning in his lungs.

The priest had risen at his usual hour, 5:00, though he had spent the night on a cot in his office. As a member of the Secretariat of State and a national of a country at war with Italy, he had a room in the German College, nestled against the outside of the Vatican walls, but still included within the jurisdiction of the Holy See.

Those quarters were useful for many purposes. The building was scarcely more than three hundred yards from his office, and his fellow tenants included several fascinating people. One of them, Hugh O'Flaherty, an Irish *monsignore* attached to the Holy Office, managed to spend most of his time spiriting Allied POWs out of Axis hands. Another was a German Augustinian monk, a professor of moral theology at the Lateran, the Pope's university, who like his Irish and American colleagues rendered unto Caesar as well as God. Father Sullivan's fluency in Italian and German and his range of contacts inside and outside the Vatican made the monk's direct links to Admiral Canaris's Abwehr as open to the Americans as was Pius XII's terror of communism. It was convenient for the Jesuit to be able to keep a close eye on his ally as well as on his enemy, but there were times when he preferred the solitude and the security that his office offered.

After rising, he had used the rest room down the hall to wash and shave, then had said Mass at one of the side altars in St. Peter's. The large number of clerics forced to live inside the Vatican enclave made for tight Mass schedules, but there was seldom great demand for 5:30 A.M.

Afterward, he had fixed himself an Italian breakfast, but his food was not of the ersatz variety that Anna and Roberto had been served. The padre had eaten rolls made from wheat flour and had smothered them in real butter and strawberry jam. He had also drunk two double cappuccinos brewed from Brazilian coffee beans that he had ground himself moments before. They were not as oily as the beans he preferred, but they made a potable drink. The sugar was American, gently refined, though he had been obliged to use a mixture of water and canned milk. There was no point, Sullivan had more than once rationalized, in allowing "yours truly" to become malnourished while he fed others. Very little of what he helped distribute found its way to his office, just a few items like coffee, sugar, and an occasional canned ham; but he took this food only to sustain his health, not for self-indulgence.

He had made the cappuccino on an old *macchinetta* that he had purchased from a bar that was going out of business. The elaborate boiler took up a great deal of space and had required special water lines run into his office. Had Archbishop Spellman been less generous in his donations to the Holy Father, Vatican officials would undoubtedly have disapproved the request instead of merely raising their eyebrows and gently reminding the Jesuit that the rumors about a war's being in progress were correct.

The *macchinetta* had turned out to be a profitable investment. Not only did it provide personal pleasure, but Sullivan's willingness to share the largesse of real coffee made his office a popular gathering place for one of the traditional Italian midmorning breaks. It was at those sessions that he did much of his work for secular government. After laboring for the Church from 6:30 until 9:30, he took a long walk around Rome, varying his route from day to day to contact different members of his net, then returned in time to preside at the morning coffee klatch.

These coffees were also among the high spots of his social life. He restricted his hospitality to some of the Allied diplomats accredited to the Vatican, most of whom were housed in the Hospice San' Marta, not far from the train station, a few members of the Secretariat of State, and several others, such as the German Augustinian, in whom he had a special interest or who might have inside gossip about the Vatican or the outside world.

Some of his less prominent friends took their exclusion from these sessions charitably enough. They attributed Sullivan's selectivity to a professional need to be on close terms with people who could help him in his work. Others were less charitable about their exclusion and claimed that he was pandering to people who might advance his clerical career or indulging a neurotic need to associate with the famous. Both groups of friends accepted F.C.—which was all his American clerical colleagues ever called him, though laymen were more comfortable with "Father Fitz"—as a name-dropper, an inveterate gossip, and an inside dopester who reveled in talking and being seen talking to people whose information and status exceeded his own.

Generally, however, he was generous in sharing, with only small exaggerations of the importance of his own role, his gossipy tidbits with the friends whom he did not invite. Always he telegraphed what he called "the straight word" by placing his right hand on the left side of his mouth and speaking "strictly *entre nous*," even to four or five listeners, as to what some important dignitary had confided to "yours truly."

In fact, the coffees did occasionally yield useful information as well as interesting rumors. In all, about twenty-five people had standing invitations, but on any given day no more than ten or twelve could find time to come, a small enough number for two or three genuine conversational groupings. The bottles of grappa, cognac, and scotch that F.C. kept by the *macchinetta* for those who appreciated *caffè corretto* did nothing to still tongues. Those moments when he heard something "hard" delighted Sullivan; they quickened his sense of being at the center of things.

His work, however, was becoming increasingly dangerous. The Fascists had been suspicious, but they were neither efficient enough to make a good case against him nor courageous enough to proceed against a Vatican diplomat. He had had no worries about his walks around Rome; indeed, he had been spending considerable time outside the city working with the Red Cross and with Italian officials trying to move food supplies around. The heart of the problem was not lack of food in Italy to feed the people as well as the Germans; rather, the system of distribution had broken down. In the Po Valley, Italy's rich agricultural area, farmers were eating beef three times a day because they had no market for their cattle, while in Rome rabbit was a delicacy and cat was becoming a necessity. The archbishop's money, a diplomatic passport from the Vatican, and an acquired but cunning Italianate talent for twisting regulations had given F.C. some success in bringing food into the south and, of course, into Vatican City, whose needs had been multiplied by the influx of diplomats and refugees.

Much of his freedom was fading now that the Germans were in command. Their ambassador to the Vatican, Ernst von Weizsäcker, had been sympathetic, even occasionally helpful in obtaining food. But his authority would pale before that of the SS; they would be incomparably more efficient than the Fascists in divining F.C.'s secular activities. Most ominous was the brutal fact that no self-respecting SS man would hesitate to erase a priest on the flimsiest of suspicions. A Vatican passport would afford little protection. He could merely disappear; the Germans would disclaim any responsibility and blame Communist guerrillas. That sort of story would deceive none of the professionals in the Holy See, but it might well convince Papa Pacelli, who was ardently predisposed to believe only the best of his beloved Germany. F.C. knew that his walks would soon have to go; and when they went, so would much of his supervision of the small but tight network of agents he had woven.

Now, just as the German squeeze was beginning, Washington had sent this Raven character to try to unlock the secrets of Enigma. F.C. did not know the specifics of the plan, but in the abstract it sounded highly impractical. He did know, however, that Raven had been told to report to Anna Caccianemici in Trastevere. F.C.'s man, the street sweeper Tommaso Piperno, had confirmed that Raven was in place. F.C., in his role as Father Christmas, was concerned by that contact. His people were reasonably sure that she was a double. He never trusted Communists to begin with, and his informants in several resistance groups had warned that she had been bent—if, indeed, she had ever been straight.

As Father Sullivan, F.C. was also worried about an agent's being housed in Anna's apartment. To his priestly self, she was an immoral woman. Death was a constant companion of a wartime spy, and it seemed to the Jesuit that it was the height of moral insensitivity to place a man simultaneously in danger of losing his mortal life and his immortal soul.

If by some wild chance Raven were successful, or even if he decided to run for cover—a far more probable outcome—Father Christmas's network would have the task of getting the young man to safety. As F.C. entered his office in the railway station, he took a key from his pocket and opened a secret compartment in the side of his old rolltop desk. From it he removed a set of passport-size pictures of Raven and three passports, the first Italian, purchased by the embassy in Rome before the war, the second American, absolutely legitimate, and the third from Vatican City, smoothly lifted from the desk of Msgr. Giovanni Battista LaTorre, one of the two papal undersecretaries of state.

The *monsignore*—by ecclesiastical standards LaTorre was a young, and by any standards an oversized archbishop, but like most Vatican bureaucrats he preferred to be addressed as *monsignore*—and F.C. had discussed diverting some food to the orphange that LaTorre shepherded. F.C. had promised the food, and LaTorre had turned away from his desk for a few moments. As an arrangement, it had been very Italian, halfway between a bribe and a tip, and for a noble purpose. Anyone who wanted LaTorre's help—and sooner or later almost everyone except His Holiness and Mother Pasqualina, the Pontiff's German housekeeper, did—first gave to the orphange. That home, F.C. imagined, must have been a luxurious ducal palace, with half of Rome showing its love for the *monsignore* and its appreciation for his influence by showering gifts of food or money on the homeless boys.

F.C. blinked several times and stared out the window toward the papal gardens. After a few minutes, he smiled to himself and carefully returned all but one of the pictures. He remembered a linotype operator at the Vatican press who supplemented his meager income by dabbling in forgery—and he was superb at it, a true artist. Padre Maria Benedetto, the French priest who was smuggling foreign Jews

59

to safety, was using him to create French and Hungarian papers. And, F.C. was certain, the man was at least partially responsible for the proliferation of cards among young Romans identifying them as papal guards. If one took those cards at face value, Pius XII could have fielded an army larger than Marshal Kesselring's. Given the raw materials available, the linotype artist could do a magnificent job for Raven. The only problem would be to replace the coat and tie on the photograph with a Roman collar. Too bad the people in Washington had not realized that the easiest way to get a man in or out of Rome was to disguise him as a priest.

Sullivan needed to do some quick thinking. He had spent his walk worrying about Raven instead of planning how to orchestrate the coffee. First he had to talk to Paul Stransky, the officially accredited secretary to President Roosevelt's personal representative to the Vatican and, more important, F.C.'s conduit to the OSS. Through his sources, Stransky might know something more about Raven. Then F.C. wanted to follow up with the Yugoslav diplomat the story he claimed to have heard from the Spanish that the Germans had captured an American agent who had crossed into France from the area around Barcelona.

If Monsignor LaTorre were there—he came only about once a week—F.C. planned to convey Archbishop Spellman's personal greetings and to hand him a check for the orphanage. (The Institute for Religious Works, the bank that the papacy had recently established within Vatican City to protect the funds of religious orders against German confiscation, could handle the transfer.) F.C. could easily have deposited the money to the orphange's account, but he preferred to give it directly to LaTorre. The *monsignore* should associate him with good things. He also wanted to pump LaTorre about the rumors that the SS were planning to seize the Jews of Rome and send them to concentration camps somewhere in eastern Europe. If there were any truth in the stories—and even if there were not—he was anxious to know what Pius planned to do or say about the Nazi treatment of Jews. His silence was becoming a scandal.

That day's coffee brought a double bonus. First, the Augustinian came. He was a dapper, delicate little man, barely five feet, six inches tall, small boned without an ounce of fat. The monk combined physical lassitude and intellectual energy: He slouched rather than walked, but his mind was a whirling force that, even outside his field of moral theology, caused him to sparkle rather than merely talk. The somber black of his robes did nothing to mask his cynical humor. Like F.C., he was dark complected with coal black hair, but his eyes, unlike F.C.'s, were brown. The man was hardly the stereotypical Aryan. Had he been Jewish he would have been described as having an excess of chutzpah; but, being Aryan by blood if not by coloring, he was merely brash enough to make a bubblingly witty performance at an occasional coffee and upstage F.C.'s less intellectually ebullient presence.

The two had formally met the previous June when the nuns who ran the refectory of the German College had staged a small joint party for the birthday they shared. Despite their belligerent nationalities, the two priests liked each other, perhaps because each saw part of his own character mirrored in the other. Each was lazy, quite bright, very gossipy, and extremely vain; each also immensely enjoyed the thrill of working simultaneously for church and state. F.C. had an advantage there: He knew that the Augustinian was a spy; the monk had only strong suspicions about his American colleague.

The morning's second bonus was that not only did LaTorre come, but he brought with him his old friend Monsignor Ugo Galeotti, a Vatican diplomat who had just returned to Italy after three years in Istanbul. Galeotti was a trencherman of some renown, as his Friar Tuck figure indicated. He also had a reputation for shrewd political judgment.

At the *macchinetta*, LaTorre put three spoonfuls of sugar into his double espress', then laced it with a slug of grappa appropriate to his physical bulk and hierarchical status. His friend took the coffee neat. "But, 'Vanni,' Galeotti was saying as F.C. approached, hand outstretched, teeth gleaming. "I know it's true, you know it's true, and he knows it's true. In charity, we must believe that he is merely waiting for the proper moment to speak out."

"When they are all dead—" LaTorre commented bitterly, then saw F.C. and immediately switched to English, turning the conversation to trivial comparisons of life in Turkey and Italy. Clearly, however, LaTorre was agitated about something, and Galeotti, who was a man of delicate tact, had been trying to calm him. On the other hand, LaTorre's explosive temper was as famous as his stubbornness. Indeed, his associates had difficulty deciding whether "the Holy Mule" or "Vesuvio" was the more accurate nickname. One story had it that Papa Pacelli had given the *monsignore* his early—many said too early —promotion to become one of the two undersecretaries of state because, after LaTorre had spoken, even a resounding no from the Pope sounded like sweet reason.

What it was that "they" all knew F.C. could guess, but it was apparent that the prelates were not going to continue their discussion while he was present. So he flitted off to join the group clustered around the Augustinian, who was playfully expounding a thesis that divine justice required the transmigration of souls. "The essence of the reasoning is simple," the monk was saying.

"How no?" an Italian *monsignore* asked. "Error usually is simple."

"Wait, my friend, hear the argument. We all agree that God has made this life a test for us—a required test. No man has a choice about being born. For that test, God has given each of us free will and an immortal soul; He has also given us a unique spark, the thing that makes each soul different from every other. That soul's performance is not predetermined. No two of us face precisely the same temptations, receive precisely the same kinds of grace, enjoy the same general cultural ambience and specific physical environment, or, if you will forgive my allusion to another Augustinian, Abbot Mendel, are endowed with the same genes. For a rich man to resist stealing five marks is hardly as virtuous as it is for a poor man; for a man who has been castrated, holy purity's demands are not as burdensome as they are for a healthy youth of twenty-one."

"*Quindi?*" the Italian asked. So?

"So? So, if God is perfectly just, as we know Him to be, we theologians confront an enigma. We know He cannot make fair interpersonal judgments about us—about who deserves eternal happiness and who eternal damnation—unless we face the same tests and under the same circumstances. And, of course, we cannot face identical tests if we each live only once. Thus, I argue"—the Augustinian smiled— "that history is merely a revolving mirror. Each of us lives one life, dies, and receives a certain grade on that particular set of tests. Then he is born again into another body and plays a new role—and on and on until each of us has been everyone and God can make perfectly just interpersonal judgments."

"But," the Italian *monsignore* interjected, "certainly an all-knowing God can extrapolate from one test to all the others."

"I answer that," the monk replied, "despite his omniscience, God cannot, consistent with His justice, extrapolate from one test to another. He has chosen, in His all-seeing wisdom, to give us free will. And a man who has free will may resist a great temptation only to succumb to a tiny one; he may fall to a certain temptation nine times and then overcome it on the tenth and all subsequent occasions. One who murders a child may risk his life to save a stranger, even an enemy; one who spends his life hating may, at the end, lay down his life for love. Free will means that moral responses are not perfectly predictable; they are not, as the logicians put it, transitive."

LaTorre and Galeotti had drifted over and joined the audience. Galeotti was smiling, but LaTorre was not amused. "Nonsense," he said heavily.

"Ah, to be sure, nonsense," the monk agreed. "The element of nonsense is the strongest empirical proof one can offer for a theory's fit with reality. For there is no history or reality as our 'rational' but very human minds have conceived them. God operates as an omnipotent stage director, shuffling men from role to role. He has allowed us to 'remember' a mythical past and to imagine a future that is not to be; but all human history has taken place within one slice of time."

"Is that how you people at the Lateran University spend your time?" LaTorre asked.

"Only when we are serious," the Augustinian replied. "When we are relaxing, we debate whether curial officials have souls."

"*Senta,*" Monsignor Galeotti intervened, "some of us have been discussing a more specific moral problem, the Nazis' treatment of the Jews. The Vatican is very concerned."

"That is something new, is it not, *Monsignore*?" the monk asked. "Are you signaling that the Holy See will now adopt a foreign policy that says we must all love our neighbor and that every man is our neighbor? Or are you implying a less revolutionary change in the Vatican's attitude toward those people whom popes historically locked in an annually flooding ghetto along the Tiber and whom our Good Friday ritual still brands as 'perfidious'?"

LaTorre cut in: "Spiritually, Pope Pius XI said, we are all Semites; and time and again Papa Pacelli has expressed his concern about German mistreatment of Jews—publicly in his messages to the world and privately in conversations with your ambassador."

"Let us hope," the monk said, "that His Holiness makes more sense in private than in public. I have never even been sure which war he has been lamenting, much less which victims."

F.C. turned his ears full on. This might be a rich jewel to display to his friends: an account of a spat between papal diplomats and a German spy.

"Do not banter with me, Father," LaTorre snapped. "I am talking to you as the Pope's representative. We—he as well as many of us in the Secretariat of State—are troubled by the SS's demanding ransom from the Jews of Rome."

"Ah, I thought your concern would be more general," the Augustinian replied, continuing his patter. Then, seeing the choler rising in LaTorre's face, he became less flippant, though hardly less cynical. "Forgive my feeble effort at humor, *Monsignore*. You wish a candid evaluation. Very well: What I see is extortion. Paying will not help for very long. Your Roman Hebrews will soon find themselves in a labor camp working against communism. They should have accepted Christianity; then they could fight courageously against communism like the rest of their Italian compatriots."

"*Ecco*, a labor camp." LaTorre could ignore a slur against Italian military virtue, but he could not keep the sarcasm out of his voice when he heard what he thought was deceit. "Take the hair off your tongue and admit that these Jews will be taken to a *mattatoio*, a slaughtering chamber, where your SS will turn these poor people along with thousands of others into slabs of dead, bloody meat."

The Augustinian shrugged. "You take Zionist propaganda very seriously, *Monsignore*. One would wish you took as seriously the awful fact of British fire bombings of German civilians. Now there is real slaughter. When I spoke of the Jews I did mean labor camps, places where they will work for victory over the barbarians from the east, like most Germans and even"—he arched his eyebrows—"a few Italians."

"Death camps," LaTorre repeated, "places of extermination for innocent men, women, and children. I do not defend the British bombings; but Germany has difficulty complaining after what your bombers

64

did to Rotterdam after the Dutch surrendered, and later to London and Coventry."

"Forgive me, *Monsignore*, but I do not believe either canard, not about Germans' bombing civilians or about imaginary death camps. You have been listening to the same sort of garbage that the British fed the world from 1914 to 1918. You remember the stories of German soldiers bayoneting babies and raping nuns? After the war even the British admitted they had made it all up. Today, you *know* about the British bombings because the British themselves boast of their murders. But you have no confirmed reports of any extermination camp, because no such camp exists. Labor camps, yes; camps, I concede, in which conditions are likely to be harsh. But hardships are a part of war, and war is an aggregation of hardships. Besides, the ancient Jews brought this suffering on their people with their cry 'Let his blood be on us and on our children.' I save my sympathy for the Christian women and children the British are roasting alive."

"*Ecco*, I have received report after report; they confirm and verify each other. They all tell the same: death camps." LaTorre spoke in a voice that was trembling with anger.

"Alas, not verified sufficiently to convince the Holy Father or any other objective observer," the monk replied. "The Pontiff has great faith in the integrity of the German people and great understanding of how repeating or even believing such vile rumors helps communism."

"*Dunque*," Galeotti intervened again, "we are all priests of God. Let us not bicker like cattle dealers. According to me, none of us here is responsible for German or British policies; each of us wants only peace and justice, not war and oppression."

LaTorre shrugged, not pacified but aware of the awkwardness of the situation. He turned to the *macchinetta* and drew another espresso. The Augustinian continued to smile blandly, outwardly unruffled by the sharpness of the exchange.

"Would you, Father," Galeotti asked the Augustinian, "put aside any personal differences and keep your ears open about reports to harm the Jews of Rome? I am certain that His Holiness would be most grateful."

"Of course, *Monsignore*, but has the German ambassador not told you everything he knows?"

65

"Perhaps," LaTorre said as he turned back from the *macchinetta*. "With diplomats one never knows. But even if he has, he may not be privy to everything. The SS is a law unto itself."

"That is true enough. But I am sure that these rumors about death camps are false. On the other hand, the British fire bombings are real, horribly real. Please assure His Holiness that his first moral duty is to protest the British murder of German Christians."

"I do not," LaTorre said as he walked away, "presume to instruct His Holiness in his moral duties." He lied, of course, but it was a white lie, even a charitable lie. Besides, since his antagonist had no right to the truth, there could be no sin in deceiving him.

THREE

The meeting took place in John Winthrop Mason's office, rather than Colonel Lynch's. That was unusual. Mason preferred to meet in other people's offices so that he could leave as soon as *he* felt that the issues were settled. His office was in the fussy Old State Department Building, next door to the White House. Lynch was there, as was a plump, balding but still dandruffy English brigadier, Sir Henry Cuthbert. He had just arrived from the British command at Bletchley, where Ultra's readings of Enigma were coordinated. The brigadier's assignment was to act as liaison with the Americans during Operation Bronze Goddess. Sir Henry's tunic was as ostentatiously bare of decorations as Colonel Lynch's.

"Bring Sir Henry up to date, please," Mason ordered.

"There's not much that the brigadier hasn't heard in his briefing this morning, sir."

"Well, then, bring me up to date." Mason's voice was an oral finger snap.

Lynch hesitated, then caught himself and spoke swiftly. "Team Able went into Holland on schedule. Our agent—excuse me, Brigadier, *your* agent—there has been bent. Able checked in with him and the Germans had them the next day."

Mason twisted his lips into what for him was a smile. "There is a serious leak in your net, Sir Henry. You must do something."

"Quite, quite," the brigadier agreed. "We really must, but then one doesn't know precisely what to do, does one?"

Lynch was not amused. He went on: "Baker made it safely into Rouen. Their contact is—or was—straight. But the Germans must

67

have broken Able pretty quickly. Two days later the Gestapo picked up Baker as they were making a reconnaissance near the airfield."

"Trust the Hun to be efficient," Sir Henry observed.

"Charlie's still at large," Lynch added. "He was scheduled to cross the Pyrenees three days ago. We've heard nothing to the contrary. I assume he's in the hands of one of the resistance groups, being passed on somewhere, probably to Marseilles. As you recall, we did not set him up with a double; but he's not very bright, and if Able or Baker talked, the Germans will know all about him."

"And that young instructor from Dartmouth?" Mason asked.

"Princeton, sir. Raven went ashore as planned, made his rendezvous, and contacted Anna immediately. That's a report from Father Christmas. He has the apartment under surveillance."

"Who's monitoring the opposition?" Mason asked.

"Father Christmas is doing that, too. It's his territory. He's nothing if not devious. The Red Cross trusts him and so does our good archbishop of New York. Paul Stransky, the special envoy's secretary, thinks he's in pretty solid with people inside the Vatican. He damned well should be. With the Red Cross's help, Spellman's money, and our connivance, he has helped get food into Vatican City and to the locals in Sicily and even Rome. The last takes some pressure off the Fascists and Germans and gives him a little freedom of movement. He even keeps in touch with an Augustinian monk in the Vatican whom we know from reading the Germans' mail is also a spy."

"Whom is Father Christmas using for close-in work?"

"He has a few people. I can't give you names or even totals. He's not a typical field man. He won't tell us any more about his network than we can squeeze out of him. And his information has been too valuable for us to squeeze him very hard. I'd guess, however, that most of his people are clerics. I know one of his agents, but only because I helped recruit him when I was with the embassy there. He's a crippled *spazzino*, a street sweeper."

"Repeat that," Mason said. "I thought you said crippled street sweeper."

"I did. I don't know what F.C.—"

"F.C.?" Sir Henry inquired. He had understood, but he needed some release from the internal tension that had built up from restraining himself from staring at Mason's enormous head and singular face.

"Father Christmas. A Roman trash man makes an excellent watcher and courier. He's got a perfect excuse to wander around town. His name is Piperno, Tommaso Piperno. Apparently a fancy midwife performed a one-handed delivery and dislocated his hip. His family was too poor to have it repaired. As a result, he's a permanent cripple. There's a lot of that in Italy."

"Typical of primitive societies," Mason noted.

"Quite," Sir Henry agreed.

"Well, he lives about a hundred yards from Anna's house on the Vicolo del Cedro. His street is called the Vicolo del Bologna. He seems apolitical. If he's blown—"

"What's your situation, Sir Henry?" Mason cut in.

"About the same. The Hun also picked up our two teams in France within seventy-two hours. That seems to be the standard time the Hun gives his doubles to 'single up,' so to speak. Like you, we sent one team to contact a known double, the other to a legitimate resistance unit. With one in hand, the Germans soon had both. Pity."

"Anything else?" Mason asked.

"We've heard nothing from our man who went into Germany. Never expected to, actually." He paused to light his pipe. "Different story in Norway. Spot of bother there."

"Yes?" An edge of impatience was beginning to invade Mason's voice.

"Our chaps there are still at work. The fellow at Trondheim we thought was a double is apparently straight. It's a bit difficult to be certain. We'll just have to wait and see, won't we?"

"You might, I would not." Mason turned to Lynch. "How certain are you about this Anna?"

"Not *certain* about much. She's been sporting a Communist party card for lots of years when carrying it would have bought her a death sentence, or worse. She lives alone, works hard, and is damned bright— and tough. She's from the Alto Adige, up in the Dolomites. It's a region that's as much Austrian as Italian."

"So why do you think she's—what's the expression?—bent?"

"Because we know that for more than a year she's had steady con-

69

tact with the Abwehr man in the German embassy, a Colonel Manfred Gratz. At the same time, she's been working with the resistance—so she pretends. The OVRA, the Fascist secret police, have had her cold several times. But they've always let her go after a day or so, except for holding her once for a week in their little home away from home in the Palazzo Braschi and roughing her up. She says there was a gang bang, but no corroboration. We have a report from Father Christmas from a friend in the Questura, the Roman police office, that once when she was under arrest, the Abwehr made some very indirect and discreet inquiries about her location. Her record is phenomenal, too phenomenal."

"Translate 'Abwehr,' please. I have small Latin and no German." Mason opened the humidor on his desk and helped himself, then pushed it toward the other two. Both men shook their heads.

"The Abwehr," Lynch explained, somewhat embarrassed by Mason's lapse, "is the German Military Intelligence Service. It's in direct and at times pretty savage competition with the SD, the intelligence arm of the SS. There's a lot of power politicking among those various services. And—"

"Unlike ours," Mason added drily.

"Ours aren't like theirs. Ropes around the neck or bullets in the brain are their ways of designating losers. In any case, Anna works for the Ristorante Remus, just off the Piazza Navona. It was run by one of the resistance groups as a flytrap for Fascists. Now the Germans have apparently become the principal clientele."

"The Hun has a way of taking things over, hasn't he?" Sir Henry broke in.

"Yes, sir. Anna's job has been mostly make-work, a pretty face—if you like 'em that hard—and a lot of body to encourage conversation."

"Sexual favors part of this crumpet's performance?" Sir Henry asked.

Mason raised his eyebrows as if to object that the question was irrelevant, but Lynch answered swiftly. "We don't know, Brigadier, not for sure. She's had a hell of a life. Swapping a night in the sack for staying alive probably seems like a good deal to her."

"To whom or to what is she loyal?"

"To herself, Brigadier. My guess is that she's an independent, playing us, the resistance, the Fascists, and the Germans all at the same time. Politically she's a total cynic, even about the Communist party. Sale, I suspect, goes to the highest bidder."

"Can we keep her under surveillance?" Mason asked.

"No, sir, not close surveillance." The colonel nodded toward Sir Henry. "Italy is pretty much a British preserve. Father Christmas and his people, whoever they may be, are about the only agents we have there. Anna knows too many of her particular resistance crowd for them to be able to follow her without her realizing it. And her group is too suspicious of the other organizations to ask for help."

"What does the priest know about this mission?"

"We have told him that Raven has come to Rome to unlock Enigma. The same story that Raven himself has. We've not gone beyond the cover. Father Christmas isn't very optimistic about the mission in general, and I don't mind telling you that he's very unhappy about involving another agent with Anna."

"The sacerdotal mentality is marvelous," Mason commented. "We use his reports to guide five hundred planes to bomb Rome and he's worried about the morality of one agent bundling with another."

"Well, from his point of view—"

"This office has only one point of view, our client's. We have nothing to do with Anna's or Raven's sexual life. Our only purpose is to keep the Germans believing we cannot read Enigma."

"Sex is only part of the problem, sir. Father Christmas has raised an interesting question: Why are we sending a man on such a critical mission and having him work through someone that we've been several times warned is a double or even a triple?"

"Your response?" Mason asked.

"I told him we thought she was ideal for this mission. She has contacts with both Fascist and German officers. I implied that we doubted she was bent."

"Simpler to say we were sure of Anna and later confess error." Mason raised his hand in anticipation of Lynch's next sentence. "I know, you Romans regard it as a sacrilege to lie to a priest. We lawyers deem it a sacrilege *not* to lie for a client."

"You're certain," Sir Henry inquired, "that your Father Christmas knows nothing about the real purpose of Bronze Goddess?"

"We haven't told him anything about it, or even hinted at the existence of our darling little Enigma-reading Ultra. But we can't be absolutely sure of what those people in the Vatican know. They're onto lots of secrets—from both sides."

"Mankind," Mason put in solemnly, "is apt to exaggerate the competence of Vatican diplomats and Swiss bankers. Who is keeping an eye on Father Christmas?"

"He reports directly to Paul Stransky, who reports directly to this office. Stransky uses the British ambassador's communication system. We don't have a radio with our people."

Mason looked incredulous, then turned to the brigadier. "Is it secure?"

"One hopes so," Sir Henry answered. "Not a pleasant thought, the Hun reading our post, is it?"

Mason switched the subject. "We can assume that all the teams talked about the substance of their mission?"

Sir Henry nodded. "A quite realistic assumption."

"The only question in my mind," Lynch said bitterly, "is whether any of them was alive enough to tell a coherent story. Give the Gestapo enough time and they can break anyone, but sometimes they overachieve."

Rome, Wednesday, 29 September 1943

Five German officers sat in the living room of a spacious suite in Rome's once fashionable Excelsior Hotel. Present were Field Marshal Albert Kesselring, the balding Luftwaffe general commanding Army Group A, which had stalled the Allies outside of Naples; Gen. Hans Mueller, obese, hard-drinking commandant of Rome; Col. Manfred Gratz, the squat, egg-bald chief of the Abwehr in Rome; and, youngest, most junior in rank, tallest, and most handsome of the officers, SS Lt. Col. Viktor Olendorf, commander in Rome of two of the SS's suborganizations, the Gestapo, the secret police of the Nazi party, and the SD, the party's intelligence and counterintelligence arm.

Before his assassination, Reinhard Heydrich had formally merged the SD and the Gestapo, but it was easier to switch names on administrative charts than to change officials' habits, especially when those habits centered on controlling the lives of other human beings. In Rome, however, the merger was proceeding smoothly. Olendorf was an efficient bureaucrat who expected rigid obedience from his subordinates and sometimes gave that same service to his own superiors. As a shrewd, professionally competent policeman, he intimately knew Rome and the Romans. Like Colonel Gratz of the Abwehr, Olendorf had been posted to the embassy before the war, and after Italy's defection he had promptly moved from assistant attaché to police chief.

The fifth officer was the director of the Abwehr, Adm. Wilhelm Canaris. The others were in properly bemedaled uniforms, but the admiral was still wearing boots and jodhpurs from his afternoon canter in the *galoppatoio*, a half mile distant. He was a short, gray-haired man in his mid-fifties, whose quick smile and brightly curious eyes made him seem more suited to the role of benevolent uncle than head of German military intelligence. His apparent candor, talkativeness, love of intrigue, and his insistence on maintaining contacts with British agents in neutral countries all made many Nazis suspect Canaris as being himself a double. The legendary success of his operations angered, threatened, and stymied those same people. Under the German military's tightly structured system, the admiral had no direct responsibility to the Nazi party. He reported to Field Marshal Wilhelm Keitel, chief of Staff of the OKW, the high command. Licking party boots was Keitel's job, not Canaris's.

The table was furnished with glasses of various shapes and an equally diverse arrangement of cognac, drambuie, sambucca, grappa, and the soft, almond-flavored amaretto di Saronno. Admiral Canaris passed around cigars. Mueller and Gratz immediately began to light theirs; Kesselring accepted one, but put it in his tunic pocket. Olendorf declined and took out a pack of Lucky Strikes.

"Where did you get those?" the admiral asked.

"My friends in the *Waffen* SS keep me supplied." Olendorf smiled. "Fortunately, the Americans smoke better than they fight, so I seldom run short."

"That meal was not," General Mueller observed as he pulled his fleshy body to the table and poured himself a triple cognac, "a notable culinary event. I fear this war has given the lie to the old saying 'One always eats well in Rome.' "

"I never ate well in this part of town," Canaris said absently. The bulk of his attention seemed focused on the rich brown of the amaretto that he was holding up to the light. "Once, this section of Rome was an area of parks and villas, but after unification there was unholy collusion among venal cardinals, corrupt governmental officials, and greedy land speculators. The result is the Via Veneto, a cheap imitation of the Champs Elysées. Its function is to harvest money from foreigners stupid enough to think this area has anything to do with the real Italy. In Trastevere now . . ."

The admiral paused. "But we are showing signs of aging, Hans. Remember what our esteemed foe, Mr. Churchill, has said: 'The pleasures of the palate are the most lasting.' They are for old men, not for youngsters like Kesselring here, who gets his satisfaction from putting together a ragtag army that slows down the British in Apulia and stops the Americans in Campania. You are to be congratulated, Field Marshal; your generalship has been nothing short of brilliant."

Kesselring chuckled in appreciation of the accuracy of Canaris's judgment. "It helps, of course," he said humbly. "if your opponent is as stupid as Mark Clark or as slow-footed as Montgomery. We should not, however, crow too loudly. We shall lose Naples in the next few days, perhaps even hours. The people are in revolt. I could put it down, of course, but I shall not besmirch German honor with the deaths of thousands of innocent civilians that it would cost to wipe out the partisans. The Allies will take the city anyway."

"The Field Marshal does not seem upset," Olendorf observed. There was a slightly judgmental tone in the SS officer's voice.

"No. We did well to hold them this long. Now we shall make them fight in the mountains north of the city and keep them tied in knots. In all honesty, gentlemen, the heart of our problem has not been the Allies, even with their overwhelming superiority in numbers and equipment. It has been our own glamorous colleague, Erwin Rommel. He had persuaded der Fuehrer to abandon all of Italy south of Florence. To me, however, it made no sense to allow the British and Americans to walk over those mountains between Calabria and the Arno without allowing our German lads the opportunity to act as angel makers. I simply moved quickly and showed what a little sound planning and a few good troops could do to not very intelligent enemies. I might add, without boasting, that if I had air power equivalent to *either* the British or American, we would have Mark Clark and Bernard Montgomery here this evening as our honored, though disarmed, guests."

Lt. Col. Viktor Olendorf carefully consulted his wristwatch. "I am deeply appreciative of this opportunity to dine with senior officers, but

I am afraid that the SS's schedule demands more work tonight." Practically, if not technically, Olendorf was outside the chain of command of all the military officers present. He could afford to be mildly insulting.

"Another woman to torture, or is it a child whose eyes need plucking?" Colonel Gratz asked in a lightly mocking tone. Gratz was not as tall or as handsome as Olendorf, but he still made an imposing figure. He was a solidly built man, two hundred pounds and a few inches less than six feet in height. In ultramilitaristic fashion, he kept his head clean shaven but, despite German military custom, sported a huge handlebar moustache of the kind that cavalry officers used to affect. He and Olendorf had known each other during their four years of service at the embassy, and they shared the mutual contempt that career officers and political police generally felt for each other. Yet each also had a grudging respect for the other's professional capacity.

For his part, Olendorf knew that however much the military might loathe the Gestapo, they also feared it. Stories about the organization's power and cruelty were legion; most had firm basis in reality. Olendorf, however, took pride in the fact that, with one exception that had not been his choice, he had never used physical brutality, at least not personally. Still, there was no point in letting his rivals understand that he considered himself a man of honor and humanity. He smiled back at Gratz. "Nothing that the colonel would find so entertaining; only a priest to strangle." His remark was a heavy-handed allusion to the rumor that during World War I Canaris had escaped from an Italian prison by strangling the chaplain and putting on his cassock. "We in the SS live rather spartan lives. I would delight in having the colonel as my guest so that he could see at first hand what gentle tabbies we are."

"Gentlemen." The admiral raised his hand. He was pleased by Olendorf's reference to the strangling, though his face gave no indication of any reaction whatever. He was not a violent man, but like Olendorf—and Machiavelli centuries earlier—Canaris knew that it was often more useful to be feared than to be loved. Thus, he never denied the strangling rumor or any other legend about his prowess or ruthlessness. "Our representative from the SS makes a valid point. We have important business to discuss. First, however, I would beg the colonel's indulgence. I have heard conflicting reports about SS plans for the Jews of Rome. Could you enlighten me? All within the bounds of security, of course."

"These other gentlemen are aware, as the Admiral may not be," Olendorf explained, "that Berlin is anxious to rid Rome of its Hebrews. Marshal Kesselring and General Mueller have protested. I am not a Jew lover, but I think they are correct. We must not push the Pope too hard. He is being pressured by the British and Americans to condemn the Reich's racial policies. I fear, and Ambassador von Weizsäcker shares my fear, that our deporting the Jews from the Pope's backyard would help our enemies persuade Pius to condemn Germany. That would be a stunning blow to morale in the armed forces."

"So," the admiral said, "you are behaving like a masterful statesman and doing nothing until your superiors come to their senses?"

"As an SS officer, I am," Olendorf replied, "always ready to carry out der Fuehrer's slightest whim. He, however, has not yet indicated his desires. My instructions are still quite general. Meanwhile, I have just extracted three hundred kilograms of gold from the Jewish community as a ransom. Tomorrow I shall send it on to Berlin with an explanation that there is much more where that came from—and probably information about Allied spies as well. I hope I can persuade Reichsfuehrer Himmler to delay action indefinitely, but—"

"But?"

"But, just in case Herr Kaltenbrunner and Herr Eichmann's views triumph, I have commandeered the records of the Great Temple."

"Thank you, Colonel Olendorf. Most enlightening. Now," the admiral directed, "we come to our main item of business. I reported to you that the Abwehr has discovered a gigantic plot."

"I hear they call it World War II." General Mueller guffawed as he poured himself another triple cognac. "The Russians, British, and Americans are conspiring to defeat us. "

"I have never been able to compete with your wit, Hans. Let me revise my former self and say that the Abwehr has discovered a subplot, a concerted effort to unmask our Enigma. With that machine in their hands, they could—"

"Might I respectfully remind the Herr Admiral," Olendorf interrupted, "that the SS are fully informed as to this 'plot.' In fact, we also captured two of the espionage teams and, if the Herr Admiral will forgive me, were able to extract from them more information than the Abwehr was from the teams it located. Two more teams are loose on the Continent, one here in Rome, one in France, and possibly yet a third in Norway. My men are looking forward to meeting the agent here in Rome. It is a one-man team, is it not?"

The admiral nodded.

"That is what our 'informant' said. I understand he seemed unsure of himself, but we felt we could trust his guessing. There is nothing like having one's testicles firmly clamped in a large pair of slowly closing pliers to enable a man to guess correctly. The SS shall serve this agent to Reichsfuehrer Himmler on a skewer, like one of those marinated shrimp we had for supper tonight."

Canaris thought for a moment that he might throw up. He tried an old trick that he had used when he himself had been an agent and had had to calm his terror. He gently persuaded himself to concentrate on imagining the space between his fingers and toes. Almost immediately, he could feel some of his tension ease. "That agent—the Allies call him Raven—is precisely why I am in Rome tonight," the admiral said slowly, as he felt his body returning to normal. "I have come to ask you, Olendorf, and you, my dear Kesselring, and you, too, Hans, not to lay a finger on this Raven or any of his contacts, not even to take notice of their existence."

Olendorf laughed out loud. "If the Admiral feels the Abwehr needs something to justify its existence, the SS will help. Perhaps I could mention in dispatches that Colonel Gratz here was of great assistance—he agreed to keep his moustaches out of the affair and let experts handle the matter."

"You miss the point," Canaris said amiably. "I do not want the Abwehr to capture Raven or his confederates. I want them all to remain free—for the time being. Without realizing it, they will play a critical role in an operation we shall call Rigoletto. It is crucial for this spy to succeed in his mission—please, for him, his friends, and his masters to think that he has succeeded. He must bring back detailed photographs and blueprints of an enciphering machine, a 'new' model Enigma that he will believe our forces will begin to use in a few weeks. With the documents he purloins will be instructions stating that, until our crippled production catches up with our needs—the British and Americans will congratulate themselves on the success of their bombings—we shall have to continue to use many of the older models."

"Fascinating, *Kieker*, fascinating," Mueller said, slurring his words and using Canaris's old nickname, "Peeper." "But what the hell is the point?"

"The point, Hans, is that we shall then fight a radio war. We shall send out dozens of messages on this 'new' model, including distress signals from submarines who earlier 'reported' their 'positions'; we shall also transmit reports of troop movement, damage estimates of bombings of factories and installations. Unfortunately, we shall have to include some factually correct information that the enemy can readily verify so he will not realize it is all a hoax. But a hoax it will be."

"Fight a radio war—damned clever!" Kesselring exclaimed. "It could be a master stroke."

"It could be," Canaris agreed. "It could well be. Can you imagine the Allies' bombing nonexistent U-boats, turning whole convoys to avoid an ethereal wolf pack only to run into an ambush laid by a real one? Dumping tons of bombs on cardboard installations? Planning an invasion of France in loving detail to strike where we are not, only to find that that is precisely where we are?"

"The British and Americans are not particularly intelligent, but neither are they totally stupid," Olendorf protested. "They would soon catch on."

Canaris rocked his head gently back and forth. "Perhaps, but certainly not *very* soon, and not necessarily ever. You are neglecting British ego—we can dismiss American intelligence. The Englishman will deceive himself. He will do our work for us, especially if we boast that our greater skill and courage produced our victories. Then he will be convinced that he has been unlucky."

Mueller laughed. "Plausible. Very plausible. After all, to have been born English is itself such tragic luck that losing a war could not seem much worse."

"Well," Canaris said much more guardedly, "even if they do catch on, it will not happen until Rigoletto has wiped out a dozen or more convoys and misdirected hundreds of their raids. The cost here is small, the returns will surely be immense."

"With all respect to the Admiral," Olendorf put in, "is this not the kind of issue that the OKW should decide? Only the high command can adequately assess global strategy."

Canaris raised his eyebrows. "My dear Olendorf, you disappoint me. I had thought that the SS, above all others, recognized the superiority of der Fuehrer's intuition to the plodding planning of the OKW. I had thought that party men always put loyalty to our glorious leader above loyalty to any military organization."

Olendorf's pale skin flushed a deep scarlet. "May I ask what the Herr Admiral is getting at?"

"What I am saying is that the plan I have just outlined has der Fuehrer's most enthusiastic approval. But just now he does not want to precipitate another dispute with the General Staff—or feed a security leak. He sees the wisdom in this plan; it fits his intuitive judgment, just as did Field Marshal Kesselring's brilliant and daring decision to defend in southern Italy instead of at Florence. Der Fuehrer has learned to trust his intuition. If a mere admiral may deign to advise an SS lieutenant colonel, I recommend that, as loyal officers of the Reich who have sworn an oath of fealty to the person of Adolf Hitler, we also should respect that judgment. On the other hand, der Fuehrer does not have faith in all his generals—or admirals. I need not stress that point in this room. I can stress, however, that he wants this operation carried out in absolute secrecy. Only a few trusted people will know about it."

Canaris paused to sip his amaretto, then went on. "And, Olendorf, let me underline the obvious: Those few do not include your immediate commander, General Wolff. Reichsfuehrer Himmler has told der Fuehrer that he is deeply suspicious of General Wolff. Fortunately the general prefers Florence to Rome—art to government, so to speak— so he will be out of our hair. In Colonel Gratz's case, the analogy is misplaced." The admiral chuckled, then continued: "With more regret, and in absolute secrecy, I must tell you that for his own reasons der Fuehrer has not brought Reichsfuehrer Himmler into his confidence on this operation."

The silence in the room was heavy. Canaris looked around slowly, then went on. "I take it that I have your solemn assurances as German officers that each of you will give Colonel Gratz your total cooperation and that none of you will ever speak of this plan without explicit orders from me or from der Fuehrer himself?"

Everyone nodded except Olendorf. "If the admiral will forgive me, may I ask if he has written authorization for such a sweeping plan?"

Canaris reached inside his riding jacket and removed a silver cigarette case. Inside was a twice folded, handwritten note. He passed it to the SS officer. "Read it aloud, please."

Olendorf obliged:

"To All Loyal German Officers:
You are to treat any request from Admiral Canaris or his authorized subordinates regarding Operation Rigoletto as a direct order from der Fuehrer. Further, I command you to tell no one, subordinate or superior, about the existence of Operation Rigoletto unless Admiral Canaris or I specifically command you to do so. This plan must be kept secret from friend as well as foe. Coupled with the miracle weapons German science is now developing, Rigoletto will insure the ultimate victory of the Reich over the subhumans who oppose its destiny. *Sieg Heil!*"

"You recognize the signature, Olendorf?" Canaris asked.

"Yes, Herr Admiral."

"Very well. Please initial the note and pass it to the other officers so that they may do the same." The admiral smiled benevolently. "I apologize for this formality, but we do not want any jealousies among departments to interfere with German victory. Now, Colonel Gratz will be in full charge here in Rome. He has been with our embassy for some years and knows the area. He also has a small network of agents on whom he will rely to 'assist' this spy—this Raven—and his contacts."

"Strange name." Mueller chortled and half choked as he swallowed his cognac in a single gulp. "But these Anglo-Americans are strange birds."

"Yes, Hans," Canaris said patiently. "We would hope that all Colonel Gratz need do is to telephone your commands and say that he wishes to speak to you about Operation Rigoletto and each of you would give him your full, immediate, and personal attention. You, my dear Olendorf, will be most affected, though probably only to the extent of looking the other way. I want no surveillance of any kind, no hint, unless Colonel Gratz asks for one to deceive the enemy, that you even know that this Raven fellow or anyone he contacts exists." Canaris nodded to the other two officers. "I felt that as a matter of courtesy you should know of our plans. We would not want to inter-fere with each other, however inadvertently."

The admiral did not add the obvious: The SS officer had, in the presence of a field marshal and another general, received a direct order and had acknowledged receipt, in writing, of that order. Ostensibly, the SS was locked in—or perhaps locked out.

"If I may append a specific note, Herr Admiral," Colonel Gratz put in. "From time to time, as we learn more about the situation, we shall inform the officers who Raven's 'protected' contacts are. But I would mention right now that this Father Christmas—the American spy in the Vatican we have all heard rumors about—will apparently be Raven's main link with his masters in Washington. As much as we would love to capture Father Christmas, for the present we must leave him completely alone, free to play his part in *our* plan."

"I object," Olendorf protested. "That man is one of the most dan-gerous spies in Rome. He runs a large net, probably several dozen agents; we think he is a priest and many of his operators are also clergy. In a few days the SS will be certain who he is. We should get rid of him as quickly as we can."

"What doth it profit a spy," Canaris asked whimsically, "to gain a whole Enigma and lose his ticket home? Sorry, Olendorf"—the Ad-miral's tone hardened—"but Father Christmas is, for the present, essential to Operation Rigoletto. And Rigoletto takes precedence over catching a mere spy—and over damned near everything else. I assume that is clear, absolutely clear. Now, gentlemen, our business is done. May I offer you another drink?" Canaris picked up the bottle of amaretto.

The officers, even General Mueller, declined and quickly made their excuses, leaving Canaris and Gratz alone in the suite. "What sort of man is your colleague Colonel Olendorf?" the admiral asked after the door closed behind the guests.

"SS, Gestapo—typical in some ways. I knew him in Spain, and then we have both been here for almost four years. He is not the worst of those people. In fact, he is reasonably bright and more willing to take chances in not blindly following orders than most of those swine. There may even be a streak of decency inside, just waiting to be born. I would hate to wait for the birth, however."

"Can we trust him?"

"Trust him? Who would trust an SS man, Herr Admiral?"

"We have already put trust of a certain kind in him—for Operation Rigoletto."

"That is a different matter. A direct order from der Fuehrer will drive him farther and straighter than a direct order from Yahweh would propel a Jesuit."

"Der Fuehrer? Der Fuehrer?" Canaris smiled innocently.

"I meant, sir, your getting der Fuehrer's personal approval welds Olendorf to us. I mean psychologically, not merely legally. He worships der Fuehrer. The man will be like a puppy. Our only problem with him will be the carpets."

"Alas, Manfred, I must warn you to be extremely careful in this operation. I am not in good repute in the inner circles these days. Ernst Kaltenbrunner hates me, and even Walter Schellenberg distrusts me, though I think the lad is fond of me. Then there is Himmler, cautious, calculating Heinrich. And, of course, that pig in a potato field, Martin Bormann, is always skulking around in the background. He would happily murder us all—and probably will someday. Who knows? I may even become a liability to Keitel. In any event, I certainly could not get near der Fuehrer, not these days. I wish I could. I believe I could persuade him. You can tell him things. First, however, you must get in to see him; that I cannot do."

"But the letter? I recognized the signature, even Olendorf recognized it, and he would doubt his own mother."

"True, true. Der Fuehrer himself would think it was his own signature." The admiral gave a shrug that owed much to his Italian ancestors. "If one commands the most expert forgers in the world, one cannot be blamed for putting their talents to some useful purpose."

"Good God, what a risk!"

"Life is a risk, Manfred. Life in wartime is a great risk. And life in wartime as a spy is a very great risk. Let me be honest with you. Without a miracle, Germany is doomed. The Russian army is rolling west. Stalingrad was not a defeat; it was a catastrophe. Moreover, the British and Americans have changed their antisubmarine tactics, and they have begun to win the battle of the Atlantic. Soon they will have enough men and material stockpiled in England to please even a man as slow witted as Montgomery. Then they will invade France. We shall be caught as tightly as that poor devil's testicles in the Gestapo's clamp. Oh, we shall fight gallantly. No doubt we shall win some heroic victories. But every night we shall lose cities we cannot repopulate, and factories we cannot rebuild; every day we shall lose Luftwaffe squadrons we cannot replace and Wehrmacht divisions whose ranks we cannot replenish. Soon, Germany will become a pyramid of rubble inhabited by stinking corpses. Then the Communists will outsmart and outmuscle their allies, and what is left of our people will become bolsheviks. I see nothing but disaster."

"Unless we have a miracle, you said, Herr Admiral."

"Unless we have a miracle. Rigoletto could be a part of that miracle, Manfred. It could be. At any rate, it is worth trying. Let me add, we in the Abwehr need a miracle, too. Those jackals around Hitler have no understanding of what intelligence is all about, but they envy us. Sometimes I think Germany's real enemies all wear the black uniform of the Nazi party."

"You should be careful what you say, Herr Admiral."

Canaris smiled again. "I have said too much too often for my opinions to be secrets. I am not a discreet man. I have found that candor is often the cleverest form of deception. Our initial problem is that the SD wants our mission, and they want our network of agents. I am afraid I helped them when I was slow to report what we knew of Italy's peace plans. I was concerned that der Fuehrer would throw a tantrum and destroy this beautiful country. I love Italy, Manfred. When I was a child my mother used to croon Goethe to me, as a lullaby. Do you know it?

> Know you the country where the lemon grows,
> In deep green leaves the golden orange glows,
> Where gently blows the breeze from azure sky,
> And myrtle stands beneath the laurel high?
> Do you recall?
>> That is the shore
> Where I would dwell with thee, my love, for evermore.

"I remember. My mother sang it to me, too."

"Goethe made Italophiles out of generations of educated Germans. Well, it is still the one place on this continent—perhaps in the world —where one can find culture without pretense. These people, most of them, never wanted any part of this war. They cheered Mussolini and

83

they lapped up his bravado, but not his war. I thought it best for them, and for us, to let them slip into some kind of neutral status. On my way in from the airport this morning I saw a crudely lettered message on a wall: '*Non vogliamo ne Tedeschi ne Inglesi. Lasciateci piangere da soli.*' We want neither the Germans nor the English. Leave us to weep by ourselves. Militarily, our friend Kesselring has been brilliant, but every day we occupy cities like Rome and Florence we make it more probable that animals like Kaltenbrunner or Bormann and their slavish bureaucrats will do things that will disgrace Germany forever."

"Is it Himmler himself who is trying to destroy us?"

"Yes and no. For years Heinrich and I have had a love-hate relationship. He wants the Abwehr, but he will not try to take it over, not directly. He has a few skeletons he does not wish to dance in front of der Fuehrer. No, it will be someone like Kaltenbrunner or Bormann, athough Schellenberg might think he was doing it. He is a bright young man, but he is in a cage with tigers. They will eat him alive."

The admiral paused to pour himself another half glass of amaretto. "I do not mind losing a power struggle, Manfred. I have been part of and the object of so many cabals that they bore me. But whoever takes over will destroy our organization—and destroy Germany's chances to survive this holocaust. That I must try to prevent."

"I do not know what to say, Herr Admiral."

"Why should you? These problems are mine, not yours. The 'Old Father' may yet have a miracle or two up his sleeve. All you need worry about is whether you can pull off Operation Rigoletto here in Rome."

"I think we can. As you know, this man Raven has come straight to one of our agents, a lady who also works for the resistance."

"Can you trust her?"

"No, sir; she is loyal only to herself. But I can use her. She says that the Americans have found a weak spot in Mueller's command at the villa. It seems that Major Otto Schwartzkümmel, the man in charge of cryptography, is vulnerable. He is that rather handsome man you met this afternoon—about forty, short and slender, has a strong but still pretty face. He taught mathematics at the university in Munich for almost ten years—brilliant, but was never offered a chair. I do not know exactly why, but I can guess."

"Guess."

"He has a thing for boys. He is strange in other ways, too, but other mathematicians would not notice those. The best he can hope for is to inherit something from his father-in-law. The old man is fairly well to do, but he is also a moral prig. He would cut Schwartzkümmel out of his will if he had any inkling of these deviations. The major's wife is just about as priggish. They have no children; I doubt if either was ever interested in consummating their marriage. Nevertheless, she would walk out on him if she learned about his boyfriends."

"So." Canaris stood up and began to pace the room slowly. "Those American moralists stoop to blackmail. How quickly they have learned about realpolitik."

"They have had expert teachers in the English, no doubt."

"No doubt, no doubt." The admiral shook his head. "But this plan displays a natural talent for evil. It disappoints me. I had hoped one nation in the world actually took its own propaganda seriously. Well, this news also warns me not to sell these people short. They have learned to sin. That means they are human, and there is nothing in the universe as deadly as a human, Manfred. Give me animals like Kaltenbrunner or Bormann as enemies. They react in predictable ways. Humans are something altogether different. Now, you have the unpleasant duty of securing Schwartzkümmel's cooperation."

Gratz shook his head. "When I joined the Abwehr I never thought I would be arranging a tryst for a bloody *Warmer*."

"For the Fatherland, Manfred, for the Fatherland. What explanation will you give your lady double? What is her name, by the way?"

"Anna. I shall not volunteer a story at all. If she pushes me—*when* she pushes me—I shall think of something appropriately venal to appeal to her sense of plausibility. Perhaps I can insinuate that I am selling Germany out."

"Good, very good. We all feel comfortable with corruption. Under no circumstances, however, can you ever let her have even the vaguest clue about Rigoletto. And what do you plan to tell this cryptographer?"

"That is more difficult. I had thought of invoking his soldier's oath, but he is not a professional officer. The most direct way would be to confide in him about Rigoletto, but that is not possible."

"Definitely not possible."

"The best thing to do might be to let nature, in its own perverted way, take its course and then assist him once the squeeze from black-mail began."

"Mmmm, that might work. I can think of nothing better, but you try."

As Gratz was leaving, the admiral called him back into the room. "Manfred, I know I do not have to repeat how important Rigoletto is, how many hundreds of thousands of German lives—even Germany herself—are depending on this operation. Rigoletto must go!"

"It will, Herr Admiral; it will go."

When they left Canaris, Field Marshal Kesselring returned to his own headquarters near Frascati, in the hills south of Rome, while General Mueller was chauffeured back to the Villa Wolkonsky and his private stock of cognac. Olendorf went down to the lobby of the Excelsior, then walked hastily down a flight of stairs to the basement. He used a set of pass keys to open a double-locked, steel door. Inside in the darkness, a sergeant was attentively listening to the conversation in the admiral's suite.

The NCO did not acknowledge Olendorf's presence until he heard the door click behind Gratz. Then he spoke: "There is something at the beginning that the Colonel should hear." He reran the spool of wire and let it play from just before the place where Canaris explained the forgery of Hitler's signature. Olendorf listened to the spool a second time, then picked it up and put it in his pocket. "Sergeant," he said in his most authoritarian tone.

The man leaped to heel-clicking attention. "Sir."

"Sergeant, what we have overheard tonight is of the utmost importance to the Reich. But I am not sure exactly what that importance is. We have either a genius or a traitor at work, and possibly both. Certainly we have a defeatist. I can count on your total silence, can I not?"

"Of course, Herr Colonel."

"Of course. You are a good man or you would not have joined the SS. What is your name, Sergeant?"

"Schmidt, sir, Heinrich Schmidt."

"Very well, Sergeant Heinrich Schmidt, you are to work closely on this project, this Operation Rigoletto. You will discuss it only with

Major Priebke or with me. No one else—not with your comrades, not your mistress, not your wife, not even with your confessor, if you have one."

The sergeant grinned. "I do not have a confessor, sir."

"That is a relief. You are to take a desk outside my office and concentrate only on Rigoletto. Is that understood?"

"Yes, sir."

Lieutenant Colonel Olendorf got out of his staff car and went into an ugly yellow apartment building on the Via Tasso, a few hundred meters from the Villa Wolkonsky, where the embassy and General Mueller's headquarters were located. He was greeted in the entrance hall by a full-length portrait of Adolf Hitler, resplendent in military uniform. Olendorf had hung the painting there himself, and he paused for several seconds of silent worship at his shrine. Then he walked down the corridor toward his office, barking at the orderly on duty, "Get Major Priebke, *schnell!*"

Kurt Priebke had obviously been asleep, but he had quickly come alert, at least as alert as he ever appeared. He was the sort of man few people could recall meeting—average in height and weight, with mousy brown hair and soft brown eyes. His only unusual facial feature was a badly pockmarked chin, his sole noticeable idiosyncrasy a habit of scratching his behind when he began to think. His voice was quiet, and he seemed shy as well as diffident in a sleepy sort of way. The man, however, had a finely honed capacity for obeying orders unquestioningly, as well as a feral cunning whose edge was dulled but not blunted by a lack of subtlety. Very early in life he had learned that being a good listener could open as rapid a road to professional advancement as hyperactivity, especially if, as was true in his own case, one's ears were more acute than one's brain.

In contrast to Kurt Priebke's anonymity, Viktor Olendorf was the sort of man one instantly recalled, even after a lapse of many years between meetings. In some respects, he was almost a theatrical carica-ture of the professional German officer—tall, slender, and muscular, with soft, slightly waving blond hair cut rather long, clear blue-gray eyes that could focus an intensely interested or an angrily withering gaze, and a thin face that men thought handsome and women mag-

87

netic. The bright scar running along his left cheek could, in an earlier age, have been made by a rapier during a duel with a fellow student at Heidelberg.

Olendorf, however, was a policeman by profession, not a soldier. Furthermore, he had never attended a university at all and, of course, had never dueled. His father had been a chauffeur. Young Viktor had received no more education than a child of a working-class family could reasonably expect in Kaiser Wilhelm's Germany: training at the equivalent of an advanced technical high school. His scar was the result of a motorcycle accident that had claimed the life of his passenger.

Education and proper family background had not been requirements for the Nazis' fellowship. And in the party, Olendorf had found genuine appreciation for his shrewd, practical intelligence and his unswerving loyalty. He had also found there an outlet for his burning personal ambitions. From 1928 until 1934 he had been a policeman in Hanover. His reputation for smart, hard work was slowly advancing him in the bureaucracy, but he soon gave up being a full-time policeman and part-time Nazi for the more interesting and rewarding work of being a full-time officer in the party's political police force, the Gestapo.

Olendorf's loyalty to the party was real. And, with his ability to thrust himself obsessively into whatever task he chose to attack, his dedication to the cause of Germany, Fuehrer, and self was equally real, consuming almost all his physical and mental energies. His only redeeming social grace was a touch of sardonic humor. As John Winthrop Mason would have immediately guessed had he read a sketch of the lieutenant colonel's character, Olendorf had been born in mid-November; he was an archetypical Scorpio.

"Come in, Kurt, come in. Sit down. I want you to listen to a recording, but first let me brief you." In less than five minutes Olendorf had neatly summed up Admiral Canaris's plans for Operation Rigoletto; then he played the wire reel. "Well," he asked when the section on Canaris's explanation of Hitler's "signature" was done, "what do you think?"

"I think we nail those bastards in the Abwehr once and for all, yes? We give this reel to General Wolff immediately. He can take it to Reichsfuehrer Himmler, and in a few days Canaris will be under arrest and the Abwehr will be crushed as a rival of the SD."

"No, Kurt, definitely not. You have the right idea, but your swiftness is an inadmissible tactic. No, for now we play the British game of masterful inactivity. We watch patiently, as a cat watches a fat mouse edge farther and farther from its hole. Who knows? That sly old Canaris may pull this thing off."

"Do you think he can?"

"No, but if we act now and force the issue, he may be able to persuade der Fuehrer that he could have pulled it off had we not intervened. We would have egg on our faces then."

"So we do nothing, yes?"

"Yes, we do nothing, but we do it masterfully. We watch, we analyze, we explore. When the Abwehr makes a mistake, we pounce. If the operation begins to succeed, we take it over. If it begins to fail, we expose the fraud. But we must be circumspect. For now we must cater to Gratz's every wish. He is not a bad sort actually—just a typical, pompous military snob who thinks he is too good for people who fight for the party as well as for the Reich. At first, Kurt, we give him all the help and cooperation he asks for—even more. We pounce only when the time is right for us."

Rome, Wednesday, 29 September 1943

By six that evening Anna was at her place behind the cash register at Ristorante Remus, where she collected ration coupons as well as money. It was not a large restaurant, but, situated near the fashionable Piazza Navona, it was modestly elegant. Before the war, Michelin had awarded it two stars, an honor unique in Rome and one that caused competing restaurateurs to whisper that the management of the Remus had presented Michelin's investigators with "a small bag." The chef—a huge, hairy Libyan who emerged from his kitchen at least once an evening to proclaim, in shouts that would have done a Trasteverina proud, that he was only a poor servant of Allah caught in a savage struggle among heartless infidels—could work minor miracles with what passed for food in wartime Rome.

Before the war, Michelin's rating had ensured that tourists and wealthy Italians packed the place. During the early stages of the war, Fascist officials filled the tables the tourists left vacant. Now, armed with prewar copies of *Le Guide Michelin*, Germans had quickly become the principal clientele. Usually officers came together in small clumps or brought Italian prostitutes. A few Fascist officials occasionally reappeared, but rarely did Italian civilians wander in; when they did, they were likely to be *monsignori* who not only worked in the Vatican but also carried passports from the Holy See.

The same trio who had serenaded peacetime guests still held forth each evening. The accordion player's voice was less lusty, though his eyes were more so as he ogled the prostitutes. The basso was a bit feebler, and the soprano heavier in the throat as well as the bust. The music, however, remained strictly Roman stornellas, tunes so plaintively sung in the thick slur of the local dialect that the trio was able to heap vulgar insults on the Germans without the least fear of being understood. Even the Fascists, their pride constantly wounded by Teutonic arrogance, pretended that the songs were of love and joined with the staff in secret ridicule of their Nordic masters. The prostitutes offered no services for which they were not paid, and nothing in their oral contracts included duties as translators.

The chef's skill was boosted by his clientele. The Nazis were often able to see that the restaurant got such precious items as a sack of real flour, a cask of olive oil, or even a side of veal. Sometimes a group of officers would bring a few kilos of uncooked food from their mess and ask the chef to turn their dross into his gold. Some of the Germans had already begun a habit of bringing to the restaurant—and keeping there—a bottle of liquor. They suspected that the management sold a few glasses and the waiters tippled a bit; but these officers appreciated the personal warmth of the people who ran the restaurant, as well as their culinary skills.

For obvious reasons, the Remus made an excellent listening post for the resistance. The two ancient waiters, the two boys who were learning the trade, the three singers, the owner, his wife, the girl from the Abruzzi who helped in the kitchen, and Anna, all belonged to a resistance unit and duly passed on everything they could remember their clients' having said. That Anna and the girl from the Abruzzi sometimes spent fifteen minutes or half an hour in a Fascist's or German's staff car after the restaurant closed was regrettable. In peacetime, such conduct would surely have caused blood to be spilled, of either the girls, their clients, or both. But war is war, and, as good Romans, the restaurant staff realized that ordinary morals were for ordinary times. Thus, at worst, these liaisons were venial sins. God must understand. After all had He not given them a war? If He sent troubles, He must have meant for them to cope with those troubles and to survive. This male dispensation to females, however, was valid only so long as the women produced useful information and on the added condition that they sincerely professed each assignation to have been distasteful.

Before the war, Col. Manfred Gratz had become a regular client of the Remus—and, for the past year, of Anna. Thus, no one seemed surprised when the colonel arrived just before midnight, had a single glass of wine, and invited her to join him in the Mercedes parked outside. Gratz motioned the driver to take a walk, and he and Anna settled down in the back seat. She swiftly began to unbutton her sweater. "That won't be necessary tonight, *Liebchen*. Our visit will be strictly business."

He opened a small compartment in the car and removed a flask of amaretto. "I have become quite fond of this *Zeug*. Would you join me?"

"Yes."

The two sipped the liqueur in silence. With his bald head and full cavalry moustache, one almost expected Gratz to affect a monocle; instead, he used a small pair of steel-rimmed glasses for reading. His family had originally been Austrian on his mother's side, Bavarian on his father's. After a long convalescence at Mannheim during World War I, the elder Gratz, then a major, had bought some vineyards along the Rhine nearby and moved his family west.

A young man of Manfred's intellectual capacity was no more likely to seek fulfillment in tending vines than in tilling soil. And, thanks to the family's small but real wealth, he had studied at the faculty of law at the University of Cologne, not far from where the Augustinian monk's family had lived. Gratz had scored such high marks on his examinations that he had received the signal honor of being invited to join the Finance Ministry. It was the army, however, that drew him. During the days of the Weimar Republic, he spent several years in the *Freicorps*, attracted to and at the same time appalled by the violence of the loose, paramilitary organization. After this apprenticeship, the Wehrmacht, despite the severe restrictions of the Treaty of Versailles, managed to find a place in its officer corps for the son of a wounded major who had not only won the Knight's Cross but was himself the son of an eminent general. Manfred's marriage to the daughter of an Austrian general had not hurt his case.

"Tell me some specifics about Raven," Gratz ordered. "What sort of man are we dealing with?"

Anna quaffed the rest of her drink. "What do you want, a character sketch or a psychoanalysis?"

"Neither, just tell me about him."

"Well, he's fairly tall, dark—"

"I know what he looks like. I have several sets of photographs. What sort of person is he?"

"Stupid in some ways. He's educated and probably intelligent with books, but in the streets he's stupid. At least the American part is stupid. He's half Italian. He's one of those soft, fuzzy-minded intellectuals whom universities everywhere produce in colorless vats. He's worried about my safety."

"Touching. No one has ever worried about Anna before except Anna. Very touching. Could be the blossoming of true love."

"It's the blossoming of a pain in the bung. Anna takes care of herself."

"And she does it very well. But tell me about our brave young spy's Italian side."

"Except for the language—he speaks like a Florentine, even when he's talking Romanacc', although he thinks he sounds like Trilussa—except for the language, he doesn't let the Italian side come out much. If he does or when he does, he might be more difficult to control. Why are you asking me all of this?"

"We are letting him live a little longer. I want to know if he can take advantage of the opportunities we shall give him."

"What opportunities?" There was a suspicious alertness in Anna's voice.

"The opportunity to blackmail our cryptologist and to learn all his masters want him to learn about Enigma. And then the opportunity to escape. If we are to give him those opportunities, we must know if he can exploit them. There are others we might choose."

"What are you saying?"

Gratz smiled a bit more ironically than Anna could tell in the darkened back seat of the car. "This is not the proper time for explanations. Just accept that some of us believe that this Raven—or someone like him—should learn all there is to know about Enigma and escape to tell the American high command."

Anna laughed out loud. "All out of charity! What are you planning?"

"What we are planning does not concern you, my dear."

"Does not concern me? I work for you and risk my neck with the resistance, the Americans, and those clumsy Fascists; now the Gestapo will probably be watching me if they see me talking to you. All those people are thinking it may be a good thing to kill Anna dead but maybe torture her a little first to hear what song she sings, and you say it doesn't concern me? *Che stronzo!*"

"Keep your voice down. All right, you may have a point, but the less you know the better off you are. Look, you are a sensible woman, you figure it out. Germany has lost the war. The Russians are pushing us back toward Poland. The Allies have driven us out of Africa and Sicily, and now they have landed here on the peninsula. But Italy is just a small thing to divert us from their major effort, an invasion of northern France. We are caught in a pincer. The only question is who gets to Berlin first, the Russians or the British and Americans. Personally, I prefer the British and Americans. With Enigma they may do it; without it they certainly will not."

Anna snorted. "Nothing is that simple. No one would try anything this risky just to be able to choose masters. How much do you plan to sell it for?"

Gratz reached out and slapped her across the face. It was not a powerful blow, but it stung and surprised her. "You filthy slut! You forget you are addressing a German officer."

Anna put her hand to her cheek. There was no blood. "You just saved your German honor by striking a woman; now you can tell the truth."

Gratz cocked his arm as if to hit her again, then relaxed. "You are a bitch. All right, I can promise you a great deal of money."

"I don't want promises. Bankers, police, and shopkeepers never accept them. I want American dollars or British pounds, and I want them in my hand, not on your lips. We both know that the Americans would pay millions of their dollars for one of your machines. I'm taking more than my share of the risks. I want a full share of the beans."

Gratz sighed. "We are all taking risks, Anna. I am talking high treason. The SS would love to have evidence that an officer of the Abwehr was plotting treason with an Italian whore."

"I know that. That's my security against your betraying me along with your country."

"I guessed you might think that way. Therefore, I took the precaution of alerting the Gestapo that a certain double agent might be a triple. I noted that I was not sure but I sensed she was hinting that I might sell Germany out. I was, I said, going to continue dealing with her to find out if my suspicions were correct and, if so, whether others were involved. I sent a copy of that memorandum to Admiral Canaris so that there will be a record outside Gestapo files. I have also taken the liberty of arranging for a Communist in Monte Sacro to receive a copy of your file of cooperation with the Abwehr *if* anything unpleasant happens to me. So, my dear, betray me and both sides will be after you."

"You are a swine."

"No, I am a prudent man who deals with swine. 'When in Rome . . .' but you know the saying."

"You know I'm loyal," Anna jeered.

"To Anna."

"Yes, to Anna. Now then, how much?"

"I cannot answer your question because I am not the one who is making the negotiations. I hope, however, that you will receive fifty thousand American dollars in a numbered Swiss bank account, a Swiss passport that the *Bundespräsident* himself would think legitimate, and a pass that would clear you through any German checkpoint."

"That isn't nearly enough. I want at least a hundred thousand American dollars."

"Anna, I cannot bargain. I do not control the resources, and I am not even sure that we shall use Raven."

"No, you're sure, or you'd never have mentioned your plans to me. And don't forget, I *do* control the real resource—him. Tell your 'colleagues' what my price is. And I want something right now."

"This minute? Absurd. I have only"—he took out his wallet—"here, three thousand lire, ten British five-pound notes, a pair of American one-hundred-dollar bills, and one hundred fifty marks. I do not carry much cash."

"Why should you? You Germans just steal whatever catches your eye. I'll take what you have, all of it, but in two nights I want another ten thousand American dollars as a real down payment."

"I shall do the best I can; that is all I can promise. Enough, we must talk about our Herr Doktor Major Otto Schwartzkümmel. How do you wish to—what is the American expression?—set him up?"

"Is he onto the plan?"

"Of course not. He is too vulnerable to blackmail. I do not know how he ever got a security clearance to become a cryptologist except that perhaps those perverts in the Gestapo look on heterosexuality as the abnormality. All the poor devil does is dream about inheriting his father-in-law's marks and fantasize about sleeping with his students."

"See that he comes to the Remus, then leave him to me. But be there in case I need you. Wait, give me a couple of days. Those cretins from the United States didn't give Raven anything to take pictures with except a tiny little camera."

"A camera that takes microfilm?"

"Something like that. It may work well for pictures of your machine, but we'll need something bigger if we're going to frighten your brave *fròcio*. Will that be all, mein Herr?"

"Enough for the present."

"All right, give me a tidbit of information that I can use to show that I wasn't just enjoying your manhood." Her voice was once more sneering.

"Here is a juicy piece: Kesselring detests Rommel, thinks he is an *Angeber*, all show, no substance. They have a personal feud going. It looks as if Kesselring has won. There is a rumor that Rommel has given up command of Army Group B in northern Italy and is being reassigned, maybe to Russia or perhaps to France. That should please your friends."

"I hope so," Anna said as she opened the door.

Gratz reached out and grabbed her wrist. His grip was strong. "Do not forget, one word of our conversation tonight and the whole plan will collapse. Betray me and you will die, too—and you will die in a Gestapo torture chamber or by the equally tender hands of your Communist friends in the resistance."

She pulled her arm free. "We're in the same business, after all, aren't we, Colonel?"

"Not quite," Gratz said softly, "but we are closer than I like to

95

admit." He paused. "Anna, that boy you use as a messenger. He is very young and he's very frightened. Be careful with his life. The Gestapo would crucify him."

Anna shrugged her shoulders. "He'll have to take his chances like everyone else in this war."

FOUR

Rome, Thursday, 30 September 1943

Anna had left shortly after dawn, while Roberto was still asleep. He had gotten up by 7:30, fixed himself some of the ersatz coffee, lopped off a chunk of the "bread" that one bought in a store, and gone up to the terrace to eat and think. The view was pleasantly relaxing. To his right the green of the Gianicolo was topped by the church of San Pietro in Montorio and the Spanish Academy. Ahead the campanile of Santa Maria in Trastevere rose above the red-tiled rooftops, and the other two sides presented a jungle of similar terraces, abutments, and chimneys poking at odd angles out of tenements like cigars from the mouths of big-city politicos. Down below, in the walled church garden, several dozens swifts, survivors of the Trasteverini's rocks and slingshots, were fearfully nesting in the trees.

Roberto was trying, without great success, to put aside dreams of a safe exit. As of now, Anna was his sole link to the world. She had not yet so much as hinted about the identity of other Italians with whom she was working; and, Colonel Lynch had said, she did not have direct contact with Father Christmas. Obviously, a real need for security was enmeshed in an Italianate delight in secret maneuvering. While all of that was understandable, it left Roberto with no place to run, at least no place he himself could choose to run. He was utterly dependent on Anna and, in a less visible way, on Father Christmas.

The mission itself was a further source of anxiety. Arranging the script and staging the scenario for blackmail would be very difficult, even if Anna were able to secure a willing partner whom they could trust, as she was confident she could. The obscenity of the mental picture he conjured up sickened him, but there were hundreds of thousands of lives at stake. He hoped that when the time came he could rationalize evil as easily as he could now. But even if he himself could pull it off, the cryptologist might not be able to do his part. The poor devil might panic and kill himself, or tell his superiors, which would probably amount to the same thing. Even if he surrendered to the blackmail, he might be inept and get caught or bring back inadequate photographs.

Anna, of course, was vital to the operation as well as to his own safety, and she left him completely puzzled. She was blasé about the mission and cynically unimpressed about its importance. Yet she seemed to be prepared to risk her life to carry it out.

The contradiction was only one of many she displayed. Even in Tuscan, her speech was as vulgar as any Trasteverina's. On the other hand, her apartment was cluttered not only with the writings of Marx and Lenin but also with works by Vico, D'Annunzio, Mosca, Pareto, Panunzio, Bottai, Oriani, and translations of Dickens, Freud, Jung, LeBon, Sorel, Michels, Hemingway, and the remnants of an anthology that contained a few of Yeats's poems. There was even an ancient volume of Belli's satirical poetry. Moreover, many of the books in that peculiar mishmash of literature, history, economics, politics, and psychology were dog-eared, with passages underlined and comments, usually terse and coarse, scribbled in the margins.

Her moods were as varied as her reading, and much more volatile. In the space of a few minutes, she could flash from hot red to cold blue, then halfway back to burnt orange. Her sudden sullenness at breakfast in the Santa Maria two mornings earlier had continued as icy silence until she left for work that afternoon. She returned home after midnight, slamming the door behind her. She threw two *bigne* and several medallions of veal onto the table and stalked into the bathroom. Five minutes later she emerged without her clothes and practically raped him. It had required a few athletic contortions on his part to keep the two of them from tumbling onto the floor from the narrow couch. An hour later, after they had eaten and carefully saved the crumbs, she had repeated the sexual assault, this time in the loft. Then she had immediately fallen into a deep, snoring sleep.

It was marvelously apparent that she took great physical pleasure in sex. For her, however, that pleasure included neither joy nor sharing. She reacted more like a distraught, housebroken pet who, after a full

98

day in the house, was finally allowed outside to relieve itself, than like a human being engaged in sensuous communion with another person.

Now, Roberto was persuading himself, might be the time to contact Father Christmas. Although he knew the name referred to a priest, he could not be certain who the man was. All he was sure of was the laundry code for making contact. His instructions were very clear not to attempt that contact unless the matter were urgent. But he felt an urgent need to talk freely and fully to an American—or at least to a person—whom he could trust, and he did have the excuse of requiring photographic equipment. His small camera would not be particularly useful in capturing the loving panorama of vile tenderness that he and Anna were setting up. Roberto checked his watch—it was Swiss-made, but a Nivada, a model widely sold in Italy. It was shortly after nine, still plenty of time to put out the signal. He went to the footlocker where Anna kept linen and hooked the proper pattern of sheets and towels onto the line connected to the wall across the street.

Rome, Thursday, 30 September 1943

Six kilometers and as many centuries distant, Capt. Karl von Bothmer, Colonel Gratz's assistant, sat in his office in the Minister's House on the grounds of the Villa Wolkonsky, staring alternately at a map of Europe and at one of the city of Rome. The European map was marked with six red circles, one blue, and one green. The reds indicated where each team had been captured, with short dotted lines linking the areas in which they had landed (or, in the case of the Basque, had crossed the border) to the places where they had been apprehended. The blue circle that was around Trondheim contained a question mark. The green one surrounded Rome, with a line connecting the city to the beach near Civitavecchia, where Roberto had come ashore.

The chart of the city was much larger, covering most of one wall of the office. It had four large pins stuck in it, one at Anna's apartment on the Cedro, a second at the Remus, a third at the Villa Wolkonsky, and the fourth at St. Peter's.

Von Bothmer was supposed to be revising and improving Gratz's story to Schwartzkümmel so that it would be sufficiently plausible to ensure the cryptologist's cooperation yet deceive him about the purpose of Operation Rigoletto. It was not an easy assignment. Von Bothmer knew the major well enough to realize that, despite his problems, the man was extraordinarily intelligent, with those strange but brilliant mental flashes that distinguish truly able mathematicians. And, with scientists, one could never be sure where their first loyalty lay. Their view of politics was apt to put nationalism on a low rung of priorities.

The captain had just about decided that Gratz had already outlined the only usable scheme: to let Schwartzkümmel be seduced and blackmailed and then intervene as a kindly father and provide the model and blueprints of the phony Enigma for Schwartzkümmel to copy—or, better, copy them for him. A simple "we have known about you and are prepared to help; you are too valuable to lose" sounded more convincing than any other story von Bothmer could dream up.

That part of his mission was troublesome, but something else was eating at him. Somehow the whole Allied effort to kidnap Enigma did not sit right with him. Everything had been too easy. The Abwehr was good. Before the war, Karl von Bothmer had been a journalist, and, even though he was now in uniform, he still distrusted the military. Yet he had to admit that the Abwehr was an efficient machine. Nevertheless, no organization was as efficient as men like Gratz wanted to believe. Canaris, the captain judged, had a more realistic estimate of the high percentage of failures that any intelligence organization inevitably suffered. And for the Abwehr to locate four of seven teams and the clumsy oafs in the SS two more bothered him. It was not an incredible feat—even the stupid American FBI had captured all the sabotage teams Germany had landed in the United States last year—merely improbable. And von Bothmer's journalistic instincts were always bothered by the improbable.

Finally, the captain mustered his courage and rapped on the colonel's door. He heard "*Herein!*" and entered the office.

Before he could speak, Gratz asked him, "Tell me about what we say to our 'warm brother' to ease his suffering." Von Bothmer explained his inability to improve on the basic idea. Gratz twirled the ends of his moustache as he listened. "All right. I concede he is bright, very bright. But, *Scheisse*, I do not like the idea of a German officer—" He paused for a few moments. "What was it that American general said? 'War is hell.' He should have seen our war; the Poles and the

Russians could tell him a few things about hell. I suppose it is time for our Herr Doktor Major to sacrifice his honor."

"I doubt that he looks on this activity as involving a loss of honor, sir. I knew some people like him when I was a reporter. They have peculiar ideas about sex, but most of them are pretty decent people."

"Probably. That does not make our job any easier—or less important. All right, we go with the plan, but do not stop thinking about it. I would prefer an alternative."

"Yes, sir." Von Bothmer hesitated. "Colonel, there is something else."

"What is it?"

"I do not know where to begin."

"Try the beginning. I am very busy deciding what the British and Americans are doing around Naples. They cannot be so idiotic as to try to slug their way up the peninsula. Kesselring thinks they are, but I doubt it. I have got a mass of reports to sift through for evidence of collections of shipping and troops for another landing up the coast. If I had their air and naval power, I would make a show at attacking north of Naples and then stage another landing at Genoa and leap right into the Po Valley. But I am on the other side. That is the biggest frustration of being an intelligence officer; you always have a clearer idea than the enemy of what his best strategy is, but you never get a chance to put your ideas into practice. Now, what is your problem?"

"Operation Rigoletto, sir. It does not fit together."

"How so?" Gratz's voice became clipped. Von Bothmer tried his best to explain his gut feeling, while Gratz listened patiently.

"I am afraid, Colonel," the captain concluded, "that this whole infection of agents may be nothing more than a diversion to distract us from the real danger to Enigma or perhaps to conceal something else."

"Yes," Gratz said, stringing out *ja* for two full seconds. "Yes, I confess that thought had crossed my mind. These agents might well be only human sacrifices for us to munch on while another team makes the job. It is possible. It has a certain English touch to it—to speak piously of the sanctity of the common man while slitting his throat for the advancement of the elite. You may be right, another team, this one going about its work in a more clever way."

"That is one possibility, sir. There are others."

"Yes. Thank you, von Bothmer; this is good work. I shall talk to the admiral about it. Now, do some more thinking about Schwartz-kümmel."

The captain saluted and returned to his desk. Gratz quickly picked up his phone and called Canaris's office. With one mention of the word Rigoletto, the chief himself was on the line. The colonel pushed the scrambler button on his phone, but he still spoke guardedly. Undoubtedly the SS tapped the admiral's lines, and probably his own in Rome as well. "About our horse race, sir," Gratz began. "We seem to be winning rather easily. Do you think it is possible that the other side has another entry and is allowing us to exhaust ourselves pacing the wrong horses?"

"Manfred," Canaris said, "we must have mental telepathy. The same thought was running through my mind. You have a fine sense of horsemanship."

Rome, Thursday, 30 September 1943

Tommaso Piperno stopped at the corner of the Via della Scala and the Cedro and carefully noted the pattern of laundry hanging across the street between Anna's apartment and the high wall that enclosed the church garden opposite her building. He was a short man, about five feet, four inches tall; his hip displacement made him seem shorter. His face was flat, almost dishlike, with a broad, short nose that looked as if he had spent his youth in a boxing ring. His ears lay back close to his scalp. His once thick hair—fifteen years ago it had been as deep an ebony as his eyes—was now thinner and silkier, white at the temples and salt and pepper on top.

Tommaso Piperno was a *spazzino*, a street sweeper, an occupation vital to health and traffic in Trastevere. He had had a busy morning pushing the garbage along the alleys to corners wide enough for other workers to load it onto horse-drawn carts and haul it away, the horses leaving a steaming trail that created employment for their drivers' morrow. It was a pattern of life that Piperno had followed for thirty of his forty-seven years. His hip had kept him from many forms of private employment as well as from the clutches of the army. But the government, for all its other faults, always tried to help the crippled and the blind, providing the cripple or the blind had a relative who was in politics or the civil service. And Piperno's mother's brother had a stepson who drove a dray for the Department of Sanitation. Thus nepotism had combined with Roman wastage to produce Tommaso's fate.

It was not a fate that he resented. By nature he was a neat man. Since early childhood he had been appalled at the indifference of his fellow Trasteverini to dirt and garbage. It was not cleaning that he minded, but the fleeting term of its effect. Now with all the shortages, people threw out less unconsumed food than they had before the war; but every other form of waste, sometimes including contents of *Zii Peppi*, chamber pots, came tumbling out of the windows to join the wrappers and bags and horse manure that passersby left. It was a pleasure to bring order to that chaos. No sooner, however, had his powerful broom cleared the length of a block than the far end would begin to fill up again. His more philosophical colleagues, most of them from the *Mezzogiorno* or Sicily, rationalized that if Romans were not pigs they themselves would be unemployed. But Tommaso Piperno wanted more than a job; he also wanted clean streets.

The pay was meager, hardly enough to feed himself and his wife and to send something to the Abruzzi, where they had moved their three children after the first American bombing of Rome. Tommaso's work, however, brought certain fringe benefits. He had always made friends with the people on his route, forgiving them their easy acceptance of filth; and for many months he had found it worthwhile to keep the length of the Vicolo del Cinque in sight as he slowly pushed his broom down that street. Whenever he noticed someone or something suspicious he would give one of the signals he had worked out with the shopkeepers. It was a small service, but the owners appreciated his help in keeping their black market safe and showed appreciation for their watchdog in many tangible ways. Some sausages, a half dozen eggs, a chunk of veal, a chicken, some cheese, or even a kilo or two of white flour would find its way into his hands. There was a bit of money, too, but that was less useful. There wasn't much to buy, and he had other sources of lire.

Occasionally, a fellow Trasteverino or even a member of the resistance might ask Tommaso to keep his eye on a person or an apartment as he went through the streets and alleys. From these people he accepted no money or other reward—not at the time. But with the shrewdness of an urban peasant he kept mental notes of debits and credits, and knew that some day he could call in those debts for small favors. From outsiders, the German and the American priests, however, he took what he could bargain for, and immediately. They were here today, but tomorrow? Who ever knew anything about foreigners? Besides, although he was not Christian, he was Italian; and no Italian could bring himself to trust a priest, unless he were a close blood relative.

To play for all sides raised no ethical problems for Piperno. He considered himself a small businessman who needed a great deal of insurance. If the Germans won, a man would have to be favorably remembered if he were to survive at all. If the Americans triumphed, positive remembrance would be less critical to life, but it would still be very useful. And an American victory seemed the more likely outcome. He had a cousin who had returned to Rome for a brief visit before the war; and, if half of what he said about the United States were true, the Germans were as good as beaten. If the Americans occupied Italy, some members of the resistance would take over the real government. And there, too, Tommaso had made friends, though not with all the groups. Adonai Himself would have difficulty counting their factions much less understanding their differences, but His servant Tommaso had done an occasional thing for Communists and socialists as well as Christian Democrats and even monarchists.

With his morning's work for the Commune of Rome about done, he could attend to other business. First was a stop at the Franciscan church on the Via della Scala, about a hundred meters from the Cedro. Inside the altar rail, a short, heavy nun was making a show of rearranging dust. Despite the fact that her coarse and much stained brown habit was tightly bound at the waist, it fell in a straight line from breast to ankles. Her open sandals allowed dirty toes to protrude inquisitively into the world. She was the mother superior of the convent, but everyone called her Sister Sacristy because she spent all her spare moments cleaning and recleaning the altar.

Piperno walked up the center aisle to the front pew, and, although Jewish, gave a passable imitation of a Roman crossing himself as he genuflected and apparently knelt to pray. After a few minutes, Sister Sacristy came down from the altar and sat next to him. Like many clerics, she made a show of not observing the sacred amenities in church. Piperno sat back and reached his hand inside his *spazzino's* blue jacket and extracted the long links of fat sausages that he had just collected from his clients on the Cinque. "God will bless you for your charity, Tommaso," the nun said as the meat vanished into the spaciousness of her habit.

Piperno hoped that Adonai would do so, for his wife, Rebecca, would not. Yet, with the full kilo of white flour he had brought home yesterday and the half kilo of veal he had brought home the other yesterday, the two of them were eating well. The Franciscan nuns, on the other hand, had almost two dozen French Jews hidden in their convent, and none of those poor people had ration cards. Here there was real hunger, more than enough to overcome most inhibitions against eating nonkosher meat.

"I have a message for our holy friend, Sister," Piperno whispered. "The colors are out."

The fat nun nodded silently, rose, genuflected, and, the sausages concealed within her waddling habit, left the church. Inside the convent she dialed a number in Vatican City. Like every Roman, she assumed the line was tapped—after all, Marshal Kesselring himself had warned that calls would be 'monitored'—so the message to Father Fitzpàdraig Cathal Sullivan, S.J., was succinct, plausible, and coded. "Padre, one of our penitents told me that he would like to consult with you on a matter of conscience."

"Of course, Sister. I shall be waiting for him at five this afternoon in my office." F.C. put the receiver back in its cradle. "Five this afternoon" meant 3:30; and his "office" meant the Franciscans' confessional in the transept to the right of Bernini's papal altar in the Basilica of St. Peter.

He pushed his chair back and put his feet up on his desk. That morning's coffee had brought unhappy news. Monsignor Galeotti had come, this time alone, and said in strictest confidence that Papa Pacelli was not planning in the near future to speak out any more clearly against German treatment of the Jews. *Il Papa,* so Galeotti reported LaTorre as saying, was convinced that tactful and very private protests were the only means of doing good. Moreover, despite warnings, the Pope refused to believe that the Germans would arrest and deport the Jews of Rome. The gold the SS had collected demonstrated, he asserted, that the Nazis were now quits with the Jews of the Eternal City. Besides, *his* Germans would never show such disrespect for the Pontiff's authority. The SS and people around Hitler might detest the papacy as a symbol of religion, but they would not dare so flagrantly to insult his conscience and that of the German people.

F.C. flipped a pencil across the room. "So much for speaking out against evil," he muttered to himself. He realized that he was grateful for the call about Raven. As a rule, he strongly discouraged agents from contacting him. It was safer for him to initiate messages and action. But Sister Sacristy's call had piqued his curiosity, and brooding on what Raven had in mind would distract him from mourning over Papa Pacelli's timidity.

After her conversation with Father Sullivan, Sister Sacristy walked to the pharmacy nearby and used a public phone to call Anna's apartment. "*Pronto*," a man answered. The nun had been in the business of smuggling humans too long to miss the tension in the voice.

"Antonio?" she asked. It was the coded question for whether it was safe to talk.

"Antonio is well. This is his nephew, Roberto." That was the all-clear signal.

"Ah, Roberto. Here is your cousin Chiara. Your uncle wanted some priestly advice, and I have a friend, a theologian, in the Vatican who would see him in his office at five today and try to help him. He is Father Perini, a Franciscan. You should tell Uncle Antonio to go to the Porta Sant' Anna and wait there."

Roberto thanked the caller and hung up. He ran through the deck of cards stacked in his memory, trying to decode the time and place of the meeting. It required a few minutes of mental effort. The weather was beautiful, the walk was straight. It would take no more than twenty minutes—well, thirty with his limp.

After he left the Franciscan church, Piperno stopped at the bar near the marriage of the Cinque and the Cedro, and telephoned the German Augustinian. His message was simple: Nothing of any significance to report. Anna had left her apartment before seven, crossed the river at the Ponte Sisto, near the foot of the Cinque, and headed in the general direction of the Remus, though it was far too early for the restaurant to be open. (Tommaso felt no need to tell the German

106

the last piece of information.) He walked a few more meters, then turned left and stopped at a small bar on the San' Dorotea. There he ordered a coffee, managed to get it down despite his distaste for chicory, then went into the men's room. There was no toilet paper, only some pages from an old issue of *Il Messagero*. He took several sheets and placed them in the crack on the right side of the wall, his signal to the Communist resistance unit in this part of Trastevere that he had nothing to report.

FIVE

Rome, Thursday, 30 September 1943

Roberto limped up the Via della Scala and through the ancient arch of the Porta Settimiana, where the street twice changed names, eventually becoming the Lungara. The buildings on the left side shaded the passageway—narrow by American standards, wide by those of Trastevere—from much of the warmth of the afternoon sun, leaving the shadows with a touch of autumn chill, a threat that winter would soon bring wet, cold winds, sheets of rain, short, dingy days, and long, dark nights.

The halfway point was marked by a typical touch of Roman artistry. From the south, the campanile of Santa Maria dominated the skyline of Trastevere; ahead, on a direct line, a matching campanile—indeed, almost the twin—rose out of the rooftops of the Borgo, outside Vatican City. A heavy, foul odor distracted from the beauty. It came from the Regina Coeli, stuffed as it was with petty thieves, anti-Fascists, foreign Jews, and people without identity cards. Roberto shuddered as he realized where he was and moved on as rapidly as he could while still affecting a limp.

Up ahead, the Lungara climbed out of the dank of Trastevere and met the Lungotevere, a broad avenue that swept the length of Rome along the banks of the Tiber. In another few hundred meters, he was at the corner of the Lungotevere and the road that tunneled under the Gianicolo Hill. He crossed that street and entered the Borgo, the *quartiere* around Vatican City, an area neither as ancient nor as dirty as Trastevere, but equally steeped in its own tradition. Slicing through it was the Via della Conciliazione, the great boulevard Mussolini had built to celebrate the signing of the Lateran agreements between the Pope and Italy. The street—whose construction had required demolishing a considerable section of the Borgo—started at the Tiber and ran straight and wide into the vast Piazza of St. Peter.

As he turned onto the Conciliazione, Roberto stopped, as he always had since childhood, to gawk in awe at the magnificence of the basilica. The gray hulk of Michelangelo's massive dome, the dirty ocher of the façade, and the crablike arms of Bernini's colonnade surrounding most of the piazza had never inspired in Roberto any emotion except awe. At no time had he felt a dram of admiration for St. Peter's demonstration of a mélange of artistic geniuses, only awe at its immensity and solidity and the eternity they symbolized. The scale was tremendous, and it seemed ever larger in Italy, where most things from automobiles to apartments to prepared foods seemed to one accustomed to America to have been constructed for Lilliputians.

Roberto had relaxed for a few seconds too long. He had missed the flash of trucks ahead, just outside the piazza on the Roman side of the border of Vatican City. Suddenly he realized what was happening and turned to retrace his steps. But a truckload of police had already blocked that way, and some were moving toward him. He was caught in one of the raids the Fascist police regularly staged around Rome. They would cordon off an area and stop everyone. The principal targets were military deserters, but the Fascists were happy to scoop up people with no identity papers, obviously false papers, or just warm bodies that could be forced to perform slave labor.

Roberto was one of seventy-five or so persons whom the advance of the police was pushing toward the center of the Via della Conciliazione. Some delay was inevitable, but he knew that if he were to keep his appointment that afternoon—or even to survive the afternoon—he would have to act aggressively. Carefully accentuating his "injured" ankle, he pushed through the gathering crowd of potential prisoners to the command car, where several officials were watching the roundup.

"*Vergogna! Disgrazia!*" Shame! Disgrace! As he shouted he held his discharge papers up in his right hand, displaying them for all to see. "*Senta, Capitano,*" he said loudly as he approached the commanding officer, obviously a lieutenant. "*Eccomi!*" Then he began to spew out rapid Romanaccio: "Here I am, a wounded veteran being herded like some animal with these dead-of-hunger, bombed-out peasants, and shanty Jews. It's an outrage!"

Wordlessly a sergeant snatched the discharge papers from Roberto's hand and scanned them. He looked at Roberto's face and then the picture. The image was different, but sufficiently similar not to arouse his suspicions. He handed the papers to the lieutenant, who merely glanced at them before using them to beat impatiently on his thigh. "What are you doing in this neighborhood, soldier? Your papers say you've lived in the Abruzzi and Trastevere. The Borgo is a foreign country to you."

"Ah, *Commendatore*." Roberto tried to look a bit sly. "I need work. Times are hard. Often there are problems with the mail and my pension does not arrive. Sometimes when I receive it, there is nothing to buy with the money. I have come to Rome to find work. Here in the Borgo I thought I might find a priest who would help me. Besides, the British and Americans may invade the Abruzzi. I fought for Fascism in Africa when I had a gun, but I have no desire to face the enemy unarmed."

"And unable to run very fast," the officer said drily. "Soldier, I don't believe you. There's plenty to eat in the Abruzzi and damned little here unless you favor cat turds on your pasta. Offhand, I would guess your peasant friends have sent you to Rome to help run a black market. You have good cover. Take these." He handed Roberto back his papers. "You'll need them in the Regina Coeli. Now, get in the truck with the others. We'll check your story. If it's true, you'll be out in a day or two with our apologies, no worse except for a few extra fleas. If your story isn't true, take a good look at the world; you won't see much of it again."

Roberto took the papers, tossed off a plausible imitation of a Roman shrug, and, as he walked toward the truck, muttered loudly enough for the officer to hear, "*Che macello! Madre di Cristo!*" Mother of Christ! What a mess!

A policeman gave Roberto a boost into the open truck. "*Pazienza, pazienza,*" the man whispered as he slammed the tailgate into place and stood guard on the rear step. "*La vita è dura.*" Life is hard, be patient. Roberto looked around at his companions. Their expressions varied from the terror of the seventeen-year-old lad who was whim-

110

pering in anticipation of induction into the Fascist army, to the quiet despair of the bearded old French Jew, to the bored resignation of the professional pickpocket who looked on the Regina Coeli as a second home.

The trucks quickly retraced Roberto's route from Trastevere. As they neared the jail, he caught a quick glimpse of Anna. She was standing at the junction where the Lungara leaves the Lungotevere to descend into Trastevere. She was looking directly at him, but gave no signal of recognition. Roberto did nothing other than to join in the laughter when the driver leaned out the cab to kiss his closed fingers and throw them open toward her. "*Lahh buonahhh!*" he called out. Anna spat on the cobblestones and shouted back in Romanaccio: "*Brutto fijo d' 'na mignotta!*" Ugly son of a whore! "Go find another queer to bugger you!"

She waited to see that the trucks turned into the jail, then returned to the apartment on the Cedro and immediately dialed Colonel Gratz's private number. The orderly who answered the phone was reluctant to put her through, despite her use of clear, paced Tuscan. Finally she exploded in rapid German: "Look, *Dummkopf*, do it in your bung and tell your bald-headed colonel that his Raven has become a sick pigeon."

A few moments later Gratz took the phone from a confused young man and carefully listened to Anna's explanation of what had happened. "*Scheisse*," he half-shouted. "Those *Katzelmacher!*" He threw the phone at its cradle, missed, and kicked the whole thing along the floor. "Von Bothmer!" he called out to his assistant. "Telephone Olendorf and tell him I must see him this instant about Rigoletto. I am on my way."

Within five minutes, Gratz was storming into Gestapo head-quarters on the Via Tasso. He began talking before the door was closed. "Olendorf, those idiotic Fascist police have accidentally rounded up one of the principals in Rigoletto. They have him in the Regina Coeli."

"What wonderful irony." The SS officer smiled. "When there is fighting to be made, our allies are as efficient at it as rabbits. But now that the Abwehr has a chance to stage a masterstroke of strategy, they suddenly become supremely efficient. I trust you will forgive me if I laugh, Colonel."

"Olendorf, if Rigoletto is blown—"

The lieutenant colonel held up his hand. "I understand, Colonel, I understand. I remember everything about our meeting with Admiral Canaris and the document that we all initialed." Gratz was too agitated to catch the way the SS officer stressed "document." "Just tell me who is to be released, and I shall see to it."

Gratz hesitated. He wanted Raven free and quickly; on the other hand, up until now, the SS did not know who Raven was. They may have suspected, but they really were not, as far as the colonel could tell, certain. "We need—Rigoletto needs," he corrected himself, "every one of those people to be released. If our man gets out and the others do not, his masters in the resistance will become suspicious of him."

"All?" Olendorf paused, then repeated: "All? Some will be released as a matter of course. Your man undoubtedly has decent cover. More probably it will merely seem that that cover held up under the sort of slipshod investigation that Italians typically make."

"All. You *may* be right about how his release would be interpreted. Nevertheless, that is a chance we cannot take. Rigoletto is too important."

"Then I suggest we not blow it by letting everyone go. That would be a confession of error, and our Fascists never admit errors. They are too busy making them. Releasing all the prisoners would attract notice and require some explanation. I suggest we allow our gallant friends to keep those without proper papers, deserters, and draft dodgers. But we ask General Mueller to intervene to 'request' release of all others after routine checks. He could base his intervention on reports of unrest at the 'occupation' and 'strongly suggest' that they help ease tensions by acting swiftly to free the innocent. In view of the extraordinary circumstances, he could suspend his requests for 'labor' from the able-bodied. Would that be suitable?"

"Yes." Gratz nodded. "Quite suitable." He had not expected such cooperation from the SS. Olendorf's plan also closed the possibility of a leak within the Fascist police, a group that was undoubtedly riddled with Allied agents and sympathizers. "How long will all of this take?"

The SS officer glanced at his watch. It was a little past 5:00 P.M. "Certainly not before tomorrow afternoon; the following morning would be more realistic. Italians are not compulsive about time."

112

"I suppose it will have to do." Gratz got up. "Thank you for your cooperation."

Olendorf waved his hand. "I have my duty, Colonel." This time he did not smile.

Vatican City, Thursday, 30 September 1943

In the darkened confessional in St. Peter's, Father Fitzpàdraig Cathal Sullivan, S.J., waited, at first expectantly, then impatiently, and finally nervously. There was a limit on how long he could stay. Some Franciscan might be along to meet a penitent. He'd have the devil's own time trying to explain what a Jesuit was doing in the box. Worse, the Gestapo might have broken his code—like Sister Sacristy, he assumed that all telephone lines in Rome were tapped—and arrested Raven.

At 4:30, after an hour's wait, F.C. left the confessional and, pretending to read his breviary, strolled around the giant basilica, making sure that most of the time he could keep the rendezvous in sight. Once, as he passed a clump of people, he heard two women softly wailing to an Italian priest an account, beautifully decorated and artfully dramatized, of the round up on the Via della Conciliazione earlier in the afternoon. F.C. continued his reading stroll for another fifteen minutes in the vain hope that Raven had eluded the Fascist net, then returned to the working sections of Vatican City, stopping first at the office of Paul Stransky, secretary to the President's personal representative, to pass on the news.

Washington, D.C., Thursday, 30 September 1943

It was 10:45 A.M. in Washington when Father Sullivan visited Stransky. Three hours later, John Winthrop Mason, Col. Brian Patrick Lynch, and Sir Henry Cuthbert were sitting down to a late lunch in a small dining room for senior officials in the Old State Department Building next to the White House. Cuthbert had brought news that the British team at Trondheim had been wiped out. Together with two members of the Norwegian resistance, they had managed to sneak into German headquarters at night, but had been trapped inside. All had been killed in the ensuing fire fight. "Well, that just about signs it off for our chaps, doesn't it?" the brigadier asked cheerily.

113

"I would have preferred that someone had lived to talk," Mason noted.

"I'm damned glad they didn't," Lynch put in. "Those guys were the luckiest of all, except maybe for Raven."

An embarrassed WAVE ensign entered the room and as unobtrusively as possible—which was quite obtrusive because she was not merely the only female present but also a very attractive young woman—brought an envelope to Mason. He put down his soup spoon and signed for the parcel. The WAVE, now very much aware that every pair of eyes in the room was riveted on her, stumbled toward the exit, managing on her way to bump into a waiter and a busboy.

Mason ripped the envelope open and quickly read the deciphered message from Stransky: "Heavenly news: Routine survey by competition has chosen our bird for her majesty. Details of offer forthcoming." He flipped the message to Lynch. "Translate, please."

"Simple, sir. The Nazis or more likely the Fascists have picked up Raven in one of those routine raids they stage around Rome to look for deserters and such. He's in the Regina Coeli prison. Stransky will let us know more when he knows."

"That accounts for all of your chaps, too," Sir Henry beamed. "I think we can drink to a successful mission."

"A completed mission; I wouldn't call it successful." Lynch's tone was surly.

Mason kept his protruding eyes on his soup. "You're both wrong. This mission is not yet successful, nor is it yet complete. We have no assurance the Germans will ever learn anything about Raven's mission. 'Are you here to steal Enigma?' is hardly the typical question one asks a suspected deserter."

"Christ," Lynch injected, "can't we assume that with Anna's record, Raven's being picked up in a routine raid was no coincidence? Sounds to me like the SS or the Abwehr used a routine Fascist raid to protect Anna's ass."

"As I read her dossier," Sir Henry noted, "the Hun would be some years late in that effort."

Mason ignored the Englishman. "We can *hope*, but we cannot be certain. And we must be certain. We'll have to blow Raven while he's in jail. Can we get a man in?"

"That's easy," Lynch said. "Getting a man out is the problem."

"Another one-way ticket hardly exceeds Bronze Goddess's expense account," Mason replied evenly. "I want someone to get to Raven and plant something incriminating on him that will force the Germans' hand."

"On short notice, there's only Father Christmas. It would be a shame to risk him just to tidy up."

"He is as expendable as anyone else in this war. I dislike sounding like Scrooge, but there's nothing special about Christmas."

"Perhaps a priest could get in and out," Sir Henry suggested. "If the Eyeties have your man, and that's probable, they'd be likely to let a priest come and go to visit prisoners."

"But would a priest blow an agent?" Lynch asked. "It's bad enough to lose Father Christmas; it would be stupid to lose him on a mission he wouldn't fulfill."

"Perhaps," Mason mused, "if he thought the agent were a double. I have no understanding of the sacerdotal mentality. Let's not lose time toying with hypotheses. This priest needn't know what he's doing. Give him a simple order to deliver a packet to Raven. Stransky has the microfilm copies of the blueprints of the Villa Wolkonsky?"

"He took them with him to Rome," Lynch answered.

"Very well, have Father Christmas get that film to Raven. Tell Stransky to use another source and tip the Fascists that Raven is a spy and is carrying dangerous documents."

"Prudent," Sir Henry remarked, "prudent. One can't be too careful in dealing with the Hun."

Lynch pushed his plate away. "I'll start now. My stomach wouldn't hold food."

Mason returned his full attention to the soup.

Vatican City, Thursday, 30 September 1943

Four hours later, shortly before midnight Rome time, F.C. was still puzzling over Stransky's request. He was supposed to deliver the small capsule to Raven while he was in the Regina Coeli. F.C. had examined the object with considerable care. It was not a poison pill. He had used tweezers to open the capsule and look at its contents through a magnifying glass. It seemed to be microfilm, but of what he couldn't tell.

The bedeviling question was why Stransky wanted—no, had insisted, and against F.C.'s objections—it smuggled to Raven when he was in prison. Stransky offered no explanation. Indeed, he claimed to know no explanation, only that Washington had said it was imperative that the object be delivered in the Regina Coeli, immediately.

The pieces were not fitting together. He had warned Washington that Anna was unreliable. Yet they had insisted on using her for this mission, a mission of the utmost importance. F.C. knew little about soldiering, but he could grasp what a difference it would make to the war—to the casualty lists—if the United States had an Enigma and could listen to the Germans talking among themselves. Now he was being asked to jeopardize that critical mission in a second way. He was also being asked to impose grave risks on the life of an agent, and for no apparent purpose. Microfilm readers were hardly standard equipment in the cells of Regina Coeli, nor was the commandant apt to provide one on special request. Even having the film on his person would further jeopardize Raven. Most perplexing, if he got free, delivery would present only minor problems.

F.C. put his feet up on his rolltop desk. He kept wondering exactly what it was he was getting himself into—morally, not just physically, though that was bothersome, too. Devoting his life to God and the Church was not a sacrifice he had ever equated with martyrdom. His conscience was stirring, and he was not sure why; but it was tugging at the edges of the wonderfully exciting world where God, Church, nation, and self made the same demands and were all pleased by the same actions. Now something was threatening to unravel the unity of his universe.

Getting in and out of the Regina Coeli might not be difficult; complicated but not difficult. He knew the Italian chaplain. In fact, the priest was one of those on whom Father Christmas called for help or information. Thus, the Italian had asked no questions when F.C. telephoned to volunteer to take communion to the prison the next morning. It was a dreary assignment, Sullivan knew. After a time, trying to bring spiritual comfort to people who were suffering and were about to suffer more became emotionally draining. The chaplain promised to make all the arrangements. F.C. need only show up at the jail at 7:00 in the morning, carrying the Holy Eucharist. However bestial they were in most respects, the Fascists always put on a grand show of respect for Holy Mother Church.

F.C. decided to sleep on his problem. He could go to the jail, hear a few confessions or give general absolution if there were too many penitents, and distribute Communion. He could talk to the guards and arrange to see all prisoners who had been picked up during the past twenty-four hours. If necessary, he could offer a plausible story about a missing nephew of an important *monsignore* in the Vatican. All Italians, even Fascists, understood the importance of family. He quickly remembered to call Monsignor Galeotti and alert him to the possibility of an inquiry about a "nephew." The *monsignore* chuckled, any qualms of conscience soothed by recollections of the reports he regularly read of Nazi atrocities.

Vatican City/Rome, Friday, 1 October 1943

It was 6:45 A.M., and the American priest was still mulling over his problem as he made his way across the piazza, around the corner by the Holy Office, and started into the tunnel under the Gianicolo. Before the war, pollution from trucks, buses, and private cars had made the tunnel's air as poisoned as any World War I battlefield. Now, with only a few taxis—many of them powered by bottles of natural gas lashed to the roof or even towed behind in small trailers— and an occasional bus or German truck, the air was sweet and cool.

At the Regina Coeli things went as smoothly as the Italian cleric had predicted. As befitted a priest carrying the Holy Eucharist, F.C. was silent. The guards were superstitiously respectful of his cargo, though they may not have been personally convinced of his divine mission. A few whispered words to a sergeant were sufficient to allow him admittance into a large, smelly chamber—a bullpen, Americans would have called it—where most of yesterday's catch huddled in frightened ignorance of their futures. As protection against the wet cold of the marble floor, each prisoner had only a thin, dirty blanket. In the corner, several communal chamber pots flavored the entire room with their ripeness.

F.C. had memorized Roberto's photograph and could parrot his vital statistics: age, 26; height, 73 inches; weight, 175 pounds; eyes, brown; hair, black; complexion, dark. Unfortunately, at least five people in the room fit those characteristics reasonably well. The only distinguishing feature would be the limp, but there was no way of telling which of fifty men sitting on a floor limped when he walked.

117

The priest spoke to the group: "I shall give a homily, a very brief homily to spare you my foreign accent, and then I shall offer general absolution and distribute Communion. After, if there is time, I shall hear confessions from those who feel the need of individual guidance. Please let me make it clear that I am absolutely forbidden to take out private messages."

F.C.'s homily was, in fact, quite brief: "You face tribulations that I have never known. Yet those sorrows are as old as humanity. Be sure the loving Christ understands your burdens, even if men do not. Put your trust and your hope in Him. Ask forgiveness for your sins and pray for His grace to guide you always. I have found in my own life that when I faced trials, it was a source of comfort to pray to Sant' Antonio, who, in the early days of the Church, helped create what became the monastic movement. He has been like an uncle to me, a kindly uncle to whom I could take my troubles and who, like a loving uncle, would intercede for me. I shall remember each of you and your families in my Mass today. Now I offer general absolution."

After that ceremony and the distribution of Communion, F.C. retired to the corner of the room farthest from the chamber pots. Several men wandered over, one limped. The priest spoke to each man as best he could, calling on all his clerical training and worldly experience to produce some comforting words for people who faced terrible suffering. When it was the limper's turn, Father Sullivan whispered quietly, "How is your Uncle Antonio?"

"I don't know," the man replied. "I have not seen him in some time."

With the exchange of signals complete, F.C. switched to English. "I have something from Father Christmas. Washington said it was to go to you even though you were here." He reached out and gently clasped Roberto's hand, as a priest might touch a person to whom he was giving spiritual advice. Roberto could feel the hardness of the capsule as it was transferred.

Twenty minutes later, the Jesuit was out of the damp cold of Regina Coeli and was on the Lungara, returning to the Vatican. The early morning sun was faint, but he could feel its warmth on his back. Only at the last second had the decision to pass the capsule to Raven been made. F.C. was thinking in the passive voice because he was not really sure he had done it at all in the sense of a fully voluntary decision. It had been much more reflex action. Back inside his office, he dialed a number in the Hospice of San' Marta. "It's done, Paul," he said. "I'm not sure why it was done, but I am sure that I don't like it."

"You know how things are, Padre," Stransky said softly. Most of what I do, I don't understand."

"Yours truly knows how things are; that's why he doesn't like it." He quickly replaced the phone in its cradle.

Stransky looked puzzled for a few moments, then shrugged and began an intricate system of calls within Rome.

Thirty minutes later, a woman left a modern apartment building in the Parioli, double-checked the instructions she had been relayed, and then telephoned the Regina Coeli. After a long series of delays she was finally put through to the commandant's office. A lieutenant was as high-ranking an officer as she could get. He would have to do. "*Senta*," she began, "yesterday you arrested a group of people in the Borgo. One of them is a spy. He is tall and has a limp. His first name is Roberto. That is all I know."

"Who are you?" the lieutenant asked.

"A loyal Fascist." The woman cut the connection.

The lieutenant sighed as the line went dead. More work for nothing, he thought. Probably another crank trying to spite someone. If he filled out and filed a form he could spend hours being questioned by his own people and perhaps even by the Gestapo. In the end, everyone would probably be angry at him. He would make a *brutta figura*. He weighed the chances of being found out if he did not file a report and decided to do nothing.

An hour later, the lieutenant's phone rang again. It was the same voice with the same message, except for the notation that this was the second call. The lieutenant sighed once more, but this time recorded the call in his log and reached for the first of the many forms he would have to fill out. He was gratified when the informer called a third time. He was able to tell her that the commandant himself was looking into the matter.

At 1:15, the prisoners in the reeking bullpen were still awaiting processing. They were eating lunch—a hunk of ersatz bread, some cold zucchini, and a cup of water. Between the smell and the fear, no one had much appetite. As he was trying to force down some of the

119

food, Roberto heard the clank of cleated boots on the metallic stairs outside. The heavy door grated open and a pair of black-uniformed guards called for Roberto to come with them. They led him to a plain, sparsely furnished office on the floor below. Carefully positioning themselves behind him, they ordered him to strip.

Terror was making Roberto's adrenal glands pump wildly. He realized that the "gift" from the priest—he had not been able to examine it with any care, but it looked like microfilm—and the search were anything but coincidental. The capsule was in his watch pocket. It was small, but too big to be missed in an exacting search. Somehow he had to destroy it. He'd probably have to eat it. But first he had to get to it. "Senta," he protested angrily, "I am a wounded veteran, not a Roman *fròcio* or some common criminal. I was a sergeant in the army. I demand to see an officer."

"Strip, *cretino*," the smaller of the two guards repeated. "You'll see an officer when you're mother naked, not before." He underlined his message by using his rubber truncheon to prod Roberto roughly in the kidney.

Roberto swiftly whirled, grabbed the truncheon, and pulled the surprised guard forward and stuck out his foot for the man to trip over. As the first guard's cheek smacked into the marble floor, Roberto spun and faced the second, who was only beginning to draw his truncheon. Roberto lowered his head at the man's ample stomach and propelled himself forward. The contact was solid, and the Fascist struck the back wall, gasping for breath. Roberto was on him with a wild right hook to the temple, then grabbed the semiconscious body and spun it in the path of the first guard, who was now lurching groggily toward Roberto with his truncheon held high above his head.

As the first guard tried to untangle himself from the second, Roberto twisted and jumped toward the door. It was locked, as he had expected. But by turning his back on the guard, who was still half dazed from hitting the hard marble deck, he gained a few seconds to conceal the transfer of the capsule from his pocket to his mouth. He forced himself to swallow as he felt the searing pain from the blackjack's collision with the back of his skull.

Several hours later, as most of Rome was recovering from its siesta, Lt. Col. Viktor Olendorf entered Colonel Gratz's office in the Minister's House at the Villa Wolkonsky. "You said it was urgent," Gratz noted coldly.

Olendorf looked wryly amused. "The code name for your man should have been Bull, not Raven."

"What is off?" Gratz's face flushed. Evidently the SS had identified Roberto. Under the circumstances it was not a surprising discovery.

"Trouble. Some loyal fan of il Duce telephoned the Regina Coeli that your man was a spy. When our gallant allies tried to strip him prior to interrogation, he beat up two of Fascism's finest."

"Oh, God."

"Colonel, I assure you that the SS will cooperate in any way we can, but your man is making it difficult."

"Yes, yes." Gratz waved his hand. "One must be patient in dealing with amateur spies, and the Americans are all amateurs, stupid, bungling amateurs. Did the Italians find any hard evidence that would identify this man as an agent?"

"No, on that score, we are fortunate. They found nothing in his clothes, and he has not yet had time to talk. He was only coming to a few minutes ago. Your average Fascist is inept at bringing his gospel to unbelievers. The guards got carried away in retaliating."

"Those dunderheaded swine!" Gratz beat his fist on his desk.

"Der Fuehrer will be displeased," Olendorf said smoothly. "I assume that you will keep him informed and that I need not file any special reports."

"You file nothing," Gratz spoke harshly. "We do not disturb der Fuehrer with reports about petty matters. Right now you and I have all we can do to keep a bumbling amateur alive. The fool must have panicked. Now we have to get him out alive and without any pall of suspicion so he can go about what he thinks is his work."

"The simplest thing," Olendorf suggested amiably, "is for one of my people to claim jurisdiction. We could transfer your man to the Via Tasso and conduct our investigation there. I would personally supervise the interrogation, making sure that he was worked over enough to convince his friends that we had been serious but stopped before frightening the fool into saying anything incriminating. He would be marred and scarred, but still serviceable."

Gratz thought of what Olendorf might be able to pump out of

121

Raven were he to be in the house on Via Tasso—enough to take over Rigoletto and claim full credit for the SS. "I appreciate the offer, but—"

"There is a 'but'?"

"Yes. That 'but' is a belief among resistance groups that seldom does even the toughest and most professional of agents leave any Gestapo headquarters alive without having compromised himself, his mission, and most of all his friends. Were this blunderer to be your guest, he would never be trusted again by his own side. Even they cannot be so stupid as to think him very professional. It would be better if you would call the Regina Coeli and 'suggest' a joint interrogation. After all, spies are really Germany's problem now that we officially occupy Rome. I shall sit in as the ranking officer of the Abwehr. Please instruct the Italians that I am to be in complete charge. I shall listen to the evidence and belittle the whole business and recommend that the man be let go with the beating as his punishment."

"That scenario has a familiar ring to it; something comes back to me from my Sunday-school days," Olendorf mused. "As I recall, it did not work then either. I think I should go along to make sure that this time the story has a happy ending."

"I do not think that is necessary."

"Possibly not, Colonel. But I have a great deal of experience dealing with Fascist police. One has to handle them with a delicate combination of tact and authority so as not to arouse their suspicions or unduly offend what they consider to be their honor, all the while making them lick German boots. I would be remiss in my duty if I did not provide my professional services in dealing with such jackals."

Gratz shrugged. There were limits as to how far he could make the SS back off, and Olendorf's point about not raising Italian suspicions was valid. "Very well. I appreciate your concern. Let us meet at the jail in an hour."

Washington, D.C., Friday, 1 October 1943

At about the same time, Colonel Lynch telephoned John Winthrop Mason's office in the Old State Department Building. Even though he was using a scrambler, the colonel spoke guardedly. "An update

122

on our bird. The packet is in his nest, and Romulus is doing it to Remus again every hour via the queen's switchboard."

"Thank you," Mason replied absently. "That should take care of the matter."

Rome, Friday, 1 October 1943

At the Regina Coeli, Gratz and Olendorf listened to the accounts of the two guards. Both Germans were fluent in Italian and were able to question the Fascists fully. Only after ten minutes did one of the guards say anything about Roberto's demand to see an officer before stripping. "Is it the custom of Italian police," Gratz asked, addressing his question to the commandant of Regina Coeli rather than to the guards, "to strip and search wounded veterans of your armed services?"

"*Allora*—" the officer began.

"When," Gratz continued, "that wounded veteran is an NCO, the searchers are enlisted men, and the NCO has asked to speak to an officer?"

"*Ecco*, it was not yet established, *Colonnello*," the commandant explained, "that the prisoner was a wounded veteran."

Gratz riffled through the papers on the table. "These seem authentic to me—and apparently to you. On the face of it, the prisoner behaved in an undisciplined way and deserves punishment; but, *Comandante*, he was provoked. I suspect any good soldier would have reacted as he did. It was a matter of honor, after all. And you certainly understand what a man will do to protect his honor."

"How no?"

"How no, indeed. Well, let us see what evidence of espionage there is other than a crank telephone call. What did you find in his clothes?"

"Nothing." The commandant shrugged, managing to glare at the already very uncomfortable lieutenant who had filed the initial report of the telephone message. "They are cheap clothes of the sort a peasant from the Abruzzi might think stylish—or a *tizio* from Trastevere."

"Italian made?" Gratz asked.

"Yes, and available in fifty stores here in Rome. When," the commandant added as an afterthought, "clothes are available at all."

"Did you make a search of the body?" Olendorf asked the guards. "After you subdued him, I mean."

123

"How no?" the senior guard replied. "We took his clothes off and made a thorough search of everything."

"Of everything?" Olendorf raised his eyebrows slightly.

"Everything, *Commendatore*, everything."

"His rectum?"

The guard's mouth twisted in disgust. "His rectum?"

"His rectum—his bung, man. Did you probe around in his rectum to see if he had anything hidden there?"

The guard looked as if he were going to vomit. He shook his head, but did not speak.

Olendorf turned to the commandant. The Italian shrugged. "*Ecco*, we are not as thorough as you Germans."

Olendorf returned to the guards. "Did you examine his mouth?"

"Well, it was open, *Commendatore*. There was some blood. But obviously he had no poison capsule."

"Obviously," Olendorf said drily, then looked again at the commandant. "His family?"

"Peasants, now; once they were petty thieves in Rome—apolitical thieves, however. Probably on the black market or soon will be."

"I'd like to talk to the prisoner, *Comandante*," Gratz cut in. His sentence was declarative, but his tone was imperative.

The commandant snapped his fingers, and the two guards leaped to their feet, quickly went outside, and within a few seconds pushed Roberto into the interrogation room. He was stark naked, with his hands tied behind his back. There was still a trickle of dried blood on his chin and a much larger congealed mess on the back of his skull. Both eyes were rapidly blackening, and there were the beginnings of heavy bruise marks on his ribs. One could almost see the imprint of a boot on his left side. Gratz found the sight morally revolting. Olendorf viewed it as appalling evidence of undisciplined anger—rage. But then the foolish amateur had probably asked for it.

Roberto was shivering as he stumbled into the room. The damp chill of the marble floor had done nothing to warm him. The two Germans, the commandant, and the police lieutenant seated themselves behind a long table at the end of the room. The space was well lit, although there were no spotlights. In front of the table was a straight-backed chair. The guards pushed Roberto toward it, and he tried to twist his body to sit in it, a difficult task with his bruises.

"The prisoner will stand at attention!" Gratz snapped. The guards grabbed Roberto's arms and jerked him to his feet. One of the guards kicked the chair across the room. Roberto managed to stand, though he swayed a bit.

"Tell us what happened in this room this morning, Sergeant," Gratz commanded. "And speak only the truth."

Roberto started to spew out Romanaccio, but the commandant interrupted and told him to speak in Tuscan—if he could.

"*Signor' Ufficiali*, I am a wounded veteran. I was crippled in the glorious struggle against British imperialism in Africa. My pension, even when it comes, which is not always, is not enough for me to live on and help my family. They are very poor."

"And stealing is not as easy in the Abruzzi as it was in Rome before the war, eh?" the commandant asked.

Roberto shrugged. "A man must eat, *Comandante*. My medals fill my chest, not my belly. I came to Rome to try to find work. Yesterday, the police arrested me and threw me in a truck like I was a deserter or a Hebrew seller of cooked pears. They put me in a cage with common criminals. I showed them my papers, but no one paid attention. This afternoon, these two *fròci* brought me here and told me to strip mother naked. As an NCO superior to them in rank I refused and told them I had a right to see an officer. Then they began to hit me with their blackjacks. I have a temper, I confess it; but they had offended my honor. I reacted with violence."

"Do you know that some woman has telephoned us that you are a spy?" Gratz asked.

"No, *Commendatore*."

"Why would a woman do a thing like that if it were not true?"

Roberto looked angry. "Because she is a jealous bitch. She wants to hurt me. She thinks I have another woman." It was both the simplest and most credible lie Roberto could imagine.

"Is she right?" Gratz asked.

Roberto tried to look sly, but his face was aching too much for him to do more than grimace. "*Commendatore*," he reasoned, "I am only a man."

Gratz and Olendorf began to laugh. The two Italian officers joined in. Finally even the guards allowed a few chuckles.

Gratz turned to the commandant. "What other evidence is there?"

"*Ecco*, I am afraid the *Colonnello* has seen and heard it all."

Gratz stood up. "If you do find a spy, *Comandante*, we want to know about it. My colleague and I will take whatever means are needed to punish such people. But please do not waste our time with lovers' quarrels. Give him back his papers and let him go."

In the car on the way back to the villa, Gratz managed to overcome his distaste for Olendorf enough to thank him for his cooperation. The admiral, Gratz assured him, would hear of Olendorf's work and would undoubtedly pass the information on to der Fuehrer. Olendorf waved the thanks aside as not due. "We in the SS are merely instruments of der Fuehrer's will. We are his Jesuits. But, Colonel, in that regard, I must tell you that your man is a disaster as a spy. He—and you—are fortunate that the commandant is an idiot. If the man had a policeman's brain in his head he would have realized the prisoner was not truly an Italian."

Gratz was nervously twisting the ends of his moustache. "How so?"

"What Italian would ever attack two armed guards on a matter of personal honor? He might have cowered and cried like a baby, then complained to the world that he had been raped. But fight? Never."

"I think you misjudge both the Italians and this young man. That the Italians recognize Mussolini as a fat pig for whom there is no honor in dying says nothing about a lack of courage—but a great deal about good judgment. As for our spy, a fight always makes an effective diversion. He may have used the time to destroy some incriminating evidence."

"Our views of the *Itaker* differ, Colonel. But, even if you are correct about his destroying evidence, what sort of fool carries such evidence around with him, especially in an enemy jail?"

Gratz tapped the driver on the shoulder and instructed him to drive by the Trevi Fountain on the way back. He looked again at Olendorf and smiled weakly. "Here is the problem. We are dealing with a rank amateur being controlled by other rank amateurs. Who knows what fools will do?"

"Who knows indeed? With your permission, Colonel, I would make a suggestion that may provide some warning. Your man is not only an amateur, he is unlucky. First, he contacts one of your agents, then he walks into a random roundup, then someone betrays him, then he antagonizes his guards, who beat him up pretty messily. Let me provide him with a guardian angel or two who will keep him from dashing his feet against the local cobblestones."

"Around Rome we could all use a guardian angel or two," Gratz agreed. "But even if the Americans are too stupid to understand espionage, there are enough people in the Italian resistance who know what they are doing. At some critical time, they will have Raven under surveillance, and it is likely they will spot your angels and we would be lost again. No, we let him stay free, completely free. I hope you understand that as a direct, categorical order."

"Of course, Herr Colonel. You have my word—and my initials," Olendorf added slowly.

Rome, Saturday, 2 October 1943

The morning after the interrogation, Roberto was released, as were most of the others with whom he had been arrested. His head was splitting with pain. He was slightly dizzy, and focusing his eyes to read the documents thrust before him for signature made him nauseated. Both eyes were swollen almost shut, and his legs, back, and rib cage ached from kicks by heavy black boots. As he left the jail and headed down the Via Lungara toward the apartment, he found it easy to limp.

As much as the pain wracked him, Roberto was more troubled by questions and doubts. Being caught in a police net was a risk that all Roman males ran. He could dismiss that as mere happenstance. On the other hand, to be visited by an English-speaking priest and given a roll of microfilm could not be the result of mere chance. The priest had said that Washington knew where he was, and the man gave the recognition code. Whomever the priest was working for—he might even be Father Christmas himself—he had used the opportunity to plant damning evidence. Then a woman had apparently telephoned and named him as a spy.

The whole pattern showed a careful frame. But then the door had suddenly opened again. The interrogation had been easy, too easy. No threats or shouts, much less torture or even tough questioning.

127

The Germans had given the impression of being busy and uninterested. But why had two high-ranking German officers bothered to come at all?

Betrayed. The word kept popping into his very tender brain. Stop babbling, he told himself, and start thinking. Accept that you have been betrayed. Who has betrayed you? Why? And why have you been released?

There were very few people who could have betrayed you. You've talked only to one person in Rome, Anna; and she didn't know that you were going to the Vatican that afternoon. On the other hand, she did see you in the truck, and she could have called. But how could she have known about the film? The other possibilities were Father Christmas or one of his people. And it was a priest who had delivered the film to the Regina Coeli. Settle the first question for the moment: Father Christmas or one of his elves was more likely than Anna, unless Colonel Lynch had been mistaken and she was one of the priest's agents.

Next question: Why? As with the first, Roberto could think of no answer, plausible or implausible, other than that someone in Father Christmas's organization was a double.

All right, let that answer ride for now. Why did the Fascists let me go? The answer was obvious even to an amateur: to lead them to others. He glanced over his shoulder but saw no one who looked suspicious. Of course, even the Fascists were not likely to use uniformed police to shadow a spy. At the Porta Settimiana, he ducked into the bar on the corner and stationed himself where he could see anyone walking down the street. At that hour of the morning only a half dozen people came by, and only one entered the bar, a hunched-over old woman who hobbled on obscenely swollen ankles that would not have allowed her to keep pace with a quadruple amputee.

Roberto could feel the barman, an old gentleman without dentures, staring at him. He fished around in his pockets and found a few coins. The guards had confiscated most of his money—fortunately, he had stashed all but a hundred Lire in Anna's apartment. "Un caffè, per carità," he asked. The old man turned, worked the machine, and pushed toward Roberto the steamy efforts of the boiler to extract something potable from ground chicory and oats, then resumed the

128

long, frank stare that Trasteverini feel it their right to give to anything or any person who arouses their curiosity.

Finally the old man spoke in Romanaccio: "*Sua moje è 'na donna molta in gamma, eh?*" Your wife is some woman, isn't she?

Roberto tried to smile. "Yes, but the Fascists did this work."

The barman's face darkened. "I"—he stressed both syllables of the word "*io*"—"do not know about such things." He pulled another steaming cup of the phony coffee, added an equal portion of raw Sicilian grappa, and put the mixture in front of Roberto. He threw it down in a single gulp and let the steam carry the fire through the roof of his mouth into his brain. "Is there a back exit?" he asked when his tongue cooled.

The man shifted his eyes to a door that apparently led to a store-room. As soon as he was certain that no one was looking into the bar, Roberto ducked through that door and made his way through a maze that eventually led him out to the Via Garibaldi, a street that ran at right angles to the Lungara. Within a few minutes he was twisting and stopping in the narrow alleys of Anna's neighborhood. It took him almost fifteen minutes to complete a walk that should have taken less than five, but he was certain that he hadn't been followed. As he turned onto the Cedro, he almost stumbled over a street cleaner who was trying to scrape something off the cobblestones.

Shortly after noon, Tommaso Piperno paid his daily visit to the Franciscan church on the Via della Scala. As usual, Sister Sacristy was at work near the altar. Along with some eggs and a kilo of cheese, Tommaso passed on his information: "Our man has returned. He has been badly beaten, but he will live. Which is more than I can promise for you and me, eh, Sister?"

Fifteen minutes later, at a bar on the San' Dorotea, Tommaso called the Augustinian monk and gave much the same message. In all, he concluded as he hobbled home, it had been a good day. He had earned the equivalent of thirty-five cents from the Italian government, two dollars from the American priest, and fifty cents from the German; and his friends on the Cinque had presented him—even after the deduction for the Franciscans' guests—with a half kilo of flour and a small piece of veal. Moreover, the young foreigner was

129

alive. That news was both interesting and pleasant. He seemed like a nice lad, too nice to be in the apartment of *la Strega*. On second thought, Piperno decided, there were worse fates than to be in *la Strega's* apartment, providing one had a great deal of youth and much manly vigor.

Washington, D.C., Saturday, 2 October 1943

As customary, Col. Brian Patrick Lynch had arrived at his office by 7:00 A.M., read over the night's radio traffic, and organized his day, giving priority to the more difficult problems that seemed solvable. Naples had fallen yesterday, but the Joint Chiefs were still unhappy about the war in Italy. The prospect of slugging up the marble-flecked Apennines promised only a long campaign and longer casualty lists. More imaginative military minds pleaded for an amphibious attack that would surround Kesselring's army. It was a situation that made Lynch ache to get rid of his desk in the Pentagon and his cold master in the Old State Department Building and go back to the troops. That was wishful thinking, he knew.

At 11:00, as he was slurping his fifth cup of coffee, a WAC entered the room and presented him with a top-secret cable. He signed the receipt and quickly ripped the envelope open: "Bird has flown queen's cage minus only a few feathers."

Lynch broke into a broad grin. He was unsure whether he was more pleased that the young man was alive or that John Winthrop Mason might lose his icy calm and throw a tantrum. Two quick telephone calls and a short drive later, he presented the cable to Mason and Sir Henry Cuthbert. As Lynch had hoped, the news made Mason explode in rage. For a few moments, the colonel thought that the lawyer's eyes would pop onto his desk. "Dagos! We serve them a fatted spy and they let him go!" He ignored Lynch and addressed the brigadier. "What do you make of it, Sir Henry?"

"It's a tough knock. We committed a mistake common in this war, underestimated the ability of the Eyeties to blot their copybooks. Apparently, some of that talent has rubbed off on the Hun. Rather makes one sympathize a bit with him, doesn't it? Well, there we are. Now the question is what we do next."

"What we do," Mason said, "is to compromise him again. The question is how."

130

"Why not just get him out?" Lynch asked. "If they let him slip away after the way we blew him, the Germans are playing some sort of cat-and-mouse game. They probably know all about him and are only waiting to see if he will lead them to Father Christmas."

"Not good enough," Mason replied. "As Sir Henry says, the stupidity of the Italians may be contagious; even under the best of circumstances, Germans tend to be more meticulous than intelligent. No, 'probably' is not good enough. Where Bronze Goddess is concerned, absolute certainty is the bare minimum. The Germans must be totally impressed with our fanatic determination to unlock Enigma. What Raven buys is a smug sense of security among the Germans."

"Forgive me, Mr. Mason, but that poor bastard doesn't 'buy' anything. That's the price we sell him for."

Mason lit one of his cigars. "Put it as you please, Colonel, but the Nazis must get their talons into Raven while he's able to tell them about every sugarplum dancing in his wee little head."

"Yes, yes." Sir Henry nodded. "That's bang on. Our Bronze Goddess is worth the human sacrifices she demands. But we face a delicate problem now that the Eyeties have mucked up the easy chance. We'll have to give the Hun a second shot, but it can't be too easy, can it?"

"No," Mason agreed. "It must look difficult and it must be done swiftly."

SIX

Rome, Saturday, 2 October 1943

Climbing the four flights of stairs to Anna's apartment had been hard, grinding work for Roberto. Twice he stumbled before Fabriziana Donatello came out of her apartment and helped him. Like most other middle-aged women housed on the Cedro, she had seen him come in the back way, weaving and reeling slowly, like a man who had spent too much time too close to a fiasco of wine. At the door, she handed him over to Anna without speaking. Helping a man who had had too much to drink and had been beaten up besides was an act of charity; speaking to a witch-whore would have made a *brutta figura*, a loss of face.

Anna guided him to the sofa, took off his shoes, and pushed him gently back against the pillows. She returned in a few minutes with wet cloths to put on his face. "Jail does not seem to agree with you, Roberto americano. You stink—among other things. What happened?"

As best he could, Roberto gave her a brief summary. He had decided that since it was unlikely that Anna had betrayed him, she could be trusted, though only a little. She interrupted only to ask what had been on the microfilm. He tried to grin. "We may know in a day or two." When he was done, all she said was, "*Cretini.*" It was a statement of fact, not a moral judgment. "*Cretini.* I risk my neck working with fools."

"What do you know about Father Christmas?" Roberto asked.

"Very little. I've never met him or known anyone who claimed to have met him in person. But he's real, a foreigner probably. He works with several resistance groups and the 'running voices' say that he has an efficient organization of his own. I guess he's a priest in the Vatican."

132

"Would he betray me?"

"How no? If he's a priest, betrayal is his business. But I am not yet convinced that you were betrayed. You are here, after all."

"It's all too pat: spot arrest, planting the microfilm, thorough search, two German VIPs standing by ready to grill me. Then release —and don't worry, I wasn't followed. I checked a dozen times."

"I am not worried, Roberto americano. The Fascists have always known where I live, and by now I suppose the Germans know, too. But you don't understand what happened. If you were betrayed, it was more probably by stupidity than by design. What you're imagining would have taken intelligence, and the people you work for are incompetent fools, the worst sort of amateurs. I can hear them now: 'Raven must get this film immediately.' 'But, sir, he's in prison.' 'I don't care if he's in the bathroom, get it to him.' And always someone who should know better carries out such orders to the letter. Have you ever met a government official who was not a fool?"

"I thought so; I'm less sure now. Well, whatever's eating at Father Christmas, I have to try to see him again today."

"How do you know he'll be there?"

"I don't, but we have a system for meeting if one party misses the first one. It should have taken place yesterday, but Father Christmas knows that I was in jail. And if he knew that, he knows that I'm out today. Besides, we need the photographic equipment, so I have to take the chance. Meanwhile, I'd like to try to get some sleep."

"After you've scrubbed with a week's soap ration. You not only stink, you probably have fleas."

"Probably. I'll shower soon. Just let me rest for a few minutes." He settled back into the couch.

Anna walked over and put her hand on his forehead. "How badly did they hurt you?" she asked.

"Aside from my face? The back of my head feels like it's been torn off, I may have a broken rib or two, and I've got a lump on my thigh the size of an apple from a Fascist boot."

"Whore's sons," she said quietly. "I do not think you have to wonder now why I became a Marxist. *Allora*, the beating will wear off your body easier than off your mind. Live with the pain, remember it. Someday the whip will be in the other hand. Patience; as my countrymen say, life is hard."

133

"Very hard," Roberto agreed and closed his eyes.

"No, no sleep now, not yet." Anna spoke sharply. "Take a shower. I'll heat some soup and get some wine."

Roberto wearily pulled himself up again. "I guess you're right, but I'd rather just sleep."

"You can sleep later, after you eat something and we make love."

Roberto shook his head. "I'm tired and I hurt too much for love making."

Anna looked at him if he were a not very bright child. "That's why we make love, Roberto americano. You still have your manhood, but you need to prove that fact to yourself. I shall help—and I shall be gentle as with a young virgin."

When Roberto wakened, he was alone in the apartment. Everything was still. He looked at his watch: siesta. He forced himself to get up and dress. It was time to go to the Vatican. He presumed that Father Christmas or his stooped helper from the Regina Coeli would be waiting that afternoon in St. Peter's. Roberto decided he would arrive at 3:30 and perhaps watch the priest, though he was unsure what he expected to learn from that exercise.

Even after the shower, Anna's surprisingly tender ministrations, a decent meal, a half bottle of wine, and three hours of sleep, the walk back to the Vatican had been painful. He'd almost panicked when he passed the Regina Coeli. For the rest of his life he would smell that rancid odor of unwashed bodies wet with fear, mixed with the aroma of chamber pots overflowing from nervous stomachs, just as he would hear the clank of cleated boots on iron stairs and feel the electric current of terror magnetize the prisoners as the door ground open on dry iron hinges. It had been like a nightmare from which one cannot awaken. But he had awakened and he could not go back to sleep, not yet. Intellectual discipline provided enough emotional discipline to allow him to walk by in his now customary limping gait.

Roberto had planned to patrol the giant Basilica of St. Peter and keep his eyes on the Franciscans' confessional, but he was too exhausted to stand any longer. The only place to sit was in the chapel at the rear of the building under the symbolic chair of Peter, set high in the rear wall. The afternoon sun was burnishing to a bright gold

134

the circle of stained glass around the dove that represented the Holy Spirit. It was one of the basilica's more majestic displays, but Roberto sat with his back to that particular beauty, his eyes fixed on the transept to the right of the papal altar.

At 4:00 P.M., thirty minutes ahead of the scheduled meeting, he got his reward. The black-cassocked cleric who was crossing the center of the basilica had the unmistakable stoop, the silver-spackled black hair, thick eyebrows, and flashing blue eyes of the priest from the Regina Coeli. At the right side of the papal altar, the Jesuit opened his breviary and pretended to read; then, as his eyes swept around the rear of the church, they locked onto Roberto's. The priest continued his slow stroll for a few minutes, then entered the confessional. He did not, however, turn on the light that signals the presence of a confessor.

Roberto's American soul pushed him to go over immediately to the box and confront the man. His Italian soul urged him to wait ten minutes, both to see if anything more was going to happen and to let the priest stew for a bit in his own curiosity. Roberto was Italian that day. Finally, he limped over to the confessional and softly pushed aside the heavy purple drapery that served as a door. Quickly, the wooden panel between penitent and confessor slid open, leaving only a thin veil between them to protect the sinner's anonymity. "Yes, my son?" F.C. whispered.

"Don't 'my son' me, you son of a bitch," Roberto hissed in English. "You betrayed me. Why?"

"Betrayed you? How?"

"Don't play cute. You planted that microfilm on me and then tipped the Fascists. A couple of hours later, they stripped and searched me. Why?"

F.C. was silent for a few moments. "I gave you the microfilm, but I did not tell anyone."

"Are you claiming all that was coincidence? That's bullshit and you know it."

"No, I only give you my word as a priest of God that I did not knowingly betray you. And I'm not sure that you were betrayed or, if you were, by whom."

"All I have is your word."

"Yes, all you have is my word. That's all you'll have when you

135

come to me and say it's time for Father Christmas to get you out of Italy—with the diagrams of Enigma, I hope. Don't forget that Father Christmas's people are your lifeline. If we wanted to betray you, you'd be dead—or still in the Regina Coeli. But you've got a point. I have some ideas about what may have happened. I'd like to check them out."

"So would I."

"If you thought I'd betrayed you, why did you come this afternoon?"

"I'm not sure. To confront you. To let you know that I know—or if it isn't you, to let you know that somebody in your organization is rotten."

"I'll pass that on to Father Christmas."

"Do that, if you're not Father Christmas himself."

"I'll say it just one more time, Roberto. I did not knowingly betray you. I had explicit directions to bring you that microfilm. Washington knew you were in the Regina Coeli, but they told me to deliver it anyway."

"Then someone in Washington betrayed me."

"But why? Why would they send you here to betray you? It doesn't make sense. Nor does it make sense that there's a German sympathizer inside the OSS—too many good things are happening. I suspect Anna. I have warned Washington that she may be a double agent. She could have betrayed you."

"She didn't know about the rendezvous."

"But did she know about your being arrested?"

Roberto hesitated. "Yes, she did. But she didn't know about the microfilm."

"You have been assuming," F.C. noted, "that the guards were looking specifically for the microfilm. That they were highly suspicious of you is evident, but they might not have been looking for the film."

"The coincidence is too striking. Besides, Anna could have betrayed me a dozen times in as many ways. Why wait until I'm in jail?"

"Perhaps to protect herself from the resistance and from Washington. I really can't say. I merely suggest that you be very careful of that woman. The Italians call her 'the witch.' I think she's a German agent."

"We're not getting anywhere."

Neither man spoke for a few minutes. Finally, F.C. broke the silence. "I admit it, I was worried about bringing that film to you. I almost didn't do it. It seemed like a very stupid thing to do then, and it seems even stupider today. But I'd have bet my life that those people knew what they were ordering me to do."

"Instead, you bet my life. Now we both know better. I hope. We're still getting nowhere. I came here because I need some photographic equipment. I brought a miniature camera that is great for taking pictures of small objects, close up. It turns out we need some shots of large objects from a distance of fifteen feet or so—and indoors. I've got to have two cameras good enough to take pictures indoors without flash attachments. I don't care what kind, so long as they can be held in the hand. And film—I'll need one roll of eight or ten exposures for each camera, something fast enough to take shots indoors."

"Mmmm, I don't keep equipment like that around. Maybe Father Christmas does. How soon do you need them?"

"A couple of days ago. I have a lead. If I can strike before it cools, I may get what we want. Break your butt, Padre. We may not get a second chance."

F.C. sighed, "My son, don't you know there's a war on?"

"I've heard. By the way, I'd like them delivered. This walk is getting tougher.

"You do want service. Well, I'll try."

"Good. And, Padre, on the business of betrayal: You may be right, I don't 'know,' but I still have something a hell of a lot stronger than a suspicion. I've told you so you can check to see if it's somebody in your organization or even if it's Anna. I've told Anna, so she may be checking on you. And I've made other arrangements," Roberto lied, "to make sure that somebody will know if none of us gets out alive. You can relay that little message back to Washington. Your people may have forgotten that I'm half Italian. I'm on home ground. As your military people would say, I'm familiar with the terrain."

"You've been prudent to protect yourself," F.C. agreed, "but I hope you haven't said too much to any Italian."

"*Abbastanza.*"

"Very well, I'll pass the word along. I only ask you not to take what Anna says at face value."

137

"I'm not taking what anybody says at face value."

Roberto stood up slowly. Kneeling had kinked his already sore muscles. "Wait a minute, please," F.C. said. "Whatever else I may be, I am a priest, and you're a Catholic whose work makes him walk on the rim of death. Would you like to talk to me as a priest?"

"You mean confess my sins?"

"Absolution is prudent for a spy, and you speak like a prudent man." F.C. had tried to keep a light tone, but he realized he hadn't succeeded. "I'm sorry, I didn't mean to joke about such a serious thing. For you, on this mission, death is a constant companion, and Anna is not a moral woman."

"Perhaps, but she's one of ours. Our masters threw me in with her, so it must be all right."

"No, it isn't. Don't blame me for what others do against my advice. I'm only trying to help you obtain the extra grace to overcome temptation that could take your soul."

Roberto smiled. "My life is fair game, but my soul is not. I'm not sure of your rules, Padre. Just bring me the cameras. The quicker you do that, the quicker I'll leave that proximate occasion of sin you call *la Strega*."

Vatican City, Saturday, 2 October 1943

"Padre," Paul Stransky explained patiently, "I don't have a supply of photographic equipment. I've got my own camera; it isn't very sophisticated but you're welcome to it. It's all I have. I'll do my best to round up something over the next few days. If you need the gear sooner, try the black market, contact the British ambassador's batman."

"You work on the British, I'll try some other sources."

Back in his office, F.C. dialed Monsignor Galeotti's number and explained his need, though not the reason behind it. The Italian asked no embarrassing questions; still, he promised no more than to look around. "At coffee tomorrow," he said, "we meet and perhaps I have something."

An hour later, Colonel Gratz's telephone rang. It was the Augustinian monk. "You must have second sight, Colonel. The request came this minute for two cameras and film that can be used indoors. How did you know?"

Gratz chuckled. "It helps if your opponents are Americans and amateurs, *Herr Pater*. Who made the request?"

"Monsignor Galeotti, the diplomat who recently returned from Turkey. He is the one, I believe, who has been goading LaTorre about the Jews. He has the undersecretary really believing that Zionist propaganda about 'death camps' and mass extermination."

"The British. They are the world's great experts on propaganda. They pick up a Zionist rumor and the next thing you know it is a documented fact attested to by phony pictures. Herr Goebbels could learn a lot from them. At least His Holiness does not believe that garbage."

"I think not, but a lot of people are trying to persuade him it is true."

"Do what you can to fight that, *Herr Pater*. Germany has enough problems saving Europe from communism without worrying about being stabbed in the back by naïve clergy. Now, the cameras: I have a lovely pair of Leicas here in my office. I can have them to you in fifteen minutes."

"Good, but it might be better to wait a day. I would not want to seem to have been prepared. Perhaps one of your people could drop them off at my office at the Lateran University in the morning."

"Fine. One other thing. I have mentioned our suspicions that your American colleague Sullivan is Father Christmas. How do you feel about that now?"

"I could not prove it in court, but I think you are correct."

"So do I; and, fortunately, we are neither lawyers nor judges. Where does Galeotti fit in?"

"I do not know. He has only been back a few weeks. I believe he is merely sympathetic. You would not expect Sullivan to ask me for the cameras himself. Are you sure you want me to cooperate with him?"

"Absolutely sure," Gratz replied. "Sometimes you learn more about your enemy if you help him than if you try to frustrate him; and Father Christmas fascinates me. It must be my German sentimentality, but he makes me sing 'O *Tannenbaum, O Tannenbaum*' and dream of home. So, the cameras will be at your office in the morning. And do keep an eye on both Sullivan and Galeotti for us."

Rome, Monday, 4 October 1943

The orderly admitted SS Capt. Erich Danzig into Lieutenant Colonel Olendorf's office. The young officer was short and pudgy, with a slug of baby fat still hanging from each jowl. Nevertheless, his tailor's considerable skill allowed the captain to present a passable military appearance. He clicked his heels and gave a smart Nazi salute, then stood erectly at attention. "Heil Hitler," Olendorf muttered, but did not return the salute, offer his hand, or otherwise acknowledge Danzig's presence.

The lieutenant colonel felt neither a need nor a desire to learn more than he had read in the man's dossier. That information allowed Olendorf to dismiss the captain as an oily, servile thug, whose only claim to professional advancement was a voracious appetite as a *Judenfresser*—"a Jew eater." He was an Austrian who shortly after the *Anschluss* had abandoned his role as a student at the University of Vienna to join the SS. Except for a brief tour with *Einsatzgruppe* A in the Baltic states, commanding firing squads overworked with the tasks of executing local Jews and Russian prisoners of war, he had spent most of his career in Adolf Eichmann's office in Berlin, enthusiastically planning mass deportations and annihilations of Jews.

After several minutes of renewed silence, Danzig felt obliged to speak. "Sir, I have my orders for the Colonel's inspection." He reached inside his briefcase, took out a thin folder, and placed it gently on the desk.

Olendorf pushed the folder away. "Give your orders to the sergeant outside. I know what they say."

"With respect, sir, I think the Colonel should read them—carefully." He leaned toward Olendorf and pushed the orders back toward the senior officer.

Olendorf shoved the orders back toward Danzig. "Captain, understand one thing: I do not give a damn what you think, or even if you think. You do your job; I do mine. And I did not give you permission to stand at ease."

The captain instantly returned to stiff attention. "Sir, the Colonel must understand that Herr Kaltenbrunner has personally made me in complete command of the *Judenaktion* in Rome."

"I fully understand that, Captain; and fully I shall cooperate with you. My second in command, Major Priebke, will be at your service. Incidentally, we have seized the records of the Jewish community from the temple and put them here. Major Priebke will show them to you. You can get all the names and addresses your little heart desires. The major can also introduce you to the Italian race officer—a knowledgeable man who will sell anything you tell him to the local Jews."

"I thank the Colonel. I shall keep those points in mind. From my examination of our files in Berlin, I estimate I shall need five hundred troops to execute the action."

"That sounds correct. Let me know if you need help billeting them when they arrive."

"Sir, I expected the Colonel to provide the manpower."

Olendorf narrowed his eyes and stared at Danzig for a full half minute. Then he fished around in his tunic for a pack of Lucky Strikes, took one, and lit it. He did not extend the pack toward the junior officer. "Captain, the Colonel does not have five hundred troops. What men the Colonel has are all very busy tracking spies or chasing partisans. Ask Marshal Kesselring or General Mueller."

"Sir, the Colonel knows those officers have opposed a *Judenaktion* in Rome, as has the Colonel. Those who are sympathetic with the Jewish scum—"

"Captain," Olendorf cut in, "understand another thing: Some of us have opposed a *Judenaktion* at this juncture. That does not mean we oppose a *Judenaktion* period, at least not in my case."

Olendorf stood up and paced up and down behind his desk. When he spoke again, he was not looking at Danzig. "I have explained to Berlin that, on the one hand, we do not want to drive the Pope into some sort of public protest that would harm Germany. And, on the other hand, the Jews here have access to money and information that we can exploit. Last week I sent three hundred kilos of gold to Berlin that the local Jews raised as a 'ransom.' There is much more there, gold that the Reich could use. Rich Jews in America are financing an organization located here called DELASEM. We can tap them for a few hundred kilos of gold every few months. Furthermore,

141

DELASEM may be a conduit for spies and saboteurs. I want to let it run, infiltrate it, and perhaps uncover spy nets and partisan groups. I am willing to accept several million marks in gold and the Allies' network in Italy as the price of letting six thousand subhumans live a few more months. That is not sympathy, Captain, that is logic."

"Berlin does not see it that way. The end of the Jews is fate-determined, and to bring about that end is the critical task facing the Reich today."

"Really? I had thought it was stopping the Russian army and the invasion of France that we all see coming."

"If I may say so with all due respect, the Colonel's thinking is not in tune with Berlin's."

"You do not need to say so, Danzig. Your presence here makes that abundantly clear. Berlin has spoken, the matter is closed. I am ready to cooperate with you in any way I can, but I cannot give you what I do not have."

"Does the Colonel have office space and quarters for me and my staff?"

"The Colonel has accommodations for you and for your staff. The orderly will show you where. Keep Major Priebke closely informed of your plans. I have several undercover agents at work around town. I would not want any of them scooped up in your shovel and shipped off to a camp in Poland." Olendorf lit a second cigarette from the butt of the first. "That is all, Captain. Dismissed."

Rome, Monday, 4 October 1943

Shortly after 8:00 P.M. Colonel Gratz and his assistant, Karl von Bothmer, entered the Remus. As they walked by the cash register, Anna nodded toward a table in the rear, where Maj. Otto Schwartz-kümmel was deeply involved in conversation with a thick shouldered young Luftwaffe captain. Each man had a hand under the table. Gratz nodded but said nothing. Later, between courses, he went to the men's room and stopped at the register to pick up a folder of matches. "I have canceled all SS and Fascist sweeps in the Borgo and Trastevere for the next few days," he said in a low tone. "It should be safe for your man to move around a bit."

Anna inclined her head slightly. "He has the cameras."

"Good. When do you want to start working on our major?"

"Why not tonight?"

"Why not? I shall set him up for you."

It was after 11:00 when the cryptologist and his friend from the Luftwaffe got up from their tables. They were talking too intently as they approached the cash register to notice Gratz's joining them. The colonel grasped the pilot's left elbow very firmly. "Captain," he whispered.

The officer turned, recognized Gratz's rank, and snapped to attention. "Sir?"

"Just walk along." He turned to Schwartzkümmel: "Stay where you are, Major."

As soon as he was alone in the vestibule with the captain, Gratz's tone became sharper, although he was still almost whispering. "I want you out of here immediately. You are to consider this place and that officer"—he motioned toward Otto Schwartzkümmel, who was obediently standing at the cash register—"as off limits, absolutely off limits. Now go, before I send you to the Via Tasso."

The captain's blush covered his cheeks and was spreading to his scalp under his thin blond hair. All he could do was mumble "*Jawohl*," and rush out into the piazza.

Gratz turned and motioned for Schwartzkümmel to join him. "Major, I shall repeat to you what I told that 'warm brother': This is the last time you shall see him."

"Sir?"

Gratz's voice softened. "Look, Major, I consider myself a man of the world. I accept sex as a fundamental part of life. I make no more moral judgments about another's taste in such matters than I do about his eating snails or octopus. But I have a war to fight—and so do you. Your friend is as obvious about his homosexuality as anyone I have ever seen. Worse, the way our planes are getting shot down, he will probably end up a prisoner of war. If the Americans capture him, you might not have problems. But if the British do, they will recognize him for what he is, and they will tease out every drop of information he has, including the names and positions of his 'friends.' The blackmail that would follow would be bad for you; it could make a disaster for Germany."

"I have all my security clearances, Herr Colonel."

"I know that, Major. You are a brilliant man and because of that brilliance we have overlooked a few things. But when you start taking chances like this one, you become a grave risk to the Reich. I would not want our colleagues in the Gestapo to take an interest in you."

Schwartzkümmel's handsome face whitened.

"What I am saying in a fatherly way is to be prudent. I do not ask for celibacy any more than I practice it myself. I recommend that 'good woman' behind the cash register. She is discreet, resourceful, and inventive. She can procure whatever you need."

Schwartzkümmel did not respond.

"So," Gratz concluded, "my dessert is served. Feel free to talk to the lady. I have already discussed your situation with her." The colonel turned on his heel and marched back to his table; he did not acknowledge Anna's existence as he passed the cash register.

Schwartzkümmel's face was flushed. He said nothing, but Anna was not about to let him slip quietly away. "Major, I have a young friend who has seen you here in the restaurant. He finds you attractive. He's boyish yet, and I understand that no beard promises certain erotic satisfactions. It also means he could make no demands on you."

Anna could see Schwartzkümmel's embarrassment turning to anger, but she did not give him the opportunity to speak. "Think about it. The colonel and I have our arrangements. They have been private, harmless, and also pleasurable. You can contact me here most evenings." With that she turned away and slowly walked into the kitchen. There was anger bordering on rage in Schwartzkümmel's eyes as he watched her leave. Anna, however, considered him hooked, and hers was the judgment of an expert.

Rome, Tuesday, 5 October 1943

The next morning, before Roberto was awake, Anna left her apartment and went to the bar on the Santa Maria. She ignored both the hostile stares of the women seated outside and the males' groping for their genitals when she looked them in the eyes. She walked inside the bar and took her usual position near the *macchinetta*, where the light was least and the privacy greatest. Stefano was swiftly beside her. He reached under the counter, extracted several dozen real coffee beans, ground them, and put them into the machine. Anna softly touched his hand as he placed the steaming demitasse in front of her. "*Grazie, caro, grazie*," she purred as she savored the almost forgotten flavor.

"A cousin from Naples sneaked into town last night with a kilo of American coffee. He gave me two *etti*. I'll save it all for you."

She kept touching his hand but said nothing more.

"You understand why I cannot do this thing, even for you?" he asked.

"No, *caro*, I do not understand." She watched his olive complexion tinge a faint red and his lips puff into a half pout. "Stefano, it is you who do not understand. What I am asking you to do is not a small thing. I know that. I will hate every second of it as much as you will. But you must trust me when I tell you that it is more important for the party and the resistance than anything you have ever dreamed of. It is also more important for us. It could mean the war will end months, perhaps years sooner. Think of what a difference that will make in our lives, yours and mine together." She sidled around the corner of the bar and lifted his hand inside her sweater. He started to pull it back, but she was easily able to overcome his effort.

"Poor *bello*, poor *caro*. You do not yet understand that we must pay for everything in life. The price is often something we do not like, sometimes it is something we hate. But when the thing for sale is survival, we pay without thinking about the cost."

"But with a man, Anna! With a man! That is degrading!"

"*Caro, caro*," Anna whispered, "you remember a few months ago before we met, you had some friends, some boyfriends—"

Stefano's pout turned to anger as his face reddened. "I was a child then, young and stupid and in bad company. I was not a *fròcio*. I just didn't understand what life was all about!"

"I know that, *caro*, I know that. You were coming awake after a long sleep and the person who awakened you was another boy."

"I am not a *fròcio*!"

"Of course you're not. You are a man, made to give pleasure to a woman. But I was the one who taught you that. It was Anna, wasn't it? You had taken care of me after those pigs at the Palazzo Braschi had used me. Then those same pigs took your brother, and you came to me for help. What help I had I gave you—the knowledge

145

that you were a man. Now I ask you to sacrifice something, not for me but for the two of us."

She moved his other hand inside her sweater. "Ah, that is good, very good. You remember that afternoon? It was your second awakening, your real one." She leaned over and flicked her tongue in his ear. "You will have to do it, *carissimo*, not for the party, or the resistance, but for us. It is a small thing. Just do nothing. Be passive."

"But if he touches me—" There were tears in the boy's eyes.

"*When* he touches you, pretend it is me on that afternoon—because it soon will be again."

"*Cos' è?*" the *signora* bellowed out from behind the cash register. "*Basta!* Enough whispering back there. If you want to pee, *signorina*, use the toilet. Don't do it behind the bar and don't distract the boy from his work."

"The *man*," Anna whispered as she went to the restroom.

Vatican City, Tuesday, 5 October 1943

F.C.'s contact in the Questura, a lukewarm Fascist official who knew who was going to win the war, called at 8:15 in the evening and left a brief message. The American priest hurriedly passed it on to the Monsignori LaTorre and Galeotti and to Paul Stransky. Then F.C. walked out to the Piazza of St. Peter, hoping to intercept the Augustianian monk during his after-dinner stroll. Shortly before 9:00 the monk showed up, his gait more a moving slouch than a normal walk. As usual, he was alone. Sullivan fell in step beside the German. The American's stoop made it easier for him to converse with the dapper little man. "May I join you, Father?" Each was fluent in the other's language, but both always chose Italian as a neutral medium.

"Of course, Father; I am honored. I enjoy your coffees, but you and I seldom have an opportunity for real conversation."

"Yes, life races by; we never seem to have time to do what we really want to." F.C. paused a few seconds. "And our situation is more delicate than that of most priests. Father, what I'm trying to say, and not doing a very good job of it, is that our nations may be belligerents, but we can never be."

The monk arched his dark eyebrows. Had they not been meticulously plucked, they would have been as bushy as F.C.'s. "Yes." He spoke the word as much as a question as an answer.

146

"Remember our days in the seminary, how they carefully—and frequently—explained that each priest was *Alter Christus*, another Christ? One Christ cannot be at war with another Christ." F.C. swore at himself. He was trying to be straightforward, but he was succeeding only in sounding pompous, even more so in Italian than he would have in English.

The Augustinian smiled. "We should tell that to some of our colleagues in the Curia. Their feuds must turn Christ into a marvelously polyglot schizoid. No wonder the world is in such chaos; Christ must be spending all His heavenly time casting out His own demons."

Both men chuckled at the mildly sacrilegious image.

F.C. tried a different but no more subtle tack. "Father, I have heard some grave rumors."

"Next to a cemetery, Rome is *the* place for grave rumor."

"Your pun is apt. But I'm afraid these stories have a solid basis in fact and will lead to many deaths."

The German took several lazy steps before he replied. "Father, under many circumstances, you and I could have been close friends. I find you *simpatico*. In addition to being priests and lovers of good coffee and conversation, we share many interests. I know that you have more than dabbled in moral theology in your concern for social justice in your country. I have read several of your articles in *America* and admire them. What is more, I have used them to prepare my lectures. I also admire your work here—in feeding the hungry of Italy, that is. Truly God's work. But I have studiously avoided ever speaking to you about politics or even about rumors concerning politics. Despite being a monk and a theologian, I am very much a German patriot, for ideological reasons as well as because of an accident of birth. I have avoided what would inevitably become bitter, pointless arguments that would destroy our relationship and settle nothing. I accept you as an American patriot and do not try to convert you, even though I am absolutely convinced that Germany's cause is just, that she is fighting a just war."

"A just war?" F.C.s tone reflected shock. It simply had never occurred to him that an intelligent, educated, and sophisticated Christian would invoke such a concept to defend Nazism.

"Yes, my friend, a just war. You are familiar with St. Augustine?" The monk's usual light irony had turned to heavy sarcasm.

147

"Augustine?" F.C. fenced. "Augustine? Oh yes, he is the man of whom St. Ignatius Loyola spoke so highly."

The Augustinian laughed. "*Touché*, my friend, *touché*. You see why I do not wish us to become enemies? I would miss your Irish wit, and it would be uncharitable of me to deprive you of my German culture. Let us speak no more of this world and its war. Instead, let us resurrect the great problems that befuddled our predecessors and leave the modern world to its own hideousness. Let me ask your opinion: When Luther came to Rome, was he already a heretic or did the Curia and Pope Leo drive him into heresy?"

"Well, he was an Augustinian, and that's already as close to heresy as a sane man would want to come."

"Ah, I am glad we are alone. If we had an audience, my reputation as the bright star of the Lateran would be in jeopardy."

F.C. was suddenly serious again. "Father, I, too, have been careful to avoid politics in our discussions. If I bring up a political matter now, it is because of its seriousness. Indulge me."

"Indulge? That is a dangerous word among Augustinians, Father; at least it has been since the sixteenth century. Very well, go ahead, but only for a few minutes, lest our friendship dissolve in the acid of angry words."

"The rumors I have heard concern the Jews of Rome."

"Again? Only the other day, I was talking to Monsignor LaTorre and his friend Galeotti—"

"I know. I was there. But something more has happened, something more specific and much more ominous. Berlin was not satisfied by the collection of three hundred kilos of gold as ransom. The local Gestapo commander received explicit instructions to prepare the local Jews for 'liquidation'—that was the word used, 'liquidation.' He dragged his feet, and now Berlin has sent another officer to arrest and deport all the Jews of Rome. They will go to death camps."

"Father, Father," the monk said, patiently repeating an oft-told explanation, "first of all I do not doubt that some Italian, indulging the national propensity to dramatize, has told you this. And I do not doubt that sooner or later the Gestapo, the SD, or some other SS organization will send some Roman Jews to labor camps. It would be politic for the Reich not to do so, not to offend the Pope. But political deftness is not among German virtues. Thoroughness is our great

148

virtue; sometimes—often—we carry it to a fault. The error comes in the invention or misuse of the term 'liquidation.' These people are sent to labor camps."

"Labor camps?"

"Labor camps. You must have also heard me express my opinion of the conditions there—deplorable, but still safer than being at the Russian front, where millions of German Christians are fighting and dying to hold back the advance of communism."

"I misunderstood, Father. I thought that Germany invaded Russia."

"Only because the Communists were about to attack us. But, my friend, already we are arguing. Tell me, what is it you wish me to do about this rumor?"

"I want you, as a priest and as a German, to go with me to the Pope. LaTorre can get us a private audience. The two of us can urge him to speak forcefully to Ambassador von Weizsäcker, Marshal Kesselring, and General Mueller and warn them that he will speak publicly if the SS attempts to deport the Roman Jews. We can help prevent a massive crime."

The monk stopped and stood almost perfectly still for several minutes. "Do you have a cigarette?" he asked.

"Of course." F.C. fumbled in his pocket and brought out an unopened pack of Camels. He handed it to the monk. "Keep them. I've given up the habit. I've been carrying these as a security blanket in case I panic someday."

"No, only one, thank you. I have also given them up, but my philosophy is 'Lead us not into temptation.' I look on an open pack as a proximate occasion of sin." He accepted a box of *cerini* from the American, lit the cigarette, and inhaled deeply. "A filthy habit. It probably causes all sorts of dread diseases. The Pope should forbid clergy to use them—perhaps a special vow could be required."

"It might be simpler to start a rumor that cigarettes cause venereal disease."

The Augustinian chuckled. "You are good company, Father. I know you are also a good patriot—of the North Pole, of course. If you were German we would call you Kris Kringle."

F.C. said nothing. The monk might have suspicions, strong suspicions, but it was unlikely he had any hard evidence.

"Still, Father, I must tell you two things, one about Jews, the other

149

about crimes. First, I do not like Jews either theologically or personally. They rejected and continue to reject Christ, not out of ignorance but out of stubborn, deliberate choice. I see malice in choosing to reject God's grace. Personally, I find them unpleasant people—clannish, secretive, and unethical. They have lived with us for centuries, but during all that time they have hated Germans and Germany."

"But, Father, charity—"

"Charity, yes. Perhaps I am deficient there as in many other aspects of my character. But I am weighted down by experience, Father. You did not serve in the Great War, did you?"

"No, I entered the minor seminary when I was sixteen."

"Wise. I was hardly more than a child when they called me up in 1916, barely seventeen. I was old enough to spend long months in the trenches. I was a front soldier, and I love my country as only a man who has bled for it can love it. And Jews betrayed us—and worse."

"Surely, you—"

"We believe what we believe. I am not trying to justify, only to explain. Enough about Jews. Let me tell you about crimes. There I speak as an expert. You remember the great thousand-plane raid on Cologne that the British boast so much about? My mother and my sister were burned alive there, like thousands of other German Christians who meet that same fate every night. Your English allies aim for the centers of population so they can kill the maximum number of civilians. They make, I suppose, targets that are easier and safer than military installations." The monk crushed the cigarette on his heel, field-stripped it as neatly as a soldier, let the few remaining pieces of tobacco blow in the wind, and put the tiny scrap of paper in his pocket.

"I'm sorry, Father," F.C. mumbled. "There isn't much I can say. I lost a cousin in the South Pacific and a nephew in the North Atlantic, but it is not the same."

"It is not the same, and there is nothing to say. Just understand why I am less than charitable toward Germany's enemies. Also you must understand—no, you cannot, you are too American, too optimistic. You have not seen your civilization decay around you. But try to understand what we central Europeans dread, the specter of communism, ruthless, godless, still gathering strength. I concede that

Nazism is evil, but Hitler has mobilized Germany into the only bulwark against communism that Europe has, that the Church has."

"You know all the arguments about the end not justifying the means," F.C. replied.

"Know them? I wrote many of them. It was, after all, Jesuits who invented such immoral arguments." The Augustinian was bantering, trying to end serious discussion.

F.C. laughed. "Perhaps, but they were wrong. Don't you, a truly great moral theologian, see Nazism as a horribly evil means that can't justify the good end of stopping communism?"

"I am not a Nazi, and I have never supported or defended them, but I lived through the Weimar Republic, a terrible period of semi-anarchy. I can understand the popularity of Nazism. In any event, like sin, Nazism exists. My dilemma and that of many other Germans is that if we oppose Nazism we help communism. That I will not do. We live in a world we did not create. It is, God help us, hard, mean, and bloody. Precisely as I did not make this world, I cannot change it."

"We differ there," F.C. said quietly. "Together the two of us might change it, only a little, but for the better. We could help save thousands of lives."

"It is not merely our nationalities that separate us," the Augustinian observed, "but also an ocean of centuries. We are exactly the same age—we share the same birthday, the same calling. Yet you are much younger. Some would say you are more hopeful than I; others that you are more naïve. You truly believe in Kris Kringle—and I mean that as a compliment, a sincere compliment. No, I cannot join you in this thing, my friend; but if I could be of service in some other way, I would be honored to try. We are, as you say, priests before we are citizens. It grieves me deeply that we must view our priestly roles through the eyes of citizens. *Alter Christus, alter civis.* Another Christ, another citizen. It is difficult to know which one speaks within us."

Rome, Wednesday, 6 October 1943

It was getting dark earlier. By 6:30 dusk would have fallen. There were few enough taxis by day, and at night, with a curfew for most Italians, there would be none at all. These problems, as well as the

151

unspoken danger to a German, even in civilian clothes, of walking alone in Trastevere after dark, had made it plausible for Anna to set Wednesday at 2:00 in the afternoon, during siesta, as the time for the major's assignation in her apartment. He had said that getting the afternoon off presented no problem.

Daylight, of course, would make the pictures clearer. The cameras that had been left outside the apartment door were big Leica 250s. Neither needed a flash attachment. Supposedly both had such fast lenses and used such sensitive film that they could operate in ordinary room light; Anna, however, felt safer with sunlight streaming into the bedroom. Roberto had found it ironic that the cameras were of German make. When he mentioned that fact, Anna smiled. She was unaware of the equipment's exact route to the Cedro, but she knew the line eventually ran back to Manfred Gratz.

Anna had left the skylight open above the bed and the door to the terrace unlocked. She had also oiled the hinges so the door's opening would be almost silent, certainly not so obtrusive as to disturb a man whose attention was desperately riveted on more pleasurable things. She had carefully constructed a scenario to provide the most light and best camera angles. Just as carefully, she had instructed Stefano where to place himself in the bed so that the major would be most visible from the skylight as well as from the study level.

The identity of Schwartzkümmel's partner had raised sharper problems for Roberto. He had not asked who the person would be until, shortly before the rendezvous, Stefano had appeared at the apartment. The boy was embarrassed, reluctant, and petulant. Roberto, who had been on the terrace, glimpsed him through the skylight, and called for Anna to come up to the roof.

"He's no more than a child," Roberto hissed.

"That makes it more erotic, I hear."

"We can't corrupt a child."

Anna grunted. "You've come too late to save that child's soul, Holy Father. Besides, we can trust him. Generally, you can't trust priests or queers."

"He's not a queer. He's pretty. That's not his fault. He's just got growing pains."

"*Va bene*, he's a child. You take his place and I'll send him home."

"Ha!"

152

"Then we call the whole operation off. I never wanted to read the Germans' mail anyway." She started back inside.

"Wait." Roberto grabbed her arm and led her back onto the terrace. "Wait, damn it. Wait. Let me think."

"About what? You know the choices. Choose—and quickly. Look." She pointed down toward the junction of the Cedro and the Via della Scala. "Our *fròcio* is coming."

"Shit. All right, all right. I don't see any choice." Roberto stayed on the terrace and Anna went back downstairs.

The sound of Schwartzkümmel's heavy tread on the steps was Anna's cue to begin to kiss Stefano passionately and to stroke his body with probing fingers. When the German's sharp rap came on the metal door, she quickly pulled away from the boy, so that the major's first sight on entering the apartment was Stefano's flushed, excited face. Anna inhaled the strong scent of Schwartzkümmel's after-shave lotion, then looked as innocently as she could at Stefano, and left via the rooftop terrace.

Stefano took several steps backward, obviously nervous and resentful. The major seemed not to notice. He gently grasped the boy's hand and began speaking in soft, remarkably fluent Italian, asking about his school and work. Schwartzkümmel was using the flowing rhythm of his voice to mesmerize the slender boy, much like a snake stalking a small bird.

During the critical moments of the assignation, Roberto was able to slip the camera under the open skylight and snap a series of pictures. As the same time, Anna quietly slid back inside the terrace door, but she got only one shot of the writhing bodies before the German sensed her intrusion. Instantly he realized that he had been betrayed and tried to recover his pistol. Unfortunately for him, his clothes and weapon were in a tangled heap on the floor, and Roberto was easily able to get down onto the bedroom platform before the cryptographer could recover the gun. Anna's pistol looked even more authoritative with a silencer attached to the muzzle, and it had hardly been necessary for Roberto to order the major to sit back on the bed.

Stefano said nothing. He picked up his clothes and walked quietly past Roberto and Anna. Roberto did not dare take his eyes off Schwartzkümmel, but Anna leaned over the edge of the loft and watched the boy dress in the living room. He saw her but did not acknowledge her presence. When the door closed behind him, she shrugged and sat at the foot of the bed. The German instinctively moved toward the wall. Anna smiled at his reaction. "Don't be frightened, *Liebchen*. We mean you no harm. In fact, we are here to do you a favor, to protect you against scandal."

Schwartzkümmel said nothing. The hate in his eyes was enough.

Anna stood up and slipped out of her clothes. "Just another pose or two, *Professore*." She pushed him back on the bed and tried to pull herself astraddle his hips. But with a burst of strength that was surprising from a man who looked so utterly defeated, he kicked her off, sending her back against the thick beam that transected the lower end of the bed platform. A split second later, Roberto tugged at the trigger and a bullet from Anna's pistol whooshed into the pillow only a few inches from the German's head. He froze, only slightly more terrified than Roberto.

Anna moved slowly and painfully forward again. "*Liebchen, Liebchen*, don't try to hurt Anna, she might have to hurt you." Then she swiftly slammed the butt of her right hand into Schwartzkümmel's crotch. He doubled up in agony. Anna waited a few minutes, until he was only writhing in pain, and climbed astraddle him. Roberto put down the pistol and took another rapid string of photographs.

Anna leaped off the bed and picked up her clothes. "That should end our picture taking, *Liebchen*. Your contortions should make it look like you were enjoying an ecstatic moment." Clearly, she was immensely pleased with herself. "You Germans do burn the candle at both ends."

"What do you want from me?" As Schwartzkümmel's pain began to recede, his mind oscillated between panic and hatred. Roberto recognized the similarity to his own emotional reactions in the Regina Coeli and suspected that the cryptographer's analytic intelligence would soon—probably much sooner than Anna realized—abstract itself from his body's pain and fear and begin to reason as a detached person might play a game.

"What do you think you are worth to us, queer?" Anna was speaking the lilting, sliding German of Alpine Italy, but she used the Romanesco word '*fròcio*.' Its root meaning was 'nostril' and had once been applied to some Germans who had big noses and large nostrils;

then, in appreciation of what the Romans from Rome perceived as Teutonic sexual preferences, to homosexuals generally. "You're not good for much besides buggering young boys. But we might protect you if you do a small favor for us."

"And if I do not?" The man's voice was still slurred from pain, but Roberto recognized signs of the German's intellect taking command of his body.

"First of all," Anna replied, "the Gestapo gets the pictures of you *in flagrante delicto* with the boy. The act won't bother them. Half of them will probably envy you such a young lover; but the fact that someone took pictures will concern them. Pictures like these mean blackmail, and blackmail of a man in your position means trading in military secrets. And the Gestapo thinks that's a bad thing. And, in case their envy overcomes their political judgment, we'll send a few snapshots of our joyous 'copulation' to your wife. She can see what you've both missed."

"You are thorough."

"Oh, we're thorough, much more thorough than I've indicated yet. We have still other plans. We'll send the picture of you deflowering Stefano to the rector and members of the faculty of your university. Like the Gestapo, your colleagues may envy your good fortune in lovers, but also like the Gestapo they'll fear the implications of photographs. You'll have no more academic career. Your father-in-law, bless his marks, will also receive a set of the pictures we'll send your wife. That should end any hope you have of inheriting his money." Anna paused for a moment. "And lest you think we've forgotten something, if you commit suicide we'll see that all those copies go out anyway."

"There is not much you have left me, is there?" Schwartzkümmel half-moaned.

"We leave you nothing. We have learned from you Nazis."

"I am not a Nazi."

"You wear their uniform, take their money, and do their killing. That's close enough, *caro Tedesco*. You've strutted around Europe like a great conqueror. The time to pay *our* price has come."

"And what is that price?"

"Major," Roberto broke in. His German was heavily accented and halting, but adequate. "You know the tactics in such situations. We ask for something small, something that won't hurt Germany at all. You give it. Later we ask for something else, only a trifle less innocent. And on and on, until not only do we have you with the incriminating pictures but we can also blackmail you on counts of espionage. Then we twist your arm to do things more and more important to us and more and more damning to you until you're caught by the Gestapo. But we won't go that route. We have too much respect for your intelligence, and we want to get this damned war over while someone is still alive to enjoy the peace."

"So what is it you want me to do to betray my country?"

"We want you to betray the Nazis, not your country."

Schwartzkümmel waved his hand. "You—whoever you are—you have me. You have humiliated me, ruined that young boy, and—"

"Ha!" Anna cut in. "We ruined that boy? We weren't doing it in his bung."

"No, but you put him up to it, you filth." Schwartzkümmel spat the words out in a torrent of rage. "You turned him into a whore, violated every shred of his dignity along with mine. It is inadmissible to ridicule what is left of my honor by asking me to rationalize treason. Just tell me what you want."

"All right," Anna said. "We want Enigma."

"Scheisse!"

"That, too. But we want detailed pictures of Enigma as well as other photographs my colleague will describe to you."

"We also want," Roberto explained, "photographs of blueprints or of a repair manual and any code book you use or schedule of changes of initial settings for the machine. We have a small camera you can use."

"Impossible. No one could do these things."

"You can," Anna said. "You are in charge of cryptography for General Mueller. He may be a drunken fool, but he has all the equipment of a German general. You're trusted, not liked, but trusted. You can *make* opportunities to get exactly what we want. We know that. That's why we picked you rather than some other *fròcio*," Anna sneered.

Schwartzkümmel fumed in silence.

"And don't consider going to the Gestapo. The best you could hope for would be a quick death—and that only if they didn't believe that you'd already tried to pay us off with some spying. And, as my colleague said, that's what they'd suspect. Anyway, trying to have us caught wouldn't stop the pictures from reaching your family and university. Ten minutes from now the film will be on its way to our organization—and we're part of a very large organization. Who knows?" she teased. "We may even have sources inside the Gestapo to warn us if you tattle."

The major looked up. He'd heard rumors of corruption, not ideological corruption, but old-fashioned venality, among those who wore the Death's Head emblem. "Give me the camera," he said.

Roberto reached in the wardrobe and flipped the small apparatus to the German. "It's Lithuanian, a Minox. It doesn't use microfilm, but it's close enough. It's loaded with enough film for fifty exposures. Hold it very still. Its shutter works at one-thousandth of a second. Bring it about thirty centimeters from the target. Make sure there's plenty of light, and push the button like any other camera. Here're four more rolls of film."

"How long do I have?"

"I want to see you at the Remus on Friday evening with the film," Anna responded.

"And your film?"

"Our film?" Anna laughed. "What about *our* film?"

"Do I get it?"

"Don't be absurd, *caro Tedesco*. When our experts have checked out *your* film, all of it, we'll cancel shipments of our film. We're socialists, not capitalists. We don't return merchandise."

"What guarantees do I have?"

"Why our word, Major, our word," Anna jeered. "The world has lived for years by the word of the Germans. Now you have to live by ours."

"You also have something else," Roberto added. "If we have Enigma, we have no more reason to harass you. There's a certain risk for us in this kind of operation, and you would no longer have anything we want that would be worth that risk. It's the strongest guarantee you could have."

"I am not in a position to bargain." Schwartzkümmel's voice was flat; his rage seemed to be waning. "May I leave now?" He gestured toward his clothes on the floor.

"Of course," Anna said, "but we'll keep the bullets from your gun. You understand, I'm sure."

When the German had dressed and was starting to leave, Roberto went out the door with him. "I'll walk you to Piazza Trilussa. It will be safer for you in this neighborhood."

The major strode in rigid silence down the Cedro and the Cinque toward the lovely little piazza at the head of the Ponte Sisto. He kept his eyes straight ahead, as if neither Roberto nor Trastevere existed. He did not break stride even at the bridge until Roberto grabbed his arm. "I know this isn't the time, but we've got to talk."

"Everything has been said. You have me by the throat."

"That's not what I want to talk to you about."

Schwartzkümmel turned and looked at the fountain on the piazza. "Your accent in German is not quite right for an Italian, almost but not quite—an American, I would guess, one who also speaks Italian fluently. Well, my victor, let me remind you of an old Hebrew saying: 'Do not appease your fellow in his hour of anger; and do not strive to see him in his hour of misfortune.' Leave me some vestige of humanity. Let me mourn my loss of dignity and let me revel in loathing you and your slut."

"There may not be another time."

"So? If I can survive the memory of the past hour, I can survive the loss of your wisdom."

"I realize that, Major, but—"

"That boy was not what I thought. His spirit has been crushed. I have suffered a great deal for what nature has done to me. I would not have heaped similar suffering on another, especially not on a mere boy. When we degrade another human being we degrade ourselves. I am not innocent, but you are contemptible."

"I am truly sorry. That's why I want to speak to you. We are both academics. Whatever our other differences, we share certain values. Surely they are not those of the Nazis."

"Less than they are the values of blackmailers—or of Communists, like your whore up there probably is. We are both trapped."

"Not completely. For the moment try to forget about the black-mail."

"Forget my humanity? My pride?"

"No, just put aside the hurt. What about your future?"

"Please, do not compound the cruelty by offering me a bribe as insurance. Let there be some limit to evil."

"That's not what I meant. Major, you can't sympathize with the brutality of the Nazis, and you also know Germany has lost the war. The important question is what will be left of Germany—and Germans—when it is all over. If the Russians get there before the British and Americans do, they'll turn what's left into a slave labor camp—and there won't be much left if the bombings continue for many more months. If we get Enigma, we'll be more likely to occupy Germany than the Russians. Then you'll have a chance for a decent future."

"You hope to get to Germany through my betraying my people. You ask me to save some of my people by helping you murder others."

"No, I ask you to save most of your people by helping us defeat your armed forces quickly. The hard point is that those forces are going to be bloodily beaten, the only question is when. The sooner they're defeated, the fewer will be killed. Certainly fewer, far fewer, will be killed by the bombings."

Schwartzkümmel managed a flicker of a smile. "You argue like a Jesuit. You try to persuade me to commit treason and justify my crime by saying it will make it easier for you to stop murdering."

"I argue like a realist. What we have done to you today is deeply wrong, morally wrong. I can only square it with my conscience by thinking of the lives that shortening the war will save. I am a pawn no less than you."

"We are both pawns; but do not think you can shirk moral responsibility that way. Even pawns have a duty to sacrifice themselves for the queen. They have no right to betray her."

"Who betrayed Germany? The Nazis have led you down the road to total destruction. Read your own army's estimates. They know the end is coming."

Schwartzkümmel sighed and walked toward the bridge. "There is no point in talking. We are enemies. For now you have won and I must surrender. But do not try to make me think my collapse is noble or to despise myself—or you—any the less."

"Despise whomever you want; God knows you're entitled to hate. But I don't speak of nobility, only of the survival of values that people like you and me treasure."

159

SEVEN

Rome, Thursday, 7 October 1943

It was a magnificent morning, and Col. Manfred Gratz was annoyed with himself that he felt depressed. The weather was as gorgeous as only Roman days can be in October. A warm breeze was rustling the papers on his desk as gently as it was stirring the leaves in the villa's gardens. The war was going well. Kesselring's troops had occupied strong positions north of Naples and had bogged down the British and Americans in bloody fights for individual mountain peaks. The terrain was such that a platoon could hold off a battalion. Obviously, the Germans could stymie the Allies for months, even years, unless, of course, they demonstrated some imagination and made an amphibious landing farther up the coast to outflank Kesselring's army.

The war in the south, however, was someone else's problem. Gratz religiously read the intelligence reports and pored over aerial photographs, hoping to discern something that Kesselring's staff might have missed. So far he had found nothing. Operation Rigoletto was the colonel's primary assignment, and that, too, was progressing. Last night at the Remus, Anna had given him a sullenly tense report of Schwartzkümmel's fiasco earlier in the day.

Her mood had brightened when he had given her $10,000 in Swiss francs as her second payment. "Remember, I want more. This is only a down payment."

"My dear lady," Gratz had explained with exaggerated patience, "when we have it, you will have it, not before. These are, so to speak, company funds that I am advancing to you—and doing so without authorization. We have only just begun serious negotiations with the other side."

"This will do for a short time, a very short time. You keep in mind that Raven doesn't leave Rome without my approval; and, before he's free to go, I want the full amount, a passport, and a pass. And if anything happens to me, I've left instructions for the resistance to kill him as a double agent."

"That would be an amusing scene—self-righteous, heroic Anna fingering a double agent. The mind boggles at the thought." Gratz was certain, almost certain, that she was lying, but there was nothing to be gained by antagonizing her. "You can be sure that we share an interest in having all accounts paid in full before Raven leaves Rome with the plans for Enigma."

When they met in his car later in the evening she had given him the film. He had sent her off without any lovemaking. It was not essential to his plan that she betray him by undercutting his supposed sale of the photographs to the Americans, but it would be helpful. He was counting on her greed to push her into making her own deal with Father Christmas. If, on the other hand, she stayed faithful, she would still be helping to use Raven as delivery boy.

Her account of the tryst with the young barman had left a melancholy hangover that was lingering through the morning. It was not the major; he had asked for whatever humiliation he had received. It was the boy for whom Gratz was concerned. Anna had used him as a courier many times, and Gratz had found him a nice lad, still untouched by either the brutality of war or the cynicism of Rome. Obviously he adored Anna, and she, no doubt, had converted him to communism as well as to other, less political, beliefs. Well, it was done and could not be undone.

Gratz took the pictures out of the envelope. As art they would never win prizes; as evidence, however, they clearly convicted Schwartzkümmel under Article 175 of the Criminal Code as a sodomite. They also damned him as a heterosexual philanderer. It was not likely that both charges could be legally maintained; but, for blackmail, they formed an effective pincer movement.

The colonel picked up the photographs again. The shots of the cryptographer and the boy became more revolting each time he looked at them. On the other hand, despite himself, he was fascinated by the pictures of Anna apparently convulsing on top of Schwartzkümmel. With her mouth open, sweat glistening on her skin, and breasts thrust out, she was the incarnation of Venus in heat, a powerful stimulant to a lonely soldier, even a middle-aged soldier. Reluctantly, he put the photographs back into their envelope and mentally rehearsed what he would say when, in a few moments, Schwartzkümmel entered his office. The colonel had hoped that the man would come to him to explain his troubles; just in case, however, Gratz had an alternate plan to summon the major. Fortunately, Schwartzkümmel had made the alternate plan unnecessary by scheduling an appointment himself.

The cryptologist's thin face was ashen; the muscles around his mouth were pulled tight, straightening his lips into pink bands. He kept his pale blue eyes focused on the floor, as if he were afraid of the injury they might burn into someone. Gratz pretended to be unaware of the tension and motioned the major to a chair. "Sit down, Schwartzkümmel, sit down. Let us dispense with military protocol and talk man to man."

"As the Colonel wishes."

"Otto, Otto," Gratz said affably, "you seem cross with me this morning."

"The Colonel is playing with me, just as he toyed with me last week in the restaurant and his whore taunted me yesterday."

"She is a bitch," Gratz agreed. "Tell me honestly, Otto, is she trying to blackmail you?"

"You knew! You knew she would! I was sure of it. Why? How could you, a German officer, permit a Latin slut to strip another Nordic officer of his honor? That was inadmissible!"

"Wait, wait, Otto, not so fast, please. Hear me out. We in the Abwehr suspected she was a spy, but we were not certain. She is very clever, as you saw. But now, thanks to you, we know and we can deal with her. I can understand your anger. You were bait. I am sorry that I could not warn you. But even if you had agreed to cooperate, you are not a professional actor. Something you would have done—or not done—might have given you away. A mistake could have cost you your life—she plays for very high stakes—and deprived us of both your services as a cryptologist and an opportunity to trap the spider in her own web."

"But to allow a German officer to be disgraced by an *Itaker!*"

Gratz's tone hardened. "We used you as a pawn, Major. That is not the preferred way to treat a German officer. But the possibility of being so used is one every soldier accepts when he takes his oath—

162

and draws his pay. Think of an infantry unit out in front of the Wehrmacht on the steppes. They are there to draw Russian fire so the main body of troops will know where the enemy is. They are pawns in their way; you were a pawn in a different way."

"To die from an enemy's bullet is an honorable death. There is only abasement in having one's soul killed by a prostitute's sneering blackmail."

"Death is death, Otto." Gratz's tone softened again. "I fought in Spain and I saw a lot of corpses. They were all equally dead, no matter what the cause. I saw no honor on any of the bodies, only a putrid smell. Now, Major"—the Colonel's tone shifted once more, this time more subtly—"enough recriminations and self-pity. Let us get on with the business of dealing with this good woman. What does she want you to do? Something trivial at first, I would guess."

"Hardly trivial. She wants detailed photographs of Enigma plus a repair manual or blueprints, and our code book."

Gratz whistled. "*La Strega* has high ambitions, you must admit that. She must also feel she has you in a powerful vise, or she is in a terrible hurry."

"Or both."

"Or both." Gratz nodded. "The usual pattern is the salami technique: slice the victim thin piece by thin piece until he is used up. Well, we must not disappoint the lady, Otto. *Noblesse oblige* and all that sort of *Scheisse*."

"Sir? Give her Enigma?"

"Not quite. We give her what she will think is Enigma. Let my people work on it for you. Did she give you a camera?"

"Here, sir." Schwartzkümmel produced the Minox and the film. Gratz examined the equipment carefully, then handed it back. "Standard stuff—the camera is Lithuanian, the film German. We shall use it to take the pictures for you. When is the delivery date?"

"Tomorrow evening at the Remus."

"Hmmm, that does not give us much time; but we shall come up with something that will fool even experts."

"Colonel, we might deceive experts for a few days, but even idiots will know they have been duped when they build one of those machines and try to monitor Enigma's traffic. And when they realize what has happened, they will ruin me."

163

"Of course, they will realize they have been tricked, but not for a time."

"Colonel, in mathematics the simplest solution is usually the most elegant and the most likely to be correct. Why do we not simply have the Gestapo arrest her and her friends?"

Gratz smiled as reassuringly as he could. "Otto, I think it wisest to keep the Gestapo out of what is an affair of the armed forces. I doubt that you would enjoy their mode of interrogation. Besides, despite their reputation, they are more brutal than efficient. *La Strega* and her friends could probably carry out their threats against you before the Gestapo made a single arrest. And strictly between ourselves, Otto, I do not trust the SS at all. Even Reichsfuehrer Himmler is worried about certain of his high-ranking officers. Perhaps you have heard rumors."

"Some, but I do not put any stock in them."

"Put some stock in this one and you will live longer. Look, it will take a week or more for Anna to get the film into Allied hands, and probably that long again before they can build a duplicate machine. Within a few days from now, you will have been quietly transferred to a secret post. Trying to punish you carries a real risk for them. Once they no longer know where you are, and so cannot exploit your weakness again, there will be no point in their trying to punish you."

Schwartzkümmel looked unconvinced.

Gratz sighed. "All right, it is chancy. I would not try to deceive you. You have done useful work in proving for us what the Fascists suspected for months, that this good woman was a spy. Within a very few days, we—with your help—were able to prove it. Typical German efficiency. We owe you something here. Write me a memorandum precisely detailing the sanctions she has threatened against you. Let us handle it from there—perhaps quiet visits from a senior officer or letters from Admiral Canaris himself would explain that enemy spies are trying to blackmail you with all sorts of horrible, and *false*, charges, and they are using doctored photographs. We could ask for their cooperation in reporting receiving any derogatory information about you. You might emerge a double hero."

"More likely a double fool."

"It is the best I can offer, Otto. We are—Germany is grateful for

164

your sacrifice. But I cannot erase the pain of your sacrifice any more than I can bring dead soldiers back to life."

Schwartzkümmel nodded but said nothing more.

"Very well, Otto. Give me the memorandum as soon as you can."

"May I ask what will happen to the Italian slut?"

"We shall see that she meets an appropriate fate. Leave her to us."

"Will you let me know?"

"I shall, Otto. That is a promise."

As the major left, Captain von Bothmer entered Gratz's office. "You heard our conversation?"

Von Bothmer nodded. "I kept the intercom open. It is a sad business."

"War is a sad business, Captain. Every day in every way we better learn how to maim and slay."

"How can we carry out your promise of letters and visits without jeopardizing Rigoletto?"

"We cannot. Both Enigma and Rigoletto come before the reputation of the Herr Doktor Major, as they also come before his life."

"What happens when he finds out we have not been able to make good on our promises?"

"One problem at a time, Captain. As a child were you never taught the prayer: 'Sufficient unto the day is the evil thereof'? The admiral has arranged for Schwartzkümmel to be buried somewhere. He will not understand what is happening, but he will be practically incommunicado until Rigoletto has delivered all its rewards. Schwartzkümmel is a casualty. Still, he is luckier than most; he will survive. Enough. Let us have our experts in photography transfer the *Zeug* the admiral prepared to the film that Raven gave the major. Then we must help Raven return safely to his masters. Given his luck and level of skill, we are not facing an easy task."

That evening in the Gestapo's house on the Via Tasso, Lt. Col. Viktor Olendorf listened attentively to the spinning wire spool that had recorded the day's conversations in Gratz's office. When the SS officer heard Gratz's response to von Bothmer, he turned off the machine and began to weigh alternative courses of action. Because he had not yet decided how best to turn Rigoletto into an organizational victory for the SS and a personal coup for himself, he was unsure precisely what to do about Schwartzkümmel. But whatever his decision, he could not allow the cryptologist to vanish into one of the Abwehr's black holes.

Olendorf picked up the phone and called his second in command, Maj. Kurt Priebke. His order was sharp if not altogether clear: "I want Maj. Otto Schwartzkümmel brought here when he tries to leave town. He is scheduled to be transferred very soon. I want him taken into custody as he is leaving Rome, and I want it done so quietly no one will ever know. Use your sources at the villa to find out when and how he is leaving."

"*Jawohl*. May I ask what the charge will be?"

"Just hold him for questioning."

"How much?"

"Interrogate him gently. I repeat: It is critical the Abwehr not get the slightest hint that we have this man."

Rome, Thursday, 7 October 1943

At 9:00 A.M. Tommaso Piperno watched Anna walk with Roberto down the Cedro, turn into the Sant' Egidio, and lazily stroll to the bar on the Santa Maria. Tommaso followed no farther than the mouth of the piazza. He made a mental note of the time and their easy manner, then, in the tradition of King Canute, pushed his broom against the tide of Trastevere's garbage. Later he would telephone his priestly patrons in the Vatican, but not until he had swept the Cinque and collected tribute from his clients on that street.

In the piazza, Roberto and Anna took a table outside, where they could enjoy the parade of Roman life. Roberto could feel a thick, almost tangible atmosphere of hostility. The other customers pointedly ignored them. And, when the men did glance at Anna, hate, not lechery, was in their eyes. The couple sat with their backs to the entrance to the bar and to the coldness of the other clients. After ten minutes without service, Anna turned angrily toward the door and stared at the elderly proprietress behind the cash register until she finally looked up.

The instant she recognized Anna, the woman jumped up and hobbled as rapidly toward the table as her swollen feet permitted.

"*Via!*" she bellowed. "*Scatta! Sanguisuga! Strega-mignotta!*" Get out, you blood sucking witch-whore!

Roberto was completely surprised by the outburst. His only reaction was to stare in disbelief. Anna, however, responded as if she had been a Roman from Rome, instinctively gesturing with her index finger as she snarled: "*Fa' in culo, Befana!* We can get better coffee from a stable floor."

The old woman shouted a battle cry and leaped on Anna, beating her small fists on the young woman's head and chest. "*E morto,*" she shrieked to the world as she pounded away. "*E morto mio Stefano! Assassina!*" Dead! My Stefano is dead! Assassin!

"She's crazy," Anna yelled back as she shoved the old woman down. Roberto gently helped her up and sat her on a chair at the next table. For a few moments she was unable to control her sobbing. Then she gathered her strength and pushed him away. "*Mignottaro!*" she spat contemptuously. Whoremonger!

Anna stopped her counterattack but not her shouts. "I didn't touch her precious Stefano. I didn't even know he was sick."

The old woman stifled her sobs long enough to appeal to her clients. "She bewitched him! He hanged himself, but she made him do it with her evil eye and slut's body. She put that rope around his neck, witch-whore! Kill her! Kill her dead!"

Roberto tugged at Anna's arm, and the two of them left the bar. As they turned their backs and took a few steps, a volley of wineglasses and coffee cups shattered on the cobblestones around them, all thrown by other patrons. A coffee cup struck Anna painfully in the lower back. She spun around and, with green fire dancing out of her eyes, pointed a long finger toward the tables. Her gesture sent the customers into frenzied gropings for genitalia, a quest that ended thoughts of more cannonading.

On the way back to the apartment, neither spoke. Once inside, Roberto walked up to the terrace and sat there alone. Fifteen minutes later Anna came up and handed him a cup of ersatz expresso. "*Ch'è fatto, è fatto,*" she said. What's done is done.

Roberto remained silent.

Anna shrugged. "Far worse things are done to boys every day. Before I met him, Stefano was already beginning to be a queer. I taught him to be a man. What Anna gives, Anna can take away."

167

"Blessed be the name of Anna."

"Don't be sarcastic, *caro*. I am not in the mood."

Roberto continued to look over the rooftops. "Most children are confused by sex. He may have been finding himself when you met him. You take too much credit."

"I want no credit—or blame. In this war Stefano was lucky. What if he had been born in a Polish or Russian or Jewish family? As an Italian 'Christian' he had fifteen years of *la dolce vita*."

Roberto paid no attention. "We were so intent on getting Enigma that we murdered a boy." In contrast to the harshness of his words, Roberto's tone was cool, distant, as if he had no real interest in what he was saying. "God damn us both as blind fools."

"Whatever I may be," Anna responded angrily, "I am not blind. And do not lie to yourself, Roberto americano. You knew what the risks were. You didn't want to consider them; but you knew what they were. Right here on this terrace you judged that Enigma was worth a boy's self-respect, even his life—his soul, too, if you believe in such superstition. You accepted all the risks. You've lost, now you pay. Mourn for yourself, not for Stefano."

"Mourn for myself? That's exactly what I am doing, mourning for *my* self-respect. I let you talk me into having a queer bugger a child."

"*Senti*, brave soldier, don't blame it on Anna. You came to Rome with the idea of blackmailing Schwartzkümmel. I staged the drama, but you were the playwright. You could have taken Stefano's place or you could have stopped the whole mess. You could have insisted I find someone else—it would have been difficult, but I probably could have done it. You wanted that *fròcio* blackmailed and you went along with Stefano because he was convenient."

"You're right." There was still no emotion in his voice. "I'm lying to myself. I wanted Enigma so badly I violated every rule of decency I believe in, and I did it without even stopping to think about it."

"Now you are beginning to talk like an adult. Rules of decency don't bind when they chafe. That's one of Anna's adages you can quote to your grandchildren—if you live to have grandchildren. And if you live that long, Stefano won't be the only person you will have sold for some cause. People are pawns. Accept that simple truth and life will be easier—and longer. Kant could say never treat other human

168

beings as means, but anyone with an asinine philosophy like that wouldn't survive two weeks on the streets of Rome."

She paused a few moments, but Roberto made no reply.

"*Va bene*, wallow in self-pity over the loss of your moral virginity. It won't grow a new hymen for your soul, and it won't bring Stefano back."

"I'm not wallowing, I'm mourning. But you wouldn't know what that is, would you?"

Anna's eyes narrowed to two cold green slits. "No, I wouldn't know about mourning, not for my brother who was a guest of the Gestapo for eleven months before they killed him, and not for myself. Certainly not for a mincing boy who helped me up those stairs after the OVRA had gang-banged me, not for a young boy who bathed me and fed me and begged me to live. Afterward, when I was whole again, he came to me when he needed solace. I 'converted' him—it was the least I could do to repay his kindness. And then I exploited him because he was so convenient for your noble mission. He was in the neighborhood, and I could trust him. No, I don't know what it is to mourn because I can't help feeling sorrier for Anna than for Stefano. He pleased me. But if he was too tender to survive Schwartzkümmel, he was too tender to survive Rome. That is the way life is, as your Englishman Hobbes says, 'nasty, brutish, and short.' The true mystery is why we all don't commit suicide; but then perhaps we do, each in a different way."

Roberto turned and faced Anna. "What can I say? That I hate you or hate myself less because I fight for a noble cause? I wish I could say that. I wish I could feel that."

"What you say or feel, *caro* Roberto, is no concern of mine. Only keep in mind that tonight I bring back a gallery of portraits of your precious Enigma."

"You'll bring back pictures of what we hope is Enigma. I don't trust Schwartzkümmel. We may have killed Stefano for nothing."

"Don't worry about the major. He left here a broken man. He hasn't got the stomach to fight back."

"I'm not sure. Schwartzkümmel is a brilliant mathematician. His mind can function without his consent or even awareness. And right now it's trying to find an escape."

Anna laughed. "You're an incredible romantic. You Americans may

169

beat the German army, but the Germans and your own allies will beat
you at the peace table. You do not understand human nature. As a
Catholic you should know something about original sin and how it
'weakens our will, darkens our intellect, and inclines us toward evil.' "

"I'm not in the mood for a lecture on sin this morning. I feel too
much like an expert in that field."

"You're only an amateur, Roberto americano; you've only barely
started to play with the big boys and girls."

Rome, Saturday, 9 October 1943

It was 2:00 A.M. before Anna returned to the apartment. Roberto
had been waiting, twisted by guilt, grief, and expectation. He tried to
curtail the last emotion, and his failure to do so only increased his feelings of guilt.

She sauntered into the apartment and took a paper bag out of her
purse and set both on the table. "A *bigne*, a dozen pieces of fried squid,
and two medallions of veal—not a feast, but it won't be bad, especially
if you bought some wine."

"The film?"

"I'd really love some chilled Riesling from the Trentino, but I'll
settle for Frascati. What did you get?"

"*Vino sciòlto*—Castelli Romani. It was all the wineshop had.
Where's the film?"

"Fortified vinegar. Most vintners in Lazio think wine is made from
wood chips and paint scrapings, not from grapes. *Allora*, pour me a
glass while I go to the bathroom."

"Anna, where's the film?"

"Safe, *caro*, Anna has it all very safe. Pour me the wine. I'll be back
in two minutes." When she returned, she took a long swallow of the
yellow liquid and grimaced. "I'd cut it with a little lemon, if I had
a little lemon. I should have liberated one of those bottles of
Gewürztraminer that German officer brought to the Remus tonight.
He had a whole case, and he was too drunk to count."

"Enough play, Anna. Give me the film."

" 'Give me the film! Give me the film!' " Anna mimicked. "You
are a romantic, Roberto americano. I tell you that again and again.
Understand me carefully: I have the film, three small capsules of it,
each one in its own very safe place. You can have them, but not as

gifts. The price is two hundred and fifty thousand green American dollars and a valid Swiss or American passport."

"Don't tease, Anna. I don't have any sense of humor left."

"Not even a kind thought about how you've been laid a half dozen times as you never dreamed possible."

"The film, Anna, the goddamned film. No more *mèrda*."

"Do it in your bung, *Monsignore*. This is your war, not mine. Hitler, Mussolini, Roosevelt, Churchill—they're all the same to me, a pack of capitalist pigs. The resistance has used me like a whore; the OVRA has used me to rape; and you have used me to steal, blackmail, and kill a friend. I've risked my life for all of you and your noble causes. Now I want to be paid for my services."

"You know I haven't got that kind of money."

"I know that, you fool. I also know how many hundreds of millions your government would pay to get its fat hands on these pictures. When do you see your priest friend?"

"I put the call out this morning. The response came this afternoon. We meet tomorrow—it's today, I guess—at noon."

"Fine. Ask him to come up with the two hundred and fifty thousand for me. Better still, add on something for yourself. Nobody respects an amateur in any profession."

"Obviously you've never been an amateur at anything."

"Don't be snide, *caro*. Your role is to be that of the sweet, honest, naïve young American hero who is appalled by the cynical corruption of Rome but still carries on for the glory of motherhood and all the other virtues of the New World."

"Anna, I don't think you realize just how badly these people want Enigma and how far they'll go to get it."

"I do realize it. That's precisely why I ask for only two hundred and fifty thousand dollars. They'd pay a Gestapo general ten million dollars, but for a poor little Italian girl to ask for more would seem greedy. You Americans have a word: 'uppity.' I won't act uppity and tempt your masters to discipline me. I ask for only a paltry sum. For them it isn't much money and, while it won't make me rich, it'll make me comfortable. The price is prudent, *caro*, quite prudent. A bargain is fair when each side thinks it has won."

"They're very determined people," Roberto warned. "If you stand in their way, they're more likely to pay off with bullets than with dollars. Don't forget, the U.S. government has been playing footsie with Mafia families to undermine Fascism."

"The Mafia? The Mafia? You joke. They're pale Sicilian shadows compared to the OVRA or the Gestapo. The Mafia will have to stand in line, a very long line, if they want to kill Anna. Besides, if I die, I take the hiding places with me."

"They might not let you die until you told them all they wanted to know."

Anna looked at him disdainfully. "Do not threaten me with torture, *ragazzo*. The OVRA have already tried it. You just tell your Father Christmas what I want. He'll understand. After all, he's a priest; they're used to charging handsome fees."

Vatican City, Saturday, 9 October 1943

"I'm glad you called this meeting," F.C. whispered through the veil separating priest from penitent in the Franciscans' confessional. "It shows trust."

"It shows that I have no one else to trust," Roberto responded. His voice was subdued, listless.

"That may be true, too; but at least you have someone. Now, why did you call me?"

It took Roberto less than ten minutes to narrate a heavily sanitized account of the procurement of a set of possibly authentic photographs of Enigma and some supporting documents. Explaining Anna's demands added only a few moments.

Trying to keep the elation out of his own voice and curious about why Roberto sounded so depressed, F.C. said: "Anna's greed is something we hadn't counted on. Probably we should have. No one ever thought the lady would make it in the annals of modern hagiography. Still, what you have is basically very good news, very good news indeed. I confess yours truly never thought you could pull it off. Congratulations. I'll pass your word on to Father Christmas. He will undoubtedly inform Washington. I suspect they'll be furious, but—"

"She's counting on that 'but.' She knows how desperately we need that film. She claims her price is fair, even cheap."

"She may well be correct. All right, great work. Father Christmas

172

will contact you soon. Stay put and wait for his signal. I don't want you on the street any more than is absolutely necessary. I'll leave first. You wait in here for five minutes."

"Before you go," Roberto said tentatively, "you made me an offer last time."

"Yes, I did." F.C. sat down again. "Do you want me to hear your confession?"

"I'm not a pious man, Padre."

"Neither am I."

"I suppose not; you couldn't be and do what you do."

F.C. swallowed audibly. It was a fact he did not enjoy facing. He started to say something in self-defense, then realized what his real problem was. "Just relax and tell me what's troubling you. We can skip the smaller sins. It's been a long time, hasn't it?"

"I'm not sure how long, maybe three or four years. I'll pass over the girls. There's something else, a young boy."

F.C. sat straight up, but his years of training stifled an incredulous "what?" before it was more than a small impulse of electricity in his brain. "Yes?" he asked as blandly as he could.

"I broke his manhood, crushed his spirit, and murdered his soul." Roberto's tone was flat, almost totally without emotion. He could have been giving the recipe for an especially dry martini. The details of the blackmailing of Otto Schwartzkümmel and his own role—and F.C.'s unknowing role—came out in the same monotone, as if Roberto were describing events about which he had only read or seen on a movie screen. He was detached from himself.

F.C. let him talk without interruption. When he finished, the priest spoke in a professional whisper. "I don't need to ask if you are truly sorry, my son. The self-loathing in your voice is far more eloquent than any words you could muster. In that loathing, I also hear despair; and that is an even graver sin than you committed against that boy. Our ability to sin is great, but God's capacity to forgive is infinite."

"Mine is not."

"But you are human, as your confession indicates."

"Or subhuman."

"Don't wallow in self-pity. You committed a horrible sin, Roberto; there is no blinking that. But be honest, to me, to God, and to your-

173

self: You did not do it for pleasure or personal gain, not for money, or sex, or glory, or any other earthly advantage. You sinned because you were insensitive and overzealous. You were trying to save human lives and not considering the cost of doing good. That is a very human sin, not one that a subhuman could conceive of, much less commit. It is also a sin that God can easily forgive."

"But I am not sure I can forgive myself."

"That is more difficult. The difficulty is connected with your pride, and too much pride is also sinful. You set high standards for yourself, higher perhaps than God does."

"But what I did—" Roberto's voice was rising.

"Shh," F.C. cautioned, then continued. "What you did was evil; the deed was evil. That does not make you evil. We are no more what we do than we are what we eat."

"I wish that were true."

"It is true. God's grace makes it true. He makes it possible for us to stand up again after we fall into the mud and slime of sin, and to get up time and time again. You have fallen and fallen badly. But God is giving you the stregnth to stand up again, to make yourself whole again. And you will live a more responsible life if, as a result of this sin, each time in the future you take an action that deeply affects others you stop and weigh that effect."

"You are more optimistic about such things than I."

"It is my business to be optimistic about such things. I am a witness to Christ and to a teaching of love and forgiveness. Now say an act of contrition." F.C. then repeated the ancient ritual in Latin, ending with "*Ego te absolvo. . . .*" I forgive you your sins, in the name of the Father, the Son, and the Holy Spirit. "For your penance, you must pray at least once a day for the rest of your life for the repose of this poor boy's soul. And I promise you I shall remember him in my Masses.

"One other thing," F.C. added. "You must not return to the apartment on the Cedro. Go to the Franciscan convent on the Via della Scala, the one by the school and the pharmacy. Ask for Sister Sacristy. Give her this." He slipped a small silver Celtic cross under the veil. "And tell her that your Uncle Antonio sent you and wants to see her before Christmas. She'll take care of you."

"And then?"

"Then we will have to work out some way of slipping you south inside the Allied lines."

"Won't work. Anna would never trust you if I disappeared."

"You may be right," F.C. agreed. "But I fear we have badly under-estimated *la Strega*. For some time I've suspected her of being a double agent. Washington has pooh-poohed me. We may both have been wrong. She may be an independent who sells to both sides. She's certainly brazen enough to try it. Anyway, I want you in a safe house for the time being. We may have to put you on the street again for a few hours when we get clearance to pay her, but I want you out of her clutches as much as possible between now and then."

"Are you worried about my body or my soul?" Roberto asked.

"Both."

"All right. I have little choice but to trust you."

"None whatsoever. Now, as I was saying a few minutes ago, I'll leave first. Give me at least five minutes before you go out; then go straight to the convent. And, Roberto, be at peace with yourself."

As soon as he left the confessional, the American priest hurried into the huge sacristy of St. Peter's and borrowed the telephone. Minutes later, Sullivan was chugging up the stairs of the Hospice San' Marta, toward Paul Stransky's office on the second floor. Then it hit him, just as he reached the top of the staircase. The pressure on his chest increased so suddenly that F.C. felt as if he had been punched by a giant boxing glove. His chest was pushing, exploding inward. His breath came in burning gasps, and his whole left arm radiated the pain. As quickly as he could, he got a nitroglycerin tablet under his tongue, then sat down on the steps and waited for relief. His prayer for forgiveness was far more intense than usual. He was frightened, almost panicked by the ferocity of the attack. His angina had been getting worse over the years, but slowly, gradually. No previous bout could compare with this one's savage assault.

It took a full ten minutes and another tablet of nitroglycerin—he had a third ready—for the pain to begin to subside and his breath to seep easily through his lungs. He should, he realized, see a doctor or at least go to bed for a few hours, but his news was too important to wait. He pulled himself unsteadily to his feet and lurched toward the door of the American mission. "We need to talk, Paul," he said brusquely as he pushed open the diplomat's door.

Stransky looked up from the first course of his lunch—*tortellini in brodo,* a *bigne,* and a small carafe of yellow wine, each surrounded and almost obscured by the papers on his desk. "So sit down and talk. You look awful. Can I get you something? The kitchen can fix you a bowl of soup. How about some wine?"

"No, no, nothing." F.C. shook his head and sank into an easy chair.

"I'm worried about you. You look as if you just ran into a truck."

"I'm all right, damn it! Just let me rest for a minute."

"Sorry." Stransky pushed his wineglass toward the priest. F.C. took it and drained it in one long gulp.

"That's more like the hard-drinking Irishman who lives under that black cassock," Stransky said.

"I'm getting old."

"Aren't we all?"

The Jesuit leaned back and closed his eyes for almost five minutes, then snapped to. "I need some fresh air and so do you. The exercise will be better for your body and soul than all that food and wine."

"Maybe, but you know that saying." Stransky grinned. " 'When in Rome . . .' "

"Rome is hungry, so you'll be doing as most Romans do if you push yourself away from the table. Besides, there's another old saying that's appropriate to this Roman enclave: 'Even the walls have ears.' "

Stransky scooped the remaining *tortellini* out of the broth and washed them down with a swallow of wine. "This stuff's not my favorite, but the second course is *cannelloni* made with 50 percent real flour. Ah, well." He sighed in mock anguish. "For God, country, and Yale."

"In that order, I hope. Offer up your hunger pangs for the thousands who are starving all over this continent." F.C. could feel himself returning to normal. His usual self-confidence was overcoming his fear.

"Won't help them a bit. It's a problem of relative distribution, not absolute consumption." Then, as they moved down the corridor: "Is my office bugged?"

"If it isn't, it's a minor miracle, and here in the Vatican we deal only in major miracles." F.C. waited until they were outside and ambling toward the gardens. "Speaking of major miracles, I have one for you. Raven has come up with what he believes are full diagrams of Enigma, all neatly recorded on film."

Stransky stopped walking. He said nothing for several minutes, while pretending to admire the Galleon Fountain at the edge of the gardens. "Say again your last transmission, Padre. I must have swallowed that wine too fast. Something is sloshing inside my ear canals."

"Raven has come up with what he thinks are full diagrams of Engima."

Stransky laughed out loud. "Are you sure, absolutely sure?"

"No, and neither is Raven. He didn't do the actual photographing himself. A German contact did that for him, so there's always the chance of deception. Roberto thinks, however, that the chances are good the stuff is genuine."

"*Mamma mia!* What a coup! Professional spies get caught all over Europe trying to lift an Enigma, and an amateur and a prostitute pull it off! How in hell did they do it?"

"I couldn't say. God moves in strange ways."

"God? Oh, yes; sometimes, when it's quiet and I hear the Pope's silence, I forget God is on our side. Well, how they did it isn't important. The film is the thing. Do you have it with you?"

"I don't have it at all. There's a small problem. Raven doesn't have it either."

"A small problem?" Stransky almost shouted. "A small problem," he said more softly as he looked away from F.C. toward the fountain. "Padre, compared to that problem, Kesselring's army is a small problem. Who the hell has the film?"

"Roberto says that Anna has it, and she wants two hundred and fifty thousand dollars for it."

"Christ—I beg your pardon. I don't like that one little bit. She wants two hundred and fifty thousand dollars for something we're not sure is genuine? I wonder if Washington would stand still for a deal like that."

"She's running, as they used to say in the Old West, the only game in town. Roberto says she claims the price is fair."

"What whore doesn't think her price is fair?"

"I wouldn't know."

"I wouldn't either"—Stransky smiled—"except for what I've read in cheap novels. But there's something else here that bothers me. We have only Raven's word that it's Anna who wants the money."

"It fits her character."

"It does. It also might explain Washington's apparently stupid orders about the microfilm in the Regina Coeli. I'd watch your lad."

F.C. nodded.

"Well," Stransky said cheerfully, "I'll deliver the message. Stand by for an explosion."

"They'll pay, I assume."

"This has been a strange chapter in my life, Padre. I've pretty much decided that most of you people in the Vatican are sane. But if you're sane, the rest of the world, including me, is crazy. So the short response is, I don't know. I'll tell you, though, maybe tomorrow."

Rome, Saturday, 9 October 1943

"What is loose, *Herr Pater?*" Gratz asked as he settled back in his swivel chair.

"As you suggested," the Augustinian monk began, "I have kept my eye on Father Sullivan, the Society of Jesus's American gift to Papa Pacelli via Archbishop Spellman and his bags of gold." The monk hesitated. "Forgive me, Colonel, that sounds petty. In actual fact, I am fond of the man. He is a decent human being."

"Unusual. Typically spies are weasels or thugs."

"He is neither. A little boorish, perhaps, in his hunger for flattery and his need to be seen with important people; but he is decent—and intelligent. Anyway, he went into the basilica a little before noon today and entered a Franciscan confessional."

"Is it not odd for a Jesuit to confess to a Franciscan?"

"It is odd for a Jesuit to confess at all. But he did not go there to be shriven, rather, it seems, to shrive. He went into the priest's door. In a few minutes a tall young man with a limp went into the penitent's side—your Raven, I believe."

"Could you get close enough to hear anything?"

"No." The monk frowned. "And I would not have done so if it had been possible. And if by accident I had heard anything, I would carry it to my grave. The secrets of the confessional are sacred, even more sacred than national existence."

"As a nonpracticing, nonbelieving Lutheran, I shall pass on that

178

one. But do you really believe it was a confession rather than a meeting?"

"I do not know, but if it was a confession, the young man must have recounted all the sins of his life. He was in the box for at least half an hour, perhaps longer."

"And then?"

"Our good Jesuit hurried to the sacristy, made a telephone call, and almost ran to the Hospice of San' Marta, where the American special envoy and his secretary have offices. About twenty minutes later Sullivan and the envoy's secretary came out of the building and took a walk. The conversation was very agitated at times. That is all I can say, except that Sullivan looked pale, either ill or very concerned."

Gratz rubbed his hand over his chin, then straightened his moustache. He spoke slowly. "Everything is falling into place. If all goes well. . . . I cannot finish the sentence, *Herr Pater*, the seal of *my* confessional. But I also cannot overstate what this may mean for Germany—a great victory, maybe even the end of the war."

"Do you truly think so, Colonel? Sometimes I wonder if the wisest course might not be for us to sue for peace with the British and Americans, give them whatever they want, and concentrate on the Russians. The way the war is going, we are being squeezed."

"No, not at all. No defeatist talk, not this afternoon, not on the verge of a magnificent coup, one, I should add, that will cost hardly a drop of German blood. We shall win; we shall win because we Germans have the courage, the stamina, and the discipline to stay just one minute longer than our enemies."

"I pray, Colonel, I pray. If Germany loses, Europe will be communist for generations, and Christianity will be exiled, only a memory of our older people." Then the monk brightened. "Now, may I have a touch of your cognac?"

Gratz poured an inch of the brandy into each snifter. "It is a big day in another way. You have also helped confirm that this Jesuit Sullivan is the notorious Father Christmas. The OVRA have suspected as much for months, but they are too inefficient to have done anything about it."

"It is difficult to act against a cleric assigned to the papal Secretariat of State," the Augustinian noted, "especially when the Pope himself knows the man helps feed the hungry."

179

"And helps bomb German civilians as well as soldiers. He has a network of spies around the city. I suspect most of them are also clergy. According to our good woman Anna, he also runs Raven. I do not know"—Gratz began speaking as much to himself as to the monk—"when to arrest him. I cannot move against him until this particular operation is finished."

"Arresting him at any time will be difficult, Colonel. During the last few days, he has not left Vatican City at all. He may sense you are catching on to him."

"Yes, a good spy would have a premonition about that sort of thing. But, sooner or later, he will have to go out to contact his people or to do his work for *il Papa*. We can snatch him so neatly that not a soul in the Vatican will be any the wiser."

"Hmmm. I would advise against that. Papa Pacelli is hardly a decisive man; but, as I have told you, he is being pressured to condemn Germany for allegedly persecuting the Jews. The sudden disappearance of one of his diplomats might push him over the edge. At the very least, it would make my position much more difficult. Monsignor LaTorre and perhaps a few others are suspicious of my activities. They might hold me responsible."

"All right. We do not want to lose your services. I shall think about it and consult with you before I act—if there is time. Olendorf and the SS are also concerned about Father Christmas. If I find they are about to move, I shall have to act immediately to beat them to the prize. But, as I say, until this operation is done, he is safe. More cognac?"

Washington, D.C., Saturday, 9 October 1943

"What is it, Ensign?" John Winthrop Mason asked impatiently as he came out into the entrance hall of the Cosmos Club. "I do not like my dinner interrupted."

"It's a message for you, sir," the WAVE replied nervously. "It's marked Urgent, Top Secret. Colonel Lynch said I was to let you read it, then bring it back to the Pentagon."

Mason looked up and noticed the pair of armed marines a few respectful feet behind the officer. He sighed. "The military mentality. Bad for the digestion as well as for the intellect." He reached for the envelope.

"I'm sorry, sir, you'll have to sign this receipt first."

"You're not listening, Ensign." Then seeing the blank look on her face, he sighed again. "Very well, give it to me. He scribbled his name on the slip of paper and ripped open the sealed envelope: "Our blackbird has probably laid the golden egg. Alas, mother hen sees the picture and wants to feather her nest 250 times. Advise."

"What is this gibberish, Ensign?"

"I couldn't say, sir."

Mason crumpled the paper in his fist and handed it back to her. "Telephone your office and have them direct Colonel Lynch here 'on the double,' or whatever is the proper military jargon for 'instantly.' I shall be in the dining room, trying to finish what's left of a cold meal."

"Yes, sir."

Twenty-five minutes later, Lynch arrived at the Cosmos Club and sat down at Mason's table. The attorney had been dining alone. "Translate, please," Mason commanded as soon as Lynch's hand touched the chair.

"I knew you'd want to know, sir; that's why I sent the young lady over," Lynch said as he deliberately tried to draw the matter out. He paused until impatience spread over Mason's oversized face. "I'm afraid you'll look on it as bad news."

"I am never interrupted at dinner with good news. Get on with the translation, please."

"Simple: Raven and Anna have probably been able to get film of Enigma. Anna has control of the photos and wants two hundred and fifty thousand dollars for them."

Mason's eyes bulged even more than normal. His hand was shaking as he returned his coffee cup to its saucer. He snapped his fingers at a passing waiter: "Two courvoisiers, quickly!"

Lynch sat back and grinned. He had the double pleasure of Raven's success and Mason's discomfort. "He did it, the son of a bitch did it," the colonel said triumphantly. "I knew you'd want to know."

Mason waited until the waiter had brought the brandy and moved away before he spoke. When he did, his voice was low, and the tone suggested he was discussing the brandy's bouquet. "He has done nothing except complicate our work. As soon as you have finished your drink, please ask Sir Henry to meet us in your office."

Forty minutes later, the three men were seated around the conference table in Lynch's office in the Pentagon. "Quite a good show for your Raven chap," Sir Henry commented. "I am impressed. He must be a keen lad."

"He's an adolescent academic who doesn't know enough not to urinate into the wind," Mason replied.

"Then either there's no wind in Rome or he's lucky," the Englishman noted. "And you recall what Napolean said about lucky officers."

Mason neither knew nor cared what Napolean said about anything. He ignored the brigadier and turned to Lynch. "Can Father Christmas eliminate Anna?"

"I have no doubt he could have it done; and I also have no doubt that he won't."

"The sacerdotal mentality again. God save the United States from pious fools."

"Not sure it would be a wise move anyway," Sir Henry observed. "After all, two hundred and fifty thousand dollars is a paltry price to pay for such a gem as Enigma. A million pounds would not have been unreasonable, actually. If the Hun ever learned that we balked at such a trifling sum, he'd be on to us in a moment. Whatever else we do, we must pay what she asks."

"Pay a prostitute two hundred and fifty thousand dollars for something we already have?" Mason's face contorted as if he had swallowed some very nasty medicine.

"Only thing to do. We began this game, now we have to play it as if we meant it, don't we? Paying her is the only thing to do."

"The first thing, perhaps," Mason responded, "but *not* the only thing. When Raven has the photographs, we must compromise him so that the Germans get him *and* his film. As soon as we've paid her, Anna will sell the Germans the information that Raven has the film."

"Maybe that's the strategy," Lynch put in. "Let Anna take care of Raven."

"Too risky. She might not be quick enough, or the Germans might not believe her. Father Christmas might have Raven in Naples before the Germans reacted. Then Enigma would become a relic and we would be deaf and blind again."

"Bang on," Sir Henry muttered.

Lynch tried again: "How about getting Raven out right now and Anna along with him? We can tell her that the Gestapo's onto her double game and is closing in. We can give her the money and promise she can keep it. Once she's in our hands, we can hold her incommunicado until the end of the war."

"And the Germans never learn about Raven? Absolutely not. We have covered this ground before."

"I know that," Lynch pleaded, "but we face a new situation. And don't forget Raven's threat to have told some Italian the story of the Regina Coeli."

"If you would examine the situation with cold logic rather than warm sympathy, you would recognize the situation as merely more complex, not new. As for Raven's threat, we must assume it is a bluff. Even if it isn't, how can it hurt us? Sir Henry has stated it correctly. We pay her and, what is it? 'blow' him. Then we destroy Anna. I shall never allow an extortionist to profit from my client."

"Quite, quite," Sir Henry agreed. "It's the only way." The brigadier looked at Lynch. "Sorry, Colonel, I know how you feel about your lad, but Bronze Goddess demands human sacrifice."

"So you've said."

"Hear it again," Mason snapped. "The only question on the floor is how we do it. Does Stransky have the funds to pay Anna?"

"No," Lynch said sullenly, "and Father Christmas doesn't either. I'll instruct our man in Switzerland to have a Swiss bank transfer the money into the Vatican. It shouldn't be very difficult, but it will take a few days."

"Do it," Mason said. "Next, how do we blow Raven? Sir Henry?"

"Your priest chap, Father Christmas, would know when the payment was made and could ensure that Raven had the film and arrange a rendezvous inside the Vatican. He could see that the word leaks to the Hun and let him arrest Raven outside Vatican City."

"But would Father Christmas do it?" Lynch asked.

"Leave that aside for the moment," Mason ordered. "The more difficult question is how do we make the Germans arrest Raven? Another series of anonymous calls? That's had little success. The Germans may ignore it totally. They seem to be remarkably inept in Rome."

"But there really isn't much else to do, is there? Unless, of course, you have a chap inside the Gestapo."

"I wish we had," Mason mused. "This whole operation would have been much easier. Perhaps we should tip OVRA instead and play them against the Gestapo. Yes, that's it. If the OVRA knows, they'll try to upstage the Gestapo. The Germans will move in and eject the Italians to save their reputations. That's it. Very well, the decisions are made. I want the instructions out tonight."

"Wouldn't it be wiser to sleep on it?" Lynch asked.

"Postponing decisions never helps. Tomorrow brings its own problems. Give me a pad; I'll draft the basic message. You can put it into your nonsensical code and then have it enciphered. I want it out tonight." Mason pulled his watch out of his vest pocket. "It is six and a half minutes past ten. Sir Henry, would you join me in a nightcap at the Cosmos Club?"

EIGHT

Vatican City, Monday, 11 October 1943

It was pitch black outside. Fitzpàdraig Cathal Sullivan, S.J., could feel the darkness in his bones; there was no need to open the heavy blackout drapes or even his eyes. Yet the banging continued. He rolled over onto his other side, but even that heroic measure did not stop the noise. Slowly his conscious mind slipped into gear. *"Basta!"* he shouted. *"Basta! Vengo subito, subito!"* Enough, enough! I'm coming as fast as I can! He pulled on his robe and cursed the baby elephant who had crawled into his mouth during the night and died there of jungle rot. *"Chi è?"* he muttered as he stumbled in the dark toward the door. Who is it? *"Chi* the hell *è?"*

"Open up, Padre; it's me," Paul Stransky replied. "Reveille! Reveille in the boondocks! This is urgent." Once inside, Stransky flipped on the lights.

"You've waked me," F.C. slurred as he covered his eyes with his hand, "for the love of God don't blind me." He staggered to the bar, switched the *macchinetta* on, and began clumsily tamping fresh coffee into two double rings. Then with a quick "Be right back," he padded down the hall to the bathroom.

"Let's roll, Padre," Stransky urged as F.C. returned. "You and I have a war to fight, and we've got a hot flash from one of the big chiefs who rule us poor, miserable Injuns. We're late. It should have been delivered yesterday, but our Limey friends were too busy sipping tea."

"I don't care if we've had a trumpet blast from the Archangel Gabriel. I refuse even to die without a cup of coffee." He inserted a pair of plain white demitasse cups under the taps of the *macchinetta* and pulled down the levers. *"Un doppio,"* a double, he said as he

185

quaffed most of his steaming cup in a single long gulp and handed the other to Stransky.

The diplomat pushed it away. "It's unchristian to offer a man hemlock because he brings bad news."

F.C. cut his eyes menacingly as he gulped down the second double, shook his head, and blew through his mouth like a winded horse. "Now I can think," he said as the caffeine began to pump through his system and clear away the fog from his brain. At the same time, the flavor of the beans fought bravely against the gamy aroma from the elephant's carcass. "What sin have you committed that's so grievous you need forgiveness in the middle of the night?"

"It's four-fifteen in the morning, and I have something for you to read. Here, if you can."

"I can," F.C. replied, as he groped around his desk for his glasses, a pair of clever Italian design that folded up into a size not much bigger than a single lens. The compactness when folded made the glasses easier to carry, but much more difficult to find if one were not wearing another pair while looking for the first. "Shit," he swore as his thumb made contact with a lens, leaving a thick smudge.

"Now, now, no vulgarity here in Peter's home," Stransky teased.

"Peter wasn't at his best this time of day either. He'd understand. I like getting up early, but this is ridiculous. Shut up and let me read this *billet-doux*. 'Mother's request up to standard of Tinker, Evers, and Chance and confirms both birds are Texas Leaguers. Urgent you make purchase but order Horace to find Raven with merchandise.' Hmmm," F.C. muttered. "You people have difficulties with the English language. Can you translate?"

Without looking at the message, Stransky said, "Just remember your baseball and it's simple. Anna's request is a double play and confirms that she and Raven are double agents. You must buy the pictures, but make sure that the Gestapo—we advance one letter for Nazi agencies so Horace, *H*, means G for Gestapo—picks up Raven with the film— which is phony anyway—on him."

"The code may be simple, but the message isn't. I don't believe that Roberto is a double."

"You'd better believe it. That message is signed by our chief himself." Then, after F.C. had said nothing and done nothing for several

186

minutes, Stransky spoke again, half-wondering if the priest had fallen back asleep with his eyes open. "Why don't you believe it? Washington knows more about its agents than we do."

"In some instances, yes. But only in some. I met this Raven three times, once when I was giving out Communion in the Regina Coeli, and twice in a confessional. That's my territory, my territory as a priest, not as an agent. I've seen a few people, maybe a few thousand people, under those circumstances, and I've developed a damned good professional judgment about character under those circumstances. Roberto's a straight arrow. He's young, a bit impulsive and inexperienced—"

"Not now, he isn't, not after sharing a tiny apartment with our Anna." Stransky guffawed.

"Don't judge others, Paul. It's a dangerous business." F.C.'s tone was that of the professional priest. "He's not an experienced agent, but he's not a traitor either."

"Sorry, Washington disagrees about Raven, or Roberto, as you prefer."

"That's obvious. It's also obvious that they used us to set Roberto up in the Regina Coeli."

"If Washington thought he was a double, their action was logical."

"Was it? It seems stupid to me. Look at what they would have accomplished if Roberto were a double: Not only would they get yours truly inside the Regina Coeli face to face with a traitor who with one wink could fix it so I'd never leave except in a small box, they also would have destroyed a chain of agents. The only purpose this mayhem would have served would be to have a male double agent work with a female double to set up a game of let's pretend we're stealing Enigma. The United States would have gained nothing and have blown a damned good network. Explain to me how all that makes sense, Paul; at least try to explain it."

"I admit there are a few questions here and there." He broke off. "Look, I can't offer you a logical explanation, not an entirely logical one; but some things you take on faith, as you people argue all the time. I don't know the right answer, but I can think of a number of plausible ones, the most obvious of which is that we're part of a decoying operation. While everyone is watching Anna and Roberto, who the Gestapo believes are in their pockets, the real agents steal an

Enigma. Part of your net is blown and your cover goes, too. That cost makes the Germans think that we consider the caper with Anna and Roberto playing touch-me, touch-me in the loft is legitimate."

"Washington was willing to take a net loss," F.C. commented. "In fact, however, I wasn't caught inside the Regina Coeli because the supposed double agent isn't a double at all." He put his right hand on the left side of his mouth and continued in a stage whisper: "Incidentally, it was kind of our people to warn yours truly that he was being thrown to the wolves."

"Fortunes of war, Padre; every general uses somebody or some unit for bait."

"I dislike quoting Dominicans, but 'I answer that' your story is totally implausible, and not merely because it makes me nothing more than a pawn."

"It's not 'my story.' It's a possible explanation. I don't know what the right one is, but I have faith that our leaders know what they're doing."

"Faith in people who, you argue, were willing to have me killed? Don't be absurd. Besides, there's a gaping logical hole in the scheme you outline—or any other I can think of: If Roberto is a double and we blow him, in effect we send him to a safe place and rub the Germans' noses in it. We'd be saying, 'Here's your double agent and here's your phony Enigma. We have the real one.' And absolutely the last thing we'd want the Germans to know was that we had Enigma, if we had it."

"If we had it," Stransky put in. "Maybe, maybe the game isn't for Enigma at all, but for something else. And don't ask me what. I don't know, and I couldn't tell you if I did. Padre, if Roberto is a double, then blowing him won't hurt him. You're right there. So what's the big deal?"

"The big deal is that I don't believe he's a double. He's an American officer in civilian clothes, spying behind enemy lines. If captured he'd be shot, even under the laws of war that civilized nations follow. And we both know the Gestapo would torture him before they killed him. Death would come as a mercy. That's a big deal to me, Paul—murdering an innocent human being who thinks he's helping his country."

F.C. walked back over to the bar and began making more coffee.

"I've got to get ready." He yawned. "I'm scheduled for a five-thirty Mass."

"I thought that you priests were like us lay folk and had to fast before Communion. Do you get a special dispensation for working for *il Papa?*"

"No, but military chaplains are exempt from the rule, at least to the extent of being allowed coffee. And"—F.C. twinkled—"yours truly served for several years as the chaplain of a naval reserve unit at the Brooklyn Navy Yard. I've looked very carefully through the correspondence about my transfer to Rome, and nowhere did anyone say that I lost my chaplain's privileges."

"Hummpph. Sounds lawyerish to me."

"The law is an instrument, not an idol. Like the Sabbath, it was made for man, not the other way around. Canon law is no exception to that rule, nor is an order to betray a young man." F.C. paused to pull down the lever on the *macchinetta* again and watched it squeeze out rich brown liquid, drop by thick drop, into the cup. "It's final, Paul," he said quietly. "I won't blow Roberto, unless I'm sure he's a double."

"Padre, ours is 'not to reason why' and all that poetic garbage. This is a war and you've received a clear order."

"Mine is to reason why. And while we're quoting authorities, how about rendering to God and Caesar?"

Stransky snorted. "It's late for that one. Sorry, but you've been playing with a two-headed coin for too long to make that argument stick. Forgive my moralizing to the all-wise clergy, but when you agreed to serve as a spy, you were an intelligent, freely consenting adult. You were sophisticated enough to know that you might have to do things that would offend your conscience as a man or even your obligations as a priest. You knew those things and you agreed to serve anyway. Any conflict of conscience is your *private* problem. As an official of the United States government you're as legally and morally bound to obey a superior's orders as I am or any GI in the mountains around Naples."

"But no legal order can command an immoral act."

"Irrelevant. No one has ordered you to commit an immoral act, merely to do something you think is stupid and, at worst, morally doubtful. Christ, Padre, if stupidity were immoral we'd all be damned

189

to hell within minutes of being born. And if we had to wait to act until we were absolutely sure that what we were going to do was perfectly moral, we'd quickly die of uremic poisoning. The short of it is that you really don't know whether this Roberto or Raven is a double. You're setting yourself up as a better judge of that than the people in Washington who have far more complete and more accurate information than you do. If there's any sin here, it's pride—your pride. You can't accept someone else's judgment when that judgment conflicts with your intuition."

F.C. shook his head. "You may be right, Paul, you may be right, at least about my pride. But you're wrong about my allegiance." He held up his hand before Stransky could interrupt. "I know what you're going to say—or repeat. Suddenly I wish I hadn't agreed to accept this job. I'm facing a terrible conflict of interest. I glossed over that possibility when I said I'd help your people. It was an easy thing to do. Nazism is a moral abomination, and Pearl Harbor stirred up hormones that years of Jesuit training had diverted into other channels. I was more patriotic than wise. But your recruiters were also sophisticated; they should have known that, when a moral question arose, I would answer to a higher law than theirs. Ultimately I am a witness, a witness to Christ; and this whole situation doesn't sit right with me. I smell evil."

"Don't you think you've caught a bit of melodrama from your Italian colleagues?"

"Possibly. But there's something very wrong here. The pieces don't fit."

"So you pick up your marbles and go home?"

"Not quite. I just pass when it's my turn to shoot."

"An apt analogy. I have to tell Washington, you know, and they'll probably only have someone else do the job, someone who won't be at home in Rome like you and will run far greater risks of ending up in the Palazzo Braschi or that new place on the Via Tasso."

"You do have a moralizing streak, Paul. It must be the atmosphere here in the Vatican." F.C.'s voice softened. "My answer is no. It's a matter of conscience. Now get out of here and let me get dressed so I can say Mass. I'll remember your soul—if you professional spies have souls."

Stransky walked to the door, then stopped. "Padre, have a little

190

faith. We're fighting against Nazism. You say that's a moral abomination. Nothing I've seen questions that judgment. And you know how important this operation, whatever it's about, is. Washington told us it was top priority, ahead of anything else, anything whatsoever. Their putting your neck in a noose may anger you, but it also shows how critical this caper is. You've got the only real American net in Rome, and they'd blow you and the net along with you. They must think something is damned valuable. Agreed?"

"Agreed."

"The problem is, we don't have the full picture. It seems to me you might give the benefit of the doubt to the good guys—and don't forget *we* are the good guys, probably the only good guys in this whole, goddamned rotten world."

F.C. made no immediate reply. He walked to the window and pulled back the heavy drape. It was still deep black outside. "My answer is still no, at least for now," he finally said. "But I'll pray on it."

"Hallelujah, brother! May you see the light! Sweeeet Jesus, save this po' chile's soul from Satan."

F.C. grinned. "Out, out. Let me pray in peace."

Washington, D.C., Monday 11 October 1943

"He says he won't do it, at least not now. The most Stransky could get was a promise 'to pray on it.' " Colonel Lynch put the deciphered cable on John Winthrop Mason's desk.

"*Pray* on it?" Mason asked. "We gave the man a direct order."

"That's true enough, but you've often said you don't understand the sacerdotal mentality," Lynch noted. "Besides, many people other than priests find praying over difficult decisions to be a useful practice."

"Nonsense. Decisiveness is the only solution to a problem. Poking into animal entrails, examing tea leaves, or invoking some supernatural being only delays the work."

"But not looking at horoscopes?"

"That is a before-the-fact precaution based on empirical evidence, not mumbo-jumbo Latin incantations and incense burning to a mythical deity."

"You don't have much regard for the Catholic religion, do you?"

"I have little regard for religion, Catholic or otherwise; but I have

191

great regard for the Catholic Church as an institution. It is one of the principal guardians of our culture. If your druids lost their ability to restrain the creatures who populate their pews, that rapacious, ragtag collection of ignorant immigrants and their snapping, shiftless spawn of savages would take over our civilization. We would soon be living in the jungle again."

"Present company excepted from the category of savages, I assume, sir."

"This whole conversation is irrelevant. Our mission has nothing intrinsically to do with religion. The problem would be no different were we dealing with a militant atheist. Our task is to deceive our client's enemy. To do that we must 'convert' an obstreperous individual who happens to be a priest. Now, fetch me his personnel file, the complete file. There must be some way to reach him."

"I doubt that."

"I appreciate your faith. I admire its innocence. Nevertheless, I want that file."

Three and a half hours later, Lynch and Sir Henry Cuthbert came into Mason's office in response to his summons. "It's done," he greeted them. "To paraphrase the bard, vanity's the beast wherewith I'll catch the conscience of the priest."

"Beg pardon?" Sir Henry asked.

"I have put my finger on Father Christmas's weakness. He is a Gemini and a typical one: versatile, intellectual, witty, adaptable, with a marked facility for languages. On the other hand, he is also restless, changeable, inconsistent, full of nervous energy—even though really lazy—and tends to be a superficial gossip."

Lynch and Sir Henry exchanged silent glances. "Interesting, old chap, even fascinating. But how does all that shed light on your Father Christmas?"

"The restlessness and inconsistency suggest insecurity, a search for reassurance. That insecurity helps account for his adherence to religion and his joining the clergy—external indicia of his having been saved. His file supplies more specific cues. He's vulnerable to flattery of a special sort. He's been a 'society priest' much of his career. In New York, the walls of his office were covered with autographed pictures of famous people, politicians, movie stars, artists, judges, millionaires. On the slightest chance of shaking a senator's hand, he would hop a train to Washington. Spellman saw through these charades, but he was tolerant because Sullivan was useful. He has a sharp nose for gossip, is a master of flattery, and any commitment he made in the archbishop's name could be easily repudiated."

"Rather a terrible boor, isn't he?" Cuthbert muttered.

"Yes and no," Mason went on. "He's quite bright. Some of his articles in *America* were well done—he was an inveterate name-dropper there, just as in conversation. A true Gemini. Still, he did see and talk to the people he claimed to. They usually couldn't remember him the next day, but he shook their hands and hung on long enough to catch an occasional pearl."

"Such people can be useful in our work," Sir Henry remarked, "but I still find them boors."

Mason went on as if Sir Henry hadn't spoken. "In the Vatican there's a similar pattern: coffee parties each morning for important people, visits to the influential, such as Monsignor Montini. Stransky's judgment is very like that of the people in New York. Our cleric is a vain, insecure, smart, ubiquitous gossip and a social hanger-on who is also good at his work."

"And you intend to exploit that eccentricity?" Sir Henry asked as he suppressed a yawn.

"Exactly."

"He certainly does," Lynch said curtly, handing the drafts of the cables to the Englishman. "Read these. The President thinks the work that Father Sullivan is doing for the United States is 'magnificent.' Even the archbishop gets into the act with a message expressing understanding of his troubles along with confidence in his faith in America's crusade against Nazism."

"A particularly elegant touch," Mason noted.

"Sir," Lynch said deliberately, "I find it despicable. It's bad enough to lie to and double-cross our own people. Worse when you deceive someone into thinking the President personally approves. But to forge an archbishop's name and use his moral influence to persuade a priest to kill another human being is more than I can stomach."

"Now, now, Colonel," Sir Henry clucked, "those are stronger words than we mean, aren't they? Things like that have a tendency to pop out when we're overwrought, and we've all been working rather hard on this operation, haven't we?"

"Have we? I'm not overwrought, only fed up with this whole sordid business of killing our own people to distract the Germans. Mr. Mason, with all due respect, you are a one-dimensional man who has no concern for anything except your mission. You may be a civilian, but you are an ugly caricature of the ruthless military mind."

Mason did not look up from the papers. "If you would say 'ugly caricature of the brilliant but ruthless military mind,' your comment would be more apt. I am a unidimensional man—and by design. I come from a very old but also very poor family. I have made my way in this world solely by my ability, not by beauty or charm. People engage me because of the power of my intellect and the force of my will. I focus solely on my client's interests. I do not concern myself with costs, as long as I do not violate the letter of the law. But my biography is irrelevant. I weigh your advice; you follow my orders."

Lynch twisted inside, desperately wanting to tell Mason to stuff his cables. But once again institutional loyalty triumphed over his voice and the urge to exit. The colonel was silent.

"See that these papers go out today, please."

Lynch took the drafts, nodded to the brigadier, and left.

When the door closed, Sir Henry leaned toward Mason and said, "He's not an Aunt Sally, you know, only a good soldier who worries about his men. It's one of the best traits an officer can have. My Australian chums are keen on him, and they aren't taken with many of you Yanks. You will go a bit easier on him, won't you?"

"Lynch is not genetically able to cope with work like this. Celts are ideal for wild charges against machine-gun nests. Like most savage tribes, their genes produce a surfeit of raw courage. But they are incapable of cool planning—all emotion and no intellectual discipline."

"Yes, yes, I know. We've had our bother with the Irish over the centuries. They are a hotheaded people, much taken with religious superstition. All this republican rot will be the ruination of what once was a smashing spot for holidays. Mark my words, in another decade they'll be begging to be reunited with England under the Crown."

"Lynch's problems," Mason went on, again ignoring Sir Henry, "are compounded by his being a Cancer."

"Beg pardon, a what?"

"A Cancer. He was born in late June. Cancers tend to be hyperemotional and hypersensitive—the syndrome that appeared a few minutes ago. They fret about others, and their paternal instincts—what you dub concern for his men—are often exaggerated. They frequently have a hard exterior, but it is generally no more than a thin veneer that covers a soft, intellectually flabby interior."

"Sorry, old chap, but that sounds like twaddle to me. A sensible man wouldn't have anything to do with it, would he?"

"A sensible man would not ignore empirically tested patterns of behavior. But it's natural for you to feel that way. You're a Taurus. You were born in early May."

"Yes, the fourth. How did you know?"

"I checked before I accepted you as liaison officer."

"Astounding!"

"No, prudent. I knew there would be problems with Lynch, despite his experience in this field. Celtic Cancers are not stable. I took him against my better judgment."

"But you do understand his problem, don't you? It is not easy for an officer to help kill his own men."

"If one finds killing difficult, one should look for another occupation."

"And you, Mason, do you find it easy?"

There was no response.

"I rather think not," the Englishman said after a few moments of silence.

Mason arched his thick eyebrows. For a brief second, his lips traced a real smile. "One can always take comfort in the contemplation of suicide."

Vatican City, Monday, 11 October 1943

"*Allora,*" Monsignor Ugo Galeotti said as he sauntered up to join Father Fitzpàdraig Cathal Sullivan, S.J., outside the train station, "you told the matter was of some importance."

"Yes." F.C. nodded. "Let's walk toward the gardens."

"*Ecco.*" The *monsignore* used one of those marvelous throwaway words that Italians employ with equal eloquence to punctuate speech or silence.

"I would hope that whatever I say would be under the seal of the confessional."

195

"You would like me to obtain a stole?"

F.C. smiled. "No. That might look a little out of place here in the great outdoors. I am caught in a double dilemma. I need both spiritual and practical advice. I'm not sure how best to cope with a moral problem centering around my duties as a priest, as a citizen, and as a human being."

"*Ecco*," Galeotti repeated, wisdom dropping from each of the four syllables the word acquired from his tongue. "Let us begin at the beginning. What is it that you seek to preserve? What value?"

"Human life. I want to end this slaughter *and* to end the horrors of Nazism."

"Those are noble ends, Father. Here there is no moral problem."

"You know something of my peculiar position here in the Vatican, my relations with my government."

Galeotti held up his hand. "*Basta, basta.* I prefer not to know all the things of which I am aware. Simply explain the problem and permit me to retain my official ignorance."

"All right. The heart of the matter is that there is an American agent in Rome. My government assures me that he is a double."

"A double?" Galeotti asked. "*Cos' è?*" What's that?

"Someone who pretends to be on one side while actually working for the other. Governments aren't fond of such people."

"No sane man makes the goat his gardener. And how does this double thing touch you?"

"My government wants me to make sure he has incriminating evidence on him, arrange a rendezvous, and alert the other side so he'll be arrested."

"Strange."

"Very. First of all, if he is a double, tipping the enemy would only mean the end of this particular mission for him. The Nazis are not likely to punish their own man, except perhaps to discipline him for failure."

"No." Galeotti frowned. "No, that does not necessarily—how do you say?—follow. *Senti,* I have learned that some German organizations hate each other, or at least fear each other, more than they do the Allies. They are all constantly at each other's throat. According to me, it is always thus when gangsters combine. We view it here in Italy in

196

the vendettas among the Mafiosi. What I mean is that if your double labors for one German agency, his being captured by another may signify something much more serious to him than discipline."

"I hadn't thought of that, but that is only a side issue. I just cannot believe this young man is a double."

"You have met him?"

"Several times, twice in a confessional."

"Then I must have care of what I ask."

"No, *Monsignore*, but I have to be careful what I say. He is a Catholic, and I believe in that box all his childhood training pushed him to be honest."

Galeotti gently shook the wrist of his right hand several times, then rotated his palm skyward. "*Forse, forse*," he said softly. Perhaps, perhaps.

"Even more, that is my territory," F.C. continued. "I think I have a capacity for professional judgment in that situation. As priests we all do."

Galeotti rolled his eyes to heaven. "*Preghiamo, preghiamo.*" Let us pray, let us pray.

"I think my government is wrong, absolutely wrong. Furthermore, there are logical problems in the story they have given me. In sum, I believe—no I suspect, only suspect—that I am being asked to betray an innocent man."

"I yet do not visualize the problem. Without other, as a priest—as a Christian—you cannot betray an innocent man. You may have difficulty persuading your government, but you have no moral dilemma, only a moral duty."

"It is not quite so clear, *Monsignore*. My government makes two arguments. First, they insist that yours truly is wrong, the agent *is* a double. Second, they stress that it is absolutely essential to some larger scheme that will save thousands of lives that I carry out my orders. The choice is not clear cut."

"*Ecco.*" The *monsignore* inhaled the word. "It is an ancient dilemma: 'It is expedient for us that one man die for the people.' But that is an inexact parallel, let us hope."

"Indeed."

"Let us proceed without haste. You wish to preserve life. Yet if you

197

do not seriously jeopardize this young man's life, you may be taking the lives of thousands of others. On the other hand, can you morally sacrifice another human being even for so great an end?"

F.C. nodded.

"It was for such dilemmas that the Angelic Doctor constructed his principle of double effect. *Quindi*, let us apply the tests for his principle to your obeying your government. First, is the end you seek good? The end you seek here is to preserve life and that is securely good. Second, assuming that an evil result will also ensue, do you want that result or do you merely foresee it? Here, you foresee the probable death or punishment of this young man, but you do not wish that end. So far you have a *votum* of one hundred percent."

Galeotti paused to watch a covey of small birds take flight before them. Then he resumed his disquisition. "Third, does the good end flow—you say that?—from the evil? According to me, you are in the pasta there. You save thousands, but by killing or at least seriously jeopardizing the life of an innocent human being. That is a morally bad act, and, in facts, the good end comes directly from that bad act. Fourth, is the act you commit evil in itself? There is room for doubt, but I have fear that it may be so."

"Is it that easy?" F.C. protested. "I do not know that it is the agent's death that will produce the good end, only his arrest; and there is a chance—from talking to you I now realize a smaller chance than I had originally thought—that he will suffer no harm after the arrest. I do not know that he will die. My government claims he will not. Furthermore, is picking up a telephone and calling the Germans an act evil in itself?"

"You have reason," Galeotti agreed. "I have often doubted the utility of the concept 'acts evil in themselves.' To kill a man I need only twitch my first finger; securely, that is a morally indifferent act."

"Unless you have a pistol in your hand."

"Sì, unless I have a pistol in my hand. To speak on the telephone is not evil in itself, though my father truly believed it so. Yet to say the other person something that will cause him to injure or kill cannot be called neutral." Galeotti paused for a few minutes, then added, "I have taught moral theology at your Gregorian University, even though I am not a Jesuit; and I am acting *prepotente*—you say showing off?"

198

"No, you are demonstrating detached judgment."

"Theologians are much more adept at solving old riddles than new ones. No doctrine can make absolutely clear to us the exact point at which a neutral act's contribution to an evil result turns the act from 'neutral' to 'evil in itself.' That answer lies with practical judgment—prudence. *Allora,* let us substitute a new test for the third: Does the good outweigh the evil?"

"How can I weigh the value of a single life by itself, much less against the value of thousands? But, if it is wrong to take a single life, isn't it just as wrong not to save a thousand lives?"

Galeotti sat down on a bench across from a small stone fountain. "*Senti,* Father, we have explored your problem in an intellectual mode; and always the signs point in all and two directions. What does your heart say you to do?"

"It tells me not to betray this young man; it also tells me to keep him hidden so that no one else can betray him either."

"You do not think you are responding as a sentimental priest and not as a prudent man? You have considered that? You will also be exposing yourself and perhaps others to great risk when you aid this agent. If he is an enemy, some innocent people will die regardless of the veracity of your government's assertion about thousands of other people. Have you considered that also?"

F.C. nodded. "I have considered all those things. I think I can take the risks."

"And after, if the risks fail?"

"After, I think I could live with not betraying him. I do not know that I could live with betraying him. On the other hand, my duty as a citizen to obey my government in the middle of a war is crystal clear, especially in the middle of a just war."

"*Ecco,*" Galeotti remarked, "on the other hand. 'On the other hand there are five fingers,' as one of my colleagues was habituated to tell. You yourself, I believe, have quoted Aristotle that to be a good man is not necessarily the same as to be a good citizen. And for us priests the selection is obvious. According to me, Father, there is where your response finds itself. I pray you find the courage to execute it. I shall pray also for your consolation against the sorrow you will inevitably experience whatever you do."

199

The *monsignore* lifted his ample frame from the bench. It required some effort. "Sometimes our God does not always give us a selection between good and evil, but only between evils. It is His mode. Who are we to question it? I recall one of your poets telling 'Glory be to God for dappled things.' In this affair, He will have much glory, for securely your selection must be very dappled."

F.C. laughed. Then, as they started to walk back, he said quietly, "*Monsignore*, thanks for not preaching to me about my having been unwise to put myself in this position. I appreciate the absence of a sermon."

Galeotti gave a northern Italian's somewhat inhibited imitation of a Roman shrug. "We are men, Father, subject to all the passions for which we chastise the laity. It is not a sin to defend the weak against the powerful bully. You know you were overzealous, but. . . ." The *monsignore* shrugged again. "*Senti*, when a poor Italian prelate has discovered informations that might shorten this war, he has not felt it wrong to pass those things to a friend. Evil is a problem for us all. We do not lose our obligations as men when we become priests."

Rome, Monday, 11 October 1943

Maj. Kurt Priebke entered Lieutenant Colonel Olendorf's office. He threw his right arm up in a perfunctory Nazi salute. "We have Major Schwartzkümmel in custody and have completed our preliminary interrogation."

"You were not seen detaining him?"

"Positive. He boarded the train at the main station, and, with one of our men standing softly behind him on the train, got off at the Stazione Tiburtina. He got off alone, I might add; he knew, of course, that there was a gun pointed at his back. He followed instructions perfectly—walked down the stairs, again alone, and waited for us to pick him up after the train had left. It was all very clean. The major is not an aggressive or courageous man, yes?"

"That is reassuring. Did he say anything in his, ah, 'preliminary interrogation'?"

"Something. When we confronted him with what we knew, he readily admitted to having received the film from Gratz and to having passed it on to this woman, this Anna Caccianemici, who works at the Remus restaurant."

200

"The good woman discussed on the tape. And from Anna where did this film go?"

"Schwartzkümmel says he has no idea, unless it was to the American who was working with her. Schwartzkümmel swears on his honor as a German officer that he knows nothing further." Priebke leered as he said "honor as a German officer."

Olendorf kept a straight face. "He is probably telling the truth. But," he mused, "he might know more than he thinks. Perhaps we need to ask sharper questions."

"Do I ask Sergeant Hoess to pose those questions?" Priebke scratched his behind vigorously as he spoke.

"No, Kurt, not yet. But the temptation to use force is always strong. I have become sympathetic with the Grand Inquisitor. No, we put the major in easy detention for the time being. Let us see what develops."

Priebke nodded.

"I have also become," Olendorf went on, "curious about that film, very curious. My policeman's intuition tells me that we must get a look at it. There is something about this whole Operation Rigoletto that bothers me. Tonight I shall visit with our lady Anna when she leaves the Remus. Can you arrange for Colonel Gratz and his assistant to have some business that will require their presence elsewhere tonight?"

"Of course. I can produce some urgent information on a band of partisans in Lazio. We shall have to work late into the night with the Abwehr, yes?"

"Excellent. You are very efficient, Kurt."

"Thank you, sir. Could I ask if you intend to board the lady with us?"

Olendorf paused to light a Lucky Strike. "It is not impossible, not at all impossible."

"She is a Communist; that alone should be grounds for arrest." Priebke laughed. "I am certain we could convert her to National Socialism, yes?"

"I am sure Sergeant Hoess could. He is a most persuasive missionary. But, as the theologians tell us, it is often prudent to tolerate a lesser evil in order to secure a greater good. Here we must bide our time. Walking the streets, so to speak, the lady may be quite useful to us. Apparently both the Abwehr and the American OSS trust her. That indicates she has other talents than those that meet the eye. It also indicates that she, too, understands the nature—and necessity—of prudence. I doubt if she will need much persuasion to work for us against the others."

Rome, Tuesday, 12 October 1943

A few minutes before 1:00 in the morning, Anna left the Remus and, armed with the pass that Gratz had given her, started to walk home. She had not quite reached the Piazza Navona when a powerful arm reached out of the shadows of a foyer and clamped around her mouth. She swiftly kicked backward as hard as she could, but felt her heel glance off the side of a heavy boot. At the same time, her right arm was twisted up behind her so that her fingers were touching her left shoulder blade. The sharp pain brought her close to fainting.

"*Liebchen, Liebchen,*" a voice whispered harshly in German, "in a moment I shall release your arm, and I shall also let you breathe again. I do these things because I know that you are a sensible woman and would not want the Gestapo angry at you. Then we shall talk."

"Swine," she muttered as she tried to catch her breath, "who are you?"

Olendorf thrust his handsome, blond head close to hers. "It is dark, *Liebchen,* but try to see me and memorize my features. You will want to remember me, for we shall soon become very close friends. My name is Viktor Olendorf, Lt. Col. Viktor Olendorf to my troops; you can think of me as the Deity—and every bit as temperamental as Jehovah was in the days of the Old Testament."

"You're already famous in Rome."

"One tries, *Liebchen,* one tries. It is expedient to enjoy some immediate succcess, for, in this sort of work, success begets success. And I do so much want to succeed with a creature as lovely as you."

"I don't give it away, Fritz," she sneered. "And I don't accept lire or occupation money. I deal only in hard currency."

"*Liebchen,*" Olendorf said soothingly, "you misunderstand. I am the dispenser of favors, the patron; you are the receiver, the client. You exist to serve your patron, not to sell to him."

"Oh? And how am I serving?"

"Not with your body, not just yet. When I want that, you will give —gladly, eagerly, hungrily."

202

"*Mèrda*," she spat out.

Olendorf slapped her across the face—far harder than Gratz had. "Never use vulgar language in my presence." He paused. "And never call me Fritz again—if you wish to keep your teeth."

Anna put her handkerchief to her mouth to stanch the blood. "You Germans are brave when it comes to fighting women. Too bad the Russians and the Allies have men in their armies."

Almost as a reflex action, she moved backward to roll with the expected blow. Instead, Olendorf laughed loudly. "You have spirit. I like that in a woman. One seldom finds it in a Latin. You Mediterranean females tend to beg and plead rather than fight."

"Perhaps because you pure Nordics put guns in our bellies or knives at our throats."

"Perhaps, but you must admit it is quicker than the rituals of courtship we have to go through with the racially pure. And that reminds me: Time moves on and so must we move to the point of our meeting: You have some film from a 175."

"Who told you such foolishness?"

"The *Warme* himself. Oh, as an officer and something of a gentleman, he was reluctant to involve a lady. Nevertheless, some of my people are quite adept at nonverbal persuasion. Eventually, he told us many interesting things about you. It seems that you are a clever as well as a good woman, Anna Caccianemici."

"If I had this film, why would I give it to you?"

"For two reasons: First, we can make our client-patron relationship permanent. Such relationships can be very profitable when the patron commands the Gestapo in Rome. Second, I can arrange for you to meet Sgt. Walther Hoess, one of my persuasive underlings at the Via Tasso. Were he to try his silent rhetoric on you, you would happily provide the film, but you would be somewhat the worse for wear."

"I don't frighten easily. Your colleagues in the OVRA have already worked me over."

"Amateurs." Olendorf laughed again. Then he stepped back and peered at her as if he could see her distinctly in the dark. "Well, perhaps you are right. You are a strong, intelligent woman with an attractive face and a beautiful body. Even without money that combination makes for success in this world. Perhaps you should have no fear." He paused again. "Well, only one fear: losing your physical charms."

Anna said nothing, less because she could not think of a reply than that she feared her voice might tremble.

"My Sergeant Hoess," Olendorf continued, "is a frustrated surgeon. He loves ladies. His specialty is the double mastectomy. Alas, he does not believe in anesthesia. Still, he is a humane fellow. After such surgery many women feel desexed, so he also removes the clitoris. He says that without anesthestic it gives the patient one last jolt she can remember all her life. The troops in the audience always applaud that little maneuver. And, as a frustrated showman as well as surgeon, he offers an encore: a small slice twelve centimeters long and three centimeters wide from each eye to the jawbone. He says it puts the right face on things. You will love his sense of humor—a very subtle man."

The German grabbed her wrist and felt her pulse. "Judging from the way your heart is pounding, you must be feeling a wild burst of passion for me. That rapid heartbeat could not be caused by fear."

Olendorf snapped his fingers loudly and called out "*Kommen Sie!*" The motor of a staff car parked on the Piazza Navona immediately cranked up and the vehicle turned onto the side street, stopping beside the pair. "See, we provide a limousine, though some people think of it as an ambulance."

"All right," Anna said sullenly, "you win."

"I always win, *Liebchen*. It is wise of you to recognize that in time to profit from your vision. Where is the film?"

"In the restaurant. It's locked up; you'll have to wait until tomorrow. I don't have a key."

"Wait? Why? Locks are not a problem for the Gestapo. Just tell me where in the restaurant."

"The film is in two small capsules. One is under the cash register, the other is taped behind the water tank in the rest room."

"How clever. Now, you and I will go to Via Tasso—no, no, *Liebchen*, do not panic. I am a man of my word. After all, I am a German officer. You will be a very temporary visitor, not a guest. I simply want you where I can put my hands on you if the film is not where you say it is and if it is not genuine."

"How do I know if it is genuine? I took what the *fròcio* gave me."

"Do not trouble your pretty head about it. If the film is there, we can check with the 175 to make sure these are the same. The whole process should not take more than a few hours. You can be home for breakfast. I am certain that you and I can find something to do to amuse ourselves while my people come up with the right answers. I have very comfortable quarters."

Four hours later, Major Priebke rapped perfunctorily at Olendorf's bedroom and, seeing the light coming from under the door, opened it and came in. Olendorf sat up, instantly awake; Anna continued to snore gently. The major stopped and began a rapid retreat. "I am very sorry, Colonel," he stammered, "I did not realize—"

"It is all right, Kurt, no matter. The lady and I were done—for the time being." He ran his hand softly down her back. "Her body is a lovely thing. Soon you will have your turn. But we have other business this morning. Let us go to my office." He pulled on a robe and led the way down the hall.

As soon as the door closed behind them, Priebke spoke: "The film was where she said it was, and it is genuine."

"Good. Schwartzkümmel identified it with no hesitation?"

"Schwartzkümmel has not seen it."

"Say that again. I have not had much sleep tonight."

"Sir, Schwartzkümmel said that he had passed on to the lady the film that Gratz had given him."

"That fits with what we know. I take it we now have that film."

"I do not know whether we have *that* film; the film we do have is of a real Enigma. The pictures are of a dismantled Enigma and some pages from a repair manual, with diagrams and instructions, yes?"

"You are positive?"

"Absolutely. We have an Engima here in the building, and I had our operator go over the photographs with the machine in front of him. He swears it is the real thing. And the manual is identical to the one he has."

Olendorf whistled. "I knew it, I knew it. There has been something rotten in this whole operation. You see, Kurt, my strategy has paid off. We have waited—masterfully waited. Now we pounce. Canaris is a traitor. He is the leak Berlin has been worried about. This whole thing has been a clever means of getting an Engima to the Allies."

205

"I wonder how much they paid the Abwehr bastards?" Priebke asked, as he began scratching the seat of his pants.

"Not enough, not nearly enough when Reichsfuehrer Himmler hears of this."

"The Reichsfuehrer will fly Canaris's head from his own yardarm," Priebke chimed in. "He will fix it so that all the senior Abwehr officers, including that bald-headed snob Gratz, will be looking down the barrels of SS firing squads, yes?"

"Gratz is a good officer even if he is Abwehr—and a snob. But—" Olendorf got up and began pacing the room nervously, as he fumbled for his cigarettes. "Fundamentally, you are correct. Heads will roll. This débâcle will mark the end of the Abwehr. Reichsfuehrer Himmler will be highly gratified. You and I now have a way to overcome Berlin's anger about their stupid *Judenaktion*. What are a few thousand Hebrews compared to a coup like this? I think you can count on soon being Lieutenant Colonel Priebke. You may even be taking over here in Rome when I am promoted to a more important post."

"I would like that, but what is our next move?" Priebke was vigorously scratching his behind.

"Moves, our next moves. We operate at two levels. First, we, the SS, continue to carry out the scheme that Canaris outlined, but we carry it out to deceive the Americans, not to betray Germany. At another level, as soon as possible, I fly to Reichsfuehrer Himmler's headquarters at Hochwald and talk to him personally."

"But General Wolff in Florence is commander of the SS in Italy. Should you not go through him? He will be angry if you avoid the chain of command, yes?"

"Let him be angry. Canaris was right about one thing: Reichsfuehrer Himmler does not trust General Wolff. Therefore, I do not trust General Wolff; and the Reichsfuehrer will appreciate my not trusting General Wolff. The Reichsfuehrer and I recognize Wolff as a *Streber*. I shall go directly to the top. One must show initiative, Kurt; that is essential to being a successful commander, initiative. Remember that when you are in charge."

Smiling broadly, Olendorf continued to pace the floor, his cigarette spewing ashes around the carpet like a tiny volcano. "Tell me again: Is our brave Major Schwartzkümmel well and happy?"

"Reasonably, sir. As you instructed, our interrogation was gentle.

He spent the night in a room on the second floor. It is not the Excelsior, but it is not too uncomfortable."

"Good, good. Apologize to him for the inconvenience we have caused him and move him to a better set of quarters—yours. Impress on him that he has a chance to save Germany from traitors. Treat him with respect, great respect. In a few days, a week at most, he must build us a machine enough like Enigma to deceive the Americans. And he will also have to prepare a repair manual. Have our people work with him to arrange for the phony radio war the Abwehr promised."

"My quarters? With respect, Colonel, can we trust the man?"

"We can trust his genius, not his loyalty. You can have your quarters back when he has completed this project. We shall not need him then. But for the meantime, impress on him the importance of his mission. Promise him anything he wants, including Anna's and Raven's heads on silver platters. There is no limit; we can dispose of him very soon."

"What if this Father Christmas, who Anna says is in charge of the operation, wants the film immediately?"

"We shall have to stall him; but, of course, we cannot do it for very long. That is why the major is so valuable to us. This whole operation would be difficult at any time, but our hours are limited and our lives complicated by this damned *Judenaktion* that Berlin is so obsessive about."

"What do we do about Anna?"

"She is a problem," Olendorf agreed. "If we keep her here or in some safe place, Gratz will become suspicious. Worse, if Raven cannot contact her, he might get frightened and run without the film. On the other hand, if we let her go, she might talk."

"Sending her back under guard is also out of the question, yes?"

"Of course. Even an amateur might become suspicious if his contact shows up with a Gestapo agent on her arm. Wait a minute!" Olendorf snapped his fingers. "Why not an Italian on the run?"

"What Italian could we trust?"

"Not a real Italian. Do I recall that we have a sergeant from the Tyrol? Someone from Brixen, or Bressanone, as the Italians call it? What is his name?"

"Yes, sir. You are right. His name is Vilpiano or something like that. Close enough so I can find him in a few seconds."

"Do that. He is probably bilingual; those people usually are. Anna is one of them. Have him go home with her. She can palm him off as an old friend hiding from the OVRA. Tell him to stick with her when she is in the apartment and when she goes out in the neighborhood. When she goes to work, he can telephone us then walk with her as far as the Piazza Farnese. We can pick her up from there and trail her back home."

"That is all possible, Colonel, but the rope would be loose, yes?"

"It could very quickly tighten into a noose around her neck. I shall etch that fact into her memory. I shall also let her know that if she tries to contact *anyone,* she will be shot—not killed, only shot in the leg so we can detain her for surgery."

"What about her regular meetings with Colonel Gratz at the Remus?"

"Hmmm." Olendorf frowned. "Those will have to be exceptions. We do not want to alert him."

Olendorf hesitated while he lit a second cigarette from the butt of the first. "All right, that part is done. Now, I must get to Hochwald as rapidly as I can, tonight if possible, tomorrow certainly. I want *our* Operation Rigoletto under way immediately; and I want to be back here before Captain Danzig starts his *Judenaktion.* Saturday is still his target date?"

"Yes, Colonel."

"All right. Even if I cannot get to Hochwald until tomorrow, I could see the Reichsfuehrer and be back here by Friday at latest, in place for Danzig's show on Saturday. I know that little bastard, Kurt. We must watch him or he will have the Vatican on our backs and tear up the morale of Catholics in the armed forces."

"Yes, sir."

Olendorf pushed the buzzer on his desk. A few moments later a sleepy orderly responded. "Coffee, a full pot—and quickly." The SS officer turned to Priebke. "It will be a long day. I want you to get started right away on finding the Reichsfuehrer and setting up an appointment for me. If you have any trouble with his staff, transfer the call to me. Put me on the next flight to Milan. At worst there is a transport out of Ciampino after dark, after the Allied fighters have gone home for the day. I am willing to chance a daylight flight. Make sure that I have copies of the recordings from the Excelsior. If there is to be a trial—*if*, I said; the Reichsfuehrer may feel it expedient to move more swiftly—if there is to be a trial, we shall also need Schwartzkümmel and Anna as witnesses. It would be useful to have this Raven fellow, too."

"I am sure Sergeant Hoess could easily coax some interesting answers from such a foolish amateur, yes?"

"Yes, I am certain that Hoess could. We may find that useful, but only after we are positive that Raven has passed our edited version of the film on to Father Christmas."

Vatican City, Tuesday, 12 October 1943

Stransky waited as the last of F.C.'s morning coffee klatch were straggling out the door. "Safe to talk, Padre?" he asked.

"I think so, but let me make sure." Sullivan turned on a new automatic record player and set a stack of 78s on the spindle. The first was The Warsaw Concerto, the next few were the album from *Oklahoma*. "That should fool any bug," he said as he adjusted the volume so that the piano came booming out. "Did you notice that Monsignor Montini was here today? He shook my hand very warmly. Soon"—F.C. put his right hand on the left side of his mouth and whispered loudly—"the *abbraccio* for yours truly. Just wait, Paul, just wait."

"Yes," Stransky said absently. "How goes your praying?"

"About the same. I see no reason to change my mind."

"Well, I've got a lot of reasons. Washington is sore as a blister about you. They're talking mean."

"Talking mean is one of many governmental prerogatives."

"They think you're a fool—or worse."

The pain in F.C.'s ego caused his eyebrows to droop.

"Or a hell of a lot worse, Padre, a hell of a lot worse. They want Raven so badly they can taste him."

"That's too bad." The priest spoke slowly, almost ruefully. "But it's too late now. He's gone under. I've already started the process of getting him out."

"You've what? Good Christ, man, you've lost your marbles."

"I've told you before, I think he's fundamentally a decent human being."

209

Stransky paced up and down the office for a few minutes. "You could still get him out of your pipeline, I suppose."

"I suppose I could, but there's no need. You've said that the film will be fake. There's no point in risking his life for some false documents."

"Padre, Padre, I can't believe you. Look, we're fighting a war against the most evil and powerful force this planet's known since the last dinosaur kicked off. Your intuition about a decent human being isn't worth diddleysquat. We deal in hard facts. And I'll lay it to you straight. You were right about Raven, he's not a double. I've had a stack of cables on him since yesterday."

"I told you that."

"Yes, you told me that. But you didn't tell me that he's in business for himself. I'll let you read those cables if you'll come to my office. He and Anna have gone independent. The traitorous bastards are out to make a bundle out of the blood of the American army and navy."

"I didn't believe he was a double and I don't believe he's an independent."

"Convincing you shouldn't be my job. We're supposed to be on the same side, and I keep telling you we're the good guys. What's come over you? Have you taken to believing *Mein Kampf*?"

"That's not funny, Paul."

"I don't think it's funny either, but the question has occurred to some people. Here, I've got a pair of cables for you to read, but before you do I want you to hear a message that isn't written anywhere. I got it orally from a source I trust, someone buried deep in the German apparatus. He says your Raven has made the Gestapo an offer, via Anna, to blow Father Christmas for a hundred thousand dollars and a pair of Swiss passports."

F.C.'s eyes narrowed. "I don't believe it."

"Believe it and live; doubt it and wake up as the Gestapo's house-guest."

"Your word?"

"My word." Having double duty as a diplomat and a spy, Stransky rationalized, made it doubly necessary to lie.

"I trust you, but your source could be wrong."

"He could be, but not likely. Making contact is risky for him. He won't try it unless he's sure of what he has. Now read the cables."

210

F.C. picked them up, retrieved his glasses from the pile of papers strewn around his desk, and read out loud:

> WE ARE PLEASED AND PROUD. YOUR WORK MAGNIFICENT
> AID TO OUR FIGHTING MEN. NEXT IN TOWN VISIT FOR
> ONE OF MY SPECIAL MARTINIS. YOUR BOSS WILL CONTACT
> ON MATTER OF DEEP MUTUAL CONCERN. FDR

"Are you pulling my leg? This is hard to believe."

"One doesn't forge the name of the President of the United States, not even in this business. I told you we're not playing for peanuts. Read on."

F.C. picked up the second cable:

> PRESIDENT AND I DISCUSSED YOUR WORK. HE IS ONE OF
> YOUR ADMIRERS, AS IS PONTIFF. I HUMBLY JOIN CONGRE-
> GATION. CURRENT CASE, HOWEVER, CONCERNS PRESIDENT.
> HE CANNOT UNDERSTAND YOUR DOUBT. I CAN AS EVIDENCE
> OF YOUR HUMANITY. BUT TIME NOW FOR FAITH IN JUS-
> TICE OF CAUSE TO PREVAIL OVER PRIVATE FEELINGS.
> NEW ITEM. PLEASE SEEK AUDIENCE WITH POPE AND ASK
> HOW CAN FURTHER EFFORTS TO FEED HUNGRY. SPELL-
> MAN.

F.C.'s cheeks reddened. "Did you arrange for these to be sent to me?"

"I didn't," Stransky replied. He spoke the truth, though in a carefully rationed amount. "I'm sure Washington did, however. They probably talked to the President and had him talk to your boss— your other boss," Stransky corrected himself.

"You've hit me with a one-two punch."

"I'm giving it to you straight. Now, let me show you something I shouldn't." He unloosened his belt and reached inside his trousers into a secret compartment sewn along the inside of his waistband, and pulled out a much folded cable. "This one is to me. Eyes only. Forget you ever saw it, but don't forget the message."

F.C. took the paper, unfolded it, and read it to himself:

> DOES C UNDERSTAND MISSION OR HAS HE GONE INTO
> BUSINESS WITH RAVEN? CANNOT OVEREMPHASIZE IMPOR-
> TANCE OF TASK. WAR IN WEST AT STAKE. MESSAGES COM-

211

"You've brought out some heavy artillery, Paul."

"Our side, at least *my* side, doesn't have any heavier. That should
tell you something about the importance of what's going on. The
President knows the situation better than any of us, and the archbishop is a man as steeped in theological training and tangled up in
moral scruples as you are."

"That's true, but I can't bring myself to believe that Roberto
would turn."

"I don't doubt he was once a good man, but he's as bent as a safety
pin now. Anna may have done it. He wouldn't be the first male to
lose his sense of values over a female's charms. As I recall, it happened to a guy named Adam some time ago."

"But—"

"No buts, Padre." Stransky was determined to turn the screws as
tightly as he could. His voice became harshly quiet. "I've got to respond immediately. If it's negative, Spellman will have you out of
here as soon as *il Papa*'s boys can arrange passage across the German
lines. And I guarantee you, Washington will make sure that after the
war you'll be known as the man whose pigheaded pride cost a
hundred thousand American soldiers their lives. You can spend the
rest of your clerical career explaining to church sodalities how you protected a traitor and killed their sons. You'll be known as the holy
fuck-up."

"Don't use that kind of language with me!"

"I'll use whatever language I think is necessary. And I think strong
language is necessary here. On the one hand, your 'decent human
being' is trying to sell a phony set of photographs to us and at the
same time is trying to sell you to the Germans. On the other hand,
the President of the United States and your archbishop are telling
you to get off your black-trousered butt and help us save lives, including your own. Your pride elevates your judgment, based on three
brief conversations, above the judgment of the people who have all
the facts. Good Christ, you and Lucifer would have made a great

212

pair. I've got a suspicion, though, that hell won't hold two sets of pride like yours."

F.C. stood up and spoke in a tensely cold tone. "I think you'd better leave before I do something I'll regret."

"Okay, I'm on my way, but think about it. You've been conned by an artist. He's no wet-behind-the-ears kid like you want to think. He's more Italian than American, and he's been a professor."

"An instructor."

"Whatever. He's educated and sophisticated and sleeping with a whore you know is twisted. He's got a lot to gain, two hundred and fifty thousand from us for the pictures, a hundred thousand from the Germans for your hide—all tax free with Swiss passports to match. A stunning ensemble in which he could live comfortably for the rest of his life."

"That won't be long if Anna shares it."

"That's another story, Padre, another story. I don't think Raven will have a happy ending either, but his loss won't bring back the dead soldiers—or you, for that matter. Just focus on the evidence, the word of the President of the United States and the archbishop of New York. As you say, that's pretty heavy artillery to stack against the popgun of your intuition." Stransky walked to the door and opened it.

"Close the door, Paul," F.C. said wearily and slumped back into his chair. "I'll take your word."

"My word? You can take my word about the plan to sell your body, but take FDR's word about the importance of this mission, and Spellman's word about the moral judgment. Now, where have you hidden Raven?"

"At the Franciscan convent on the Via della Scala."

"I know the place. Can you contact him?"

"Yes."

"Can you contact Anna?"

"I don't see why not. She doesn't know me, but I've left messages at her apartment before."

"Do it again. Assure her that we'll meet her price. The money won't be available for a few days. Talk about an exchange, but stall. Tell the truth. We don't have that much cash on hand. It'll have to

213

come from Switzerland. Tell Raven we'll bring the money directly to him. Have Anna give him the film—if he doesn't have it already."

"I doubt that he does; but why not get the money directly to Anna? It would be simpler."

"Riskier. The two of them are working with the Gestapo or the Abwehr or some other German organization. The less directly we get involved, the better. I don't want any of our people arrested."

"I still don't understand why you're willing to pay a quarter of a million dollars for something you think is false."

Stransky shook his head. "Good Padre, naïve we're not. Look, for reasons I don't pretend to understand, Washington says that it's critical we go through the motions of making the purchase. That's another indication of how important this mission is. We're throwing money away. It pisses me off, too; but so does this whole war. After Raven has the film, after, that is, we're *sure* he has the film on him, have him come directly here to your usual spot. It's in St. Peter's somewhere, isn't it?"

"I'll tell him; but, Paul, I still don't like it."

Stransky smiled a little. "I don't like much of what I have to do either, but nobody said war was a bed of roses. Padre, I'm sorry I was so rough on you, but I had to shock you. There are too many lives at stake in this mission."

"I wish I understood the situation completely."

"I wish I did, too. Just keep the faith. Think of all those young men who're going to live because of you. That's not a bad thought to hold onto."

Vatican City, Tuesday, 12 October 1943

"Something new already, Padre?" Stransky asked as he and Father Fitzpàdraig Cathal Sullivan, S.J., apparently met by chance as they strolled around the Basilica of St. Peter in the late afternoon.

"Yes. I'm concerned. Anna didn't come home to Trastevere last night. She showed up about eight-thirty this morning with a man in civilian clothes. The Trasteverini believe he's a foreigner."

"Which could mean anything from his coming from another part of Rome to his being a German."

"True, but my sources lean toward his being a German. Those old dollies are eagle-eyed. They said he walked like a soldier."

214

"Curious, curious," Stransky muttered. "Raven's gone under—we don't *think* Anna or the Germans yet know where—and a soldier moves in. He's probably some variety of SS. Very curious. Seems they don't trust her either. That's prudent, but only in one respect. They've run the risk that somebody would spot their man as an agent."

"They've lost that gamble. They probably don't know that those old *dondrone* spend their lives watching the world walk by."

"Yes," Stransky said absently. "It may also mean that the Germans have decided that Anna shouldn't go independent after all. Who knows? Have your people keep their eyes open."

"How could I stop the Trasteverini? Any word on the money?"

"A few more days. Stall Anna."

"I don't know how long we can put her off."

"What are her options?"

"She could sell the film back to the Germans."

"Not likely they'd pay off except in her own blood. Still, I'll goose our man in Switzerland."

Rome, Tuesday, 12 October 1943

"What is loose, *Herr Pater*?" Gratz asked, as he and the Augustinian monk met by chance as they strolled inside the Basilica of St. John Lateran in the late afternoon.

"I am concerned, Colonel. Anna did not come home to Trastevere this morning until eight-thirty, and she had a strange man with her, someone in civilian clothes."

"And Raven?"

"I do not know. My agent has not seen him since Saturday. He left that morning, walking in the general direction of the Vatican and, as far as we know, has not returned."

Gratz stopped to admire the twin tombs of Popes Innocent III and Leo XIII, set high up in the walls flanking the apse. He was hoping that Raven's absence meant he had taken the bait and run. Anna's return with a new male in tow supported that hypothesis. "This man in civilian clothes could be merely a client in Anna's other line of work."

"He could be," the monk conceded, "but my source thinks he is a soldier. He walked very erect and he did not swagger."

215

"Certainly not a Trasteverino then, and probably not an Italian. This could be very good news, *Herr Pater*—if, that is, our good woman has taken up another romantic liaison."

The monk frowned.

"Sorry. I meant only that a venial sin was less odious than a mortal sin."

"The Church does not classify casual sexual liaisons as venial sins."

"Forgive my insensitivity. All I meant was that it would be better were Anna engaging in a romantic dalliance than if she were dallying, so to speak, to betray Germany as well."

The monk nodded. "Using a lady of easy virtue as an agent does create moral difficulties."

Only if you care about moral theology, Gratz thought but did not say. "On the other hand," he went on, "if this man is from the SS, we may be in for trouble. You are fortunate to have been spared the bitterness with which organizations supposedly working for the same end fight each other."

"Spared?" The monk raised his eyebrows. "Does Holy Mother Church not have Jesuits?"

"Yes; well, perhaps you can understand that in this operation the SS is more of a threat to Germany than are the British and Americans. The SS would sacrifice anything—sometimes I think even the Fatherland—to spite the Abwehr."

"Surely you exaggerate. Even the Jesuits would stop short of crippling the Church—at least deliberately crippling the Church," the Augustinian added wistfully.

"The SS could give your Jesuits lessons in both cunning and evil. These people are thugs, gangsters, torturers, murderers—a disgrace to all that German civilization stands for. Scum." Gratz paused. "But," he continued in mock cheerfulness, "Winston Churchill said he would ally with the devil himself to defeat us. So we must enlist our own devils to survive. We live in a convoluted world."

The monk remained silent.

"The SS," Gratz said finally, "is my problem, not yours."

"I wish that were true, Colonel. I never liked those people, but I had never thought they were as bad as you picture them."

"Worse, far worse than I have said or you have imagined. To more immediate problems: Do you have anything at all on Raven?"

216

"Nothing more than I have indicated, except that when he left he was carrying nothing in his hands."

"Thanks, *Herr Pater*. Let me know anything you hear, no matter how trivial—and at any hour of the day or night. Either this operation has ended in success or is in danger of coming apart. It would be helpful to know which."

When he left the Lateran, Gratz started walking toward the Via Tasso. He motioned his staff car to trail behind him. He wanted time to mull over the evidence before confronting Olendorf.

The SS commander greeted Gratz with courtesy, but he also made it plain that he was, with great difficulty, creating space in a very crowded day to accommodate the colonel. "I am sorry to be able to offer you only a few minutes, but," Olendorf explained, "we are about to launch a *Judenaktion*."

"So I have heard. I have also heard that Berlin has sent another officer to take charge of it. Congratulations on showing some decency."

Olendorf stiffened. "Berlin was not pleased with my plan for handling the Hebrew question. No congratulations are in order on that score. You know my feelings. Now, how may the SS assist you?"

"Operation Rigoletto."

"Rigoletto? Operation Rigoletto. I had almost forgotten. Sorry. You know how it is." Olendorf pointed to the files on his desk. "Programmed activity tends to drive out unprogrammed activity. It is an iron law of organizations. How is Rigoletto progressing?"

Gratz ignored the query. "Where is Raven?"

"Raven?" Olendorf asked in genuine surprise. "Where you put him I suppose. I assume safe with Father Christmas."

"He is missing."

"Missing? *Scheisse!*" Olendorf swore. "Damned amateur! Probably lost his way walking around Rome. My men are already overcommitted, but I shall do what I can to locate him for you."

"That is not necessary. I can find him myself—unless you have him."

"I do not, Colonel. On my word as a German officer, I do not have him. I have not seen him since our session in the Regina Coeli, and to the best of my knowledge neither has any member of my command."

217

"Very well. I accept that for the present. I understand that there is a new man sharing the apartment of Raven's contact. Do you know anything about him?"

Olendorf controlled his panic. He had assumed that Father Christmas had Raven stashed in a safe house somewhere near the Vatican, probably in a nunnery. Stupidly, he had not drawn the obvious conclusion that Raven was sleeping with Anna. The SS officer tried to speak slowly so that he could test his lie for plausibility before Gratz heard it. "I do not even know Raven's contact. If you give me his name and address, I shall make an investigation of whoever he is and of whoever is sharing his apartment. That is the best I can offer."

"Never mind. I have warned you, Olendorf, to stay away from this operation; Admiral Canaris has warned you; and der Fuehrer has ordered you. If you are meddling and Raven gets suspicious and this operation topples, your head will topple with it. Remember that paper you initialed."

"I remember it well, Colonel. There is no need to remind an officer of the SS of his sworn duty. Now, if you would excuse me, I must be about my Fuehrer's business."

The instant Gratz left, Olendorf picked up the telephone and called Anna's apartment. She answered. "Let me speak to Vilpiano," he said curtly.

"*Subito, Padrone.*"

"Sir?" The click of the sergeant's heels came over the wire.

"How is our lady behaving?"

"Beautifully, sir, absolutely beautifully."

"I did not mean in bed, *Dummkopf*. I meant has she tried to contact anyone?"

"No, sir. No one at all."

"Very well. Screw her all you want, Sergeant; but do not be taken in by her. She is a professional and will be using you far more than you think you are using her. Let me speak to her."

"Yes, *Padrone*?" Anna came back on the line.

"Cut it. You did not tell me that Raven was sharing your apartment or that he is missing."

"You didn't ask."

218

"Do not play games," Olendorf snapped. "Vilpiano might have frightened him off and ruined the whole operation."

"*Calma, calma,*" Anna mocked. "Your handsome sergeant didn't frighten Raven. He left here Saturday and hasn't come back."

"Where is he?"

"I don't know. I'm his contact, not his mother. Father Christmas probably has him tucked away somewhere. Why are you so concerned about that bumbling amateur?"

"We want Father Christmas," Olendorf said swiftly. He could feel his blood pressure drop ten points. "Raven will lead us to him."

"Then don't be worried about Raven. Father Christmas is in touch with me. Raven must have told him that I have the film. He wants it. Shall I tell him to contact you instead?"

"My patience is being sorely tried, Anna. Shut up and listen. Play along with Father Christmas and do it smoothly and quietly. Raise his suspicions and we become very angry. How did he contact you?"

"There was a note in my mailbox downstairs in the entryway."

"Very clever. The man is careful. How are you supposed to reply?"

"If I have the film I'm to hang out two sheets and a blue towel on my laundry line."

"Clever again. Do it. And keep in mind that I have a quick temper." Olendorf's voice became very cold. "I also have a long memory and an ability to concentrate on a specific problem. I assume that you are going to try to sell the film to Father Christmas. That is your business—up to a point. If it causes problems, it becomes my business. I can be very sudden, *Liebchen.* Keep that in mind. And let me know what happens, everything that happens. I mean everything."

NINE

Rome, Friday, 15 October 1943

In the smoky predawn darkness a light rain had begun to fall. It was hardly more than a thick drizzle, but the first sharp winds of autumn drove it painfully against human flesh, and the early morning chill penetrated even the polished black boots of an SS major. Kurt Priebke paced up and down the tarmac to keep his circulation churning. In the distance he could hear the heavy drone of a multiengined aircraft approaching from the northeast. A few seconds later, lights carefully hooded to be visible only in a fifteen-degree arc flickered along the runway, then beamed steadily until the plane's groping tires slapped the wet concrete. Then the blackness returned.

The six-motored Me-323 taxied to the remains of what had been an administration building, and a ground crew pushed out a portable stairway. Lt. Col. Viktor Olendorf was the first person to emerge from the cabin. In the darkness he was little more than a moving shadow, but Priebke needed no more evidence to recognize his commanding officer.

The major tapped the fender of the staff car, and the vehicle arrived at Olendorf's side just as Priebke did. The salutes were perfunctory. The major held his lighter for the lieutenant colonel's cigarette. In the dancing light, Olendorf's face shone pale with fatigue, his eyes red rimmed. "Christ." He exhaled smoke and exhaustion. "I have been bouncing around in those flying boxcars for three nights. If I take my boots off, my feet will swell up like barrage balloons."

"How was the Reichsfuehrer?"

Olendorf took two more long drags from the Lucky Strike then tossed it aside. "Driver," he ordered, "find yourself some other transportation back to Rome. The major will drive us." Olendorf settled into the passenger's side of the car and drew his black leather over-coat tight around him. His teeth were on the verge of chattering. "Do you have a drink?" he asked.

Priebke pulled a small silver flask from his own overcoat pocket and offered it. Olendorf sniffed then sipped it tentatively. He coughed and half choked. "What the hell is this, bottled St. Elmo's fire?"

"No, sir, Sicilian grappa."

The lieutenant colonel took a second, deeper swallow, coughed again, and returned the flask. "Sicilian fire," he muttered. "At least it puts some warmth in your bones. Any problems while I have been gone?"

"No, sir. Danzig is all set for tomorrow. He has borrowed troops, mostly *Waffen* SS, from the Wehrmacht. He has about 365 men."

"Not enough," Olendorf said wearily, "not enough. Well, to hell with him and to hell with the filthy Jews. Let Danzig fall on his fat, baby face. Nobody can say I did not warn them. Where does the turd plan to take the Jews, straight to the train?"

"No, sir. There are problems. Our superefficient captain cannot muster enough priority to have anything before Monday. He will billet the *Untermenschen* at the *Collègio Militare* until then."

"Right under the Pope's nose, not a kilometer from his palace. If he does not squawk at that insult, he is truly an old lady. If he does yell, no one can say I did not warn them."

"No, sir. No one can say that."

Olendorf lit a fresh cigarette. "And Raven?"

"Nothing, sir, absolutely nothing. We followed your instructions and did not conduct a search of any kind, but Vilpiano—"

"Vilpiano? Who the hell is Vilpiano?"

"The sergeant you assigned to stay with Anna, yes?"

"Go on."

"Vilpiano reports nothing, and our other sources report nothing. Raven seems to have vanished, but give the word and we will turn Rome upside down and shake him out—if he is still here."

"He is still here, I feel it in my bones, cold as they are. But do nothing to upset the Abwehr, not yet anyway. We have enough problems. Raven and Anna must have some deal between them, but I am not sure what and we cannot squeeze her . . . yet."

"Maybe he simply does not trust her."

221

Olendorf chortled. "That would not be surprising, even from an amateur. Here we have to sit tight for the time being. What about Major Schwartzkümmel?"

"Proceeding. He says he should have a machine that would pass inspection on film in twenty-four more hours. I borrowed a couple of technicians from Florence to prepare the repair manual as he goes along—only old SD hands. Once we have one machine, we can reproduce a second very quickly, yes?"

"And Anna?"

"As far as we can tell, she has been a model of deportment. Other than the laundry signal we agreed on, she has communicated with no one; and, it seems, no one has tried to reach her other than Gratz. He visited her twice at the Remus—waited for her outside in his staff car, so there is nothing we can say—although I can make a pretty good guess as to what went on."

Olendorf brushed aside the lecherous tone. "Anything else to report?"

"No, sir. May I ask how the Reichsfuehrer received our news?"

Olendorf stared ahead at the narrow road, barely visible under the slits of the blackout lights. Priebke thought that his question was going to be ignored for the second time. In a few minutes, however, as they neared the walls of the old city at the Gate of St. John Lateran, the lieutenant colonel began to speak in subdued tones, his voice so low that Priebke occasionally missed a word or even a phrase.

"The Reichsfuehrer was cool, very cool. I had the distinct impression that neither my presence nor my news was welcome. He reminded me of his annoyance at my opposition to what he called 'cleansing of the Roman temple.' To be sure, he congratulated me on work well done on Rigoletto, and he hinted the conspiracy might go much deeper than you and I imagined. He is convinced that some people, not just one person, have been leaking information to the Allies. The British seem to know exactly where our submarines are, too exactly. But, Kurt, here is where I am confused. He reacted almost lethargically, and I have never thought of Heinrich Himmler as lethargic—cautious, carefully calculating, but never lethargic. In any event, he ordered us to do nothing and say nothing except at his specified command. He will conduct his own investigation."

"Strange."

"Very strange. I am an honest, blunt professional policeman. I neither like nor understand deviousness. I am afraid, however, that more political games are being played in Berlin, even in Hochwald, than der Fuehrer realizes. My policeman's instincts tell me that Canaris is going to slip away."

"I thought we had him."

"We had him and we still have him, right by the balls. But apparently he has the same hold on several other people at the top. If we twist, he twists; and God alone knows who will scream in agony. It is an ugly situation."

Olendorf fell silent again until they pulled up outside the house on the Via Tasso. "Incidentally, the Reichsfuehrer is keeping the film and the recording to present to der Fuehrer when he feels the time is right. Nevertheless, that he does not immediately lay that evidence before der Fuehrer shows how bizarre—and serious—the political maneuverings in Berlin are. I am concerned, deeply concerned. As a professional policeman my job is to carry out orders, but I cannot help wondering what policy—and whose interests—are behind those orders."

"Perhaps you are overtired. Things may look clearer after a long nap."

"I hope so, I hope so. I have never felt so depressed about Germany's future."

"What priorities do we get for the manufacture of false Enigmas?"

"Whatever is needed," Olendorf said absently. "The Reichsfuehrer himself will handle that part. All we have to do is to send him the original when Schwartzkümmel is done. . . ." The SS officer's voice trailed off.

"Colonel, are you all right?"

"Did you ever make a *Blutkitt*?"

"Yes . . . yes. My 'blood cement.' It is required, often."

"Yes, it is often required. A true SS man must have pledged himself to party, Reich, and Fuehrer by committing a bloody crime. Do you know what mine was?" Olendorf's voice was almost trancelike.

"No, sir. We should be going in now. You will get a chill out here in the rain."

"Mine was a girl, a girl in Spain—Barcelona. We suspected her of being a Communist spy. There were plenty of Franco's boys who could have worked her over, but my commanding officer said I was soft. He gave me the chance to prove myself, to make my *Blutkitt*."

"She was a spy, yes?"

"Was who a spy?"

"The girl in Barcelona?"

"I do not know. She died before we found out. No more questions, Kurt. It is too cold and wet out here."

Rome, Friday, 15 October 1943

At noon Olendorf entered his office. He felt somewhat refreshed after a three-hour nap, but still his muscles ached from long nights of sitting up in cramped airplanes. Capt. Erich Danzig was waiting for him and snapped smartly to attention as soon as Olendorf came in the doorway. He ignored the junior officer while he glanced through his mail. After several minutes, he sat down heavily. "All right, Captain, what additional help can I give you?"

"I thank the Colonel, but the answer is none, sir. I have everything under complete control. The *Judenaktion* begins before dawn tomorrow. I have locked up all the Italians who were involved in the planning, and our troops are confined to their barracks. The Hebrew scum have no inkling of what will hit them."

"Splendid, just splendid," Olendorf said as he picked up a memo from SS General Wolff snidely complaining that weeks after the German occupation of Rome the British escape line for downed airmen was still running through the Vatican, and the American spy network operated by a person known as Father Christmas was flourishing.

"Sir?" Danzig's voice brought Olendorf back to the Via Tasso. "Sir, begging the Colonel's pardon, but I have come to protest his order that Major Priebke accompany me tomorrow. It would not be functional for the officer in charge to be accompanied by an officer senior in rank. My orders were signed by Herr Kaltenbrunner himself, and they make it quite clear that I am in charge of the *Judenaktion* here. The Colonel's sending Major Priebke with me is inadmissible."

"Inadmissible? It is inadmissible for you to use that word with me, Captain. Your orders also make it clear that I am to cooperate with you. By attaching my executive officer to your person, I am ensuring that I can provide the maximum assistance possible."

224

"Sir, the Colonel could have helped by loaning me the troops I need to round up the Jews."

"I said 'maximum assistance possible.' I have explained to you that my men are totally engaged chasing partisans and spies. I cannot give what I do not have. What I do have is an experienced senior officer who knows Rome and is fluent in the language."

"I speak Italian very well; and, if I may refresh the Colonel's memory, I vacationed in Rome on several occasions."

Olendorf raised his eyebrows. "Captain, I have lived in Rome for four years. I am only now beginning to understand it. The Middle East begins right here, and the Etruscans are alive and well in the old city. Furthermore, people in the ghetto and Trastevere, where most of your work will be, speak their own language."

"Sir, with all due respect to the Colonel, I must insist."

"No, I insist." Olendorf paused. "You plan to raid the Franciscan convent in Trastevere. That will be a very delicate affair. In strict international law, the Vatican has no extraterritorial rights there, but your forcing your way into a convent could cause the whole operation to blow up in our faces. It well might anyway. You can browbeat and bully those nuns all you want, threaten them with hell twice over, but if you use any violence, Germany will be in serious trouble."

"I am sure that Herr Kaltenbrunner fully understands the diplomatic situation, and he placed me in complete charge of the *Judenaktion*."

"True, but to arrest these particular Jews you must first get through the nuns. And, as Christians—and possibly even Aryans—in Rome, those nuns fall under my jurisdiction. If this *Judenaktion* provokes the Pope to condemn Germany—and, as I have told you and I have told Berlin, I strongly fear it will—then you can have the nuns and their Jews. You can rob them, rape them, shoot them, or send them all packing to one of your death camps. I shall not give a damn. But as long as the Pope is quiet, I am going to do my best to keep him that way."

"The Colonel has imposed a humiliating condition."

"Merely an intelligent precaution. Of course," Olendorf added, "if you get a direct order from Herr Kaltenbrunner to the contrary, I shall accede to his wishes."

Danzig saluted and stalked out. Olendorf walked to Priebke's office.

225

"Stay with Danzig. What he does to the Jews is his business. What he does to the nuns is ours."

Rome, Saturday, 16 October 1943

At 5:30, an hour before dawn, there were only slight stirrings in the ghetto, across the river from Trastevere. The curfew kept all but the bravest in their homes. It was also the Sabbath and, besides, it was still raining. A few badly addicted souls were slinking through the wet shadows to queue up at the tobacco shop for the week's ration of cigarettes, but even the stray cats thought them decidedly odd. Then, suddenly, truckloads of SS troops began to surround the old sector, while other detachments spread around Trastevere and the rest of town. The soldiers quickly split up into small teams; each leader carried lists of names and addresses of Jews to be arrested. A mimeographed sheet the size of a postcard went with each name. It read:

1. You and your family and all other Jews belonging to your household are to be transferred.
2. You are to bring with you:
   a) food for at least eight days;
   b) ration books;
   c) identity card;
   d) drinking glasses.
3. You may also bring:
   a) a small suitcase with personal effects, clothing, blankets, etc.;
   b) money and jewelry.
4. Close and lock the apartment/house. Take the key with you.
5. Invalids, even the severest cases, may not for any reason remain behind. There are infirmaries at the camp.
6. Twenty minutes after presentation of this card, the family must be ready to depart.

As the statement warned, the Germans accepted no excuses. Infants and children joined the very old, the feeble, the ill, the pregnant, and the able-bodied. "All must come," the troops insisted, "all must come." Every Jew was going to a labor camp, they explained. Each would work according to his means; each would receive according to his needs. Not even the excuse of being Christian was sufficient. At the central collecting point, the *Collègio Militare*, officers would carefully check identities and release those who were not Jewish.

226

Despite military firmness, slippage was large. Some Jews had taken the frequent warnings of Chief Rabbi Israel Zolli and had gone into hiding. Other males, mistaking the raid for a labor levee, climbed over roofs or jumped out of windows, leaving their families to what they thought was safety. Still others, who were in the corridors or doorways, simply walked past the soldiers, whose Teutonic vision could not distinguish an Italian Jew from an Italian Christian. Nevertheless, the toll was high. The SS took more than twelve hundred people that rainy morning to the *Collegio Militare*.

Rome, Saturday, 16 October 1943

At 6:00 A.M. the rain was still coming down. Hours before it had turned the streets of Trastevere into slick trails of mud, wet garbage, and partially liquefied horse manure. Tommaso Piperno left his apartment on the Vicolo del Bologna and adjusted his cheap raincoat to divert a steady trickle of water from running down the back of his neck. Had his job been one of lesser responsibility, he would have turned over and snuggled close to Rebecca and enjoyed the sound of the rain. But Trasteverini needed, even if they did not deserve, clean streets, though only Adonai Himself could have provided them on a day like this.

Tommaso was trying to sweep the Via della Scala when the Germans arrived in the neighborhood. A staff car and two trucks came roaring down the narrow street from the Via Garibaldi and- made a slamming, skidding stop in the small piazza in front of the Franciscan church and convent. SS troops tumbled out of the trucks. Four of the soldiers, led by an officer in a black leather overcoat, trotted up the steps to the convent door. The rest fanned out around the neighborhood.

For a few moments, Tommaso watched in morbid fascination. For the poor Jews hiding in the convent, the black-clad officer was truly the angel of death. Then the full realization of what was happening flashed across the street sweeper's consciousness. The Germans were rounding up *all* Jews, and several SS had jogged off the small piazza down the Bologna—his street.

Suddenly Tommaso understood what it meant to be a Jew in an area controlled by the Reich. For a split second his mind raced over the events of the last few weeks. The president of the community,

Ugo Foà, had insisted that Chief Rabbi Zolli was wrong. The Jews of Rome were safe, especially after they had paid the ransom of three hundred kilos of gold the Germans had demanded. Now this! He and Rebecca had never been active members of the *cheila*, the community. Their grandparents, like many other Jewish families, had moved out of the ghetto after 1870, when the Italians had occupied Rome and repealed the oppressive regulations of the Papal States. But still, the Germans knew. They knew everything, the monk had boasted. He had been right.

Tommaso dropped his broom and tried to run, but he slipped on the greasy cobblestones and slid through a pile of fresh horse manure. He got up and limped on as rapidly as his bad hip would allow. As he rounded the corner where the Bologna twisted, he saw he was too late—two burly SS were disappearing up the stairs to his apartment. As he reached the entrance, he looked up and saw the door open and Rebecca appear. The Germans handed her a card. She looked at it and began to scream. Without thinking, Tommaso lowered his head and charged up the stairs, bad hip and all, into the soldier closer to him. The man fell backward in pain, his steel helmet clattering to the foot of the marble staircase. Tommaso turned on the second Nazi, throwing his full weight behind a looping right to the solar plexus. Caught off guard, the man absorbed the full impact of the blow, lost his balance, and joined the first German's helmet bumping down the stairs, his own steel hat clanging like a klaxon as it bounced alongside him.

Tommaso reached for Rebecca's hand, but he never made contact. A sergeant came down the steps from the apartment above and slammed the butt of his machine pistol against the back of the street sweeper's skull. He crumpled in a heap at his wife's feet. The first two Germans came rushing back up the stairs and started to kick Tommaso's unconscious body, but Rebecca leaped on them like a ferocious mother cat protecting her young. It took the combined strength of the two men to subdue her.

The sergeant stood on the stairs above the melee, his face covered with a large grin. "We have a pair of Hebrew tigers. I had heard the swine were so docile that there was no fun in this sort of work. Bring them both along," he ordered, "but throw some water on that pig first. He smells like horseshit."

228

Meanwhile, Captain Danzig was pounding his fist on the door of the Franciscan convent. Major Priebke climbed slowly out of the staff car and walked halfway up the steps to the convent. Two minutes of Danzig's beating brought no response. He pounded again. Still nothing. "Sergeant," he commanded, "break down the door."

At that point the heavy door swung open, and Danzig tried to enter, but Sister Sacristy was quicker. She thrust herself just outside the opening, anchoring each hip of her cannonball figure against a side of the doorway. Three smaller nuns crowded behind her. "This is God's house, what do you want?" she asked. There was no trace of humility or even deference in her rasp.

"We know you are hiding Jews in here, Sister," Danzig said menacingly. "Stand aside and let us take them out. The penalty for hiding Jews is death, but as good Christians we forgive you this time. Just stand aside."

"This," Sister Sacristy said in the same tone she used before she caned an errant schoolboy, "is a house of prayer. It is God's house. You may not enter."

"Stand aside, Sister," the captain snarled more loudly. "We are going to take those Jews. If you try to stop us, we shall arrest you as well and impose the full punishment for hiding Hebrew scum."

"You may not enter." Sister Sacristy's voice also grew louder and more confident. As a Trasteverina she was now firmly on home ground. The German wanted a shouting contest, and no male, mueh less a foreign male, could compete with a female from Trastevere when it came to shouting. "We are under the Pope's special protection here."

Despite the rain and the early hour, windows were going up all around the piazza and people began to stick their heads out to see and hear better. A few souls, more curious than prudent, even ventured onto the edges of the piazza itself.

"Send for your chaplain, Sister," the captain yelled. "A man will understand what harm you are bringing on yourself by this foolish resistance."

"Our chaplain? Our chaplain?" Sister Sacristy screamed in a derisive tone that burned a layer of skin off the German's eardrums. Lifting her right hand to the level of her lips, she rubbed her thumb and first two fingers together and waved her hand in a small, tight circle, as she continued to shout: *Non rompere le scatole! Via! Via!* Get

229

away from this holy place or the wrath of God and His Pope will turn you into a fat eunuch."

"Screw the Pope!" Danzig howled. "Stand aside, damn it!" With that, a sergeant tried to push the nun out of the way. But her weight was concentrated around a very low center of gravity, and the man succeeded only in rocking her. The three other nuns pushed from the other side, wedging Sister Sacristy even more firmly in the doorway.

"Do not touch me, you sex fiend," she bellowed at the sergeant. "You Germans love to rape nuns; that's why you're trying to break into this holy place." She then played to the larger audience in the windows and on the fringes of the piazza. "But they won't succeed, they won't succeed without killing me first! I promise all you witnesses that. Then the Pope will tell the world about German atrocities."

"I tell you—" Danzig began.

Before he could finish his sentence, Sister Sacristy easily out-shouted him. "Sisters," she called over her shoulder, "it is dawn. We shall recite our morning prayer: 'The angel of the Lord declared unto Mary,'" she began to chant, her harsh tones smashing through the rain to strike like a hammer against the building across the piazza.

"'And she conceived by the Holy Spirit,'" the nuns behind her sang in thin voices.

"'Hail Mary, full of grace, the Lord is with thee. . . .'" Sister Sacristy's decibels rang out, missing each note by the precise margin of half an octave.

The sergeant was enraged. He drew his pistol and started to point it at the nun. Priebke immediately intervened. He clamped his hand firmly on the NCO's arm. "Put your weapon down, Sergeant. That is a command." Then the major turned to Danzig. "Enough, Captain," he called across the din of Sister Sacristy's chants. "We have orders not to use force, yes?"

Danzig trembled in rage as he glared at the bellowing nun, but SS discipline was stronger than his anger, and he began to retreat. At the foot of the steps to the convent, with a dozen yards and a volume of rain to protect his ears from the nun's grating chants, the captain shook his fist and yelled out, "We shall return for those Jewish swine and then we shall take you along, too."

As Danzig shouted, Sister Sacristy was just reaching the second verse of the prayer: " 'Behold the handmaid of the Lord,' " she sang and, without missing a beat of her off-key rendition, made a fat fist, raised her right arm in a slow twisting motion at the German, and, in the best tradition of Trastevere, loudly slapped her biceps.

Fuming in anger and frustration, the captain called out to his troops: "Hold all these people in the piazza. Those without identity cards must be Jews. Arrest them!"

Hidden inside the priest's compartment in the confessional of the convent's chapel, Roberto could see nothing and hear little. He recognized, however, the slamming of the heavy door, the light tread of the younger nuns, and the slow sloshing of Sister Sacristy's large feet as sounds of victory. Nevertheless, he waited inside the cubicle until a nun tapped on the door. "They've gone for now. You may come out. Please wait in one of the pews. Sister Sacristy wants to speak to everyone."

In a few minutes, twenty-three Jews, twelve nuns, and Roberto crowded together in the small chapel. "I have grave news," Sister Sacristy reported. She spoke hesitantly in very bad French. "The attack on us was part of a larger thing. At this moment, the SS are raiding the ghetto and arresting every Jew they can find. As they were trying to break into this house, they were also smashing down doors all over Trastevere and kidnapping Jewish families here."

There was absolute silence. The story was not new to these people. They had survived similar assaults. And, being French, few if any had close friends or relatives on either side of the river.

Sister Sacristy went on: "Our danger may not be over. The Germans could return at any minute. They know you are here. If any of you wishes to go, it would be wise to go quickly. The streets in Trastevere seem clear at the moment, though there are many Germans still in the ghetto."

"Where would we go?" a woman asked.

"I do not know. Father Maria Benedetto might, but I cannot locate him."

"Can we stay, Sister?" The question came from an elderly man.

"You can."

"But, if the Germans return—" another man began.

Sister Sacristy cut him off. "Then the Germans return."

231

"But," the man continued, "they have threatened to take you with us."

Sister Sacristy offered one of the more eloquent Roman shrugs. "Then we go with you. We have pledged our lives to God's service, to live in poverty ourselves while helping the poor. We can serve anywhere. But," she quickly added, "God's service is no excuse for suicide. We must prepare ourselves for their return. The sisters will begin looking through every closet in the convent. I hope that if we work together we will have Franciscan habits for all the women. I will ask the good fathers next door to find habits or pieces of habits that we can sew for the men. Our religious community may soon blossom."

"But the children?" a mother asked.

"Why," Sister Sacristy responded, her open hands cupped in front of her and gently jiggling, "we have begun an orphange for children made homeless by the cruel American bombings of Rome. That, too, is part of our holy work." Her voice shifted gears. "But we shall need your help, the help of all of you. We have much cutting and stitching to do. And we must teach you enough of our ritual so that you can fool an SS officer. It won't be too difficult; he'll probably be a filthy heretic and a *fròcio* besides."

Vatican City, Saturday, 16 October 1943

It was shortly after noon. The rain had stopped and, in one of Rome's frequent miraculous displays, a bright sun turned the sky a brilliant blue. A tall, gaunt, ascetic figure in white, Eugenio Pacelli, Pope Pius XII, looked owlishly through the thick lenses of his metal-rimmed glasses at Giovanni Battista LaTorre, titular archbishop of Bacata, who stood respectfully before him. As he spoke, the Pope turned away and peered intently from the high window of his study toward the southeast, as if he might see something of what was still happening in the ghetto, more than a mile down the twisting Tiber. From that angle he appeared emaciated; his skin, tautly drawn across his facial bones, was almost translucent. His expression showed suffering that only El Greco's black oil could have fully captured. "Is it true, then, *Monsignore?*" he asked.

LaTorre hesitated before he spoke on such a serious and sensitive issue. His superior, the secretary of state, Luigi Cardinal Maglione,

232

was closeted with the German ambassador to the Holy See, but his availability might have made no difference. Where, as here, a problem concerned foreign affairs, it would not have been unusual for any pontiff to have consulted with the undersecretary who routinely handled such matters. But Papa Pacelli habitually dealt directly with many members of the staff of the Secretariat of State. Before his election to the papacy, he had been Pius XI's secretary of state, and he had never really surrendered that office. He preferred, he claimed, to have people execute his decisions rather than collaborate with him in making choices. Yet he constantly sought advice, even guidance.

"Sì, Holiness," LaTorre finally replied. "The SS are arresting Jews all over Rome and taking them away."

"You are absolutely certain?" Pius asked. "The *principessa* telephoned this morning to say so, but are you certain?" Even if one could not have heard the catch in his voice, the magnification of his glasses would have revealed the moistness of his eyes.

"Absolutely, Holiness. We've had warnings from what is left of the German embassy here in Rome, the British, Marshal Kesselring, German clergy in town, and even a few Jews. I have talked to people who are actual witnesses, including a member of my own staff. I have also seen the trucks with my own eyes, Holiness. Several of them got lost and drove to the edge of the Piazza di San Pietro. Even in the rain, they had no canvas; and I could see the women and children huddled up under guard."

"*O Dio, Dio mio,*" Pius moaned. "This brutal war! What further cruelty do we have to bear? Where are they taking these poor souls?"

"For the time being to the *Collègio Militare.*"

"So close to our own presence? So close? They would not allow us not to know of this shameful blot on Germany's honor?"

"So close, Holiness. It is a studied insult."

"What have these people done?"

The Pope's question was rhetorical, but LaTorre answered. "They are Jews, Holiness; and for the Germans that is crime enough."

"Say *Nazis,* not Germans!" Pius snapped. "You know the special affection we feel for Germany and the German people."

The silence was renewed. Pius continued to stare out the window. LaTorre grew uncomfortable physically as well as psychologically. To share the suffering of those made homeless by the war, Papa

Pacelli allowed no heat in his quarters; and the dampness of the two previous days still saturated the large study, making it seem colder than it actually was. Moreover, it was nearly lunchtime, and the archbishop's stomach was reminding him that, like a good Italian, he had breakfasted lightly. LaTorre doubted that *il Papa* knew what a hunger pang was. He seldom showed interest even in the few morsels of bread, cheese, and fruit that Mother Pasqualina periodically set before him.

Eventually, the Pontiff turned from the window and seated himself at his desk. He pressed his temples with the palms of both hands. Suddenly questions poured out in rapid, Roman-accented Italian. "What should we do? What can we do? How many did the Nazis kidnap? Are they being taken care of at the *Collègio Militare*? What will happen to them?"

LaTorre sighed. One of Papa Pacelli's more annoying habits was to go over the same ground again and again, like a patient, if not overly intelligent, detective questioning a suspect. "I can tell you what is going on in the *Collègio*, at least as of half hour ago. I sent Monsignor Carducci there earlier today. He has returned and has dictated this brief memorandum." LaTorre handed the Pontiff a note.

For His Excellency, *Monsignor*, the Substitute: At 10:00 A.M. this day at your order I visited the *Collègio Militare*, where the Germans are bringing Jews from Rome. The SS officers did not allow me to speak to any of the prisoners or to go into the rooms in which they are being held, but I could see enough to make me weep. There is no water and little food. Some families have been separated, parents even from small children. I saw the elderly and the ill without medical attention. I saw one woman holding her newborn infant, begging for help. The baby was too weak to cry. I learned from a physician who was trying unsuccessfully to see her that she had prematurely given birth only two days ago, and the doctor feared that without prompt medical care both mother and child would be dead very shortly. I also saw a car with three physicians from the Hospital of the Holy Spirit turned away by the guards. Last, I saw an SS officer shouting commands in German, which the prisoners obviously did not understand. When they did not obey, the soldiers struck the people, including the women, with their rifle butts and continued to kick them while they lay injured on the ground. I tried to come to their aid, but an SS officer physically restrained me. I thought it best to return immediately, lest I cause a serious diplomatic incident.

234

Pius handed the memorandum back to LaTorre. "What can we say, *Monsignore?* What can we say?"

LaTorre was not about to let up. "Their hell has only begun, Holiness. In the next few days, they will be packed on board freight cars, without food, water, blankets, medicine, or even toilet facilities, and shipped like cattle across the Alps. Finally, they will stop at one of those special camps in Poland about which Monsignor Roncalli in Turkey, the apostolic visitor in Zagreb, and other prelates have written us."

"And then?"

"Then only God can be sure, Holiness, but most likely *finiti. Saranno tutti finiti.*" They will be done for, all of them. "The Nazis will kill them dead."

Pius shuddered. "But how much reliance can we put on these reports of 'death camps'?"

Again the question was rhetorical, but LaTorre thrust his bulk into the opening. "With propaganda, censorship, and the confusions of war, one can be certain of very little, but the evidence is overwhelming. We can discount what the British and the Jews say, but we cannot dismiss the reports of our own diplomats or of local priests who have seen the trains and smelled the burning flesh."

Pius looked away again, but not so quickly as to shield the tears that wet his cheeks. Once more he stared out the window. LaTorre was becoming more and more impatient. Time was ticking away. He had reports of a freight train beginning to form in the marshaling yards near the Tiburtina station. To delay was to decide, for soon there would be no way of stopping the juggernaut; indeed, it might already be too late.

Eugenio Pacelli, however, was a fastidious man, not a person whom even the most urgent events could rush. Neither decisiveness nor firmness in decisions already made was among his virtues. Always and under all circumstances he would proceed in his slow, exasperating way, covering well-traveled paths again and again, hoping perhaps for an angel to waft down from heaven with a solution neatly typed on a note card. He knew the answers, the facts and the deductions that one had to treat as facts, but he had an obsessive need to hear them repeated.

The Pontiff looked over his desk, found some routine papers, then

235

took out a special cloth, cleaned the nib of his pen, dipped it in ink, and very, very carefully attached his signature to two trivial documents. He blotted them with equal care, then again meticulously cleaned the pen's nib with his special cloth. "The point will rust if it isn't cleaned," he explained. A hundred times before, LaTorre had seen this exacting ritual of the birth of a papal signature, and, as often, had heard Papa Pacelli's rationalization of his fetish for a clean pen point.

Pius got up and began to pace the room. "We have long prayed that these reports of deportation to death camps were all bad dreams." He was muttering quietly to himself rather than addressing LaTorre. "But now that it has happened here in Rome, within sight of our window, we can no longer pretend that the evil is not real. It is real. We confess it. But is it enough to confess it? Is that anything at all? How should we react? We shall pray harder, of course. But what official notice shall we take? What steps?" The Pope's voice was pleading, full of self-pity. "What shall we do?"

"*Allora*, we could summon the German ambassador to a private audience and His Holiness could explain how this latest atrocity cuts into a Christian heart. Perhaps the ambassador could personally intervene with Hitler. Or perhaps our own nuncio in Berlin might see Hitler or at least von Ribbentrop."

"Do you think those madmen would listen to reason?"

"I lack faith that any politician listens to reason unless it is directly, immediately, and very obviously linked to his self-interest. But—"

"*Monsignore*," Pius intervened, "we suspect that you are advising us what you think we would like to hear and not what you think we should do. We ask you to let your heart advise us in this moment of our torture."

LaTorre swallowed audibly. "Speak out, Holiness, speak out. Condemn before the world this brutal act and the other brutal acts by which the Nazis are slaughtering a whole people—children, Holiness, children, dying in their mothers' arms."

Papa Pacelli smiled gently. "The children, that bothers you so very deeply—just as it strikes at us. Strange that we should feel so when neither of us has ever been a physical father."

"Perhaps that is why, Holiness."

"Perhaps. Do you have Jewish children at your orphanage?"

LaTorre looked up in surprise, then quickly resumed what he thought was a poker face. "All the children have baptismal certificates, Holy Father."

"We are certain they do, *Monsignore*." Pius smiled again. "Do not forget that we are a Roman. There is scarcely a pastor in Italy who would not readily provide a baptismal certificate for a threatened child. And we commend them for their charity, as we do you for yours. But the way of the priest cannot be the way of the pope."

"Why not, Holiness?"

"Because we are responsible for many flocks and many shepherds, for the entire Church. Private charity is a duty for most men. For us it may be a self-indulgence. There are times when we want to cry out loud and strong; but restraint and silence are imposed on us. Where we would like to act and to assist, it is often patience and prayerful expectation that become imperative."

"Why, Holiness? I do not understand why you feel you must sit in silence while hundreds of thousands, perhaps millions, are being murdered."

"As in the British bombings of German population centers? As in Stalin's slaughter of the Russian Kulaks?"

"Condemn them all, Holy Father."

"We have, *Monsignore*; we have. Last Christmas we spoke of the Jews in our message to the world. We recall our own words, for we chose them with great care, as you yourself remember: 'Humanity owes this vow'—of ceaseless work for a return to the commands of divine law, we said—'to hundreds of thousands of people who through no fault of their own and solely because of their nation or their race have been condemned to death or progressive extinction.' There, *Monsignore*, we spoke clearly of the sufferings of both the Jews and the German civilians."

"But those words were pledges of your own holy work for peace, not condemnations of these frightening sins."

"You are right; that is our way. 'He who has ears to hear, let him hear.'" The Pontiff stopped pacing and stood face to face with LaTorre. "*Monsignore*, we know that you have come to plead with us once again to break our silence. We have had this discussion before. We are not, you see," Pius said, softly reproachful, "the only person in the Vatican who travels the same road twice. Let us ask you what

237

would happen were we to condemn the Nazis. What would their reaction be?"

"We do not know. Perhaps they would change their policies. They backed down on killing mental patients when German clergy protested loudly. After all, almost forty percent of Germans are Catholics."

"And perhaps they would not change. If these reports on which you rely are to be believed, the Nazis are slaughtering the mentally retarded with the same voracity as they are murdering Jews. And these are madmen who are running Germany. For months we have heard reports that they have plans to kidnap our own person, even to designating the man to do it, the same SS officer who rescued Mussolini. And we are not a brave man, *Monsignore*. We know it no less than you. We acknowledge our weakness. Like St. Paul, we wear our failing as a sign of Christ's love. Still, we hope that our silence is not the product of our fear, at least not our fear for ourself. Rather, we hope, it is the product of our fear for the Church."

The Pontiff raised his hand to still LaTorre's rejoinder. "We know the evils of Nazism, not all of them but enough. The Americans are merely stupid and venal, the British sly and murderously vindictive. But even Perfidious Albion seems saintly beside the specter of Nazism. Nevertheless, the greatest evil of all is Soviet communism, bolshevism. 'To be in awe of the Lord—that is wisdom, and to avoid evil—that is understanding,' as the Book of Job says. Because we understand the greater evil, bolshevism, we tolerate the lesser evil, Nazism."

"Both bolshevism and Nazism are sworn enemies of the Church, Holiness—"

"True," Pius interrupted, "but communism is the more dangerous, the more insidious because it is the more alluring temptation. As an ideology, Nazism can only appeal to a limited group of people who are already half depraved. Communism, on the other hand, is a universal though false religion, spreading its lies to all mankind. Nazism is a highly selective disease that threatens only the morally defective; communism is a deadly plague to which few may be immune. More immediately, communism poses a graver threat to the Church. We agree Nazism is also a menace. But for now, the Nazis need at least our passivity, our silence. We may become stronger before they can directly launch their final assault on us. The Communists, however, would attack and destroy us at once. And they are more efficient; they have already honed their skills in Russia."

"But, Holiness—"

"If we speak out against these atrocities, the initial result would probably be our own kidnapping; persecution of the Church would follow swiftly and surely. And the Jews? Would a regime that physically attacked our person hesitate to invade the sanctuaries where Jews are hiding? Would such a regime slow its system of death because we, another of its victims, protested? No, *Monsignore*. This is a courage we cannot indulge ourself. We would harm the Church and also make it worse for the Jews. We would fill vacant places in the camps with Catholics. Furthermore, if our message were heard among the German people and their armed forces—and we cannot be certain that it would—we would succeed only in weakening Europe's sole bastion against communism."

Pius paused to catch his breath, then continued. "A shrewd diplomat, *Monsignore*, always keeps his eye on the main objective. The Jews of Europe are the price of stopping communism. We cannot save them. It is beyond our power. We weep with them in their time of sorrow. We pray that their deaths will serve a worthwhile end."

"But, Holy Father"—LaTorre's eyes flashed back fire—"nothing could be worse than for the Jews to be slaughtered before an uncaring, silent world. Nothing could be worse for the promise you carry than to watch murder in fearful silence. You speak as if you were powerless. But you are armed with Christ's command to preach His word and also His Promise: 'Thou art Peter . . . and the Gates of Hell shall not prevail against you.' You may die, I may die, but Peter's legacy will live, just as the Church will live, even as Christ lives. Whatever the immediate pain, your speaking the Gospel and trusting in Christ's promise will be a beacon to the world, now and forever, a sign of God's living with us in truth and love, in compassion. Your sacrifice—"

"Our sacrifice? It is easy to speak of the sacrifice of others. You are young. You imagine a glorious hero leading the Church. Look at us, *Monsignore*, look at us. What do you see? A timid old man. Boldness and glory are drained from our body. We have only prudence left— prudence to save not ourself but the Church. Do not speak to us of sacrifice."

"But you speak of sacrifice, Holiness; you preach sacrifice to others —to priests who wish to leave the clergy and find solace in marriage for their loneliness, to young married couples to abstain from making love if they do not wish more children, to other couples whose lives together have become a torture to continue in marriage rather than divorce. You preach sacrifice because our religion demands sacrifice as essential to salvation. Can you, who once took the red hat of a cardinal as a reminder that you must be willing to shed your blood for Christ, now avoid risking sacrifice?"

Pius sighed deeply. "You are indeed young, *Monsignore,* and we say that with envy. You make the ancient cry: *'Fiat justitia, ruat coelum.'* Let justice be done though the heavens fall. Yes, we can avoid risking sacrifice. Just as we are the successor of Peter rather than of John the Baptist, so too we sit in Peter's chair, not Don Quixote's."

LaTorre was close to tears. "But, Holiness, if we have faith in Christ's promise, communism shall not prevail against us any more than Nazism."

"With deepest regret, *Monsignore,* we must remind you that the Sacred College of Cardinals, under the guidance of the Holy Spirit, elected Eugenio Pacelli as Bishop of Rome, not Giovanni Battista LaTorre—though with all our heart we wish that He had let this cup pass from us. And, while we are quoting scripture, let us also remember that it is written 'thou shalt not tempt the Lord thy God.' Men are weak; original sin has weakened their wills and darkened their intellects. Some lay people can withstand temptation, a few can meet persecution. But the number of souls that would be lost is enormous."

The Pontiff stopped speaking. He began to riffle through several sets of papers on his desk. LaTorre did not move. Finally Pius looked up and said very softly, "If we thought that our speaking out would save the Jews without opening the gates to communism, we would speak. One part of us fears martyrdom, another part of us welcomes it. But we do not read the risks as you do. *Allora,* we have thought much about the problem, and it is our solemn conviction that the only way to help all the poor souls who are suffering during this war —and will suffer afterwards—is by prayer and by quiet, patient, tireless diplomatic negotiation, not by open denunciation, however satisfying that would be to our personal conscience."

240

LaTorre was silent. Pius went on: "Please take this matter up immediately with the German ambassador and inform him of our grave concern, our deep personal sorrow."

LaTorre walked toward the door. Then he hesitated. "Holiness," he asked, "if the Nazis win, who will speak for the Catholics when they are marched to the death camps?"

Pius turned and once more stared out the window, his signal that the audience, like the Jewish community in Rome, was finished.

Vatican City, Saturday, 16 October 1943

When LaTorre returned to his office, he carefully closed the door and sat down at his desk. He laid his head on the blotter and wept. Ten minutes later, Ugo Galeotti came in without bothering to knock. LaTorre recognized the footsteps, but he did not look up for several moments, not until Galeotti had gently patted his friend's arm. "I tried, Ugo; I tried. Poor tortured soul, he is so piously lacking in confidence in himself and faith in God that he consistently mistakes timidity for prudence. He would like to be a martyr, but he's afraid of the nails."

"Unless there is present a question of sexual morality," Galeotti mused. "Too bad the Germans are not merely using Jewish women as prostitutes, then His Holiness would thunder at them."

LaTorre looked coldly at his colleague. "They are, they are; but, unfortunately, not 'merely.' The young and lovely are sometimes subjected to a purgatory of a few months of prostitution, entertaining German troops before the hell of the death camps."

"He knows that, too?"

"The information has crossed his desk. Who can say what he 'knows'? He is human, after all; and, as with the rest of us, his knowledge is a selective thing. *Ecco*, Ugo, I am beaten, totally defeated. In his mind, it is all so easy. He is a true diplomat; he does nothing, he risks nothing, except the lives of others and his own immortal soul."

"*Allora*, join me at lunch," Galeotti offered. "It will cheer you up. I'm eating at the German College as the guest of our Augustinian monk."

"I didn't think you approved of his activities."

241

"I do not approve, but I look on him as a lost sheep whom we might return to the true fold. Today I may put him to the test and reveal to him the dark secret that Christ was a Jew."

LaTorre did not laugh.

"And, he might be able to assist the situation here in Rome through his contacts with the German armed forces. Why not join us? The college also possesses some superb wine from the Rheingau."

"No, thank you. I have too much work to do. I shall have something sent to my desk. I doubt if the monk or anyone other than *il Papa* can do anything at this stage, and he may be right that even he is powerless to help the Jews of Rome. The German wheels are rolling; it is next to impossible to stop them. Besides," LaTorre added bitterly, "I saw too many Teutonic faces this morning guarding the Jews in the trucks. One more and I might lose my appetite or my temper."

The Augustinian and Galeotti seated themselves at the far end of the long refectory table, slightly removed from the polyglot murmur of voices from the other clergy. During the silence of grace, the *monsignore* looked around the room with wry amusement. Here he himself sat next to a German spy clothed in the proper black robes of an Augustinian. About ten plates down was Fitzpàdraig Cathal Sullivan, S.J., the American spy, next to his guest, a French Capuchin named Marie-Benoit, whom the Italians called Maria Benedetto, *il Padre degli Ebrei*, the priest of the Jews. His entrepreneurial imagination and burglar's coolness were responsible for hundreds, perhaps thousands, of foreign Jews' being safely hidden around Rome. His headquarters were in a monastery on the Via Sicilia, but he was a frequent visitor to the Vatican, where he continually if unsuccessfully sought aid for his people. Farther down the long table, Msgr. Hugh O'Flaherty of the Holy Office was lunching alone. The huge Irish theologian was the resident British secret agent in the Vatican; his principal task was to help hide escaping Allied airmen and smuggle them south.

"*Se Cristo vedesse*"—If Christ could see it—was the prewar Italian joke about the SCV on the license plates of Vatican vehicles. Here at this table, the joke lacked humor. Obviously, the Vatican had

242

become a den of spies, if not of thieves, each struggling to help his country fight brutally to win a just war.

"I have heard, *Monsignore*, of this morning's *Judenaktion*." The Augustinian's usual cynical tone was absent. "I wanted you to know that I do not approve of it, and that many Germans around Rome tried to prevent it."

"Understood, understood," Galeotti noted.

"Poor devils, they will be treated little better than animals."

"If they are fortunate."

"The trip to Germany will be difficult. Then they will spend months, perhaps years, doing hard, manual labor. I suppose that the physical activity will be good for them. Jews are like shopkeepers everywhere, they tend to be soft and overweight. And, I suppose, some suffering is functional for the soul. Still, one hates to think of lives disrupted, families separated."

"Lives disrupted? Families separated? I pray you, do not deceive yourself," Galeotti said heavily as he poured himself a second glass of wine. He sipped the liquid, holding it on his palate for several seconds before swallowing. "We, all and two, know where they are going and what their fate will be."

"Yes, to a labor camp, where they will work for the Reich's eventual victory. If, *Monsignore*, these people had only listened to the Gospel, the good news of Jesus Christ, they would not now be in this unpleasant predicament."

"*Senta*, I have fear that the only 'good news' from a Christian source these people will ever hear is that their deaths will be mercifully rapid. They are lambs going to slaughter."

"Do not exaggerate, my friend. You Italians dramatize everything. These people are going to a labor camp to work, not to die. Conditions will be primitive, discipline harsh, but no worse—probably far better—than for soldiers in combat."

"*Ecco*, they are going to a death camp, to be gassed, then their bodies burned."

"Nonsense, *Monsignore*, nonsense. Do not believe British propaganda."

"I believe reports from Germans, from trainmen who carry the Jews to Poland and bring back the poor souls' coats, underwear, and

243

hair; from Red Cross workers who give them a bit of food and water on their way to the camps but never see any Jews leave; from peasants who smell the thick, sweet odor of burning human flesh; from military men whose nightmares never stop. I believe in stories said by escapees, by priests and bishops in the Balkans and in Poland. I believe in reality, not in patriotic myths, whether Italian, British, or German."

"That must be the wine talking, *Monsignore*. Forgive me, but I cannot believe that a man of your sophistication would accept such foolishness."

"Foolishness? Nonsense? *Allora*, let us take ourselves to my office. There I shall show you the reports of which I speak. You shall know the truth, though it would be lacking in sensitivity to predict that this truth will set you or anyone else free." Galeotti stood, quaffed a third glass of wine as he slipped a piece of sausage into his pocket, and led the way back to the papal palace.

The Augustinian paced slowly as he read the documents in Galeotti's office. An hour later he put them down and half-collapsed in an easy chair across from the *monsignore*'s desk. For a few minutes he said nothing; then he began a barrage of words in German. "I cannot believe it, I cannot believe it. Raids like this one in Rome are taking place all over Europe—trains loaded with people, first mass shootings, then gassing by truck exhausts, now huge chambers and crematoria. It is so organized, so systematic."

"So German," Galeotti noted softly.

"It is inadmissible. I cannot accept it. We are speaking of hundreds of thousands of people—women, infants, old people, even converts; good God, even priests who have Jewish ancestors—all being erased like chalk marks from a blackboard. I am not a wishy-washy man. I favor putting obstinate Jews who will not accept Christ in separate areas of cities so they do not contaminate honest people. I also support making them wear their ugly yellow star so that Christians will know with whom they are dealing. But to kill them as if they were insects? That is barbaric! Especially the children; some of them might later be converted."

Galeotti could think of nothing to say to the dapper little monk. He merely leaned back in his chair, closed his eyes, and tried to pray for the German's soul. It was not a task that came easily to him.

244

Finally the monk asked, "Did you know that in the Great War, I fought in the trenches?"

"No."

"I tried to explain to our American friend why that makes me love my country. He smiled in his usual amiable way, but I do not think he understood. Do all Americans smile like that, *Monsignore*?"

"I think so. It is not the worst of faults."

"No, it is not. But if I cannot explain why I love my country, can I explain why I despise Jews?"

"For a Christian it should be easier to explain love than hate."

"Alas, the two are equally real, and I fear hate is the stronger. I was a front-line soldier. I was called up when I was barely seventeen. I was wounded during our last offensive in March 1918. We had swept close to Paris, at the Marne, when I was hit. I rejoined my unit two months later; by then we were back in Flanders again. We were losing, but we were still a magnificent machine. Some units were breaking, not ours. Our morale was high and we loved each other. You don't know—you cannot know—the comradeship of men who have shared the fear and filfth of war in the trenches. We were brothers. Education, wealth, family—none of those things was important. All that mattered was whether a man would stay awake when it was his turn on watch, stand and fight when the Tommies or poilus came, and risk his neck to rescue you if you got hit. Because we loved each other, we loved Germany. We knew our cause was just.

"When it was over in November, we cried—not like simpering babies, but like men who suddenly realized that they had been betrayed. Our lives had been wasted; our friends were dead, and our wounds ached. We were ready to fight on, but Germany had been betrayed."

"Do you believe that, truly believe that now?"

"The point is that we believed it then. When we heard the news of the armistice we were in reserve in a little French village near the Belgian border. We were shipped back home, spared, we thought, the ignominy of laying down our arms before the enemy. But there was a greater indignity waiting for us, the ultimate humiliation. When we got off the train in Germany, in Trier, we were attacked by a mob of Communist rabble. They shouted vile names at us, threw stones at us, and tried to tear off our badges and medals. They killed one of my comrades, a man—*der Älte*, we kids called him because he was all of thirty and had a wife and three children. He also had too much shrapnel in his leg to move fast enough to avoid a big paving brick. Then we fought back and beat the scum off with rifle butts; we even bayoneted a few. But routing them was no victory. The whole incident confirmed our belief that we had been betrayed. Now we knew by whom—Communists and Jews."

"Jews?"

"Jews. The mob was made up of Jews. I looked at the faces of those *Untermenschen* who were attacking us, and I saw they were not Germans at all, but Jews."

"How could you tell that?"

"In Germany one can tell. I could tell."

"And now, do you think the same thing?"

"I am trying to explain how I came to feel as I do about Jews and about Germany. I fear I am not doing a good job."

"*D'accordo*, it is not a simple thing. Perhaps it would be more fruitful to try to explain what you feel now, as a mature priest."

"That is my point, *Monsignore*. That young boy's experiences in the trenches are still part of the middle-aged priest, as is the trauma of those ugly, howling faces tearing at us. When I see a Jew, I see that mob. I wipe spittle from my face. I see a dead comrade. It is a chemical, not an intellectual, reaction."

"That is an answer we have both often heard in the confessional in other contexts."

"Do you not think I realize that? It means that I, too, am a human being who can love and hate and sin. I am no different from the laymen who implore me to impart God's forgiveness. I hate exactly as they do. And I understand what has driven their hatred against the Jews."

"You understand, that is good; but you do not try to harm these Jews, to gas them, to burn their bodies in huge ovens."

"I have lacked the opportunity, *Monsignore*. I am not innocent; I simply have missed the occasion of sin. For that I can take no credit."

The monk stood up and began pacing again. "How much can I trust these documents you have shown me?"

246

"*Abbastanza.*"

"Enough? If they speak the truth, why has His Holiness not shouted out condemnations before God and man?"

Galeotti shrugged. "His Holiness also knows the truth about the English bombing German civilians. It requires a true neutral to witness in silence each side's atrocities."

"What would you have me do, *Monsignore*? Go to Pacelli and plead with him to speak out?"

"That would be of little help. Others have tried and failed."

"What then?"

"I do not know. You might try to ask your countrymen to stop their deportation of the Roman Jews."

"I do not know if I can do that, and if I could, I doubt it would make any difference. I am not even certain that I can accept what I have read here. It is somewhat like discovering that your mother is a prostitute and at the same time realizing that you yourself may have been one of her pimps. I do not think I am quite ready to accept that news."

"*Ecco*, denial is a very human reaction."

"Yes, it is."

Again there was a long period of silence. "I must go," the Augustinian said at last. "I have many things to do."

"I am secure that you do." Galeotti nodded curtly. "Alas, I cannot wish you or any other German to go in peace. It is not a charitable thing to withhold such a wish, but all my Italian soul today rages against everything German."

"Except perhaps our wine," the monk put in, trying to smile.

"*Sì*, except your wine." Galeotti's tone softened. "But that is not a thinking thing that establishes itself as the judge of who is worthy of God's free gift of life. Perhaps as a penance for your nation, you should go to the *Collègio Militare* this afternoon and offer Christian solace to those poor souls whom you would segregate and make wear badges. According to me, it might do great good for your own soul."

Rome, Saturday, 16 October 1943

"Thank you for seeing me so promptly, Colonel," the Augustinian monk said as he sat down in Gratz's office in the Minister's House

247

on the grounds of the Villa Wolkonsky. His usually jaunty air was replaced by a funereal solemnity.

Gratz waved his hand aimlessly. "It is always my pleasure to see you, *Herr Pater*—and often my profit. And there has been damned little profit these last few days."

"Yes, I know. One cannot help feeling pity for those poor Jews."

"I was not thinking about them. But," Gratz admitted, "they also seem to be having their share of troubles."

"I have come to ask you a favor."

"If it is within my power, you have only to name it."

"Intervene with Lieutenant Colonel Olendorf and ask him to release the Jews. You are his superior in rank; he will have to listen to you. If he cannot release them, he can at least keep them in Italy. We must need them to dig trenches or carry stretchers. Marshal Kesselring has said we do."

"Yes, Marshal Kesselring claimed we do, and he was not alone. You must know something of the maneuverings within the German community here in Rome to stop the deportations. What is left of the embassy staff also said that it would be a mistake to deport the Roman Jews. Even Olendorf requested that we not act. Unfortunately, Heinrich Himmler, Ernst Kaltenbrunner, or one of their deputies took the matter out of Olendorf's hands. Berlin sent an SS captain named Danzig to take charge of the *Judenaktion*. When that happened, Kesselring backed down, the embassy backed down, and I can assure you that a certain colonel in the Abwehr also backed down."

"Is there nothing then that you can do?"

"Do? What could I do, *Herr Pater*? We confront a system. Der Fuehrer wants Jews to go to labor camps, and the SS have created an efficient organization to make sure that Jews go where der Fuehrer wants them to go. Anyone who opposes der Fuehrer's policy too loudly or too strenuously joins the Jews in the labor camps. The Americans have an expression, 'You can't fight city hall.' This is much more than 'city hall'; it is the whole Nazi party with all its armed might. As you probably know, Bishop Hudal and several other German clergy in town signed a letter to General Mueller asking him not to deport the Roman Jews. They went further than I would have dared go; but, of course, they may not know what I know."

248

"And what is it that you know, Colonel? A short time ago you spoke to me about labor camps for Jews and today you use the same expression. Do you really believe that is where these people are being shipped?"

Gratz looked away from the monk and searched around his desk for a pair of cigars, then offered one to the priest. The Augustinian shook his head. The colonel took a few minutes to prepare and light his, then he blew a large smoke ring. "The expression 'up in smoke' is widely used by Germans these days. You have heard it, *Herr Pater?*"

The monk nodded.

"That should tell you something."

"Only that the British have been fire bombing our cities."

Gratz grunted. "Really? Well, then, in the same fashion, I do not know where these people are going. But, if you want a candid answer: I am afraid to probe behind the official explanation of labor camps. I fear what I would find. The order that Himmler sent here to Rome a few weeks ago used the term 'liquidation' to describe the Jews' fate. Obviously it was a slip, but it may have been a slip that revealed the truth. What good would it do for me to know? I could not stop it from happening."

The monk stood up and walked toward the window overlooking the villa's magnificent gardens. "I spent part of the early afternoon reading documents in the Vatican. Something like scales fell from my eyes. Those reports reveal an ulcer—death camps festering on the German soul. It is a horror that is both nameless and ineffable."

Gratz blew another smoke ring. He watched it dance slowly across the room. "Sit down, *Herr Pater.* You have known for a long time that the SS were not nice people. And to handle the Jewish problem they have formed special cadres, men—and women—chosen for ruthlessness, even sadism. It is a disgrace to German honor. But the Jews are not the only ones suffering in this war. What about the German civilians who are murdered by British raids on population centers? Your own family?"

The monk was not listening. He began to pace around the room. "Colonel, I need to talk to you, to a fellow German, an informed, intelligent man who loves his country as I do. How can we permit it? How can we?"

249

"How can we permit it? How can we stop it? I see very few alternatives. You and I and a few hundred others could try an armed revolt. We would be gunned down in minutes—if we were fortunate. Or we could try to escape to the West and tell what we know. But why bother? They already know, probably in greater detail than you and I. The British are not anxious to save the Jews. I *know* that some corrupt SS have offered to let the British ransom Jews, but the British are not interested. They want no more Jews in England, and shipping them to the Near East would complicate relations with the Arabs. The Americans do not care either. They have more than enough Jews of their own. The Russians' only objection to what the Nazis are doing to the Hebrews is that they are not in on the fun."

"The Swiss? They are neutrals, they would care. They could make the whole program public and that would force the Nazis to stop it."

"The Swiss?" Gratz laughed out loud. "The Swiss government has instructed its police to refuse entry to any Jew trying to escape from the Nazis. They are not to be given political asylum, but turned back. The humanity of the Swiss has more holes than their cheese."

Gratz paused to tap the ash from his cigar. "There is yet another alternative," he continued. "It is even less promising. We could make a silent protest and join the Jews in their boxcar ride to death. That alternative not only means death, it means a death with no meaning. If what you and I fear is true, the SS are killing on such a wholesale basis that one individual's death has no more significance than a bar of soap. Martyrdom has lost its meaning to this world."

"To this world, yes; but to God?" the monk mused.

"God comes under your jurisdiction, *Herr Pater*, not mine."

"You are right, God is my business; so, I suppose, are moral questions my business. Our society insists on a division of labor that is both rigid and fine. I have no right to impose my troubles on you. But tell me, Colonel, strictly for my own information, do you think we are fighting a just war?"

Gratz snuffed out his cigar and leaned back in his chair. "A just war? Justice is not a common word in a soldier's vocabulary. Obedience, duty, responsibility—those are the words a soldier understands."

"Pity."

"Perhaps, perhaps. Look, I am not a Nazi; I never have been and

I never intend to be. I am a German officer, the son of a German officer, and the grandson of a German officer. The profession of arms is an honorable one. I justify my role in this war by reminding myself that I am a member of an honorable profession who conducts himself according to that profession's honorable rules. I do not torture prisoners; I do not make war on civilians by fire bombing women and children."

"That is enough if the cause is just."

"There is more, much more. I also justify my role by looking at our enemies: the Communists, murdering, godless swine who would destroy this planet; the British, always slyly maneuvering to rape other countries like India, Ireland, Burma, or the whole continent of Africa, while they piously proclaim only the purest of motives. Their fire bombings are the real atrocities of this war, though I have no doubt that eventually the Russians will find some way of outdoing their ally. The Americans are only naïve, blundering amateurs. They are as full of selfish evil as the rest of us, only they are too self-righteous to admit it even to themselves. Look how they bomb Rome. They say they do it in daylight to be more accurate and hit only military targets. It might be safer for the civilians if the bombardiers aimed at apartment houses. I would rather fight the English. They are rational in their evil. We can always tell where they think casualties are going to be the heaviest: where they put their colonial troops, the Australians, Canadians, or Indians. The Americans are stupid, and in a war a fool can be a more dangerous enemy than a rational man, for nobody can predict what a fool will do. So, *Herr Pater*, when I look at our enemies, the SS's blot on German honor does not seem so terrible."

"I envy you your ability to see things in such a broad perspective."

"Do not envy me. Each of us seeks his own rationalization for not committing suicide. You clerics have constructed a hell in the next world to frighten us. You have wasted your time; you need only have looked carefully at the mad world we live in. The real hell is right here. And someone is stoking the fires under my part of it."

"What has been happening?"

It was evident from the monk's tone that he would have preferred silence to an answer, but Gratz spoke. "Our operation has run aground. You reported that Raven had disappeared. I hoped that was a good sign. Apparently it was not. I have received very explicit—and agitated—instructions from Admiral Canaris himself to back off the whole operation."

"Too bad. You—whatever you were doing—put much energy into it."

"It is much more than a personal disappointment. We had an opportunity to win a great victory for Germany. I fear that chance is vanishing."

"That is too bad."

"Yes, and it will be too bad for thousands of young German soldiers and sailors. Well, we should worry only about what we can control or influence. What has your colleague Father Christmas been doing?"

"As far as I can tell, nothing out of the ordinary, although he and the diplomat Stransky have frequently been together—sometimes arguing."

"It is gratifying to know that our enemies share some of our misery. What is going on at Anna's apartment? Anything more on that man who has moved in?"

"I am afraid," the monk replied, "I shall not have more news about Anna's apartment until I can find a new agent. My man was picked up by the SS. I never realized he was Jewish."

"In Italy," Gratz said humorlessly, "one can never tell unless the Jew has a name like Levi. All these people look alike. But are you certain?"

"On the way here, I stopped at the *Collègio Militare*. I saw his name on the list of those going to the 'labor camp.' "

"A name may not mean anything. Almost every Jew in Rome has one of twenty last names. Dozens of them have the same baptismal—I mean given—and last names. Have you ever walked through the ghetto and looked at the nameplates on the doors?"

"I have never cared to have any close contacts with those people unless it was absolutely necessary. I do not approve of murdering them, but neither do I associate with them."

"I understand. I do not like them either—an untrustworthy group. But it is ironic, your man, a very useful German agent, is probably awaiting shipment to a slaughtering pen, not because he did not perform well—no, not at all. He is being erased because of his race. It is

252

unfortunate that we cannot sanitize him, de-race him. I told you we live in a mad world, even madder when you realize that the president of the local Jewish community was a leading Fascist, a worshipper of our glorious ally, Mussolini. This insane asylum is far beyond the ken of a poor colonel—who soon may be much poorer. I have heard an owl screech in the gardens here."

"Do not talk like a superstitious peasant."

"Superstitious or not, I have a premonition that our work here is about to blow up in our faces."

"Our faces?" The Augustinian looked at Gratz quizzically. "I never knew what was going on, not really."

"All the better for you. The less you know, the less difficult decisions are." He broke off abruptly. "I suggest you get inside the *Collègio Militare* and make certain that it is your man who is in there. If it is, you might telephone Lieutenant Colonel Olendorf and explain the situation. It is largely out of his hands now, but he might be able to intervene with Danzig. I would offer to step in, but a request from the Abwehr might ensure your man's getting a different kind of special treatment."

"You are the second person today who has suggested that I go inside the *Collègio*. I tried; but," the monk said slowly, "when I went, I could not muster the courage to go beyond the office the SS set up at the entrance. I am not sure they would have let me go in, and I am even less sure I would have had the courage to go in if they had let me."

"I understand, but your agent is a valuable piece of property. Try again."

The Augustinian did not try again. Instead, he went back to his room at the German College.

Vatican City, Saturday, 16 October 1943

At 4:00 P.M., while Vatican diplomats and the German ambassador were exchanging laments over the arrest of the Jews of Rome, Paul Stransky received a note from the Institute for Religious Works that his account had been credited with $250,000. He swiftly walked to the other side of the enclave where the institute was located and asked for the money in cash. The director, a bishop who had grown up in Sicily, was accustomed to dealing with men who preferred their money in that form. Still, it took him the better part of an hour to round

253

up enough greenbacks, and it was not until 5:30 that Stransky started to return to his office.

On his way, he stopped at the train station to alert Father Christmas to begin his part of the final phase of the operation. The priest was hard at work, unusual for a late Saturday afternoon. He was polite but cool and offered Stransky neither coffee nor company. He did, however, promise to do his best to set up the exchange for the following morning.

Like the Augustinian, F.C. was hampered by the loss of Tommaso Piperno. Unlike his German counterpart, however, the American had contacts among Italian clergy in Trastevere, and they had strings to several other sources of information about the neighborhood. Nevertheless, he decided to handle part of the mission himself. Anna would see his face, but Roberto already knew him and could point him out to the Gestapo as easily as could Anna. In any event, the Gestapo's efficiency meant that he was soon going to have to stay within Vatican City or perhaps return to New York. Thus, the small immediate risk to his safety was worth the advantage of being personally in command.

At 7:00 P.M., an hour before Roman doors had to be locked and most Italians off the streets, F.C. put his diplomatic passport from the Vatican in his pocket and left the Piazza of St. Peter. He walked briskly up the Via della Conciliazione, crossed the river, entered a maze of streets that emptied into the Via dei Coronari, and made his way toward the Piazza Navona and the Remus.

Then, for the first time, he saw Anna. Even after decades of discipline, F.C. could feel the twinge of a hormonal surge. The hardness of her face made it impossible to apply any of the usual feminine adjectives such as lovely, beautiful, or pretty; but she wore a coarse, pulsing sexuality with the same relaxed obviousness as saints wore their halos in Renaissance paintings.

The Jesuit walked directly to the cash register. "*Senta, signorina,*" he began in polite Italian fashion, "your Uncle Antonio said that you had some excellent old portraits for sale."

"Antonio?" she looked at him blankly.

"Yes, I met his nephew, your cousin, I believe, at the Regina Coeli. There was some small misunderstanding with the police."

"So?"

"So, I have talked to my own uncle and he agrees we should be in-

254

terested. But first he would like me to inspect these portraits. With the war, you know, there are many forgeries in circulation. We have to protect ourselves."

"Antonio" had triggered Anna's recollection of Roberto's description of his contact in the Vatican, but she kept her expression as empty as she could. "Not possible. To see these things is to learn their secrets. If I show them to you, I would be giving them away; and in my profession, one sells, one does not give."

F.C. stopped. He was unsure how far he could push. He glanced around at the dining room, half full of German officers, and decided that he had no leverage here. Besides, Washington had indicated no interest in haggling over price. He dropped his voice so that it was at a confessional whisper. "All right. Are you under surveillance?"

"I don't think so."

"Then who's the man staying in your apartment?"

"A guest, a client, if it's any of your business."

"It is very much my business if you and I are not to share a cell in some Gestapo headquarters."

"For you it might be worth it."

F.C. ignored her sally. "Where's Roberto? Our people haven't seen him in several days."

"I don't know. The last I saw of him was a week ago; he was going to see you."

"I saw him then, but not since." Like a good Jesuit, he provided the truth only in closely metered doses. "Is it possible the Gestapo have him?"

"Possible, but not likely. You and I are still free. Of what importance is he? You have the money; I have the film. I want the money; you want the film. We exchange."

"And Roberto? Nothing for him?"

"He's had a great deal. He will treasure those nights in my apartment more than money. You forget he's half Italian. You Americans are too materialistic. What's between Roberto and me is our affair, none of yours. You supply the money. I need neither questions nor advice."

"All right, tomorrow morning—someone will telephone you. Follow the directions. You'll receive additional instructions along the way. Make sure you have the film. We won't risk setting up two meetings.

And don't try to tip the Gestapo. You'll be watched, and so will the place for the exchange. The watchers will be armed."

Anna nodded. "And what assurance do I have that someone won't stick one of those guns in my face and take the film?"

"The same assurance we have that the film is genuine. We have to trust one another."

"*Mèrda!* What intelligent person would trust a priest?"

"A quarter of a million dollars is a great deal of money; we're gambling with that and with our lives. That requires mutual trust. You can sell us to the Gestapo, we can sell you to our friends in the resistance. If they realized what you were doing, they'd slit your throat."

"For the money, only for the money."

"You'd be as dead from greed as from patriotism. That's our offer. Take it or we use the money to corrupt a German officer. We have a line on several who are reachable."

"*Va bene.* I'll wait for your call."

"Do that; and keep in mind what I said about our mutual friends."

As F.C. was leaving the restaurant. Col. Manfred Gratz came in. The two men confronted each other in the entryway. Gratz started to push forward, then noticed the black cassock. "*Prego, prego,*" he mumbled, and took a half step backward.

Sullivan was quicker to recognize whom he was facing. "*Prego, prego,*" he echoed, gave the German a smile, and stood aside for him to enter.

At that point the pictures in Gratz's mind slid into focus, and he recognized the American. "Would you join me in a bite of supper, *Herr Geistlicher?*" he asked in German. "Two strangers might enjoy a meal together 'in the country where the lemon grows.' We would have much to discuss."

"Companionship is always pleasant where 'the golden orange glows,'" F.C. tossed Goethe back at Gratz, "but, alas, I have work to-night. *Buon' appetito,*" he added in an abrupt switch to Italian.

"*Grazie ed arrivederLa.*" Gratz bowed.

"Perhaps. Let us hope so, my son."

"We will meet again," the colonel whispered to himself. "We will meet when Rigoletto is finished and your 'protection' ended." Then

256

Gratz turned and went into the restaurant; he stopped at the cash register and tested Anna. "Do you have anything to report?"

"First I need more money. You're already late with your payment."

Gratz went through elaborate motions in taking off his overcoat, put his gloves in the coat pocket, and laid his cap on the counter. Deftly, Anna slipped her hand under the cap and extracted a packet of bills. "There is nothing here that feels like a passport," she complained.

"Not yet."

"When?"

"When the arrangements have been completed."

"When will that be?"

"I cannot be certain. A slight delay at the top—a day or two, not more. Raven is the main problem. Do you have any information at all about him?"

"Nothing."

"I do not like that. What more do you know? Is there anything happening here or in Trastevere that we should be aware of?"

"You saw the American priest."

"Yes. Is he Father Christmas?"

"I think so. He wants the film. I told him he'd have to wait."

"Good. He is trying to work through you without paying us. He may not know about our larger arrangements. Do not let him have the film until I tell you."

Anna nodded.

"Is there anything else to report?"

"Nothing."

"Nothing at all? Not even in your personal life?"

"Personal life?" Anna raised her eyebrows. "My personal life is none of your business, but I have an old friend from Bressanone staying with me."

"Get rid of him in the morning—early. He may frighten Raven away."

"I can't. He's a deserter from the brave army of the Italian Social Republic. He's on the run."

"That is his problem. Get rid of him tomorrow before eight. Raven is more important."

"Why care about Raven? I have the film, and the Americans are in direct contact with me now. Maybe they've given up on Raven. Why shouldn't we?"

"You may have a point," Gratz mused. He stopped for a moment to think. "I suppose," he went on, "that you are planning to sell the American the film that we are paying you to deliver?"

Anna said nothing, just stared at him blankly.

"It fits. If the priest and his friends know you, they will not trust you unless they see you trying to cheat both sides." She lifted her chin but said nothing. "Have the Gestapo been nosing around?" he asked.

"Not that I know of; if they were, it's likely that I'd know. They are not noted for subtlety."

"Let me remind you that the Abwehr *is* noted for subtlety—and for a long memory. It is not, however, noted for tolerance of betrayal. Whatever schemes are going through your lovely head, Anna, do not put yourself between the Gestapo and the Abwehr in a power struggle."

"I want no games, Colonel. Give me a passport and the rest of my money and I shall deliver the film to Raven or Father Christmas or to the Pope himself."

"My grandfather used to say," Gratz continued, " 'Greed killed the wolf.' "

Anna looked at him without blinking. "I'm for sale, Colonel, everything I have, everything I am, everything I can do. That's good capitalist business; whether it's also greed, I leave to moralists. May I show you to a table?"

"No, thank you. I do not have much appetite tonight, and I still have much work to do. One other piece of advice: Do not rely on the SS to help you if things turn sour. Rescuing damsels in distress is not in their operations manual."

A few minutes later, Anna picked up the telephone and quietly relayed the priest's instructions to Olendorf, warning him that she would be given several sets of instructions and would be under surveillance. "Prudent," he commented. "The man is very careful. We shall keep away. But, *Liebchen,* do not try to escape from us. You would not get far."

"Gratz promised me a Swiss passport and some money when this operation was done."

258

"Gratz cannot deliver on either his promises or his threats. I can deliver on both. If you are the special friend of the chief of the Gestapo in Rome, you have no need of a Swiss passport. If you are the special enemy of the chief of the Gestapo in Rome, a Swiss passport will not help you. So, we need not discuss it further. Your task is simple: Follow the priest's instructions to the letter."

"What about the film I'm supposed to deliver? I still don't have it —and I don't understand why you want me to cooperate with the Americans."

"The film will be in your sweet little hands tonight, before you leave the Remus. And do not worry about my strategy, *Liebchen*. I am playing the same game as Gratz, only I am playing it effectively—and delicately."

As he hung up the phone, Olendorf looked over at Priebke. "Get the film to Anna tonight. Stay away from her in the morning, but pick her up when she comes back to her apartment."

Priebke nodded.

TEN

Rome, Sunday, 17 October 1943

Exactly at 9:00 Anna received a telephone call from a woman instructing her to cross the river and stop at the Fountain of the Face on the Via Giulia. There a small boy ran up and gave her a note, telling her to proceed on the second leg of what became a two-hour walk around Rome and would eventually return her to the bar at the Porta Settimiana, where Roberto had stopped on his return from the Regina Coeli.

At 10:30, while Anna was still trudging around the city, a young nun ushered Roberto into Sister Sacristy's small office. "Father Christmas says that you are to take this"—she motioned to a battered briefcase—"and at eleven o'clock go to the Bar Settimiana and wait for *la Strega*. You are to exchange gifts, then you are to go directly to the Vatican. Enter at the Largo d'Alicorni from the street of the Jesuits, the Borgo Santo Spirito."

"Then?"

"Then I do not know. You will be in the hands of Father Christmas—and of God."

"I can never repay you for your help, or your courage."

The fat nun shrugged. "Help is our duty. And, as for the other thing, one can only be courageous when one has something to fear. What Christian can fear a martyr's death? It is something to pray for, not to run from."

Roberto moved toward the door, but Sister Sacristy reached out and touched him. "A little moment, please. I need to say something. You are Italian in language, but you are American in all other ways. You expect the world and all of us in it to be perfect. Christianity does not teach perfection in this world, only forgiveness for imperfections."

260

Roberto said nothing. He had been lectured about being American before.

"I was a Trasteverina long before I was a nun. I quickly learn anything of any importance whatsoever—and much that is of no importance—as soon as it happens in this neighborhood. I know of you, *la Strega*, and the German; I also know about Stefano. You must forgive her, Roberto. Do not trust her, but forgive her. And most important, you must forgive yourself."

"It's difficult to like Anna, and you're right that no one can trust her; but I do forgive her. She's a set of conditioned reflexes that respond without thought."

"*Che stronzo!* You are speaking like another 'superior male.' Anna is hardhearted, selfish, even ruthless. But she faced the same problem that you did, and she made the same choice. Why do you not think she suffered the same pain? Forgiving a child or an animal is not enough. You must forgive a human being, an adult, like yourself. And if you can forgive another person like yourself, you can forgive yourself."

"I wish it were that easy."

"I do not say that it is easy; I say only that it is necessary. You hold yourself, in your struggle for survival, to much higher standards than you expect from others in that same struggle. Your real sin, my son Roberto, is pride, setting yourself above your fellowman."

"Woman." Roberto tried a small smile.

"*Ecco!*" The nun beamed. "*Esatto.* You commence to learn. Now go with God and His love. And visit us when the Americans have driven the Germans from our Roma."

Roberto was closing the door when Sister Sacristy called his name again. He turned. "Roberto," she said gently, "it is also permissible to have cared and even still to care for Anna. She can be a trial to God and man, but, after all, she is a woman."

Shortly after 11:15 a very footsore Anna entered the Bar Settimiana. She saw Roberto sitting in a dark corner but ignored him long enough to order a *caffè corrètto*. Then she came and sat at the table. Outwardly, Roberto did not move. "Well, *caro*, you are alive. I thought the streets of Rome had swallowed you. I have been concerned."

"I'll bet."

261

"You sound Italian," she purred. "You were more *simpatico* when you were American."

"Where's the film?"

"Where are the money and the passport?"

"There." Roberto gently kicked the old briefcase.

Anna leaned over as if to adjust her shoe. She opened the top of the case just enough to peek inside. "I can see a passport and money, but are they genuine?"

"I couldn't say. I'm only the messenger boy."

"*Va bene*, I'll take the briefcase into the rest room and make sure."

"Not on your life, Anna. Not unless you leave the film as a deposit."

"*Caro* Roberto, the Italian in you is so suspicious. Let us compromise. I shall take the passport and several packets of the bills into the rest room."

Roberto nodded. In less than three minutes, Anna was back at the table. "Satisfied?" he asked.

"I am," she said, "but you're probably not. Shall we go to the apartment and have a last round of lovemaking?"

"No thanks, just the film."

"Here." She reached out and held his hand. He could feel the containers between the warmth of her fingers. "It's probably just as well. I have a new friend living with me. He's very jealous."

As nonchalantly as he could, Roberto pocketed the film. "He probably thinks he has a monopoly on you. Undoubtedly you told him that's what he was buying. We wouldn't want to disillusion him—yet." Roberto stopped short. "You said there were three rolls of film. You gave me only two containers."

"That's right, *caro*; there're only two. The third is gone, for the time being at least."

"Gone? Where?"

"It's a long story. All you need know is that the Gestapo is closing in. Take what you have and run. It's what I'm going to do. That pig in my apartment will never see me again."

"You sound almost sincere."

"I am," she said evenly, then smiled. "Almost. *Senti*, you have the *fròcio*'s film; I have the money. The only people who have nothing are the Germans. But give them a few hours and they may have us

262

both. Come with me. I know those people are closing in. I have a few friends who will hide us. After the war we can live well off this." She kicked the briefcase.

"Sure." Roberto treated the offer as a diversion. "Well, I can't force you—here—to produce the third roll, but remember that the people on both sides can play rough. It would be better to give it to me before someone takes it."

She laughed. "Roberto. You are americano again, and so *simpatico*. Do you care for Anna just a tiny bit? Did you care those nights up in the loft or down on the sofa?"

Roberto did not reply.

"If you do not care, why are you so angry?"

"You do not understand my anger or anything else about me."

"I understand, Roberto americano, far more than you realize. You did not answer. Do you care?"

"Do you?"

"Do I? Does Anna care?" She laughed harshly. "Anna is a professional, you know that. Anna cares for Anna and only for Anna." Then her voice became more tender. "I might have loved you, but in a very different world, not this one. Perhaps in our next incarnations we shall meet again and be great lovers. *Ciao*, Roberto, *arrivederci*."

Roberto M. Rovere, Lieutenant (j.g.), USNR, slipped out from behind the table, and, without looking back at Anna Caccianemici, began his slow, lonely, limping walk to the Vatican.

As he passed the Regina Coeli, he inhaled the jail's now familiar, fetid odor. Once more he could feel the cold sweat break out on his face and back. He limped faster. A few paces later, he saw a heavy guard of SS at the entrance of the *Collègio Militare* and a small cluster of curious people trying to see what was going on inside. Roberto did not stop, but kept walking at his gimpy pace.

Ten minutes later, however, he did pause as he passed through the dark street of the fortresslike offices of the Jesuit Order. From there he could see a swatch of Bernini's colonnade and above it Michelangelo's dome atop the Basilica of St. Peter. Even this fragment brought back a child's sensation of awe.

Then, after a few moments' indulgence, he trudged on toward the end of the narrow street, climbing slowly toward Vatican Hill. Two civilians turned the corner and began to come toward him. Both were looking directly at him, and Roberto's mouth turned dry with fear. "*Signore, per favore,* we wish to speak to you. It will only take a little moment." The taller of the two men flashed a card with the initials OVRA visible, even at ten yards. "Not again!" flashed across Roberto's mental screen. He glanced around to see two more men, obviously police in civilian clothes, closing rapidly behind him.

"*Cos'è?*" he asked as he limped toward the first two policemen. What is it?

"We only wish to ask you about something, please."

Roberto continued to advance slowly until he was less than a dozen feet from the police in front of him. Then he sprinted off around them in a nonathlete's imitation of a fleet halfback's dip and run, hoping that adrenaline would compensate for lack of skill and practice. The suddenness of his movement surprised the Fascists, and he was around them in a split second, dashing at top speed without the barest trace of a limp. There were less than a hundred yards to cover, all of it slightly downhill, before the double white lines and the safety of Vatican City.

"*Alt! Alt!*" the first policeman shouted. As his partner and the trailing pair of OVRA took off in pursuit, the plainclothesman pulled his pistol and fired a wild shot that ricocheted off the colonnade, chipping a piece of stone off the inscription to Pope Alexander VII. Roberto tucked his head down and tried to run a zigzag course to make a more difficult target.

A squad of five German paratroopers who were on guard between the Largo Alicorni and the Via della Conciliazione reacted instantly to the shot. They arrived at the mouth of the Borgo Santo Spirito just as Roberto raced by them, only twenty yards from sanctuary. The German sergeant's command "Halt!" was followed almost immediately by a burst from his machine pistol. The bullets cut the legs out from under Roberto, but his momentum carried him forward another few painful yards of skidding over the cobblestones. He rolled several more feet, still short of the border.

Through the blur of shock and burning pain, Roberto could see Father Fitzpàdraig Cathal Sullivan standing under the shelter of the colonnade. The priest's face was a mask of horror. "Here," Roberto

264

called out as he reached into his pocket to get the containers of film. Before he could remove his hand, an OVRA agent and a paratrooper simultaneously landed on his back and pinned him down.

With the rapid assistance of his three colleagues, the OVRA agent tried to pull Roberto out of the paratrooper's grasp. *"E il nostro!"* the OVRA shouted in Italian at the uncomprehending soldier. He's ours!

"He is my prisoner! Back off!" the paratrooper responded in German, and shoved the OVRA man hard enough to push him off balance, behind first, onto the stone street. The other OVRA agents jumped on the German and the rest of the paratroopers joined the melee. In the confusion, Roberto fought back the pain long enough to drag himself awkwardly toward the colonnade. He had completed two agonizing yards before a paratrooper stopped slapping an OVRA agent across the arms with his carbine stock long enough to smash the weapon's butt plate against Roberto's head and send him reeling off into unconsciousness.

An officer's whistle and commands shouted in two languages brought the minor riot to a close, but the noise continued as the senior OVRA agent, blood pumping profusely from his nose, began screaming wildly at the German officer, clusters of people on both sides of the border, and the Deity about the sovereign rights of the Italian Social Republic and the injustice of Teutonic interference with God's natural laws.

Rome, Sunday, 17 October 1943

"They what? In the name of Christ, tell that to me again; I cannot believe it!" Olendorf shouted into the telephone. Then he listened silently for three minutes, his face and even his scalp beneath his blond hair turning to a darkly raging crimson. Finally he yelled into the mouthpiece, *"Scheisse drauf! Scheisse drauf!"* and threw the telephone at its cradle hard enough to send both pieces of equipment crashing onto the marble floor.

"Sir?" Priebke inquired as he put the phone back on the desk.

"You will not believe it. Anna gave Raven the film. He was going to the Vatican to deliver it to Father Christmas when those *Scheisskerle* from the OVRA tried to arrest him. They managed to involve one of our paratroop units, and in the chase they shot Raven in the

265

legs. Right now he is in the Santo Spirito Hospital outside the Vatican under Wehrmacht guard while the OVRA are screaming that Raven is their prisoner. The Wehrmacht officer in charge has found the film and sent it to his commanding officer. They have turned the whole operation into a steaming pile of shit."

"Are they idiots or traitors?" Priebke asked, as he scratched the seat of his pants."

"I do not know, I do not know," Olendorf said wearily.

"I would respectfully suggest that we arrest them and have Sergeant Hoess find out, yes?"

"We may do that, but first go to the hospital and pick up Raven. You can arrest anyone who even murmurs a protest—whether German or Italian. Raven's wounds are not serious. Bring him here. We may as well get something out of this fiasco. Let us see what he knows—about everything."

"*Jawohl.*" Priebke clicked his heels and saluted in the same motion that took his usually sleepy body at a half run toward the exit.

Rome, Sunday, 17 October 1943

Ten minutes after Olendorf received the call about what had happened at the Largo Alicorni, Gratz heard the news from one of his sources. He stormed into Gestapo headquarters only seconds after Priebke had left to claim the prisoner. "Have you gone completely mad?" he half-shouted at Olendorf. "A shootout on the edge of St. Peter's and now Raven captured? Your people must be taking lessons from the OVRA."

"Please, Colonel." Olendorf's voice was unctuously soothing. "Would you care for a brandy? No? Then a cigar?"

"I want an explanation, *schnell!*"

"Colonel, I am as upset as you are, but please understand that the SS had nothing to do with this fiasco. It was the OVRA, operating without either our permission or knowledge, who started the shooting. They missed, of course, but they alerted the paratroopers, who also fired. They did not miss. Raven is in the hospital. Apparently his wounds are not serious. The Wehrmacht and the OVRA are still squabbling over jurisdiction. I have sent Major Priebke to assert our superior claim."

266

"You will get him back, of course."

"Of course. In police matters, no one can claim higher authority than the Gestapo."

"All right. As soon as you have him, I want him in my office in the Villa Wolkonsky."

"I am truly sorry, Colonel; that is not possible. Operation Rigoletto has come to an unhappy end. The Wehrmacht has the film and has probably examined it carefully by now, and dozens of people including spectators, hospital personnel, German soldiers, Swiss Guards, and even OVRA know Raven is an Allied agent. Rigoletto is *kaput*."

"That is not for you to decide."

"Somebody has to make a decision, and I am the senior SS officer on the spot. Too many people know about Raven *and* his film. Besides, even the Americans would not be so naïve as to believe that an amateur could twice slip out of our grasp, especially when the second time we catch him with photos of Enigma on his person. Anything he brought out would be considered trash."

"You may be right, but—"

"I am right, Colonel, believe me. Incidentally, I am doing what I can to get the film back." Olendorf carefully watched Gratz's reaction to the last sentence, but the colonel's expression did not change; it remained one of angry frustration without a trace of apprehension. Either the man was a consummate actor or he had been duped, Olendorf concluded.

"I am going to report immediately to Admiral Canaris and get his decision on terminating Rigoletto. Until he says otherwise, the operation is on. Canceling it may require der Fuehrer's approval."

"I am certain that if anyone can obtain der Fuehrer's approval, the admiral can. If we can be of any further assistance, Colonel. . . ." Olendorf tried to break off the conversation.

"I want Raven. He is ours." Gratz was not about to be deterred by Olendorf's efforts to divert him.

"It grieves me, Colonel. That is not possible. Now that Rigoletto is *kaput* and we have saved Raven from the OVRA, the Wehrmacht, and his own stupidity, we deserve a few days of his company. We may be able to squeeze something useful out of this farce."

"More likely you will kill him."

267

"That is a risk we are willing to run. After all, he is a spy, so little will be lost. Our bird may as well sing while he is alive."

"Olendorf, on the authority of instructions from der Fuehrer himself, I order you to turn over custody of Raven. Operation Rigoletto is still on until Admiral Canaris or der Fuehrer himself cancels it."

"I am afraid, Colonel, that orders are not quite in place at this juncture. I suggest a compromise. I shall refer the matter to Reichsfuehrer Himmler; you refer it to Admiral Canaris. Let them argue, command, negotiate, or whatever it is higher authorities do. Meanwhile, the SS will retain custody of Raven."

"No," Gratz insisted vehemently. He had to keep Himmler out of it, lest Canaris's forgery of Hitler's handwriting become known. "That is totally inadmissible. You know that der Fuehrer has excluded many high-ranking officials, including Himmler, from any knowledge of Rigoletto. If you discuss this matter with Himmler you violate the explicit terms of the order."

"I am less certain of that than you are, Colonel. But"—Olendorf shrugged in mock innocence—"I do not want to come even near the rim of violating an order from der Fuehrer. I shall leave it up to you to talk to Admiral Canaris and have him negotiate with Reichsfuehrer Himmler. When the Reichsfuehrer orders me to return Raven to you, I shall do so. Not before."

"Either you turn Raven over to me as soon as you get custody of him or I call the Admiral and tell him you are refusing to cooperate."

"Colonel, I have no desire to fight with the Abwehr as an institution or with you personally. I am a professional policeman trying to perform his duty. Throughout this operation I have cooperated as best I could; I have even acted outside of regular SS channels. Now that Rigoletto is finished, I am going to return to acting within regular channels. That is final. Please keep in mind that the Gestapo and the SD answer only to their parent organization, the SS; and the SS answers only to der Fuehrer himself."

"Olendorf—" Gratz began.

"Colonel," Olendorf interrupted, "you must forgive me. I have other urgent business to attend to. Good day." He stood up, clicked his heels, popped his arm forward, and recited "Heil Hitler!"

Gratz stood silently for fifteen seconds, then turned and walked slowly out of the room. His bluff had been called. There was nothing else to do but throw the problem in Admiral Canaris's lap.

Vatican City, Sunday, 17 October 1943

Rev. F. C. Sullivan had watched the haggling over custody of Roberto and was somewhat relieved when an ambulance arrived and took him—and several shouting Germans and Italians—away. The Jesuit walked slowly back to the giant basilica. At the altar in the apse, a cardinal was celebrating a solemn High Mass, and a half dozen priests at side altars were engaged in similar rituals for smaller clumps of people. Everywhere there was too much noise, too much activity. F.C. went into the quiet of the sacristy and spent ten minutes kneeling at a prie-dieu. Then he made a series of telephone calls, and returned to his office.

Sharply at 1:00 P.M., a rap came at the door. "*Avanti*," F.C. called out over his shoulder as he went through the rites of coffee making at his beloved *macchinetta*. "You are exactly on time, Father," he noted without looking up from his work.

"It is a Germanic trait," the Augustinian apologized, "one shared by Americans and most northern Europeans but not by our Italian colleagues. They regard it as a fault. I recall remonstrating with your friend Monsignor Galeotti about the absence of a phrase in Italian for 'to be early.' He assured me that there were many words to cover the expression; it was the concept that Italians lack."

"And they shall outlive both our people. Their only compulsion seems to be to enjoy what God has given, while we too often try to force God's hand. Here, have a cup." F.C. passed a demitasse of espresso to the German.

The monk sipped it appreciatively. "Delicious. I doubt that even Marshal Kesselring enjoys coffee like this. But, my friend, you said that the matter was of some urgency. I should not waste time with Italian customs and compliments on your coffee."

"You remember, Father," F.C. began slowly, groping his way, "I once said rather pompously that we were both priests before all else?"

"I agree now as I did then—although I often have difficulty meeting such demands."

"Yes, as do I, and all of us, I guess. Look, Father, I'll come straight

269

to the point. This morning a young man tried to slip into Vatican City. He was wounded and caught. I don't know who got credit for the capture, the OVRA or your paratroopers—both were fighting over the spoils when the ambulance came—but the Gestapo came to the hospital and took him away as their prisoner. I suspect he's at the Via Tasso. Technically, he's a spy."

"Then, I am sorry to say, Father, that he is as good—or as bad—as dead. I have learned a great deal about the SS in the last few days. They are a blot on German honor, to put the matter in its most favorable light. Your young man should have had better sense."

"It is not his fault; it's mine. I betrayed him. Technically, I said, he's a spy. In fact, he is a dupe."

"I fear such distinctions escape the Gestapo. They will extract what information he has, as a housewife squeezes the juice from an orange, then discard the useless skin. I am helpless to intervene. Those people do not listen to priests. And, if technically he is a spy, I doubt if any military organization would listen. Spies are executed."

"Only if caught."

"Only if caught? But he is caught. Or am I missing something?"

"Yes, but the Gestapo is missing more. Do you think they would exchange their technical offender for a real spy?"

"I do not know. I cannot speak for the Gestapo, thank God. I could make some inquiries. Who would the real spy be, Father? Or is that too sensitive a question?"

"No, it is not. Father Christmas."

The monk put his coffee cup down and sat on the couch. "Are you sure of this thing, my friend? Absolutely sure in your heart and soul? I am a loyal German, but if I thought the Gestapo, or the SS in general, represented the future of Germany or even had a significant role to play in that future, I would agree with your argument that there is no moral difference between communism and Nazism. Indeed, I might choose the Red over the Black. For years, I have heard rumors about the SS, but I dismissed them as Jewish or British propaganda. Now I know the stories tell only half the evil truth. These people are an unspeakable horror."

"That has been a secret that most of the world has long known."

"Forgive my ignorance. No, forgive my stubbornness. I have long

270

'known' it, but I could never admit to myself that I knew. A man can love his country too much. False gods come in many forms."

"I know, I know. Like you, I have learned that truth in spite of myself."

The monk nodded. Neither spoke for several minutes, then the German broke the silence: "Does Father Christmas know that the Gestapo get what information they want from a prisoner? No one leaves both alive and silent."

"Father Christmas is very familiar with the methods and the success of the Gestapo. He is unlikely to leave alive, but he will leave silent."

"Can he be sure? Few men can withstand that much torture."

F.C. half-smiled. "The good God has provided a way. It will not be a long experience."

"How can you be sure?"

"I would rather not discuss it, Father, but I am sure."

"Very well, I shall not pry." The monk paused. "No, I want to pry. Why are you doing this, Father? You are no different from the rest of mankind. Your judgment is not infallible. When an officer errs, soldiers may die; when a priest errs, souls may die. That is the way life is. Surely if God had meant us to be perfect He would have made us so."

"My mistake was not an error in judgment. I wish it were. Even idolatrous patriotism did not mask my mistake—if it did, only partially. I committed the sin of vanity. I wanted to please 'the right crowd.' Not because I thought they were just or morally correct—in my heart, I always thought they were wrong. Last night I had from one of your agents all the confirmation a rational man needed. But I could not admit that my great models were wrong and that I was trying to please them only because they were powerful and glamorous and I wanted their esteem.

"This morning," F.C. went on, "I knew, really knew, what my sin was. I knew it when I looked into the eyes of a young man as he lay in his own blood and still tried to throw me some film that he thought was important to his country. I saw myself as a shallow, name-dropping gossip whose highest ambition was to be seen with the smart set. I let that crass craving override my judgment of right and wrong."

271

"You and I share much, Father, including errors."

"I hope your penance will not be as heavy as mine."

"I doubt it," the monk said lightly. "You Celts have peculiar souls. You set perfection as your norm and then torture yourselves when you behave merely as humans. Alas, we Germans tend to relieve our guilt and anxiety through sadism rather than masochism." The Augustinian broke off abruptly. "Father, do you love God?"

"Of course—well, I never asked myself that question. I think so. Yes. Don't you?"

"I fear Him. How can one love an omnipotent being who has no need of anybody or anything, who can stomp out whole peoples, who can watch brothers murder each other? I fear Him, but fear is not love."

"No, but it may be the beginning of love, as it is the beginning of wisdom. I believe in a God who is a loving Father, a God who marks the sparrow's fall. Still, I cannot explain the mystery of evil and God's mercy."

"Not in words, perhaps, but you feel you understand it, and you show it. I envy you. My God is not like yours. He is just, not merciful, terrible, not loving."

"I do not know what to say."

"Nor do I. I pray."

The two men sat in silence for a quarter of an hour. Finally the Augustinian stood up. "I shall see what I can do, Father. I can promise nothing, but I shall try. Does Father Christmas have a timetable?"

"As soon as possible. His knees may soon knock together so hard he'll bleed to death." F.C. laughed nervously at his own feeble effort at gallows humor. "Tonight, if it can be done."

At the door, the monk turned. "I think I can do this thing, but I hope with all my heart that I cannot."

"Thank you, Father. That's kind of you to say. One last favor: Would you tell Monsignor Galeotti that I want him to have the *machinetta* and my supplies of food?"

Rome, Sunday, 17 October 1943

The three Germans met at an outdoor cafe on the Via Veneto. Most of the other tables were empty at 3:30 in the afternoon in

272

silent worship of the sacred siesta. The Augustinian was already seated next to Colonel Gratz when Lieutenant Colonel Olendorf stepped from his staff car and entered the café area. He clicked his heels and gave a smart Nazi salute. The colonel responded with a vague touch to his cap, then introduced the monk, who nodded in reply to a repeat of the heel clicking and arm popping. There was no exchange of handshakes.

As Olendorf sat down he snapped his finger for a waiter. An elderly gentleman, half-dozing in the sun, looked over quietly, then slowly stood up, dusted his chair, returned it to its proper place under a table, and ambled over to the Germans. *"Signori, mi dicano."* Grammatically, it was a polite way of asking how he could be of service, but only grammatically.

"Coffee," Gratz said, and the Augustinian nodded acquiescence.

"Caffè corrètto," Olendorf barked. "And bring the brandy to the table so I can make sure that it is potable—and plentiful." The waiter elaborately wrote the order onto a tiny scrap of paper with the barest stub of a pencil, then shuffled off as speedily as the ebb of a fall morning's mist. The SS officer looked contemptuously at the old man's wake and laughed. "When we have won this war, I am certain our scholars will return to their work and discover that Italians are not Aryans after all, but members of some inferior race. We shall have to find a 'solution' for them too."

The Augustinian shuddered but said nothing.

"Well, gentlemen," Olendorf noted as he consulted his watch, "we have been here almost five minutes, and I have heard neither of you do more than offer greetings. I thought you had said that time was of the utmost importance."

"Does the name Father Christmas mean anything to you?" the monk asked softly.

"Of course it means something. He is the only successful American spy in Rome. Our friends in the Abwehr, as Colonel Gratz may have confessed to you, have not been able to do much about him."

"Our record is precisely the same as yours," Gratz observed. "And counterintelligence falls more under your jurisdiction—or so you contend at our conferences."

"I may be able to deliver Father Christmas to you," the Augustinian said.

273

Olendorf looked doubly surprised. "Deliver him to me? Why to me? I thought you worked for the Abwehr. Forgive me, Colonel, I had assumed he was your man in the Vatican."

"One of ours; but he can speak for himself."

"I have talked the matter over with the colonel," the monk explained. "He cannot meet the condition for the delivery."

"Which is?" Olendorf asked suspiciously.

"You are holding a young man, someone you picked up today from a hospital near the Vatican. How is his health?"

"Better now than it will be, I am afraid. He has been shot in the legs, nothing serious. But he is a spy, and spies captured in wartime are shot dead."

"Would you exchange this young man for Father Christmas?"

Olendorf lit a Lucky Strike. He did not offer the pack to either of his companions. "Why would I want to sacrifice a spy in the hand for another in the Vatican's bush?"

"What sort of spy is your prisoner?" the monk asked. "Is he clever?"

"Clever?" Olendorf sneered. "Ask your friend Colonel Gratz. He is a rank amateur come to steal an Enigma and do it without our noticing. Ludicrous. I could have taken him anytime I wanted him, but out of deference to the colonel here, I stood aside. These Americans are like children. They think that if they close their eyes we cannot see them."

"And yet . . ." Gratz's voice trailed off.

"And yet what, Colonel?" There was resentment as well as suspicion in Olendorf's tone.

"And yet Father Christmas is still operating a network that does rather well, if I correctly read the traffic between Berlin and our respective offices."

"There are exceptions to every rule. Furthermore, I now know precisely who this man is."

"So do I," the Augustinian interjected. "I may be able to give you this American exception in exchange for your amateur."

"I do not need your bargain, *Herr Pater*. I can take him anytime that I please."

"Anytime," the monk argued, "that you care to further rile His Holiness. Look, Colonel Olendorf, I know you opposed the *Juden-*

aktion yesterday because it risked—and the risk is not yet over—turning the Pope into an enemy of Germany. To kidnap one of Papa Pacelli's favorites—and make no mistake, with American food and money for the hungry, Father Christmas is a papal favorite—would be a far greater risk than sending a few hundred Jews to work for the Reich."

"If that is true," Olendorf said less belligerently, "how can you 'deliver' this spy without irritating the Pope?"

"He will come to you; and he will clear his coming with the Vatican's Secretariat of State so there will be no protest, diplomatic or otherwise."

"It sounds interesting." Olendorf rubbed the back of his hand across his mouth. "But his masters in Washington would never approve. Even they are not that stupid."

Conversation stopped for several minutes as the ancient waiter returned and placed the cups and a bottle of cheap brandy from Trieste on the table. Olendorf looked at the bottle disapprovingly. "Take that horse piss away," he directed. "And do not put it on the bill."

"Sì, *Commendatore, sì.*" The waiter nodded. He removed the bottle with all the solemn dignity of a master of ceremonies at a pontifical High Mass.

When the old man had shuffled off again, the monk spoke. "The Americans do not and need not know until the deed is done. The Vatican is the critical element here. I can arrange a quiet word from the Secretariat of State to Ambassador von Weizsäcker."

Olendorf snubbed out the cigarette and stared off into space. "Can I trust these priests?" He spoke to no one in particular.

"The real question," Gratz said, "is whether these priests can trust the SS."

Olendorf snorted. "If I agree, I shall give my word as a German officer. But, before I agree, I shall have to have Ambassador von Weizsäcker tell me there will be no protest from the Vatican."

"I can arrange that this afternoon," the monk promised.

"Well, then," Gratz asked, "do you accept the offer?"

"Hmmm," Olendorf finished his coffee. "Let me hear more. What timing do you propose?"

"Tonight, if possible."

275

Olendorf hesitated. "That is possible, if I can have the ambassador's assurance before then. Where do you propose the exchange be made?"

"At the edge of the Vatican, at the Largo Alicorni, where the Borgo Santo Spirito intersects—"

"I know the place."

"The amateur must be alive and in good health."

"In reasonably good health. He stopped three or four bullets with his legs, *Herr Pater*. Instant and miraculous cures fall within your province, not mine."

"I meant no torture."

Olendorf looked blankly at the monk. "I agree to those terms. Father Christmas must come to us, and he must be wearing civilian clothes. I would not want even to seem to offend His Holiness. If that is acceptable, we can set nine this evening for the exchange."

The monk nodded. "If it has to be later, I shall telephone."

"I want to be there as well," Gratz noted.

"I would appreciate that, Colonel," Olendorf said almost amiably. "Since you set up this meeting, I shall hold you responsible for any foul play. It would be comforting to have you within gunshot—sir."

Gratz smiled coldly. "I am always at your disposition, Olendorf, just as I am to any inferior officer."

Olendorf stood up and adjusted his cap on his handsome blond head. "With your permission then, gentlemen, I take my leave. If all goes well, the Reich will be in your debt. If it does not . . . well, you will both be in the Gestapo's debt." He repeated the heel-clicking, arm-popping ritual and marched to his staff car, ignoring the bill on the table.

The other two Germans watched him drive off. "Thank you for your help, Colonel," the monk said.

"We owe it to you. Your work in the Vatican has been of immense value to Germany. I hope this exchange will also help Germany. It should, but what is good for the SS is not necessarily good for Germany."

"So I have come to learn."

"Yes. Take care of yourself, *Herr Pater*. I still have my black feeling of the last few days. As I said, I fear that our world is unwinding. Maybe it is this Jewish business coming on top of the failure of our mission. I do not know. It may be something far worse. Well, my driver will drop you off at the Vatican. I am going to walk back to the villa."

Vatican City, Sunday, 17 October 1943

The Augustinian went directly to Monsignor LaTorre's apartment in the Sant' Uffizio, the palace that at one time had been the central headquarters of the Inquisition and now housed a somewhat reformed Holy Office and also provided apartments for several high-ranking Vatican officials. LaTorre was at home; Monsignor Galeotti was with him. They were both deeply troubled and very displeased, but they had already talked with F. C. Sullivan and were reconciled, though only barely, to his decision. The monk passed on the few details of the exchange to which he had agreed, and LaTorre promised to call von Weizsäcker immediately. As the monk was leaving, the undersecretary shot a parting comment, heavy with Sicilian sarcasm: "There is an old legend that when God created man he scattered enough good in this world so that each man has at least a small piece of it—if only we look hard enough. Anyone who would work with the SS must have sold his share."

The Augustinian's olive face blushed. "Who knows the mind of the Lord? Who has been His counselor?"

A few minutes later, the German visited Sullivan and gave him the information. "Can you get some civilian clothes?"

"I have some here. I assume your man does not mind if I dress informally." Then the Jesuit glanced about at the papers strewn over his desk. "I am not a neat administrator, Father," he said apologetically. "Indeed, some say chaos is my natural habitat. But I should make some effort to tidy up for my successor. I thank you for your help, but could you excuse me?"

"Of course. I shall call for you at eight-thirty."

F.C. tried to put his affairs in order, but after half an hour he gave up and lay down on his cot and started to read and pray *The Spiritual Exercises of St. Ignatius Loyola*. That effort produced only a cold sweat, so he tried reading his breviary. Afterward, he shuffled down the hall to find another cleric to whom he could confess.

Promptly at 8:30 the Augustinian reappeared. With him were LaTorre and Galeotti. "It is time," the monk said simply.

277

"So soon? Let me make a stop at the men's room. The spirit," F.C. noted, "is willing, but the bladder is weak." He hesitated, then took a small vial of nitroglycerine tablets from his pocket and flipped it into an open desk drawer alongside a bottle of papaverine.

The four clergymen walked swiftly around the Vatican and exited via the Gate of the Bells into the Piazza of St. Peter. Near the edge of the colonnade, F.C. stopped, turned, and inhaled a last view of the basilica's massive hulk. "It is like the Church iteslf," he mused. "Old, pretentious, ugly, and still beautiful."

The others made no reply. At the edge of the colonnade, they stopped. Three Vatican police in civilian clothes joined them. Behind the columns in the colonnade were posted another dozen Swiss Guards, armed and in battle dress. Across the street, several squads of German paratroopers stood in the shadows. They all waited.

In a few moments, a pair of German staff cars wheeled up next to the colonnade, their tires sliding to a stop only a few feet from the double white lines. Olendorf got out of the first car, Gratz out of the second. It was impossible to see inside either vehicle. Olendorf stood in front of his car. LaTorre came to meet him. "Do you have the prisoner?" the *monsignore* inquired.

Olendorf jerked his thumb toward the back seat. "Do you have the priest?" he asked.

LaTorre nodded, walked over to the car, opened the door, and looked inside. Then he came back over to the Vatican side of the lines and spoke to F.C. "From the pictures you showed me, I would say that is the man. He's alive. He seems all right."

"I must be sure. Let me talk to him alone for a moment."

LaTorre went back to Olendorf and made the request. "Let me look closely at the famous Father Christmas first." LaTorre motioned for F.C. to come over. He did, but he kept his toes carefully within the inner white line. "Yes." Olendorf nodded. "This is the man. I hope you will be happy with us, *Herr Geistlicher*."

F.C. tried to ignore the German. "Let me t-t-talk to the prisoner," he stammered.

"Only outside the lines while you talk," Olendorf said curtly. "You are already stretching our agreement." Then he motioned to the two guards who shared the back seat with Roberto. "Bring him out,

278

schnell!" With some difficulty, they helped Roberto lift himself out of the car, half-carried him to where the others were standing, propped him against the front fender, and moved off several paces.

"Are you in pain?" F.C. asked in English.

Roberto looked at the priest. Even in the faint light his face appeared pale. "How do you think four bullets in your legs would feel?"

"What have you told them?"

"About what?"

"About the nuns."

Roberto made a sound that was midway between a snort and a nasty laugh. "Betraying friends is your line, not mine. Besides, they've only begun to work on me. I've told them about my mission and about the other teams. That's legitimate barter against unbearable pain, so I was instructed in Washington. Who knows what more I'll be saying in a few days?"

"Nothing. You won't have to say anything, except perhaps to explain to the OSS all the complications of your mission."

"What do you mean?"

"You're being exchanged. Those *monsignori* will take you in for a few days until some friends of mine find a way to smuggle you south."

F.C. turned abruptly and walked back to the place beside the car door where Olendorf, Gratz, and the three clerics were standing. "You've made him talk already," he said wearily.

"We encourage confession," Olendorf replied. "You holy men tell us it is good for the soul, and we do so want our guests to be comfortable, psychologically as well as physically."

"Do you still want to go through with it, Father?" LaTorre asked. "It's not too late to change your mind."

F.C. shrugged. "I never could do that like a Roman," he tried to joke. "And if any of you asks me to back out again, I'll run like a rabbit. No, I'm ready. Shall we go?' '

LaTorre stared at the Jesuit for a moment. "Are you all right, Father?"

"I'm cold."

The *monsignore* signaled the Vatican police, and they helped Roberto across the lines. At the same moment, Olendorf held the door open for Father Fitzpàdraig Cathal Sullivan, S.J. "I would like you to

279

ride with me, *Herr Geistlicher*. It would give me comfort to have divine guidance so near. We are anticipating the indulgences you will bring us."

"Just a moment, please." The Augustinian grabbed Olendorf's arm. "Give me your blessing, Father," he begged Sullivan and dropped to his knees. F.C. made the sign of the cross and touched the man's head gently. "Peace," he whispered, "let there be peace between us, *Alter Christus*."

"Move out." Olendorf pushed the American into the car.

The two vehicles made a sharp left turn into the Borgo Santo Spirito and, retracing Roberto's flight, sped toward the river. The Augustinian remained on his knees. After a few minutes Galeotti tapped the sobbing monk on the shoulder. "We should leave now, Father."

The Augustinian stood up slowly, painfully, like an arthritic old woman. "I want to pray," he said, "but what was it the English poet wrote? 'My words fly up, my thoughts remain below: / Words without thoughts never to heaven go.' "

"God understands all, Father," Galeotti said, trying to comfort him.

LaTorre was less kind. "Your conscience shows there is still hope for you. We know of your work for that obscene organization you call a government. Perhaps God will find it in His heart to forgive you for that. I never could."

"Nor could I, *Monsignore*, nor could I," the monk muttered as he turned toward the German College.

"*Momentino*, please, Father," Galeotti called out and rejoined the Augustinian. "Today and yesterday our American friend was inquiring about several Jewish families. He discovered that at least one was being detained in the *Collègio Militare*, Tommaso Piperno and his wife, Rebecca. *Senta*, it might be better to make a work of charity than to mourn for your mistakes. I have always found it so. Perhaps you could intervene with the SS to secure their release. According to me, Father Sullivan would consider it a great gentleness."

The Augustinian shook his head sadly. "I have no influence with the SS. That is about the only decent thing I can say for myself tonight. But"—he shrugged, affected by the Roman habit—"I can try." Suddenly the monk started laughing.

280

"Something is wrong, Father?" Galeotti asked in genuine concern for the priest's sanity.

"No, nothing in this misbegotten world is wrong, or everything is wrong; I am not sure which. I am laughing at another thing that Father Sullivan and I have shared here in Rome. I only now realized it. Yes, *Monsignore*, I should be happy to try to secure the Pipernos' release."

"Thank you." Galeotti tried to smile. "The worst the SS can do is shoot you."

Abruptly the monk was morose again. "I wish that were true. They have already done far worse than that."

Rome, Sunday, 17 October 1943

"Yes?" Olendorf barked into the telephone. "What is it you want? It is now too late to change your mind."

"I want to talk to you about something else," the Augustinian explained.

"Talk quickly then, I am busy. Your American friend needs my attention."

The monk swallowed hard. "Yes. Well, since I helped you with this operation, I thought—"

"The SS does not incur debts. The Reich is our only client, der Fuehrer our only master. But go on."

"There is a Jewish family in the *Collègio Militare*, Tommaso and Rebecca Piperno."

Olendorf groaned impatiently. "You must accept that the future of the Jews is, as Berlin says, 'fate-determined.' There is nothing that you or I can do."

"You do not understand," the monk persisted. "Tommaso Piperno is one of my agents. He has been my eyes and ears in Trastevere, a loyal and efficient man."

"I see." Olendorf's voice softened a bit. "But it is out of my hands. Captain Danzig has complete command of the *Judenaktion* in Rome. Talk to him."

"Yes, I have heard. But I do not know Danzig. Could you talk to him for me?"

"Now it is you, *Herr Pater*, who do not understand. I am very

281

busy. . . ." He groaned again. "Very well, I shall call Danzig and tell him you have been helpful to the SS and have a request. Anything more might hurt your cause. I suggest you come over here right away and try to talk to him in person. The Jews will be shipped out early tomorrow morning."

"I would, Colonel, but I do not have transportation. Could I borrow your car and driver?"

"My car and driver? Christ, you have got a hell of a nerve."

"A very valuable German agent is involved."

"An Abwehr agent."

"I could see that you received any information I get from him."

"I can take that as a solemn assurance?"

"Of course."

"All right. I am a damned fool. Be at the Largo Alicorni in fifteen minutes."

Capt. Erich Danzig looked up in annoyance. His office was little more than an oversized broom closet stuffed with a desk, two chairs, and several filing cabinets. The absence of windows aggravated his mild claustrophobia. Moreover, it was 10:30 Sunday night and he'd had no sleep Friday night, little on Saturday, and there were still hours of work to be done if the trainload of Jews were to leave by nine the next morning.

"Colonel Olendorf said that you would see me."

"*Scheisse!* You are the Abwehr man inside the Vatican. Olendorf tells me you have been useful in arresting the head of an American spy ring here in Rome, but patriotism is not reward enough for you. You also want a special favor. I must warn you, *Herr Pfarrer*, I do not wish to subscribe to a perpetual novena or even an occasional Mass. Wrong religion. In fact, I have no room for religion, astrology, phrenology, or any other superstition in my life." He pulled a wad of lire from his pocket and flipped it onto the desk. "You may put me down for a small indulgence."

The Augustinian stifled the anger that was welling up inside him. "You misunderstand, Captain. I want the release of a pair of Jews you have arrested, Tommaso and Rebecca Piperno. Tommaso is a German agent; he works under my command."

"Under your command and that of anyone else who would pay him

282

a few shekels. Write their names down." As the monk was scribbling on a pad, Danzig shouted, "Orderly!"

The door opened almost instantly.

"Take these names and bring me their files. Quickly."

Danzig ignored the Augustinian, who was still standing, and went back to his work until the orderly returned with a pair of files. "Here," the officer said, "we shall see. Tommaso is a registered member of the Jewish community, but he is a naughty boy. He neither goes to temple nor contributes to temple. That is from the temple's own records. For Italians, these Jews are very methodical. Now, here is what we piece together from our total information: Born, 24 January 1896; occupation, street sweeper; address, Vicolo del Bologna, 882; political affiliation, unknown; criminal record, none; distinguishing features, permanent displacement of left hip, walks with bad limp." Danzig looked hastily over the second file. "Rebecca, wife of Tommaso Piperno. Born, 23 August 1903; mother of two sons, dead as infants, and three living daughters, born 1931, 1935, 1937. Nothing else. That is interesting, *Herr Pfarrer*. I do not trust people who have nothing in their criminal records. To me, that is sure evidence of *clever* criminality; and, since these people are apparently poor, I conclude that they are likely to be political criminals—in addition to being Jews, of course; and that is crime enough."

"Captain," the monk asked, "would it help if I told you these people were baptized? Tomorrow morning I can produce the church records of their conversion."

Danzig focused his cold, yellow eyes on the Augustinian. "*Herr Pfarrer*, I am not noted for my sense of humor. Nor am I an acolyte or any other kind of fool. Give me a few thousand lire and twelve hours in Rome and I could produce Christ's baptismal certificate, in Italian and German as well as Aramaic, duly signed by John and witnessed by a low-flying dove who can speak and write. You are wasting my time."

"I am trying to persuade you not to kill a valuable German agent." The little monk raised his voice, unable to control his anger. "I have told Olendorf that Piperno is my eyes and ears in Trastevere. You may not know it, but, if an effective resistance to Germany is ever formed in Rome, it will be based on the Communist sympathizers in Trastevere. Damn it, man, hate the Jews all you want, but do not allow that hate to cost us an uprising here in Rome. Remember what happened in Naples!"

Danzig carried on as if the outburst had never happened, even as if the monk were not in the room. He simply went back to his papers. The Augustinian stood before the desk, refusing to budge until formally, if not physically, dismissed. After five minutes, the captain looked up. "What is your official position here? Olendorf told me, but I may have forgotten." His voice bore no trace of rancor.

"I teach moral theology at the Lateran University."

A slow smile spread over Danzig's pudgy face. "Yes, I thought I remembered that. You professors of moral theology like to pose difficult problems to your students, do you not? Let me turn the tables and give you one. That is good, very good. I give you one, a true moral conundrum: a pass, a single pass. That is your moral dilemma. You may visit the *Collègio Militare* and bring one of the Pipernos out with you. Your instincts as a German agent will say bring out Tommaso so he can still serve the Reich. Your instincts as a man of the cloth, as a chivalrous German, will say bring out the woman. Is that not a lovely dilemma? You can have fun posing it to your students next week. Oh, you have some excitement ahead."

Danzig picked up the telephone and barked a series of orders. He turned to the monk. "You will have to visit the *Collègio* tonight. Tomorrow morning will be too late for either Piperno, or for your dilemma."

"I have a staff car."

"Very good."

The captain started to pick up another sheaf of papers, then changed his mind and spoke again. "And, *Herr Pfarrer*, you must make your choice at the *Collègio*—not before—as you look in their eyes and smell their stinking fear. You will have to choose who lives and who dies. Perhaps that experience will teach you to respect those of us who every day must make such decisions in the real world. Moralizer, moralize thyself, as the saying goes."

Danzig spun in his chair and presented his back to the monk. "You can leave now. The orderly will have the pass ready and a visiting permit for you. I warn you, keep that pass blank until you have seen the Pipernos."

*   *   *

With the curfew, the ride was swift. It was also silent, until the car reached the right bank of the river. "Please drive on to the German College," the monk asked the driver.

"But I thought we were going to the *Collègio Militare*."

"That is where we are going eventually, but I must stop at the German College first. Are you Catholic, my son?"

"I guess so. It has been a long time since I went to church."

"Yes. Still, I think you can understand why I have to stop. The people whom I shall see have been taking instructions. Tonight I shall baptize them and give them their first Communion."

"If that were a way out, you could make a thousand converts in five minutes."

"I have a pass for the release of one man. But more important, the sacraments will release both of them from a worse bondage, sin."

"I am sorry, *Herr Pater*. One drifts away."

"Try each day to spend a minute or two talking to God, my son. Now, when we leave the *Collègio*, bring us back here. The man is a German agent."

The driver stopped outside the Vatican. And, after clearing his pass with the guards on duty, the dapper monk ran to his room, picked up his winter scarf and his heavy, hooded black cape, then raced to the chapel and took a small, gold-plated pyx, inserted a dozen consecrated hosts from the tabernacle, and hung the small box from a chain around his neck. In less than fifteen minutes, he was back in the staff car for the short ride to the *Collègio*.

The driver pulled off the Lungara and onto the narrow street alongside the *Collègio*. The Augustinian hopped out and, followed by the driver, presented his papers to the sentry. The soldier passed the pair on to the guard office, at the entrance to the hollow square around which the stately old palazzo had been built. The young SS lieutenant in charge glanced at the priest's permit. "We have been expecting you. I understand you also have a pass for the release of one of our guests. May I see it?"

The Augustinian produced the second piece of paper. The lieutenant looked at it more carefully than he had the monk's own pass, and gave it back. "Good, it is blank. Captain Danzig telephoned explicit orders that if there were a name on the release you were to be turned away."

285

The monk nodded and took the pyx out so the officer could see it. The man did not react, so the Augustinian looked inquiringly at his driver. After a few seconds of awkward silence, he got the message and spoke up. "Sir, he is carrying the holy viaticum. Under such circumstances, priests speak as little as possible. It is a sign of respect."

"I see," the lieutenant replied, though it was clear he did not see. "A guard will escort you inside. Your friends are in one of the small classrooms. I can give you only five minutes. Sorry, another of Captain Danzig's orders."

The guard led the priest across the dimly lit courtyard and under the Roman arches of the portico, and unlocked the door to a large hallway. Immediately, the dainty monk was almost overcome by the foul odor of unemptied chamber pots and too many human bodies crammed together. It was, although the Augustinian could not make the comparison, the Regina Coeli writ small. There were people all over the floor, some sleeping, some sobbing, some talking, some simply staring into space.

Off this hall was a series of smaller rooms. The guard opened the second door. Fifteen people were crowded inside. "*Raus! Raus!*" the soldier commanded, but the Jews looked at him without a trace of comprehension.

"Let me try, please," the monk suggested, and without waiting for a reply spoke in Italian, asking all but the Pipernos to leave for a few minutes. Slowly the other prisoners left, too sleepy and confused even to grouse at their awakening.

The Augustinian motioned for the guard to wait outside as well, then closed the door and turned to face the Pipernos. Rebecca did not have the vaguest idea who he was and glared at him suspiciously. Tommaso, however, seemed genuinely pleased, though badly bruised. "Ah, Padre. It's good of you to come to say good-bye. We're going to a work camp in Germany. It won't all be one big *fèsta*, but we're strong; we'll survive. However, they took us away without giving us time to gather any food or money, so if you have a few German marks or even some lire—"

The monk ignored the street sweeper and stared at Rebecca. "Good, you are tall for a woman. It may work. Pray that it does. First, the pass." He took his pen and wrote in Tommaso's name. "Here, Rebecca, you keep this and show it to the guard when you leave. It is for

286

Tommaso. Here is a visitor's permit for you. Give that to the guard at the gate, not the one outside the door."

Next, the monk removed his heavy outer cape and handed it to Tommaso. "Hold this. Rebecca, take off that bathrobe and give it to me."

"Just a minute, Padre," Tommaso broke in. "A few lire have passed between us, but you must have respect for my wife."

"Shut up, *cretino*," she snapped. "Haven't you got any sense? Can't you see what's happening?" She stripped off the robe and handed it to the priest, then took the cape from her husband and covered her chubby nakedness.

"Pull the cowl over your head," the Augustinian explained. "There. Good. Keep it up and put your hands in the slits on the sides so you can hold the cape up. That way it does not drag on the floor. Put these glasses on."

Rebecca swiftly did as she was told.

"Shoes? Mine are too big for you. Can you wear Tommaso's?"

"How no?"

"Put them on and give me yours. Tommaso can wear mine."

"Mine are bedroom slippers," Rebecca apologized, "but they will stretch a little." She handed the slippers to the priest. "Why are you doing this thing, Father?"

For a few moments the monk ignored the question as he gingerly rolled his pants legs up around his knees. Then he spoke very slowly. "Because I am German and because I am a Christian and because there is a great darkness in the world." He took the scarf from around his neck. "Make a babushka for me."

Once again Rebecca did as she was told. "You have heavy burdens to bear, Father." Then to Tommaso: "Give him your sweater. It will be cold in Germany."

He hesitated, ever so slightly.

"*Subbito, cretino, subbito*," she snapped. Do it quickly, idiot. In the Roman fashion she added an extra and exaggerated *b* to the Tuscan *subito*.

"Thank you." He pulled the sweater on, then put the floppy bathrobe on over it. It was not the costume he would have chosen for a heroic role. "Now, when you leave, hand the pass for Tommaso to the guard and give the visitor's permit to the sentry at the gate. He thinks you are carrying the holy viaticum, so he will not speak—probably. If he does, nod and point to the middle of your chest, where a priest would be carrying a pyx inside his cape. There is a staff car waiting. The driver knows where you are going—to the Vatican. He will not talk either. If he asks you anything, just say *ja*. You can manage that?"

"How no? And when we're at the Vatican?"

"Walk to a Swiss Guard and show him my identification. Here." The monk reached inside the bathrobe and fished out his wallet. "Ask to see Monsignor Galeotti or Monsignor LaTorre. One of them will take care of you."

Rebecca knelt down and kissed the monk's hand. *"Basta, basta!"* he said. "Tommaso, you must make the Germans think you are leaving half your life behind. You must walk out of the cell like a man suffering the terrible agony of being separated from his beloved wife. Weep, Tommaso, weep!"

"I am weeping, Padre." The tears on his cheek were genuine.

The Augustinian smiled at the Roman's complex simplicity. "Remember, Rebecca, if anyone here questions you, point to the middle of your chest. If you feel pressed, make the sign of the cross outward toward them, like this." He demonstrated a blessing.

"The cross, that is easy," Tommaso said as the guard opened the door. Then, like a great actor receiving his cue, he fell on the monk with tearful embraces, and continued moaning to heaven of his desperate love and shattering loss as the guard led him and the fully frocked figure to freedom.

The Augustinian monk fingered the small cross etched on the cover of the pyx. "No, my friend Tommaso," he whispered to himself, "it is not easy."

EPILOGUE

The Goth, the Christian, Time, War, Flood, and Fire,
Have dealt upon the seven-hill'd city's pride;
She saw her glories star by star expire,
And up the steep barbarian monarchs ride,
Where the car clim'b the Capitol; far and wide
Temple and tower went down, nor left a site:
Chaos of ruins! who shall trace the void,
O'er the dim fragments cast a lunar light,
And say, 'here was, or is,' where all is doubly night?
GEORGE GORDON, LORD BYRON,
"Childe Harold's Pilgrimage"

Rome, Monday, 18 October 1943

It was just past dawn and the recital of the first hour of the divine office when a shy nun ushered a young woman into the convent's gloomy, dusty reception room. She sat in one of the rickety chairs and inhaled the chamber's musty odor of ancient furniture, moldy doilies, and ashes from charred incense. A few minutes later, Sister Sacristy came bustling in, her rosary beads clacking as she waddled. "Yes?" The nun recognized the woman.

"I am Anna Caccianemici."

"I know who you are and what you are."

"Then you know I worked for Father Christmas. The Gestapo have him."

"I know the Gestapo have Father Christmas. What do you want here? This is the house of God, a house of prayer."

289

"Asylum. The Gestapo are after me. I spent yesterday hiding."

"Yes, that's logical. And there will be others looking for you if the Germans do not find you. You have offended both sides."

"That should not matter to you, Mother Superior. The Church is above politics, and it preaches love and forgiveness."

"My child, my child." Sister Sacristy sighed. "You would sell—no, you *have* sold your body and your soul and others' bodies and souls. Now you want us to risk our lives to hide you."

"I can pay you well, if that's what's worrying you," Anna said defiantly.

"I know that. You have two hundred and fifty thousand American dollars from Father Christmas. Yes, if you stay with us, you will pay well for it. Your money would help feed the others. You can stay, but first you must donate one-half of what you have."

"That's robbery!"

"Something close to it, I believe. But robbing Judas to feed the lambs is neither a sin nor a crime."

"I won't pay."

"You are free to leave, my child. Our doors keep the Germans out; they do not keep our guests in."

"You are a fat bitch, a *dondrona*. Like all clergy you are ready to suck blood from the poor."

"You have been a slender slut, my child, but you may be right that I am a *dondrona*. Still, I am not stealing from the poor but from the rich. The poor do not have two hundred and fifty thousand American dollars. Make your decision. I have much to do today."

"I have no choice."

"I know," Sister Sacristy said.

Suddenly Anna started laughing, at first a giggle, then real laughter. Sister Sacristy joined in, her large belly a quivering mass of coarse brown wool.

Rome, Monday, 18 October 1943

Fitzpàdraig Cathal Sullivan, S.J., woke up slowly. His revival was more a shift from an unconscious to a conscious nightmare than a return from a restful sleep. It was dark inside the cell. The only light came from the hallway, refracted through the narrow, barred transom.

One side of the cell was bricked in, with a small air vent at the bottom that was letting in a cold autumn draft. Undoubtedly the bricks covered what had been an outside wall before the Gestapo had taken over the building. The other three walls were plaster. With the tip of his shoestring, the priest had scratched his initials and the date near the floor, beside the door.

F.C. shivered in the cold. He got up slowly, muscles and bruises aching, and used the chamber pot. He tried to imagine the flavor of a steaming cup of espresso, but all he could taste was sour bile and dried blood. Nevertheless, the first night had not been as bad as he had expected. He'd been taken downstairs to a room in the basement and seated facing backward in a chair, his hands manacled in front of him, around the chair's back. An SS major had questioned him about American agents in Rome. For thirty minutes the Jesuit said nothing, despite the officer's threats.

Then a short, swarthy, bandy-legged sergeant from East Prussia had taken over. The questions became simpler, silence more painful. The sergeant had slapped F.C. heavily across the face after each question and hit him a half dozen times with his fist in the rib cage or kidneys. But even that intermittent beating stopped after twenty minutes. "We want you to sleep on all of this," the major had explained. "Sleep on it, and tomorrow we shall have a real session."

There were footsteps outside, then the cell door opened. It was the major, flanked by a pair of guards. "Come," he said curtly. The four men walked across the dark gray marble floor and squeezed into an elevator. They got off at the basement and made their way to the windowless room where the interrogation had taken place the night before.

"Remove your clothing," the major ordered.

F.C. stripped, feeling even more vulnerable—and cold. The guards kicked his clothes into the corner. The priest stood there for several seconds before the short sergeant entered the room. This time he had an assistant with him. The man was pushing a small table with several boxes on top.

"*Herr Pater*," Major Priebke began, "we have arrived at one of those historic moments of truth. Last night we tried to talk to you, sane man to sane man, but you refused. We gave you a taste, but only

291

a tiny taste, of what silence brings in this house. Then we let you sleep on it. Today, we get down to earnest work."

Sgt. Walther Hoess was paying no attention to Priebke's speech. He was walking slowly around F.C., carefully examining his naked body. With a fat thumb, Hoess traced the outline of the priest's kidneys, then hefted his testicles. His touch was disinterested, professional, but F.C. pulled away in instinctive revulsion. "Easy, easy," the NCO whispered, like a blacksmith calming a skittish horse. Then he turned and looked through one of the boxes on the table and took out several pairs of large pliers. Meanwhile his assistant was connecting a length of hose to a spigot. F.C. tried not to watch, but he couldn't help it.

"We prefer to act quickly and peacefully," the major droned on, "but the choice is yours. We shall have the names of your agents soon enough. You have had your last sleep until we get what we want—and you are enjoying your last pain-free moments. Do you wish to speak to me like a reasonable man?"

F.C. shuddered but he said nothing.

A guard slipped in the door and handed Priebke a note. He nodded and turned to Hoess. "I commend him to your firm hands, Sergeant." At the door, Priebke halted for a moment. "I shall return in an hour or two; but if you need me before then, just call out. I answer to 'enough.'"

Once outside the torture chamber, Priebke swiftly ran to Olendorf's office. The lieutenant colonel was standing behind his desk, feet apart, hands on his hips. Priebke could feel the fire. "He is gone," Olendorf spat out. "Your 'warm brother' has walked out of here."

"Gone? Impossible. Perhaps he went for a walk."

"That is what he told the sentry he was going to do—at midnight, nine and a half hours ago. The sentry said he had no orders to restrict Schwartzkümmel or to make a special note of his movements."

"That is correct, sir. You said treat him royally. He had my quarters, yes?"

"I did not say let him come and go as he pleases, you moron. I want him back. *Now!*"

"*Jawohl!* At least we do not need him any longer."

292

"I have tried to treat you as a colleague, Kurt. But make no mistake, I want that faggot back and I want him back now. And I want that bitch Anna back. You have had two days to find her. Do it! And stop scratching your ass when I am talking to you!"

He was drowning. His lungs were filled with water and his head was pounding. F.C. had no idea how long it had been going on, or when the pressure had started in his chest. He felt himself retch and could sense cold stone against his cheek. His hands were cuffed in front of him. His hands—they burned as if someone had inserted hot tongs under the nails. Lights began to swirl around him, and gradually a room and people came into blurred focus. It was Olendorf himself who was standing there. The two guards jerked the priest to his feet.

"You have aged a great deal in the past hours, *Herr Pater*. Perhaps there is something in our accommodations that displeases you?"

F.C. made no reply. He retched again. The pain was radiating down his left arm now. It was overpowering. He felt as if someone had moved St. Peter's Basilica on top of his chest.

"Major Priebke has given me bad reports on you. We brought you here to tell us about sin, but he says that, despite his urgings and those of kindly Sergeant Hoess, you refuse to preach a sermon. That is unchristian. You must tell us what we need to know to save our souls."

For a few seconds, F.C.'s eyes blazed defiance; then they reflected only agony.

"Do you forgive us?" Olendorf asked. "Do you forgive us our trespasses on your body?"

The priest said nothing.

"No, you do not forgive. You are not a good Christian. But I do not blame you. I would not forgive either if I were in your shoes—pardon, your bare feet."

Olendorf suddenly dropped his mocking tone. "Look, Sergeant Hoess here has only barely begun his work. The water treatment does not 'convert' everyone. You can live without your fingernails. It is painful but very possible. The balls come next. Even a man in your profession will find that part excruciating and humiliating. You will

293

survive that crushing—probably. But eventually the sergeant will wear you down, down, down, down. You know that. The pain, the lack of sleep—one of them will finally get to you. It is inevitable."

F.C. still said nothing. The pressure in his chest was preventing him from getting enough oxygen. He felt woozy. If the guards had not been holding him up by the elbows he might have fallen.

"Afterward," Olendorf continued. "You are concerned about afterward. Only natural. Afterward there should be a speedy court-martial and a swift, relatively painless death before a firing squad. That sounds like a mercy, does it not? But I offer you an even greater mercy. If you give me the names of ten of your people, only ten, I shall send you back to the Vatican—alive, as you are right now. With a week in a hospital, you could function again. But, as your country's advertisements say, my offer is good for a limited time only. You must decide immediately."

F.C. did not reply. He tried, but his brain was not able to transmit any messages except to the reflex that made him groan loudly.

"He is obstinate," Hoess admitted, and rapped the Jesuit sharply across the buttocks with a riding crop. A thick crimson welt immediately rose on the skin. "Run in place, *Schwein!*" the sergeant ordered.

F.C. did not respond.

"I said run in place!" Hoess repeated, slapping the priest again with the crop, this time across the face. Again a bright welt appeared. "*Schnell!* I shall count cadence for you. *Eins, zwei, drei, vier! Eins, zwei, drei, vier!*" he repeated more rapidly.

Painfully, F.C. lifted his knees and began mechanically to jog in place.

"He remains obstinate because he has too much energy," Hoess explained to Olendorf. "We could tire him slowly, but this will speed things up. It is like the work of the *banderilleros* in the bullring. We tire him more quickly. Keep it up! Keep it up! *Eins, zwei, drei, vier!*"

Suddenly F.C.'s body stiffened. His back arched. He let out a deep groan and pitched forward. Olendorf grabbed him and broke his fall. "No, not yet, you cannot faint again, not yet."

There was no response. F.C.'s body went limp, completely limp. Hoess reached over and felt the priest's carotid artery. There was nothing.

294

"He is dead, Colonel."

"Dead? You *Scheisskerl!*"

"He must have had a bad heart," Hoess whined. "We were careful not to push him too hard. We were bringing him along slowly, tiring him. The Colonel could see that himself."

Olendorf felt a wave of disgust twist his stomach. For an instant it was 1937, and he was looking at the face of a dead Spanish girl. "No, you did not push him too hard, you only killed him. Butcher!" The SS officer stood up. "*Scheisse drauf! Scheisse drauf!*" he repeated and stalked out of the torture chamber.

Olendorf strode past the elevator and climbed the steps to his office. He slammed the door, sat at his desk for a moment to scribble something on a card, then snatched up his briefcase and stomped out of the building into the bright Roman noon. He drew the air deeply into his lungs and marched toward the Villa Wolkonsky, only a few blocks away.

At the villa's gate, he flashed his ID and absently returned the sentries' salutes. Straight ahead up the hill, through the spacious gardens, was the Minister's House, where Gratz had his office. There the asphalt road made a gently sweeping ninety-degree turn to the right and cut through the mimosa, cypress, bougainvillea, and small umbrella pines to the villa itself. At the curve, Olendorf quickly glanced over his shoulder to make certain he was not being watched and ducked inside the house, slipping into Gratz's office without knocking. The colonel looked up in surprise. "What the devil are—"

Olendorf shook his head, pressed his hand over the colonel's mouth, and dropped the card on the desk. "Meet at Greek temple," it read.

The SS officer went outside and proceeded up the road, past a pair of dug-in *Flakwagen*, to General Mueller's headquarters in the villa, where he left some routine reports. Then he ambled back to the gardens, strolling casually away from the Minister's House, past the swimming pool and along the ruins of the old Neronian Aqueduct to the shaded grove that held the ruins of a small Greek temple. Gratz was waiting for him.

"What the hell is going on?" the colonel demanded.

Olendorf looked around. The foliage was thick and, except for a pair of paratroopers on watch in a machine-gun nest twenty-five yards down the hill, the place was deserted. "I have orders straight from

295

Berlin to arrest you. The film of Enigma that Schwartzkümmel gave Anna was genuine."

"What? Impossible! I got it directly from Admiral Canaris's hands."

"So you claim. The admiral claims otherwise. He also has a duplicate of the film that he gave you—and three machines that fit his copy of the film."

"I do not know what to say. Somebody else must have switched the film. The admiral is not a traitor."

"Somebody is a traitor, and Schwartzkümmel has disappeared. He, obviously, will tell us nothing until we find him. Canaris has too much political clout—right this minute he does, though that could change —for anyone to accuse him of being that somebody."

"This is one of your SS tricks, Olendorf," Gratz snarled.

"It is no trick, Gratz, not like forging der Fuehrer's signature on an order or helping your Lady Anna blackmail Schwartzkümmel as a 175."

"You knew?"

"We had a listening device in the admiral's suite at the Excelsior, and we have one in your office here. I do not like surprises. After you arranged Schwartzkümmel's transfer, I arranged for him to be our guest for a week. But sometime this morning he simply walked out. We do not know where he is—or where Anna is. But we shall find them both."

"Strange."

"Passing strange. More important, Berlin is seething. You are the unanimous nominee for the traitor's role."

"It must have been that *Gottverdammt schwül* Schwartzkümmel trying to get revenge for my using him with Anna."

"That is plausible."

"It is also true."

"What is truth? That is an old, but unanswered question. Fortunately, as a policeman, I do not deal in truth but in facts, Berlin's facts; and Berlin's facts are that you are the man. Schwartzkümmel is too small a person for Berlin to notice."

"Then what in hell are we doing in a Greek temple in the middle of Rome?"

"It is now twelve-twenty-seven. At precisely three P.M., I am sending Major Priebke here to arrest you. That gives you exactly two hours and thirty-three minutes to get yourself into the Vatican or the Abruzzi or wherever else you want to go to earth."

"Why? Why are you doing this, Olendorf? I do not like you, and you do not like me."

"No, I do not like you. I despise you as an arrogant snob. But you are also a loyal German officer. I think that you also believed in Operation Rigoletto, that it would mean a great victory for the Reich."

"I did believe in it. And what happens to Germany now? The admiral was right; we do need a miracle."

"Der Fuehrer will produce one for us. He has done it before." Olendorf broke off and turned away to stare at the machine gun nest. After a few moments, he turned and faced Gratz again. "Look, I do not know. Suddenly I am very tired of killing and all the obscene rituals that go with killing. Right now it would be better not to think about anything. I might arrest you. Just get the hell out of here."

Birkenau, Saturday, 23 October 1943

At 11:00 the night before, the train had slowed to a crawl. The tilt of the car and the protesting squeals of iron flanges scraping against the rails had indicated that the train was turning onto a siding. Then it had stopped, a slow, grinding halt that had had all the sound of finality about it. Through the cracks in the boxcar's wooden sides, the Augustinian had seen searchlights playing against the sky. There had been little sound and only a faint, slightly sweet odor to give any indication of where he was, but he correctly guessed Poland.

The trip had started before dawn on Monday, 18 October, when the SS at the *Collègio Militare* had herded the inmates into the courtyard, loaded them onto trucks, and drove them to the suburban Tiburtina Station. There a freight train waited, twenty wooden boxcars long, and the troops had packed the Jews aboard for a five-day ride up the peninsula, across the Alps, and then on a zigzag course across south central Europe.

The cars had no toilets, no medicine, no food, not even water. Periodically, the SS stopped the train to allow the Romans to jettison their dead, relieve themselves, and occasionally receive some water or food from friendly Italians or, later, the coldly efficient German Red Cross. The monk had traveled in one of the cars in the center of the train. The people around him were mostly from Trastevere and the ghetto. Two had died in his arms, one an eighty-year-old man, the other a two-year-old girl.

He barely knew his other companions. Except to help with the ill, he still had difficulty in overcoming his feelings about Jews. For their part, the Romans had not been unfriendly, merely consumed by their own sorrow. Some, in fact, had tried to offer him comfort, and several had shown grateful appreciation of his concern for the old man and the child. But there had been no exchange of confidences—several angry outbursts that had bordered dangerously near violence, but no intimacies. Hope that they had been told the truth and were being taken to a labor camp was slowly being asphyxiated by the dread realization that no sane man would treat a work animal as savagely as they were being handled.

Now, in the predawn darkness, the monk was silently reciting his divine office. He was doing so from memory. A few minutes earlier, he had eaten one of the consecrated hosts from the pyx. Praying took effort. The only words that seemed appropriate were "My God, My God, why hast Thou forsaken me?" It took far more effort to fight back the temptation to identify himself as an Aryan and a priest when the doors were opened. After all, the Pipernos had been saved. There was, however, a second aspect to his mission.

He was no longer hungry, very thirsty but not hungry. Indeed, he was half nauseated. After much bickering, the car's occupants had set aside a corner of the rickety old vehicle as a privy. Someone had tried several times to drape it to provide a minimal degree of privacy; each time the car's wild swaying had shaken the drape loose, leaving the makeshift privy open to the eyes and, worse, to the nose. The dapper monk was unsure that he could have chosen martyrdom had he known it was going to be so filthy and smelly.

Before he could finish his prayers, he heard footsteps crunching on the gravel roadbed and loud voices, some in French, some in Polish, but most in German. The car's door was unlocked and slid open. "Raus! Raus!" came the orders. It was one word in German that the Italians now comprehended. Groups of other prisoners in striped uniforms, each with a six-pointed Star of David sewn on, boarded the cars and helped unload the sick, the dead, and what was left of the luggage. It was some comfort that these Sonderkommandos, as they were called, were Jewish, though none could speak Italian. They indicated that the Romans should form two lines, men in one, women and children in the other.

The Augustinian joined the other prisoners in marching before a handsome young SS doctor who, whistling Wagner as he worked, chose 450 of the people to go to a labor camp, ten kilometers away. The others, he explained through an interpreter, would stay at the main camp. Separated families, the doctor said soothingly, could visit in the evenings and on weekends.

The monk was among those selected for the work detail. Wisely, he had left Rebecca's bathrobe on the train and had rolled down his pants legs so that he would seem like a reasonably healthy, reasonably young man. While the work detail milled about, the other Jews were loaded onto trucks. After a few minutes, the SS doctor came over to the Augustinian's group. "We have some extra trucks," his interpreter announced. "Those of you who do not wish a ten-kilometer walk are welcome to ride."

The monk looked at Rebecca's bedroom slippers and decided that a truck ride made far more sense than a walk along a gravel road, and joined about half the work force. Curiously, he noted, their trucks drove off at right angles to the workers' line of march and then switched back to follow directly behind the trucks carrying the other Jews.

All the vehicles swung along a muddy road that led through a maze of high, electrified wire fences surrounding a huge camp. They drove straight ahead, past row after row of neat barracks, until they reached the far end of the camp. Then they stopped between a pair of large white "bathhouses" that looked more like blockhouses. Again the cry from the SS and the *Sonderkommandos* was *"Raus! Raus!"* The Romans were directed into the bathhouse on the left where, a translator shouted, they would take showers and receive fresh clothing. Inside, in a huge dressing room, the SS and their Jewish assistants motioned the new arrivals to undress, hang their old clothes on pegs on the walls, pick up towels and soap, and go into the shower room.

Despite the body heat from being squeezed among hundreds of people, the Augustinian broke into a cold sweat. He was embarrassed at the sight of females stripping; but far more terrifying was the fact that the guards were following, precise step by precise step, one of the more gruesomely detailed narratives that he had read in the Vatican. Almost instinctively he opened the pyx and swallowed its contents, just before an SS sergeant saw the gold and snatched it, easily snapping its slender chain.

Panic hit the monk. He could not go through with it, not yet. He had thought there would be more time in the camp, a few months even weeks, not immediate slaughter. And, when the end came, he had imagined it would be like "swimmers into cleanness leaping," not like animals into filth herded. Moreover, there had always been the flicker of hope that the Vatican's reports were wrong, that his beloved country had not adopted a policy of mass murder.

Life was too precious for such a horrible ending. "I am not a Jew!" he yelled in German. "Help me! Help me!" But the press of the moving crowd pushed him into the shower room. The steel doors clanged loudly shut behind him.

For several minutes nothing happened. Then as the Romans waited expectantly, not water but *Zyklon* gas came hissing through the shower heads. Men as well as women and children started screaming in wild panic. Some tore at each other and the steel walls in frenzied efforts to escape; some husbands and wives embraced; some mothers shielded their children with their own bodies in a futile effort to protect them against the New Order's solution for their problems.

Horrified, the monk tried to hold his breath, but he could hear himself shouting, "Christ, save me! Save me! If You are a God of mercy, save me!" Shouting, of course, meant that he had to breathe in and suck the poison into his lungs. Its effects were inexorable— not instantaneous, not immediate, not even swift for those who were suffering, only inexorable. The Augustinian tried to pray, but the acid was searing his lungs, entering his bloodstream. Like everyone else, he began vomiting, then defecating, then convulsing in agony as his body's ability to absorb oxygen broke down.

In ten minutes he was dead, as was everyone in the room. Giant fans switched on to draw off the poisoned atmosphere and replace it with fresh air. High-booted *Sonderkommandos* wearing gas masks came in to hose off the vomit, blood, and excrement, while others pried the stiffened corpses apart and dragged them to another room, where gold would be chipped from their teeth, their hair cut off, and what was left lowered into gas ovens. Soon a heavy, sweet smell was saturating the early Polish morning.

Naples, Sunday, 24 October 1943

A long hot shower, ten hours of sleep, a breakfast of bacon and powdered eggs, and a fresh set of clothes had combined to restore humanity to Lieutenant (j.g.) Roberto M. Rovere, USNR. Now, as he stood in a spacious suite in the Hotel Vesuvio overlooking the wreck-strewn Bay of Naples, Anna, Trastevere, and even Father Christmas seemed only memories of dreams. Only the fear of the Regina Coeli, the bullets of the Largo Alicorni, and the terror of the Via Tasso were still real. He knew that for decades, if not the rest of his life, they would burn in his psyche like dry ice—like Stefano's death.

The door opened and John Winthrop Mason marched in; the measured cadence of his walk made him appear more like a West Pointer than an Old Blue. Roberto felt his vascular system tense and his fingertips cool as the lawyer advanced across the room. Trilussa, Roberto imagined, would have constructed a poem around that face, describing it, probably, as the product of a liaison between a lion and a pig or as the incarnation of the face on the fountain on the Via Giulia, behind the Farnese Palace. For Roberto, however, it was merely ugly, prosaically ugly.

"Sit down," Mason invited, as he himself settled awkwardly into the sofa. "The hotel has only wine left, but some of it is quite potable."

"No thanks. I'll stand. My legs can take it."

"Suit yourself, but we have a great deal to discuss."

"Yes, we do. The first item is why you betrayed me."

"Betrayed you?"

"You hear well."

"Oh, that." Mason waved his arm. "I can understand your feelings."

"Can you?"

Mason's voice hardened. He was not about to retreat. "I did not say I have experienced your feelings, only that I could understand them. You have every right to be angry. Colonel Lynch criminally mishandled your case. His mistake in ordering transfer of the microfilm while you were incarcerated almost cost you your life, and his use of a compromised cipher to communicate a request to Switzer-

301

land to transfer funds to the Vatican to pay Anna caused your second arrest."

"Go on."

"Why? Words are inadequate."

"Try some."

Mason took a silver case from his breast pocket, opened it, and selected a corona. He did not offer one to Roberto. He waited until he had it lit before he took up the challenge. "Two remarks: First, the United States is new to this work. We have very few trained, experienced men. Colonel Lynch was not among that gifted handful. He is no longer a member of our organization. Second, with that said, I was in charge. I take complete responsibility, and I apologize fully, sincerely, and abjectly. If you can think of other formulae, speak them and I shall invoke them."

Roberto said nothing.

Mason got up and walked to the window. Below was the harbor of Santa Lucia, its usual beauty marred by shell craters along the shore and pieces of debris and tops of sunken boats in the water. Far off to the left Mount Vesuvio was quiet in the October sun.

"You were bought at a great price, Mr. Rovere," Mason solemnly intoned. "We shall miss Father Christmas."

"I blamed him at first."

"Understandable." Mason nodded. "He did not want to execute Lynch's order to deliver the microfilm. In the end, he showed his courage."

"Why?"

"Father Christmas recognized that unlocking Enigma is the most important step that the United States could take to end this war. You came within a millimeter of pulling it off. Your work showed extraordinary skill, a natural talent. He knew that with a second chance you would probably succeed."

"Hold on. Don't treat me like a fool. I don't trust you, and I have no intention of going back, not now, not ever."

Mason held up his hand. It was surprisingly small, feminine. "Hear me out. Surely you owe Father Christmas that much."

Roberto made no reply.

"You know Florence well?"

"Of course, I know it well. It's the closest thing I have to a home."

302

Mason nodded. "Gen. Karl Wolff, commander of all SS forces in Italy, has his headquarters there, and he operates an Enigma. He won't be expecting another effort so soon after the one in Rome. Sit down; I'll explain our plan. Since you know the town and have outwitted the Germans once, perhaps you can improve it. . . ."

Inside his stomach Roberto could feel the noble senator from ancient Rome begin pacing in anticipation of another debate with the modern Roman from Trastevere. This time the senator seemed less confident.

A NOTE
ON BIBLIOGRAPHY

Except for a few people who have small parts in the book, such as Pope Pius XII, Adm. Wilhelm Canaris, Field Marshal Albert Kesselring, Father Marie-Benoit, and Monsignor Hugh O'Flaherty, all the characters in this novel are fictional, as is the plot. Both the Allies and the Axis, however, did have spies operating in the Vatican during World War II.

For the work of code breakers in general and Ultra's capability, see especially:

Peter Calvocoressi, *Top Secret Ultra* (New York: Pantheon Books, 1981)

David Kahn, *The Code-Breakers* (New York: Macmillian Publishing Co., 1967)

Ronald Lewin, *Ultra Goes to War* (New York: McGraw-Hill, 1978)

R. Harris Smith, *OSS* (Berkeley: University of California Press, 1972) has several chapters devoted to clandestine American operations in Italy during World War II. Peter Tompkins was an OSS agent who slipped into Rome during the Nazi occupation. His memoir, *A Spy in Rome* (New York: Simon and Schuster, 1962), makes fascinating reading.

Eugen Dollman, a German diplomat and Italophile, has written several books, translated into English, about his experiences in wartime Rome: *Call Me Coward* (London: William Kimber, 1956) and *The Interpreter* (London: Hutchinson, 1967).

There is a vast literature about the Holocaust. The best account of the fate of the Roman Jews is by Robert Katz: *Black Sabbath* (New York: Macmillan Publishing Co., 1969). Rolf Hochhuth's play, *The Deputy*

(New York: Grove Press, 1964), caused an immense wave of interest in the silence of Pius XII. Although fundamentally unfair to Pius, Hochhuth raises a significant moral question. At first, defenders of Pius claimed he did not know what was happening. But the continuing publication by the Vatican itself of its own documents on World War II shows he did know. The current defense is that his speaking out would have done no good and perhaps even harm. For fairer but still harsh evaluations of Pius's noninvolvement, see:

Carlo Falconi, *The Silence of Pius XII* (Boston: Little, Brown, 1965)

Saul Friedlander, *Pius XII and the Third Reich* (New York: Alfred A. Knopf, 1966)

Walter Laqueur, *The Terrible Secret* (Boston: Little, Brown, 1981)

John F. Morley, *Vatican Diplomacy and the Jews During the Holocaust, 1939–1943* (New York: KATV, 1980)

In his memoirs, the German ambassador to the Vatican during much of the war asserts that Pius handled "the Jewish problem" just right: *The Memoirs of Ernst von Weizsäcker* (London: Victor Gollancz, 1951). Although von Weizsäcker behaved with considerable decency in Rome, the War Crimes Tribunal sentenced him to prison for his earlier role in aiding the "final solution."